The Beard

THE
BEARD

David Clifford

51TH STREET PRESS · WASHINGTON, D.C. 2020

Published by 51th Street Press

THE BEARD. Copyright © 2020 by David Clifford

51th.street.press@gmail.com

First Printing:2020

ISBN: 9780999164914
Library of Congress Control Number: 2020904525

For Darcie

If she's into it.

Contents

Prologue

The stone in his hand skittered against the brittle rock wall. When he had started, it had been half the size of his palm, nice and sharp on one side, but with each pass a little more of it flaked away, ground down, flattened out. The mark it made now, much as the feel and the sound, resembled chalk on a slate board. This, of course, would not do: he needed to etch into the wall. He wanted this to be a lasting memorial.

They deserved a lasting memorial. All of them did, though from the look of it he would only be responsible for the one name. Thank God.

He turned the rock in his hand, searched fruitlessly for a better edge. He might've been tempted to go back for a fresh chunk of debris, but he was so close to being finished. He centered the narrowest part of the rock on the superficial mark he'd just made, as he had dozens of times now, and pressed all his weight against it to carve out a short, shallow groove. Shifting his weight back, he tilted the rock against the wall until the edge aligned perfectly with the width of the line above it, then rubbed rapidly up and down, hard as he could.

Behind him, the lantern flickered briefly and dimmed again. He leaned forward and squinted against the dancing shadows while he wore his line into the wall. This close to his work, the sharp dust burned his nostrils and made his eyes water. It was a lot of effort for such a small addition, and it was time consuming to do it right, but he insisted on taking the time, on putting in the effort, on doing it right. There was no way in hell he was ever coming back to this place to try again.

At length, he straightened up, slid back, and examined his work. Not bad, he decided, better than just legible. And a good thing, too, what with the lantern weakening by the second. He hucked the small stone into the dark, listened to it clatter away down the stairs. As the ticking of its descent grew softer, he realized that one of his companions had filled the lamp, and he had no idea whether they'd brought extra fuel. Even if they had, there was no one left here to tell him where they'd put it. He crouched to gather the rest of his belongings, determined to not be bothered. It was just as well. The lamp would be one less thing to carry.

He turned from the waning light and marched upward, first into his own shrinking shadow, then around and into true darkness. The stairs spiraled invisibly before him. He placed the fingertips of his left hand lightly against the inner wall, and carefully measured his steps against the sound of his breath. Each inhalation brought the smell of dust, of cold stone and clean dirt, and pulled him further out. He closed his eyes. There was nothing to see. There was nothing here he wanted to remember. And there was only one way out.

He could sense that he was getting closer. The echo of his footsteps grew louder as the ceiling drew nearer, and the dank from every corner seemed to lift, to warm. He raised his hand along the wall and felt the roof of the cave above him. Keeping his knuckles even with the crown of his head, he bent forward, first into a crouch, then loping on hands and knees. As he shuffled over a rise in the floor, the entrance burst into view. Bright though it was, the light did not penetrate the space, but rather appeared as a ragged, blinding disc in front of him.

So, it was still day time. It felt as though he'd been down there longer. He wondered if he might have been underground all night and into the next morning. It didn't feel possible. But he had stopped placing bets on what was possible some time ago.

Unhurried but resolute, he scraped and scooted to the light. It only now occurred to him that it had not yet occurred to him where he should go, now that this was done. There might be only one way out, but once he reached it there would be infinite options. Back east, perhaps. He had always assumed he'd eventually get back home, had even fantasized about it on occasion, yet after everything, now that it was probably time, now he wasn't sure he saw the point. He wasn't sure if he'd be able to call the place home anymore, if he went. But if not there, then where?

As he passed through the opening, he was overwhelmed. The day reflected off of every surface, glared into his retinas and baked his exposed arms. Oppressed by the light, by the silence, by the smell of hot dust and dry earth, he was suddenly aware of his incredible thirst. He reached back to grasp for the canteen he knew they'd left inside the cave entrance. Feeling it, he uncapped the container and dumped the water into his mouth, overflowing across his chin and cheeks to stream down the sides of his neck. It was cold. That was fine. He inhaled through his nose just as ravenously as he swallowed the liquid in his mouth.

His feet dangling out of the cave, swinging freely beside the path off the low cliff, he took another drink, but this one slow, deliberate. He needed to pace himself. Even if he didn't know where he'd end up, he still needed to work out what to do next. He was hungry, that was something. They had stashed some food with the baggage down at the creek bed. The baggage was another thing: he should inventory the remaining supplies. Once he'd done that, he could decide what was worth keeping and how much was worth carrying.

All of that was downright approachable. A sense of control settled over him. His eyes adjusted more every second. Gradually, he realized the extent of the mess splattered across his shirt front: patches of beige dust caked and clotted in something much darker and more sinister. He followed the ranging gore down his legs and arms, noted the still sticky drops on his wrists.

That was where he would start. Before he did anything else, he would wash the blood off his hands.

First Growth

June 1, 2015

Day 1

'*Shit-shower-shave, Shit-shower-shave, Shit-shower-shave…*'
The cornerstone of Jared's day ran through his mind on a loop as he hurriedly made the bed. He looked again at the blinking 12:00 on the alarm and wondered whether or not he still had time to set the clock, before realizing he'd pulled the blanket in front of him askew. Jared straightened his back for a moment, inhaled deeply, and softly breathed his mantra aloud, "Shit-shower-shave…" He pulled the blanket off and started over.

Sliding in his socks across the hardwood, he tossed the pillows onto the bed and ran for the door. His shoulder hit the jamb hard, bouncing him into the hallway where he used the handrail to slingshot himself to the top of the stairs. Without breaking focus from the movement of his feet over the steps, Jared called out, "What time is it?"

From the living room, a woman's voice replied, "Oh, did you just wake up? I thought you'd be shaving by now."

'*So, seven 'o clock,*' Jared thought, '*Still time to be on time, no point calling in and looking like an asshole.*' Jared moved briskly into the kitchen and poured a cup of coffee: ice cold. He looked at the coffee maker and noted the clock blinking 12:00. Jared put his mug in the microwave and busied himself reprogramming the coffee pot. He already wished he'd taken the time to fix the alarm. There was no chance of his forgetting about it now, but the idea of his possibly not thinking to fix it later would plague him all day. With one second left on the microwave, Jared retrieved his beverage and marched back to the bathroom.

Clifford

After more than ten minutes had passed, and steam from his shower had already fogged the glass stall, Jared heard the bathroom door open. "Hi baby," the woman's voice intoned from beyond the haze, "I'm sorry I didn't wake you up earlier. The power went out for a couple minutes before 6, and I didn't think about the alarm clock."

"It's okay," Jared answered, turning his head to keep shampoo from running into his eyes while he attempted to acknowledge her in some way. Through the door, he could only make out Kristin's fuzzy, dishwater blonde silhouette. "I can probably still get in on time if I leave by 7:30."

"You want me to get you some breakfast?" Kristin asked.

"Don't really think I'll have time for it."

"Well you have to eat something," she stated.

"Yeah, I'll do that," he replied absently, "I'll stop and get something on the way in, should be fine." Jared heard Kristin leave, and he returned to his inner monologue: *'lather face-shoulders-back-balls...'*

As he grasped for a towel, his foot slid across the wet linoleum, sending his knee into the wall beside the toilet. He steadied himself on the tank, retrieved his towel and, still dripping, hobbled to the sink. Jared opened the medicine cabinet beside the mirror as Kristin's voice inquired from outside, "You okay in there? I thought I heard something."

"I'm fine," Jared called, shuffling past nail polish and mascara to find his razor, "Still moving."

"Good thing," Kristin said, "It's 7:25."

Jared paused, razor in hand. *'Shit-shower...ssson-of-a-bitch.'* He looked to his reflection in the mirror and shook his head admonishingly. The pale skin of his fleshy-though-not-fat

The Beard

midsection was still scalded red from the shower. The uncut stubble on his chin shimmered in the bathroom light and extended as a dull stipple to his perfectly square sideburns. That, along with his wet brown hair, framed hazel eyes set amongst invitingly rounded features: neither notably handsome nor homely. He mumbled, "Fuck it," before throwing the razor back into the cabinet. Without actually drying off, Jared wrapped his towel around himself and ran down the hall, then back up the stairs to the bedroom.

Kristin had laid out his clothes, as she did every morning. Jared's complete wardrobe consisted of six pairs of khakis and six button-down shirts complemented by six inoffensive neck ties. None of these items were uniform, but all were completely interchangeable. For weekends, Jared kept two pairs of blue jeans and two solid-colored t-shirts folded in the back of the closet. This outfit-ratio sometimes made holiday weekends tricky, but, mercifully, vacations rarely came up. For today, Kristin had selected a combination of dark grey pants with a light blue shirt and a purple tie.

Dressed and mostly dried, Jared descended the stairs to the front door where Kristin waited with a nylon messenger bag. She handed it to him as he leaned down and kissed her forehead saying, "See you around 6:30 or so."

"You're scratchy," Kristin observed. As Jared jogged over the tiny porch of their narrow, split level apartment and down the sidewalk in front of the squat complex, she called after him, "Seriously, don't forget to eat something!" Jared smiled and waved in response.

On an ordinary morning, it would take five minutes for Jared to get from his front door to the nearest metro stop, but today he covered the distance in three. He ran down an escalator then crossed through the gate and down to the platform. The display board showed the next train arriving in three minutes: his timing would be tight, but he could still make it.

It was unlikely that Jared's tardiness would really cause problems anyways. He had started at the bank as part of a work-study program when he was 17 years old, and in the eleven years since they'd offered him a full-time role, he had never called in sick and had hardly ever been late. On top of that, he had every confidence in his coworkers' ability to cover his position. Jared took pride in how *he* did the work, of course, but he was also realistic about his performance: he played to his strengths and mitigated his weaknesses as people do, and he brought a unique perspective to his job, which could be said for everyone else in the world. The tellers at the downtown Washington, DC branch were not uniform, but all were completely interchangeable.

Jared broke off his train of thought: it had to have been at least three minutes. He looked at the board, now showing the orange line train as arriving in two minutes. As Jared watched, the display flickered off and came back up with Orange – New Carrolton – 18 minutes. In a kind of awe, Jared asked of no one in particular, "Whaaaat is this now?" He dug through the nylon bag that hung from his shoulder and retrieved his cell phone to check for service advisories. He discovered (not to his surprise) that his battery was dead, as the display on the platform went dark once again. After a brief pause, a message appeared: 'Water main break at Metro Center. Expect serious delays in both directions.'

Jared inhaled, then softly breathed, "Shit-shit-and-shit."

Day 3

At a certain point each day, usually right before lunch, Jared was reminded of his brief time in the Boy Scouts. During his first year of middle school, his mother had declared that he needed stronger male role models, that he should be challenged, that his values needed reinforcing, and that his character needed building. The Boys Scouts, in her view, offered time-honored one-stop shopping for her son's soul.

Every Monday night for a little over two years, Jared had attended the meetings. He had enjoyed the structure and the ritual of the thing: everyone in uniform, reciting the pledge and the oath, going over troop business... all the things that seemed to bore the other boys. Outside of those activities though, he spent more time building a pinewood derby car than he did building character. He had vague recollections of other educational activities: outdoor cooking, knot tying, orienteering, and similar, but he had stopped attending meetings when he'd switched to high school, and by the time he graduated, he had forgotten all of those.

One thing he did remember, though, which triggered his nostalgia now, was a perk that had come with his Boy Scouts' membership: a free subscription to Boys' Life Magazine. More specifically, he remembered the advertisements in said publication. In the back of every issue of Boys' Life there were pages of plastic schlock for sale. Everything from joy buzzers to pocket knives, X-Ray glasses to seahorses to fingerless gloves: in short, everything a boy could want that his parents would never waste their money on. One item though, which still piqued Jared's interest, was a wrist watch with a built-in universal remote control.

Clifford

If the ad was to be believed, there was no shortage of boyhood mischief to be wrought by wearing that much power on your arm. As a grown man in his fourth consecutive hour of sitting in his teller window while a TV blasted cable news into the bank lobby, it was exactly that brand of power Jared would have found most useful. The TV had an actual remote, but it was housed in the desk of the branch manager, who swore against all evidence that customers enjoyed being forced to listen to the news while they waited. This meant that Jared had to distract himself with moving those customers through the lunchtime rush as efficiently as possible, thereby sparing them the noise so far as he was able. He occasionally wondered if that may have been his manager's actual goal when he'd cranked up the TV.

"Welcome to Mid Atlantic Regional Bank," Jared said to his window without looking up, "How can I help you?"

"Hiii Jareeehhd," a woman's husky voice cooed. Jared looked up and registered a slightly heavy woman in her late 50's, neatly dressed with a close hairstyle.

"Well hey, Deborah!" Jared replied. "I was about to go on break, I was afraid I might miss you today."

"Yes, I've been waiting a little while," Deborah explained pleasantly, dropping a deposit bag into the tray below the window. "Your line was a little slow, but you're worth it."

"Oh, that's sweet of you to say," Jared answered as he pulled the tray through and began entering check amounts into his computer, "But you know, my feelings won't be hurt if another window would be faster for you."

Deborah waved a French manicured hand dismissively in the direction of Jared's co-workers. "I don't *knoow* them."

The Beard

Jared leaned forward knowingly and said, "I understand," wondering if there might be more to her sentiment than he understood. In short order, Jared emptied the bag, processed the deposits, and printed a receipt.

As he slid the tray back through, Deborah cocked her head to the side and observed, "You're looking a little scruffy today. You feel alright?"

"Yeah," Jared sighed. "I ran out of time to shave a couple days ago, and that got Kristin wondering what I'd look like with a beard. I don't really care either way, so I figured, why not try it out?"

"Couple days ago?" Deborah asked, surprised.

"Two days it would be now," Jared answered.

Deborah regarded him skeptically, "That's a lot of hair for two days." As she picked up her empty bag and receipt, she said thoughtfully, "I'm not so sure about that look for you. I think that little girlfriend of yours might be a bad influence."

"Probably," Jared laughed, "We'll see what you think of it tomorrow. Same time, right?"

"It's a date," Deborah smiled as she headed for the door. Jared looked past her and saw a man in a dark suit and pink tie gesturing wildly on the sidewalk outside. Kevin always brought everyone for lunch early. But since Jared was the only one of their group that didn't work in the office building down the block, he constantly stood accused of making them all late. Jared responded to Kevin's flailing with an exaggerated nod as he set out a nameplate with the words 'Next window please,' printed on it.

"Are you serious?!?" A deep voice crackled through the speaker in the window.

Clifford

Jared looked up and saw a very large man with a hostile expression staring back. "My break is starting," Jared explained, "But one of our other associates can help you in just a minute."

The man answered at full volume, "So you found time for your big 'ol girlfriend back there, but now that I'm here, you've got someplace to be."

"Now sir, it isn't like that," Jared started, "I got people- "

"Oh, it isn't like that," the man bellowed back, "So what's it like then?"

Jared glanced nervously from the customer to Kevin, who was now pointing at his watch through the front window. It was still technically two minutes till the hour: if the customer decided to complain to the branch manager, Jared could expect a lecture on punctuality, in addition to the 'Customer is always right,' speech. Jared shrugged toward Kevin and turned back to his window.

"I've really only got a couple minutes," Jared explained, "But if there's something quick I can help you with…"

"Well I didn't come here for the news," the man said, jerking his head in the direction of the television. He calmed slightly as he continued, "Got a deposit." The man reached below Jared's field of vision and came back with a water-cooler bottle full of change. The counter groaned as he placed the container over the top of Jared's tray. "So, how you wanna do this?"

Ten minutes later, Jared ran out the front door, pulling on his jacket as he went. "Sorry guys," he said, "Sorry. I got caught up with something. Thanks for not ditching me."

"We would have," Kevin laughed, "but we didn't want to miss the show. Dude made you *work* for that shit."

"Guys," a thin man in a light grey suit interjected, "We should probably get moving if we're going to get back on time."

14

The Beard

"Right, sorry," Jared repeated as the group moved briskly up the block and into a sandwich shop. Soft Motown filled the dimly lit dining area where a dozen well-dressed people ate in silence beside an equal number of pastel clad tourists. One employee at the near end of the polished wood counter nodded a greeting, while a second stood at her post by the cash register, contentedly humming along to the music. Jared and Kevin took a place at the back of the line while their three companions placed their orders.

"So does that happen often?" Kevin asked boisterously at full volume.

"What's that?" Jared requested, just over the level of the music.

"That thing with the change," Kevin explained loudly, "I mean, who drags that much change downtown on a weekday? Two hundred pounds of pennies isn't like popping over with a check on your break or something."

Jared nodded, "That was a lot. But it happens all the time, just usually a jar or a freezer bag's worth. I don't think people haul it down here though, it's mostly people who live in the neighborhood."

"Yeah, but do you think *that* guy lives in *this* neighborhood?" Kevin asked loudly. After a pause he followed, "Oh my god, do you think he brought all that in on the bus?"

Jared shrugged in response.

"Excuse me sir," the sandwich-maker interjected, "What can I get you today?"

"Aaaahhh," Kevin answered, tapping the counter and scanning the menu in bewilderment, "I think I need a minute. Jared, you go."

"Right," Jared answered. "I'll have a ha-,"

Clifford

"Ham and swiss with tomatoes and mustard?" the sandwich-maker picked up, "Should be down at the register for you."

"Oh," Jared blinked dumbly. "Did one of the other guys..."

"Nah," the sandwich maker smiled. "It's Wednesday: I figured you was coming, thought I'd take a chance. You all a little late though. Hope it's not cold."

Day 4

Kristin hummed to herself while she worked a corner of the worn sponge between the tines of the fork she was holding. The sound of a game show floated in from the living room where Jared sat with a magazine open in his lap, but the only noise that registered with Kristin was the rewarding clink of clean silver and porcelain hitting the plastic dish drainer beside her.

Kristin enjoyed washing dishes. Her parents' home had only had paper plates, but on holidays the family had eaten at her grandmother's house, and Kristin had always been expected to clean up after the meal. Following the chaos and altercations that were inevitably a part of those dinners, Kristin's grandmother always led her quietly out of the room to her post at the kitchen sink. Those moments of calm conversation had afforded a rare measure of peace for Kristin the girl, and, even now, submerging dirty utensils in filthy gray water only to see them come out clean still made Kristin feel oddly hopeful. So, when she and Jared had gone looking for a place to move in together, she had been secretly relieved when the property manager had apologized for the lack of a dishwasher in this unit. Kristin had known at that point that it was meant to be, because nothing said 'home' to her quite like the task of hand washing flatware.

There were, of course, numerous other household tasks that she was much less enamored with, but because her job was part-time, she had become responsible for the lion's share of chores. She was fairly certain that Jared would help out more if she asked, but it didn't feel necessary, as so much of her day was spent at her discretion, although that aspect of the arrangement did change

Clifford

when Jared returned from work. Every evening just before dinner, the fluidity of her day was quickly subsumed by his routine.

Jared was never obstinate about maintaining a schedule, but he had a strange, almost compulsive, way of enforcing it. For example, if dinner wasn't on the table by 6:30 sharp, Jared would not mutter a word of complaint or concern, but he would begin absent-mindedly eating everything within reach. The same was also true of the mornings: if Jared's clothes were not laid out for him at 7:05, he wouldn't object, but his socks would never match, and he'd be ten minutes late and distracted all day long. The routine was self-correcting, and it was absolute. It defined much of their life together, and it wasn't something either of them bothered to question, in part because, even in the absence of everything else, they knew the routine could be depended upon.

But recently Kristin had begun to feel the repetition of things more acutely. The women she worked with at the boutique clothing store had always had interesting stories. Every one of them was originally from some distant place or had travelled extensively for some frivolous reason and, if they were to be believed, these circumstances had created the backdrop for an unending series of escapades featuring far-off best-friends with exotic sounding names. Lately though, it seemed like everywhere Kristin went, less likely people had been having adventures of their own: an old high school acquaintance had volunteered for charitable work in Ghana, the next door neighbor had been visiting an uncle in Germany, even the clerk at the grocery had just gotten back from a Caribbean cruise. And because Kristin had no such stories, she had no response to them beyond listening quietly. And because she listened quietly, people became more inclined to tell her all of their stories.

18

The Beard

Kristin rinsed the last of the plates and pulled the stopper from the sink. For whatever she might lack, she still had the dishes, and the value of these little things was not lost on her. The routine, the repetition, all spoke to a stability that Kristin had only wished for before her life with Jared. And even though they hadn't seriously discussed it, she could easily imagine the more absolute security of a marriage and a family with him. All the same, she found herself pining for stories of her own, for the chance to participate in all those impressive conversations. Even if she felt like her life had everything she needed, she couldn't help wondering if she had already missed out on something.

Kristin dried her hands, hung the towel, and crossed into the living room. Jared addressed her without looking away from the TV. "Look at this jerk," he said motioning to the second contestant on Wheel of Fortune. "He's two letters short, and he whiffed it. I mean, it's one thing to keep spinning after you figure it out, but what is he doing with just the 'O's missing? It's 'A Good Night's Sleep,' idiot, where'd you think the 'R' was gonna fit?!"

"Hey sweetie," Kristin said softly.

"Hmm?" Jared replied, "I'm sorry. Some of these people are just painful to watch."

"That's fine," Kristin said, sliding onto the couch next to him and leaning her head against his shoulder. "Jared, do you think we should travel more?"

Jared blinked and rubbed his stubble thoughtfully as Kristin muted the commercials. "I'm trying to think of the last time…" he trailed off. "I guess you could ask if we should travel. Period," he chuckled.

"See, that's what I'm saying," Kristin answered brightly. "We should get away. Just a few days. A change of pace or something."

Clifford

"God," Jared said, "I must have so much time off saved... I really don't keep track any more. I'd still want to give some notice, if we do decide to go somewhere, though. And your job, you've only been there a year: do you think your bosses would mind?"

"No, they're cool," Kristin said. "They're always telling me I should get out more, and that they'd give me the time if I asked. I don't think they mean paid time, but they said they would cover my shifts."

"Then that's one catch," Jared observed, "Doing without that money, on top of spending on a trip. But we could plan ahead for that. Where'd you want to go anyway?"

"Not sure," Kristin shrugged. "I hadn't really thought about it until just now."

Jared said, "With all the arrangements and costs and everything, I feel like we should *really* want to go to wherever we're going. Tell you what, you take awhile to think on that, come up with a place, and we can talk about it."

"Okay," Kristin sighed. "I just wanted to see how you felt before I got excited about something." Kristin craned her neck to kiss Jared on the cheek. She stopped to inspect a dark patch of his emerging beard, just below the sideburn. "That is coming in really fast," she said. "I'm not sure exactly how long it's supposed to take to grow a beard, but it has to be longer than this."

"Yeah," Jared nodded, "Someone else said something about that the other day. I guess I'm just one of those people that's meant to have a beard."

"Or one of those people with a genetic disorder," Kristin teased, "It is seriously, abnormally, just... You a freak."

Jared laughed, "Well, at least it stopped itching. Not sure what I think of the aesthetic though. Kind of patchy, right?"

The Beard

"Mmm not patchy," Kristin said thoughtfully. "It's coming in full, it just has all these blonde streaks. But I think that's kind of cool."

"Yeah, so patches of different colors," Jared challenged, "So it's patchy."

"No," Kristin argued, "When I think of 'patchy,' I think bald patches. This is more like calico." Jared laughed and Kristin waved it off, "Seriously though, I'm really curious how this is going to turn out. I'm seeing red and brown in there, and then there's this black spot right…. There," she poked high on Jared's jaw line.

"Ow, damn woman," Jared said, "You got some nails."

"Sorry," Kristin giggled unapologetically. "That spot is so crazy though, like a tiny perfect rectangle."

"Is that right?" Jared asked

"Yeah," Kristin continued softly, "Square corners and everything. Then this red circle around it," she said, beginning to trace the shape on his cheek with her fingernail, "and these three weird loops underneath…"

"Are you getting lost in it?" Jared whispered, turning to look at her.

"No, hold on," Kristin said, grabbing his chin and turning his head to resume her inspection. "It reminds me of something…" After a moment of quiet reflection, she firmly stated, "Yes. That's what it reminds me of: the Lincoln Memorial."

Jared broke into laughter again. "What?" he snorted, "That was not where I expected you to go with that."

"No," Kristin said, "I'm really serious. It looks exactly like the Lincoln Memorial."

"I'm really serious," Jared smiled, "That is insane." Kristin defiantly stood up and marched out of the room. "Oh, come on now," Jared called after her, "I'm not saying *you're* insane." He was answered by a muffled clatter from the far end of the kitchen. He continued, "I love that you see things like that. It's like cloud watching with a kid. It's adorable, really."

Kristin walked purposefully back into the room with a laptop under one arm and her cell phone in her free hand. She deposited the objects on the coffee table in front of Jared's knees, then reached over with both hands and jerked his head toward the floor lamp beside him. Once she had deemed the lighting appropriate, she retrieved the phone, stood on the couch leaning over Jared's right temple and snapped a photo. "There," she said firmly, hopping down from the couch and opening the computer.

Jared sat up, rubbing his neck. "Am I missing somethi-?"

"Shhh!" Kristin stopped abruptly and raised one index finger without looking up from the screen. "I'll get to you in a second." She logged in, opened the browser and pulled up a map of Washington, DC. Kristin zoomed in over the National Mall and switched to satellite view. The Lincoln Memorial appeared as a small green rectangle surrounded by a circular lawn, with three looping roads behind it. She pulled up the picture of the black rectangle and loops of colorful hair that she had taken on her phone, and propped it on the keyboard to lean it against the screen. "And there," she reiterated, "it's the Lincoln Memorial." Jared blinked in stunned silence. "And this blonde part," she said, tracing a perfectly straight line that extended from between the lower two loops on the phone photo, "That's exactly where the Memorial Bridge would be."

"Damn," Jared said leaning forward, "I could see it."

"I hope you can see it," Kristin said, turning back to stare at Jared's cheek, "It's exactly the same. After the bridge though, it

The Beard

gets kind of light." She continued following the blond line across Jared's cheek to a spot even with his nose. "I see half of that traffic circle right here, but it hasn't really grown past that."

"Because it's patchy?" Jared asked drily.

"Yeah," Kristin said, "for now. Fast as it's coming in... Maybe in a few more days we can see it." Jared sat quietly, staring at the computer screen while Kristin continued to reflect on his face. "Oooh!!" She exclaimed suddenly, startling Jared halfway to his feet, "Next weekend we should follow it."

Jared leaned back in his seat to make eye contact, "Sorry, follow what now?"

"That. Your beard," Kristin answered enthusiastically. "Next Saturday, when it's a little thicker, we should go down to the Lincoln Memorial, and follow that blonde streak, see where it goes."

"It's hair," Jared challenged, "Where's it gonna go?"

"I don't know," Kristin answered, "That's why we have to follow it."

Day 6

Louis marched purposefully from the stand of birch trees: only twenty yards to take his place in the line. On the orders of a nearby corporal, Louis' comrades in arms raised their rifles, took aim and stood fast. He, unlike them, ran a final check to see that his canteen, cap pouch, and cartridge box were safely secured before scouting the ground for any extra-large, man-sized dry patch.

Because Louis had to die. Louis always had to die.

He half-raised his weapon in an obligatory gesture as the order to fire came down. Louis' ears rang with the sharp crack of dozens of scattered firearms discharging, and the smell of black powder burned in his nostrils. Dark smoke roiled and rose toward even darker clouds overhead, as though the violence on the ground might seed the coming storm. Louis squinted past all of it to focus intently on a row of uniformed men on the other side of the open field. After a moment, the enemy line bristled with muzzle flashes, and by the time the sound of their volley had reached him, Louis had already fallen heavily onto his stomach, his eyes staring blankly into oblivion, his head turned to face the hundreds of spectators spread out on picnic blankets and lawn chairs nearby.

At the perimeter of the battlefield, near Louis' body, a very big dog, a 150-pound black Newfoundland, lowered itself to the ground and looked through the tall grass to meet Louis' eye in a manner suggestive of a lion stalking prey. Louis hated to impose on his fellow Civil War reenactors to look after Marlow during battles, but it could be difficult to find a dog sitter without some notice, and Louis rarely planned far enough ahead to provide that. That same lack of planning was one of the reasons he was a constant casualty: Louis had to attend three reenactments each year to maintain his membership, but he never bothered to RSVP, which was an important courtesy for the event organizers who coordinated everyone's positions. By volunteering to die early in each battle,

The Beard

Louis could fulfill his obligations without disrupting anyone's plans. He might still have guaranteed his survival by joining the battle as a Union soldier (they were always short-handed over there), but all of the reenactment units near his small hometown of Selmer, Tennessee were Confederate, so the only way for him to get into a blue uniform would be to offer that service in advance which, again, would have required some planning.

Privately, though, Louis never regretted showing up unprepared. As it applied to arranging pet care, he found the sight of his companion lying on the ground with him very calming, and over time, Marlow had become a sort of mascot for his unit, which raised Louis's stock within the group. In addition, the other men were grateful to Louis for his willingness to take a hit in the first exchange: someone had to do it for the sake of accuracy, but very few men wanted the job, because for most of them civil war re-enactments were about something deep and personally meaningful, so Louis had been told.

Some of Louis' colleagues were obsessed with history in an objective sense: they didn't care so much about which unit they fought with in what position or even on which side, so long as everything about the battle was correct for the benefit of the spectators and other participants. Others were paying some sort of homage to their heritage and seemed to hope that by doing exactly as their ancestors had done (albeit in a much safer context) they might gain some insight into the people they came from, and consequently make more sense of who they themselves were. Still others appeared to Louis to be drawn by the escapism of the thing (though he knew better than to point that out to them) and wanted the chance to fight to the death for a cause, secure in the knowledge that it wouldn't make them late for work on Monday. All of these men had reasons that they held deeply enough to justify spending their money and weekends recreating history, and all of those reasons demanded of them that they fight more than the first three minutes of a battle.

Clifford

But for Louis none of that mattered: he didn't know the names of any Civil War battles he hadn't personally reenacted, and even half of those he had he'd forgotten within months of participating. The only heritage he'd ever been told about had still been in Ireland for decades after the South seceded. And, as many problems as Louis would have liked to escape from, he had never considered war in the 19th century a desirable destination. The reason Louis kept returning to this world with which he felt so little connection, was his obsession with accoutrements.

Three years earlier, a coworker had convinced him to try an event, mainly for the camping and camaraderie. In preparation, Louis had bought or borrowed the mandatory items: an ill-fitting uniform, a three-band reproduction rifle, and similar. But within minutes of registration, he could see how much potential there was for improving his impression through the collection of things. For a time, Louis' goal had been simple: to appear authentic enough that the other reenactors would not accuse him of being inauthentic, or "farby." But Louis came to enjoy the admiration he received as he progressively replaced each article of his wardrobe with better fitting and ever more detailed pieces. At some point he had internalized this motivation and had begun seriously hunting for small items to put in his knapsack, even if no one was likely to notice: antique nibs and ink-bottles, period tobacco pipes, aged pocket watches, original belt buckles... Louis found the historical figures that had inspired these events to be flat and un-relatable, but something about their possessions really spoke to him.

And, Louis figured, if he was going to go through the trouble of collecting all these things, Civil War reenactments were a great excuse and opportunity to show off his finds. All of which he had done by the time the first shot was fired, which left him available to hit the ground and stay there, just as early as he was allowed.

It was his moment. It was also his preference.

Lying flat in the tall grass was the only peace he seemed to get these days. At odd moments during the week, he actually considered driving a few miles from town to stretch out in a field

The Beard

on his own, without all the ceremony and gunplay, but he wasn't sure if a grown man could really justify doing that. Today though, as his unit pressed forward, as the sound of rifle fire and death moved further and further toward the roar of Union cannon, Louis lay easy with the knowledge that, for once, he was doing exactly what was expected of him and perfectly.

For all of the enthusiasm Louis' peers put into their fighting and dying, he wondered if his serenity and stillness weren't the truest historical interpretation. During battles he often reflected on whether a man's final moments would necessarily have been spent screaming, or if they, like him, might have spent that time quietly observing the smell of the grass, the sounds of their fellows, the first light raindrops on the back of their neck, maybe contemplating the profound value of their sacrifice, or perhaps the futility of it. If they had known the outcome of the battle, Louis wondered, would they have felt any differently about their end? Or would they have bothered to consider the future at all? Was death as complicated as the rest of life, or did its inevitability somehow make it simpler? Or maybe, Louis thought, the real complexity lies in reflecting on the nature of these things as inevitabilities to begin with. Either way, the whole exercise just left Louis exhausted and envious of Marlow.

For the dog, life appeared to be the only certainty, and he did not seem to waste his energy thinking about the alternative. Hell, much of the time it was difficult to tell if he even knew he was awake, and for now, in this field at Kings Chapel, Marlow said nothing, did nothing, but to lay his chin on his paws, his thick ear flaps bowing around his heavy jowls, while he stared patiently into his master's eyes.

Louis' gaze drifted from the Newfoundland's chocolate stare to Annabelle's shoes. Hidden as they were under a large, oblong hoop skirt, Louis had never noticed her boots. Fastened on the side with period appropriate buttons and subtle detailing at the ankle, he thought they were nice. He wondered where she got them. He wondered how that information could be useful to him. He supposed he should think about new shoes for himself: his brogans were wearing a little thin. But not as thin as his work boots. He should have known better than to buy those at the discount store. But it was so convenient: he was there all the time anyhow, and their shoe section was on the way. This was why he was certain he would make that same mistake twice. He could even stop and get a new pair on his way home from the war. That might be a good time to get something for Annabelle, to thank her for minding the dog during the battle. He wasn't sure what to get her. He would know when he saw it. And coffee, he would need to get coffee. And was there something else? Maybe T-shirts. Definitely dish soap.

The sound of fighting slowed as men in Union uniforms walked the field and checked the casualties on the ground. True to history, an old white gentleman in an officer's uniform made a pronouncement to spectators, and thus the bloodshed was ended.

Louis pushed himself slowly to one knee, plucked his kepi from the grass nearby and carefully adjusted his equipment as he stood. Taking his cue, Marlow lazily stretched his bulky frame and stood beside a slight brunette in her mid-thirties, the top of his head reaching well above her waist. "Really great job today!" Annabelle called out sarcastically.

Louis answered, "I'm a natural born actor."

"With grass stains," she pointed out as he approached.

Louis nodded. He brushed pointlessly at his knees as he noted the contrast between his dirty, disheveled grey wool and Annabelle's delicate pink dress. "Wanted to complement your shoes," Louis remembered, "Very nice."

"Oh," Annabelle laughed, picking up the front of her skirt, "Someone finally noticed."

Louis followed up, "Say, you wouldn't have an extra pair 'a brogans floatin' around, would you?"

"Well *I* wouldn't," Annabelle said, bemused.

"You or Derek, I mean."

"I don't think so," she said slowly, "Now I'm thinking about it, I'm sure we don't. He just got a new pair couple months back, and

28

The Beard

I tossed the old ones. But you know who you should ask is Gary. I just saw him over…"

Louis started to shake his head, "No need t'bother –,"

"Hey Gary!" Annabelle yelled over her shoulder, "C'mere! Wanna ask you somethin'!"

A wiry man of medium height wearing dark blue jeans with a denim button-down shirt and thick glasses sauntered over. His shoulder length hair was silver and matted, and he moved in a way that suggested he was usually nimble but did not, in this case, care enough to hurry. He nodded curtly and greeted the group in a raspy voice: "Annabelle. Louis. Marlow." The dog yawned and sat on Annabelle's boot.

"Hello Gary," Louis said politely, "No vendors today. I didn't think you'd show."

"Never know though," Gary answered. "If anybody forgot to bring something, I got a spare set of everything in my car, just in case."

Annabelle interjected, "That's perfect: Louis was just asking after a new pair of Brogans."

"Yeh," Gary said, putting his hands in the back pockets of his jeans, "I got that."

"A *new* pair?" Louis asked skeptically.

"Just like new. Only better 'cause they broke-in." Gary chuckled, mainly to himself, "Broke-in Bro-gans."

"I's hopin' for new," Louis pressed.

"Like new," Gary repeated. "Brand new ain't gonna look right anyhow. But you take or leave 'em: you the ones called me over here."

"Okay then," Louis sighed, "I'll give 'em a look." Gary nodded and turned to lead the way, but Louis delayed him. Turning back to Annabelle, Louis said, "Just remembered: I was gonna see if you could take Marlow for the next couple weekends. I've got the kids, and you know how that goes."

"A little crowded with the both of them and the both of you in that trailer?" Annabelle asked sympathetically.

Clifford

"Trailer's not *all* bad," Louis said. "Kids get bored, I just hook it to the back of my truck and tell 'em we're camping. But their mother still don't like the dog bein' around 'em."

"Yeah," Annabelle said, scratching Marlow's ear while the dog grinned sloppily, "This one is a killer. But we can handle him for a couple days at a time. Derek would probably keep him if he could."

"Great," Louis said, "So I'll swing by Friday afternoon. He looked down and motioned calmly. Marlow stood, shook out his coat, and lumbered behind Louis, who in turn lumbered behind Gary.

"See," Gary said as they walked to the car, "Shoulda never had kids, man. Complicates everything. Complicates your marriage, your divorce, now your dog... And you can't keep nice things, is the main reason I don't have kids."

"Nice things?" Louis asked curiously. "You live in a scrap yard."

"That don't mean I don't have nice things," Gary replied, pausing beside a 95 Buick with peeling paint, "Plus, can you imagine what kinda trouble it'd be, chasing kids around that place? I can tell you, I grew up there and that was no picnic for my dad, neither. Nah," he finished, unlocking the trunk, "You can keep all that nonsense." Gary sunk his arms elbow deep into the mass of grey wool, canvas, leather, and brass that filled his trunk.

"Need some help there?" Louis asked.

"I'm 'a get it," Gary grunted. "I feel one... and another..." With a flourish he freed two worn brown shoes from the pile. "And there you go: Broke-in-Bro-gans."

"Broken Brogans, maybe," Louis said, gesturing to a hole in the toe of one. "Are those all you got? 'Cause I'll have to pass on those."

"What?" Gary spat, bewildered, "You can't just pass. You can name a price, but... You had me come clear out to the car, you have to offer somethin'."

The Beard

"Clear to the car," Louis repeated incredulously, "That was all of 25 yards. That effort ain't worth a quarter."

"What about tha' opportunity cost?" Gary whined, "I coulda' spent that time findin' someone who has money to spend on a bargain like this. Can I maybe interest you in something else here?"

"Sorry man," Louis said, "But I don't need what you got to sell."

"Shit," Gary mumbled as he shifted the worn shoes to one hand and slammed the trunk lid with the other, "You don't even know what I got to sell. Y'know, you wouldn't be sayin' that if I showed you the good stuff."

"So why aren't you tryin' to sell me good stuff?" Louis asked, "And what good stuff are you talkin' about? I don't need car parts."

"No," Gary said, visibly annoyed, "Auto scrap pays bills, but the good stuff, at my place, comes from estate auctions."

"Really?" Louis asked with renewed interest. "I didn't know you were into that."

"Oh yeah," Gary exclaimed, "You'd be amazed what you find at those things. Bid on the miscellaneous lots no one wants, you can get odds and ends, lots of vintage stuff. Some of it real old, Civil War old even. Talkin' original stuff here, not re-pro or nothin'. You can't count on it every time a'course, but you go to enough auctions, set those little things aside, it adds up."

"Okay, I'll bite," Louis said, "What's it take to get a look at the 'Good stuff?'"

"No secret handshake, no special appointments," Gary said, "You know where I'm at. Any weekday between tha' hours of 8 and 4."

"Might be a couple weeks, 'afore I get out there," Louis said, "But I just show up?"

"Sure. You can show up in a couple weeks," Gary paused to flop the tired brogans onto the car, "If you buy these today for ten dollars."

Louis thought for a moment and stated, "I got eight."

"Done," Gary answered quickly, handing over the shoes and holding out his hand to receive payment, "And a pleasure as always, sirs."

"Sure hope it's worth it," Louis mumbled to Marlow. He picked up the shoes and patted his dog's neck to signal their departure. Gary waved them off without comment.

The Beard

Day 13

The soft chirping of birds in the trees along the reflecting pool cut through ambient traffic noise and echoed across the plaza at the foot of the Lincoln Memorial steps. Small clots of tourists in brightly colored t-shirts took photographs of one another with the World War II Memorial in the distance and an uneven procession of partially dressed joggers in between. Jared and Kristin crossed the plaza from a stand of trees to the North and paused near a trash can on the opposite side.

"What's wrong?" Jared asked. "Why'd we stop?"

Kristin gestured up a ramp to a tastefully concealed door in the monument's pedestal, "Thought you might want the restroom before we get into this."

"I don't think we're going all that far," Jared said. "Of course, we would be even closer if we'd just taken the train across the river. Since we know we're going that way, I don't see why we have to walk the extra ten blocks."

"Reeeally?" Kristin asked sarcastically, "Because you hadn't mentioned that. Like a hundred times." She reached up with flat fingers and caressed the hair along Jared's sideburn while continuing, "Like I told you, we're starting here because this is where it starts." Kristin playfully tapped the dark rectangle on Jared's cheek.

"Alright," he relented, "I'll hit the restroom real quick and we can go. It's too early for this nonsense though." Jared turned and walked purposefully up the ramp.

"It's after 9:00," Kristin said. "Any other day you would have been at work a half hour ago."

33

Clifford

"Still too early," he called back over his shoulder.

Kristin stepped around a wall at the bottom of the ramp and sat on a bench to wait. In front of her, the sun had risen above the Capitol dome, casting the long shadow of the Washington Monument halfway to the reflecting pool. A small flock of geese rose up from the trees to the North and swept low and loud over the plaza, prompting a group of high school girls to flee giggling past a homeless man engrossed in the contents of the trash can near the 'Refreshments' kiosk.

"Hey space cadet," Jared interrupted, "I'm ready when you are." Kristin stood, smiled, and wordlessly took Jared's hand to lead him away from the memorial and around a traffic circle to the approach of the Memorial Bridge. As the couple passed between a pair of gilded equestrian statues Jared observed, "All these years and I don't think I've actually walked this bridge."

"Oh?" Kristin said without slowing her pace, "Do you mean that like it's something you're finally getting around to, or like it's something you've managed to avoid?"

"Good question," Jared nodded thoughtfully, "Neither, I guess. Just something I never had to do, so I never really thought about doing it." A cool breeze blew across the shimmering river on Jared's left, while light traffic crowded to Kristin's right. "It's kind of pretty," Jared stated, "This is nice, I think I'm okay with this."

"Yay," Kristin grinned, "It makes me really happy to hear you not bitching."

"Give it time," Jared laughed.

As the couple exited a second bridge, Jared pointed in front of them to a brown pylon in the distance. "Train station," he stated.

The Beard

"I know," Kristin sighed, "But if we took the train, you would've missed all that," she waved back over her shoulder. "Anyway, the train station isn't on the map."

"You mean it isn't on my face," Jared countered.

"Same," Kristin shrugged unenthusiastically.

"Something else that didn't make it onto my face," Jared said, "Was a scale. Any thoughts on how far we're going?"

"Not really," Kristin answered, "I packed us a lunch, just in case. Why? Do you have to pee again?"

"No," Jared scowled. After a pause, "Well maybe just a little, but only because you've got me thinking about it now."

Pedestrian traffic began to thicken as the pair proceeded down a walkway lined with tall hedges and punctuated occasionally by bronze statues. They pushed by a group of teenagers mustered around a chaperone with a yellow umbrella, through a gate in the long hedgerow, then shifted into single file to pass an elderly couple with a stroller. Across the street, through a break in the shrubbery, the sunlight played across the tops of row upon row of low, white headstones. "I haven't been to Arlington Cemetery since I was in grade school," Jared said wistfully, "This is turning into a weird walk." Jared led Kristin by the hand to the terminus of the sidewalk: a curved granite wall with a niche in the center that contained a fountain overlooking a round pool.

A short woman in a National Parks uniform approached from a position near the end of the wall. "Excuse me," she called from 25 feet away, "Did you two need a map?"

"No thanks," Kristin answered brightly, "We've got one." The woman nodded and returned her attention to the groups approaching from the Metro escalators.

"Do we have one?" Jared asked incredulously.

Clifford

"Sure," Kristin chirped, "We have you."

"Right," Jared said, "But I don't think this," he gestured to the high memorial wall before pointing to his chin, "Fits on this."

Kristin swung her backpack from her shoulder and balanced it on one knee to dig her phone from beneath their lunches. "Honestly," she mumbled under her breath, "It's like you haven't been staring at yourself in the mirror for ten minutes every morning." She held her phone directly in front of Jared's mouth and snapped a photo. Slinging her bag over her shoulder, Kristin stepped alongside Jared and held the screen in front of him. "You see that blond streak we've been following," she said. Jared nodded as she continued, "Look for a little black horseshoe right there."

"Oh, I see it," Jared conceded. "I'd call it more like an arch, but... the blond part runs through the middle of it."

"Not the middle," Kristin corrected him, "It hooks a little to the right, and if you noticed while you were dragging me around a minute ago..."

"Holy crap," Jared said looking over his shoulder, "there's stairs over there."

"There you go," Kristin said unsurprised, lowering her phone, "So we go up."

Kristin turned and strode briskly into a recess in the wall. Jared paused dumbfounded for a moment before muttering, "I'll be damned," and settling into a light jog after her. The staircase was illuminated by diffuse sunshine filtered through a skylight that allowed Jared's eyes to adjust only enough to make the world at the top appear brighter. As he emerged, a field of identical white tombstones sparkled against the dark grass. Jared retrieved his sunglasses from the pocket of his weekend-jeans before he spotted

The Beard

Kristin at the edge of a narrow concrete terrace. "So, I guess you decided to wait after all," Jared said.

"Had to," Kristin replied, "I need you to show me where to tell you we should go."

Jared approached and assumed the position, bending slightly and tilting his head back as far as it would extend to expose his chin. "Thank you, sir," Kristin said softly. With one finger she traced a short track toward the corner of Jared's mouth, her eyes darting to the landscape and back, to compare. Her own mouth silently formed words as she consulted. Finally, Kristin declared, "This way," and charged without warning at an angle up the hill, between two rows of grave markers. Jared followed dutifully behind her.

The duo proceeded in this way across the grass and around a stand of trees to discover a long, paved staircase running the length of the hill. Each step was stretched out like so many miniature landings, to facilitate erstwhile pallbearers. In the distance, the hill's summit was crowned by a two-story stone house with a pillared portico. Kristin turned back to re-examine Jared's face. As he obediently leaned down to accommodate her, Jared asked, "Any way to avoid all the stairs? Seems like there's been a lot of up-hill on this."

"No," Kristin answered absently, "Looks like you'll just have to suck it up and get to the top."

"I guess," Jared said, rolling his eyes behind his sunglasses. Kristin turned and led the way up the elongated stairs. Jared caught up quickly, measuring his own steps in a long-short, long-short pattern to suit the new terrain, while Kristin elected three stutter-steps to a tread. As they crossed from the top of the stairs onto a gravel trail, Jared paused and turned around. He was greeted by a panorama of the National Mall with the Potomac running lazily in the foreground. "That's all?" he asked loudly. "We must have walked further than that." Kristin paused quietly. Turning to face the few remaining steps up the hill, Jared addressed her more directly, "Should we take the tour of the house? I mean, we're this close, it seems like maybe we should."

"Or," Kristin answered, "You can skip that and take a tour of the bathrooms behind the house. Just if you need to."

Jared walked sullenly past Kristin and up the trail to the aforementioned outbuildings.

Kristin followed at a short distance and paused in sight of the restroom doors. She looked back down a dirt path, through a barren garden patch, to the rear of the stately mansion, where groups of visitors milled and bounced from the house tour, to a book shop, to a display of refurbished slave quarters, and back again. As their laughter and soft conversation mingled with the smell of wet grass across the recently ploughed earth, Kristin let her attention slide to the wispy white clouds that passed calmly overhead.

Over the previous eight days, she had secretly chided herself for her growing enthusiasm over this hike. She knew, or at least she reminded herself, that there was probably no pot of gold at the end, that it was just a day trip that they would likely remember as more trouble than it was worth. And she felt confident that, were that the case, Jared would be sure to remind her of said trouble every chance he got. But she couldn't help secretly wishing that it might lead to something, to at least a funny story they could share. She wanted very much to daydream scenarios, to imagine every option of where Jared's beard could lead, but the whole exercise was so unusual that everything beyond the bridge was a total blank for her. So instead she had focused on the day: on the lunch, on the start

The Beard

point, on making sure that when she'd laid out Jared's clothes, she'd put him in her favorite shirt. And from there Kristin had found herself unusually focused and decisive because dammit, whatever it was at the end was there to be found.

The slam of the restroom door announced Jared's pending return. "Okay," Jared said to the back of Kristin's head as he approached, "That should be the last of the coffee."

"I'm sure," Kristin acknowledged, turning and standing on tip toe to kiss him lightly. As Kristin pulled away, she reached for his hand and squinted at the middle of his cheek. "And now we go this way," she announced, turning on her heel and pulling him forward.

Jared followed Kristin past the back of the stone house. Hurrying along the uneven gravel and fighting the glare of the sun on his tinted glasses, Jared focused on his sneakers, tuning out the meandering families and tour groups that filtered over from the bus stop nearby. As they neared a metal gate between the building and the road, Kristin dropped his hand abruptly. Jared blinked and retrained his focus in front of him, suddenly feeling disoriented without Kristin's lead. "You stay there," Kristin called over her shoulder, "I need to check something." She walked double-time into the crowd and vanished. After a few seconds she emerged from her human cover with a smile. "Yeah, I thought so," she said triumphantly.

"Thought what?" Jared asked.

"Have you ever noticed that weird spider web looking thing on your left cheek, back near your jaw?" she asked.

"I think of it more like a stained-glass window," Jared argued, "But yeah, I know the brown spot you're talking about."

"Well I thought it was weird how it's not really on that blonde part we're following," Kristin continued, "So I tracked it down just now: there are these garden paths on the other side of the house that match up with it."

"Then we go that way?" Jared asked.

"I don't think so," Kristin answered, "I just wanted to know if it matched." Kristin surveyed the nearby road thoughtfully. "We go there," she said finally, retaking Jared's hand. The couple moved quickly around the crowd, outside the gate and across the road to a newly paved foot path. Kristin took advantage of the solid footing and turned to walk backwards while examining Jared's cheek.

"I have to admit," Jared said, "I'm kind of enjoying all the attention today."

"Aww, that's because you're finally interesting to me," Kristin teased as she turned back around. She pulled Jared hard to the left at a small white building. "Not this one," she mumbled as they passed a cross street, "but this one riiiight here." She pulled him suddenly to the right.

"How can you even tell?" Jared asked.

"It's the red rectangle," Kristin explained, still looking forward. "The lines of red hair represent the roads we haven't been using. The blonde part is where we go, but it doesn't always line up with a road. The brown looks like boundaries and the black parts are landmarks."

"What, is there a key and a compass rose on the back of my head or something?" Jared followed up, "When were you going to share all this?"

"I'm figuring it out as I go," Kristin shrugged. "Besides: what were you going to do with that information?" She led Jared off the road toward a line of trees. Where the vegetation encroached on the neat rows of headstones, the last string of monuments was larger, more elaborate, and set further apart to accommodate. "This should

The Beard

be it," Kristin announced as she walked into a shallow clearing bounded by a semicircle of trees. She concluded simply, "The blonde part comes to a point: away from the nearest red line, but next to a black dot, and surrounded by brown on three sides."

Jared followed Kristin around the trees and discovered the 'black dot,' she had spoken of: in the deep shade of the timber stood a 7-foot-tall granite marker. Affixed at eye level was a 2-foot diameter bronze medallion cast with the bust of a distinguished looking man in profile and streaked a mottled bluish-green from more than a century in the elements. "Now, that is a beard," Jared said, referencing the portrait subject's thick, chest-length facial hair.

"Right?" Kristin replied. "I saw a stone, I thought, 'Maybe we're looking for a relative of yours,' but *that* beard... I'm sorry sweetie, there's no resemblance yet."

"My feelings aren't hurt," Jared laughed, "Even if it got that long, I still couldn't carry it like him." The couple stood silently a few feet apart, reflecting on the face in front of them, its one visible eye forever glancing slyly to the side, gazing deep into the space in between them. A warm breeze rustled the leaves overhead to throw patterns of shadow across the stone in a way that made the portrait appear to nod slightly. After a moment of heavy silence, Jared asked softly, "So who is it?"

"I know what you know," Kristin said, without breaking her stare at the stranger's eye. "Just what's on the nameplate: Major Henry Sullivan Strafford, born on July 21, 1860, died in Balangiga, Philippine Islands, September 28, 1901."

Jared answered with silence. He removed his sunglasses and squinted through the obstructed light at the detail of the relief: the individual hairs that stretched from Strafford's head halfway to his shoulders mingled with the lines of his beard, and all of it hung over the collar of a uniform with one elegantly curved epaulette in view. But wherever Jared may have intended to train his focus, he always ended back at the eye. Even with the subject's mouth so fully concealed, Major Henry Sullivan Strafford's eye seemed to be smiling. It occurred to Jared that, even though the marker was not very distant from the road, this far back in a cemetery this size, it might have been years since anyone had gone out of their way to see it. Jared was struck for a moment by the idea that Strafford might actually be happy to have visitors. But at the same time, there was something mocking if not malevolent in that look, as though Strafford had been reminded of a joke too nasty to repeat.

The harder Jared stared, the more aware he became of a chill gradually climbing his spine. Partly to prevent a lump forming in his throat, Jared finally broke the silence, "So what do we do now?"

"Don't know," Kristin answered, sheepishly for the first time all day. "I have lunch in my backpack but…"

"Yeah, and I *was* hungry," Jared said. "It doesn't feel appropriate though, does it?"

"No," Kristin agreed, "It does not." After another pause, "So do we just go home then, if this was the end of it?"

"Is this the end?" Jared asked. "I know the path came to a point here, but I thought it veered back down my cheek."

"It does," Kristin confirmed as she took a step toward Jared. She regarded Strafford's stare and pulled Jared out of the dead man's direct line of sight. "But I wasn't sure if that last part actually means something. It mostly doubles back and tapers off under your chin." Jared tilted his head back, inviting Kristin to investigate further. "Well, look at that," she said, "There is a fat black ring under there."

"Seriously?" Jared asked, feigning surprise in the hopes that he wouldn't be called out again for spending too much of his morning in front of the mirror.

"Like you didn't know," Kristin sighed, "There's a wide, red 'V' with a black circle inside the tip and another black dot inside the circle. Like a little bullseye."

"Which way was that?" Jared asked.

"I'm thinking it's sort of this direction," Kristin said turning Jared about face. She stepped around him and took a brisk pace into a sunlit field. Jared tried for one last look over his shoulder as he started forward, but through the shadows he could only see the outline of Strafford's marker.

Jared caught up quickly and retook Kristin's hand. As the couple crossed through rows of headstones, they saw an increasing number of families and small groups making their way down the roads. Jared pulled Kristin to follow them, toward the rear of a marble amphitheater. "Where are you going?" she asked.

"You said a circle in a circle, right?" Jared said. "So that's a big circle."

"I said a dot in a circle in a 'V'," Kristin corrected, "And the 'V' is red, and there's no roads near *that* circle. We want to go this way," she pulled Jared to a nearby curb where they waited for a tour bus to pass. In pulling away, it revealed a looping one-way drive across the street from where the couple stood. Forty yards distant, at the point where the drive doubled back, a large steel ship's mast, complete with crow's nest, rose from a circular granite base.

Clifford

Side by side, Jared and Kristin walked reverently down the tree-lined approach and tentatively rounded the base of the monument. From top to bottom, the granite was divided into panels inscribed with names and occupations:

John C Nielson
Seaman

Sophus Nielson
Coxswain

William Noble
Fireman First Class

After a short distance, the pair arrived at a barred bronze door, every bit as weathered as the bronze medallion they had recently locked eyes with. Above were the words:

Erected in the memory of the officers and men
Who lost their lives in the destruction
Of the USS Maine
Havana Cuba February Fifteenth MDCCCXCVIII

"What year is that?" Kristin asked.

"You'll have to give me a second," Jared said, squinting up through his sunglasses. "It's been awhile for me and Roman numerals."

"But you work with numbers every day," she said.

The Beard

"Well yeah, but the bank has sort of phased out Roman numerals. Part of last year's abacus upgrade," Jared replied absently. Kristin waved off the comment and continued her circuit around the monument while Jared silently mouthed the letters. After a moment he proudly announced, "1898!"

"Jared?" Kristin called out from the other side of the pedestal.

Jared jogged around to find her staring up at the top of the base. At a more reasonable volume he repeated, "The USS Maine sank in Cuba in February 1898."

Kristin extended her arm to point at what she'd found. Spanning the full width of the top of the panel in front of them was the inscription:

Henry Sullivan Strafford
Engineer

Lowering her hand but not her eyes, Kristin asked, "So how did he die again in Cuba three years later?"

Second Growth

Day 1

The magnet on the mirrored medicine cabinet gave up with a muffled thump, and Jared got down to business. Taking his time, he carefully, but thoughtlessly, reached past Kristin's nail polish and various lotions to retrieve his materials and lay them out on the counter, left to right, in order of use: toothbrush, toothpaste, dental floss, mouthwash, nail clippers...

In the two weeks since Jared had taken his face down to bare skin, he had enjoyed his familiar morning rituals. He could hardly be surprised that it had become so comfortable so quickly to fall back into the way he'd done things since he was 16 years old. To move fully away from their discoveries at Arlington, however, was proving to be a slightly longer process. It didn't help that the entire idea of following the map was too odd for Jared to discuss with anyone but Kristin. Unassisted then, the two of them had theorized, hypothesized, and generally wracked their brains to prescribe some meaning to what they'd found, but to no avail. They briefly tried searching online for the name Henry Sullivan Strafford, again with no luck. Considering that the man had not one, but two sizable markers in the nation's premier federal cemetery, they felt his absence from the internet was notable and took that as discouragement to dig deeper. So they were left with nothing to say about it, apart from agreeing with each other about how crazy the whole thing was, fewer and fewer times each day, until they should presumably stop thinking about it altogether.

And that would be that: A very strange thing-that- happened-that-time that went nowhere.

...deodorant, shaving cream and razor. The door of the medicine cabinet drifted wide, reflecting the surface of the mirror over the sink. Jared watched himself standing to the side, as the frame of one surface gradually revealed the other revealing itself, repeating and repeating and repeating, forming an empty corridor that bent infinitely into nothingness.

Just as well, Jared thought, that Kristin's little adventure hadn't panned out. It was a diversion from the routine he liked so well: he enjoyed shaving, at least more than he enjoyed an itchy beard, and the whole thing had been impulsive and impractical and pointless.

Jared rubbed the stubble on his chin and wondered why he was still thinking about it, now that he'd decided all that. He would never admit as much, but he couldn't shake the sense that the exercise had to have meant something. And he had loved the expression on Kristin's face each time she had discovered what she'd thought they were after. Jared was beginning to regret that they didn't do more pointless and impractical things. But to re-grow the beard just to remind his self of that one Saturday they had wasted together would be silly and sentimental.

Although, if he was really re-growing it to remind him to waste more Saturdays with Kristin, then it would serve a purpose, sort of a work/life balance kind of thing. He could maybe even sell that as a romantic gesture. In any case, he thought the look had sort of suited him.

Jared pulled the shaving cream and razor from the right end of his lineup and put them back in the medicine cabinet. The magnet on the door reengaged with a muffled thump.

Day 3

The smell of hot asphalt and sweat burned through Louis' nostrils and made his eyes water under his tinted safety goggles. Perched on the black vinyl seat of an orange road roller, Louis focused intently on nothing in particular, only vaguely aware of the steel drum in front of him as it turned hypnotically over freshly laid blacktop. In addition to his new discount-store-steel-toe-boots, he wore old blue jeans, a reflective vest and a faded blue flannel with the sleeves rolled to his elbow. The moisture from his short-cropped hair saturated the sour foam sweatband of his yellow hardhat.

Louis' cotton-gloved hands held the steering wheel steady, his large frame folded awkwardly behind the controls. His size had always been a mixed blessing. As a young man, Louis had been tapped for his high school football team's defensive line. He had been stout and immovable enough to excel up to the point that came naturally, but his lack of coordination and actual interest had prevented him from taking it any further.

In later years, Louis' physique had made him so obviously capable of defending himself that he was rarely ever challenged, but that had also meant that his friends had constantly called on him to back them up when their trash talking had gotten them into trouble. His very brief pass through college had ended with assault charges stemming from a bar fight on someone else's account. His parents had seemed unsurprised by that outcome: Louis had always been very popular, and he had never had anything to show for it.

The gravel on Louis' right gradually narrowed to meet a rusted guardrail, the weeds beyond which dropped away into a wooded ravine. He squinted over the treetops to watch a hawk circle slowly in the distance.

For most of Louis' 20's, he had just sort of existed day to day. He had lived off and on in his old room at his parents' house, had

Clifford

taken short-term jobs as they came to him, and had spent much of the rest of his time drinking. Prodigiously. Just before his 30th birthday, Louis had found out that a girl he'd made time with, named Carolyn, was pregnant. They had never been anything serious, but Louis supposed that he loved her as much as he loved anyone else, and she had informed him that getting married was the right thing to do, so he'd rented a tuxedo and a church, and he'd obliged her.

His parents then informed him that holding a steady job and moving out of their house was the right thing to do, so Louis had accepted a standing offer from an old friend who had made a career of construction. Louis did passably well in the job but never fully applied himself, as his wife had explained to him that a baby at home and another on the way precluded his taking on additional responsibilities at work. That had made sense to Louis, for a while at least, until he had realized that as important as he had been told that it was to be home with his children, they didn't seem to care much either way. So, after years of his coworkers suggesting that he should instead be out at the tavern after work, he had joined them in the hopes that his presence there would actually be noticed. For the most part he had not been disappointed.

Carolyn had been uncharacteristically tolerant. She had said that she could tell that Louis had been unfulfilled and had hoped that by taking some time for himself he could find more satisfaction in the time he spent at home. But things didn't really work out that way. Louis' evenings out eventually led to weekend camping trips and, in turn, to periodic benders. Carolyn had then welcomed his sudden interest in Civil War reenactment, if only because it was a relatively sober activity. But that had turned out to be almost more insidious than his previous mischief, as Louis' collecting provided further distraction in the increasingly rare moments he spent with his children.

For his part, Louis had noticed the degrading affect that his choices had on his marriage, and he hadn't enjoyed disappointing Carolyn with his absence. But over time he had developed a role

52

within his core group of friends, and to vacate that position would have meant disappointing all of them instead. More than that, he liked who he was outside of the house: whether on the job or after hours, he had a sense of who he should be. But at home it was a guessing game that he had never been good at, and he knew that it was only a matter of time before his children were old enough to be disappointed in him as well. So, when Carolyn had informed Louis that moving out would be the right thing for him to do, he hadn't fought the decision.

The irony was that, in giving up on meeting his family's unknowable expectations, Louis now found that he had lost his ability to deliver for everyone else. He had become directionless, distracted at work, and no longer much fun to be around. Louis wondered if that wasn't why he'd been so attracted to the idea of getting a dog: not just a living creature to be stuck with Louis, but a companion whose requirements were basic and obvious, whose devotion and approval were absolute.

"YO!!!" a baritone voice abruptly cut through the growl of the steam roller and Louis' reverie. On the shoulder of the road twenty yards distant, a short, stocky man wearing a full beard and his own compliment of safety equipment, waved his arms above his head. Louis quietly raised his hand in greeting, and the man responded by twisting his two gloved fists in front of him in the international signal for 'break time.' Louis nodded and returned his attention to the road surface, carefully navigating past the man and over a seam in the asphalt before bringing his vehicle to a stop.

"Damn, Derek," Louis called as he stepped down from his perch, "Y'startled me."

"Saw that," the bearded man chuckled. "I's wavin' atcha' fer five minutes."

"Huh," Louis shrugged. The men continued quietly along the roadside, the steady rhythm of gravel crunching under their boots interrupted only by the sound of rustling leaves in the nearby ravine. Approaching a gradual bend in the highway, they reached their destination: a mud-stained, white pickup truck parked in the closed northbound lane. Louis lowered the tailgate and took a seat, while Derek retrieved two small coolers from the cab. Once those were deposited in the bed of the truck, Louis reached into one to retrieve a pack of cigarettes and a plastic lighter. Derek sat beside him and began eating a sandwich, while Louis lit up and leaned against the side rail. After a long moment, Louis peered over the side and knocked the ash from the end of his cigarette.

"Watcha' lookin' for there?" Derek asked, motioning with his half-eaten sandwich to the ground where Louis had been staring. "Drop somethin'?"

"Nah," Louis said absently, "I keep ashin' on the dog at home. Tryin' t'train myself to pay closer attention. He don't seem t'notice, but I'm afraid I might light him on fire one a'these days."

Derek laughed, "Now it makes sense: when we had him last weekend, we noticed a grey spot on his back. I thought it was from his flea medicine, but Annabelle swore he was gettin' into somethin'."

"She was sorta right," Louis nodded.

"Mmm," Derek intoned, taking another bite, "Maybe. I don't tell her she's right if I don't have to. I'm open to sayin' we're both wrong."

"All that reminds me: meant t'say thanks for dog sittin' again."

"No trouble," Derek shrugged, "I should thank you. Little vase you brought Annabelle was a nice gesture."

"I come across it when I's out buyin' workboots, thought she might like it."

Derek grinned, "I hear you been shoe shoppin' a lot lately. Even throwin' business Gary's way."

"Oh, she tol' you 'bout that?" Louis looked at the ground again to ash his cigarette, "Not sure if she was tryin' to be helpful, or if that's her idea of a joke."

"How bad was them Brogans?" Derek asked.

"Awful," Louis said, shaking his head, "Useless."

Derek laughed, "Bet you still paid full price, though. That asshole got a gift for gettin' people's money. What line did he use on you? Did he say they belonged t'someone famous or somethin'?"

"Nah. Said this sale'd be more like a access fee. He said if I bought the shoes, he'd give me a run at more choice stuff he been stockpilin'."

"As though he'd turn you away from buyin' more of his crap if you didn't buy the shoes."

"You never know," Louis said, "He is that stubborn. An' now I'm curious about his little treasure trove out there."

"I can only imagine what constitutes treasure for that guy," Derek said, still amused.

"You don't think I should waste my time on it?"

"I'd say y'have to," Derek said enthusiastically, "You have t'waste yer time out there so's you can give me a full report. Just don't waste your *money*."

Day 4

The glass pot lid shuddered against the grumbling saucepan. Each vibration released wisps of steam from roiling water made barely visible by a film of dripping condensate. On the neighboring burner, a still-cold casserole dish stood half filled with ingredients. In the adjacent sink, two metal mixing bowls and a fork sat neatly, side by side, waiting to be cleaned, and beyond that, a tall, open trashcan bridged the distance from the counter top to a small table, itself currently covered by a handful of plastic grocery bags. The only light in the room came from a wide, arched entryway that opened into the living room, vacant now apart from a television broadcasting a reality show to a sofa buried under carefully separated piles of partially folded laundry.

Kristin emerged from the half bathroom in the corner of the kitchen. She walked quickly to the stove, removed the lid from the pan, reached into one of the grocery bags, and, in a single motion, she pulled out a box of noodles, tore the top off, and emptied the contents into the boiling water. From there she returned her attention to the table, efficiently emptying two of the bags into a tall cabinet beside the sink, before striding into the living room to sit down with the laundry. As she shook out a t-shirt in front of her, a verbal altercation escalated on the television. Kristin glanced at the clock: 5:45, making good time. She leaned back and stared absently at the screen, lowering the shirt in her hands to her lap.

The sound of a key in the front door jolted her back into action. Kristin sat up, grabbed the remote, and lowered the volume on the television by half before returning her attention to the unfolded shirt. She answered the sound of the closing door by brightly calling out, "In the living room." Kristin picked another shirt from the pile and tracked Jared's noises on the other side of the wall: the clack of the deadbolt, the high squeak of the hall closet being opened, the low thump of his bag dropping to the

The Beard

floor, and only finally the soft reverberation of his footsteps toward the kitchen.

Jared eyed the boiling noodles as he walked past and reached over grocery bags to retrieve a magazine from the table. He turned sideways to shimmy over Kristin's feet, then stopped and stood awkwardly by the laundry pile at the other end of the couch.

"You're home pretty early," Kristin observed.

"Yeah," Jared said absently, "I got into work a little early this morning. It was a slow afternoon, so I cut out a half-hour before closing." Jared tucked his magazine under one arm and began transferring clothes from the couch to the coffee table.

"Hey sweetie," Kristin interrupted, "I'm working on those."

"Oh. Right." Jared looked around, "I can help." He set the magazine on the corner of the table and retrieved two of the socks he had moved. He coupled them sloppily and tossed them next to the stack of neatly folded shirts.

"No," Kristin said with a note of mild irritation, "Please don't. I have a system. Just…" She stood up and carefully moved two of the sorted piles closer to her end of the sofa, clearing a space. Backing toward her seat, Kristin grabbed the remote control and changed the channel over to Jeopardy.

A sharp hiss issued from the kitchen: the sound of water boiling over onto an electric burner.

Kristin mumbled, "Goddammit," and hurried out of the room. By the time Jared appeared in the doorway, she had lowered the heat on the stovetop and was stirring the noodles.

He stopped near the groceries and asked, "Is there anything I can help with?"

Kristin set the pot lid in the sink and answered sharply, "No. It was all going to be done in twenty minutes anyway. Just go watch TV and stop hovering." Jared retreated without further comment, and Kristin busied herself with putting away groceries, washing what was in the sink, and taking out garbage while the noodles finished cooking. Having added those and placed the casserole in the microwave, Kristin walked slowly through a kitchen now

Clifford

populated by clean, clear surfaces and retook her position in the living room.

Jared looked up from his magazine long enough to change the channel back to the reality show that Kristin had been watching. She smiled sweetly at him and placed a small pile of unfolded socks in his lap. As Jared began pairing them off, her eyes narrowed, her grin replaced by a look of concentration. "What?" Jared asked, "Am I doing it wrong or something?"

"No," Kristin replied, "It's your face."

"My face again?"

"Not like that," Kristin waved dismissively, "Your beard is back."

"Oh," Jared said, "Yeah, it's been a few days now. I thought you would've noticed already."

"But I didn't," she said, "And that makes me feel like kind of a jerk."

"You shouldn't," he said, "It's not like I mentioned it. It's been coming in weirdly fast again for the last day, day and a half. I don't know yet if I'm committed to keeping it, but it seemed like you liked it the first time, so I thought, why not?"

"I did," Kristin confirmed as she returned to folding shirts, "But I like how you look both ways, just so you know. And something to think about: if you're going to make it your official new look, you may want to do more to maintain it. Like maybe buy a trimmer or something."

"I thought about that," Jared said, "That would be a good investment. Plus, I was thinking I might color it? Nothing extreme, just something to match the hair on my head."

Kristin nodded thoughtfully, staring hard at Jared's face. "I could support that," she said finally. "Although... it doesn't look like it's coming in as colorful this time, anyway."

"You noticed that too?" Jared asked, placing a few pairs of carefully folded socks on the table. "I thought I was just seeing things since it hasn't completely come in yet."

The Beard

"It's definitely less than before," Kristin said, "You can tell because the blonde streak is there, but not as wide. And that black horseshoe is back, but I don't see the Lincoln Memorial."

"You mean the black arch?" Jared asked casually. "It's sort of there again, but it's not in the same place though."

"What? Is that possible?" Kristin asked incredulously. She paused in her work to take a second look. "You're right: it's the same symbol, but up on your cheek. And the exact same pattern over there… That doesn't make any sense."

"I don't think it needs to make sense," Jared answered, "Last time must have been a fluke."

"But where it is now," Kristin said slowly, "It *would* make sense if you changed the size and position of the map. Then it would start near where we ended."

"So you think it's reversed?" Jared asked.

"Not reversed," Kristin said, standing up. She stepped closer and leaned to within an inch of Jared's face, "I'm not sure yet, but it looks like that bull's eye where we stopped is coming in again, only smaller and on this side. And then, if those blonde hairs do lead down that way, that would take you away from the cemetery. But I can't really tell. Even if the hair was thicker, the patterns are coming in so small."

"So, should I color it then?" Jared sighed.

"Hmm, no," Kristin said matter-of-factly, as she straightened her posture. "We're going to have to go back out and follow it again before you do that."

"Can we at least take the train to the cemetery this time?"

"Yes Janet," Kristin said exasperated, "You can take the train. We wouldn't want to wear out your dainty feet."

"Thank you," Jared said with mock aplomb.

"For now, though," Kristin jumped in, "You can stop folding socks."

"Wait… you don't want to follow it right now, do you?"

"Course not," Kristin said, turning as the microwave began to beep, "Dinner is ready."

Day 9

The smell of bacon filled Jared's nostrils and made his mouth water. He shuffled one step at a time past a pair of refrigerator cases, to follow a line of people to the sandwich station, only vaguely aware of the hum of conversation over soft classic rock. Directly in front of him, wearing a tan suit, Kevin drummed his hands on the edge of the counter while he ordered. Track lighting gleamed indiscriminately across polished wood and Kevin's hair gel.

The line took one more step, and the sandwich maker began his recitation without looking up from his work. "Good afternoon and what can I get you to-," he paused, making eye contact with Jared. Breaking into a smile he announced, "Oh hey, Ham-n-Swiss, how you been?"

"I'm good," Jared said amiably, "Trying to stay cool."

"Hear that," the sandwich maker answered.

"I was thinking I'd have a BLT today," Jared said. "That bacon smells great, I think I'm sold on it."

"Right," the sandwich maker nodded, his smile fading, "But it's Wednesday though."

"Well sure," Jared shrugged, "But a BLT... that's not a daily special, is it?"

"Nah," the man said dejectedly. "But you order ham and swiss every Wednesday: I already made it and sent it to the register for you. If you still want it, that is. I mean, I *guess* we can toss it if you really want something else, but it seems like a waste is all."

Jared nodded, slightly nonplussed, "Oh... Okay. That would be wasteful. I think the ham will be fine."

"Good t'hear!" the sandwich maker beamed. "At the register: tomatoes and mustard, just how you like it."

"Thanks," Jared said unenthusiastically as he walked the length of the counter.

The Beard

Behind the register, a young woman turned to meet his eye. "Hey... Ham-n-Swiss!" she called, "I got you down here: $6.50, as always."

Jared paid, and the young woman handed him a paper-wrapped sandwich with a smile. He accepted it, silently noted that the food was stone cold, and smiled politely while he nodded his appreciation. The sound of Kevin's voice led him around the corner into the seating area.

"All the same," Kevin bellowed, "They are poised to have a great season."

Next to Kevin, a man with deep acne scars, dressed in a black suit with a thin black tie shook his head. "I don't think a couple wins against Miami means as much as you think it does."

On Kevin's other side, a fat man in an ill-fitting sport coat chimed in, "No. Chris, all we're saying is that it's way too early in the season to get that hung up on standings. How does a Red Sox fan not get that?"

Jared pulled out a chair at the circular table and wedged himself between the fat man and a thin man wearing a light grey suit and a stern countenance. The latter stared hard into the screen of a smart phone. Jared cordially asked of the thin man, "They keeping you busy there, Anthony?" Anthony grunted and continued scrolling on his screen with one hand while eating with the other.

On the opposite side of the table, Chris shot back, "And all I'm saying is, that home-town favorite bullshit doesn't work for us. Our teams mostly suck."

"Loyalty doesn't suck," Kevin stated.

"Yeah," the fat man answered, "Boston sucks."

"Not as much as your whole league," Chris shot back.

Jared leaned back in his chair, unwrapped his sandwich, and took a cold bite. The water from the tomatoes had turned the bread limp and soggy. His eyes settled on the edge of the dark wood table in front of him, and his mind settled on his plans for the weekend.

Or, more accurately, on his lack of a plan. As had been the case a few weeks previous, Jared had no idea what he would find on the other side of his beard, but unlike the last time, he felt sure that he would at least find something, or if not a thing, then some answer or lead... anything that might make sense of what he and Kristin were doing and why they should be the ones doing it.

It was around this point in his train of thought that Jared sensed he was getting ahead of himself. After all, there was no evidence of a specific purpose behind the map. Discoveries on the last trip had lined up too perfectly to feel coincidental, but that was still a far cry from demonstrating a pointed mission of any kind, and farther still from marking Jared as *the* person somehow qualified to see it through. Jared decided that the whole thing didn't make him special, that the strongest odds still favored them reaching a dead end, and that all they would prove is that he had unpredictable follicles. That, and the fact some guy had died a bunch of times a hundred years ago.

But for the moment, Jared thought, what harm could there be in allowing for more possibilities? Even if he would ultimately be disappointed, Jared had decided to let his imagination run. Only privately. With no mention of it to anyone ever.

"So, Jared," a dour baritone interrupted. "How's things at the bank?"

Jared blinked and looked around the table. Kevin, Chris and Roger had become dead quiet, singularly focused on devouring their food. To Jared's right, Anthony still held his phone in front of him, but now looked at Jared, waiting patiently for a response.

"Oh," Jared said, disoriented. "Ahhhmmm... Let's see... what's new at the bank..." He tapered off, unclear whether he should bother to continue while the rest of the group paused expectantly. Jared legitimately wracked his brain: he had long ago given up being asked to contribute to these lunch conversations, but hated to think that he had lost the ability when called upon. "It's actually been kind of miserable lately," he said finally.

Without shifting attention from his sandwich, Kevin disinterestedly followed up, "That right?"

The Beard

"Yeah," Jared continued. "It's this damn 'Savoring Savers' promotion we have going. See, the bank came up with this limited time offer of a three-year CD with two percent APY and no penalties."

Anthony tentatively nodded, "That... sucks?"

"No," Jared enthusiastically corrected him, "It's really good. Too good, is the problem. It should be enough to get the attention of large depositors. But Mr. Sherman got so excited, that he has us pushing it on everyone who comes in. He stands around making sure we bring it up during every transaction. And 'no penalties' means there's no minimum deposit, so now we have a ton of new accounts that are basically non-existent. Just a lot more work with no reward, because the boss is hung up on the wrong details."

"You know what that reminds me of," Kevin said to no one in particular, "Is Hernandez."

"Oh yeah!" Roger replied. Pulling his round chin back toward his ample bosom, he looked over his glasses at Kevin and mockingly impersonated, "Negotiating contracts is above your pay grade."

Turning to Kevin, Chris chimed in, "But you think Hernandez will ever admit you were right if the company loses its shirt?"

Anthony returned to his cell phone. Jared considered doing the same, but remembered that his battery was dead again. He looked over Anthony's shoulder to the clock at the top of the screen and sighed to himself.

Ten more minutes of this before he could get back to work.

Day 10

Louis's truck idled up a sloped and winding driveway. He squinted under its faded visor, against sunlight made brighter by contrast as it burst sporadically through the shade of scattered trees. The sound of gravel crunching beneath his tires rode a warm breeze through the open passenger window, which was presently full of Marlow: the dog's panting face stretched nearly two feet out of the cab. As the road leveled, sparse forest gave way to an open field. Here on the hilltop, a constant wind riffled tall, brown grass and pushed large clouds across a strikingly blue sky. Thirty yards in front of Louis's dusty windshield, the pastorality was blighted by a single-story house set amongst cannibalized auto frames on cinder blocks. The shingles on the roof of the building had begun to curl up, and bare patches in the siding exposed shredded tar paper and tufts of stained insulation.

Louis pulled into an empty patch of lawn near the house's concrete front steps, cut the engine, hopped down and strode to the entrance, making a point to leave his door open so Marlow could clumsily clamor out of the truck behind him. He knocked, waited, and checked his watch. Looking at Marlow, Louis mumbled, "8 to 4 my ass," before starting back to the truck. As the dog crouched to leap back into the cab, Louis said, "Wait." Rubbing his eye with the heel of his hand, he inexplicably explained to the dog, "If he's here we should find him. I don't intend to forfeit eight dollars, and I don't intend to drive out here again." Marlow listened intently and then followed Louis around the back of the house.

Neat rows of still whole cars, interrupted by stacks of wheels, car doors, and panels, ran across the property to an enormous, weathered stable. The objects taken together against the virgin landscape somehow made Louis think of a motor oil stain on a wedding dress. As the pair made their way through the yard, Louis paused occasionally to peer through the windows of the vehicles: a

The Beard

Taurus with all the seats torn out, a Suburban with no steering wheel or stereo, a LeSabre missing its dashboard, gauges, and gear selector... every seemingly intact automobile was really somewhere in the process of being hollowed out.

The further Louis and Marlow got from the house, the wider the distance between the cars. Fresh mud and flattened vegetation transitioned to tall grass which, when viewed up close, was actually concealing more rusted axles and brake drums, scattered piles of which extended well into the field. Beyond every mess looked to be another mess.

Marlow stopped to hike his leg on a Dodge Neon with no doors or windows. The dog's reach was high enough, Louis considered, that if he popped the fuel door, Marlow could fill the tank, assuming the car still had one. Marlow paused suddenly with his leg half extended and cocked his large head to one side. Without further provocation, he trotted to the end of the aisle and out of sight around the side of the outbuilding.

As Louis neared the corner of the structure, he heard what Marlow had already noticed: a sharp hiss punctuated by high-pitched snaps and the groan of sheet metal giving up on itself. On a dirt patch outside the large rear barn door, Gary sat on an overturned plastic bucket, intensely focused on running a torch under a rear quarter panel of the Buick he had been driving two weeks earlier.

Once Louis had taken up an impatient stance next to Marlow, the dog wagged twice and gave one hard bark. "The Hell!!!" Gary exclaimed, dropping his torch in the dirt. He spun around and yanked a pair of heavily tinted goggles away from his thick glasses. After a moment's recognition, Gary shouted, "Dammit Marlow! Sneakin' up like that." He picked up his torch and turned off the gas.

Louis gestured to a patch of smoldering grass behind the car and asked, "You gonna get that?"

Clifford

Gary reached under the car and pulled out a second bucket, half full of water, which he used to douse the embers. "You gonna train your frickin' dog, man? Dog that size gotta be trained."

"He don't jump on people an' he don't shit inside," Louis answered casually, "So he's in good shape, far as I'm concerned." Gary stood up and shook out one leg. He took a moment to regain some measure of composure. Louis nodded to the car and asked, "You tearin' this one up? I thought it could run."

"Well sure it *could* run," Gary said, "Any car *could* run if you care 'nough to make it run. But runnin' ain't the most valuable thing this one can do for me today. The body shop needs a rear panel. I got plenty of other cars around here to ride around in." Gary paused expectantly. After a moment he asked, "So? Wanna fill me in? Why you out here?"

"Came to see the good stuff," Louis answered.

"Good stuff?" Gary asked, squinting at Louis incredulously, "To what 'Good Stuff' are you referring, sir?"

"Last time I saw you," Louis sighed, "You tol' me to come out and see all the good stuff you leave at home."

"Ohhh," Gary said, "Civil War stuff. God, that was weeks ago, man, I totally forgot."

"Yeah, well, I tol' you it'd be a couple weeks, now it has been, and that's what I come for."

"Tell you what," Gary said, "I's about ready for a break anyhow. You wanna step into my office here, I think I got some things might interest you." Without waiting for a response, Gary led the way to a padlocked man-sized door on the back of the building and pulled an enormous key ring from his pocket. "Too damn many keys," he muttered. "Any given time, all but three of these keys goes to something that's about to be garbage. But you'll want doors off and steering columns out before you feel right about tossing the keys."

Gary sorted through quickly, selected a key, popped the lock and put his shoulder to the rotting, wooden door. It scraped across a dirt floor with a groan and a shudder. Gary stepped through into the

The Beard

half-dark with Marlow following at his heel, and Louis bringing up the rear.

The interior felt large and open: portions of a former hayloft had either rotted away or been removed, exposing the eaves high above and allowing more daylight to filter in through gaps and holes in the roof. Several of the horse stalls on either side of a central aisle were in similar condition: missing gates, rotted walls or caved-in partitions. Compared to the land outside though, the space was very tidy. There were no vehicles or vehicle parts, and aside from a few puddles, the floor appeared to be regularly swept. Louis followed Marlow who followed Gary to a surviving stall halfway to the front door. "Here we are," Gary announced. He pulled the chain on an overhead light and swept an arm theatrically before them, "Civil War shit."

Louis stepped into the space, which had been opened into the contiguous stalls to create more room for assorted bulk goods. A pile of trousers in one corner, a crate of dippers and canteens in another. A paper shopping bag full of drawers and socks. A stack of rolled up tents. A ten-foot rod hung with uniform jackets, a fifty-gallon trash can full of slouch hats and kepi, a small pyramid of knapsacks and, leaned clear back in a corner, a handful of rusted three-banded muskets.

"Browse to your heart's content," Gary instructed, channeling a carnival barker. "Find something you like and I'll quote you a price."

"No offense," Louis said, nudging one of a dozen skillets with his toe, "But this looks like a whole lot of the same ol' stuff. I don't see anything looks antique."

"'Cause it ain't," Gary answered unoffended. "All used, some from enthusiasts, mostly from quitters. You ever think about the life cycle a' people's hobbies? Folks get into something like reenacting, first thing they do is run out an' buy everything they think they might need. Then after a year they do one of two things: they do like you and get way too into it, in which case they figure out that none of what they bought early on is good enough, or they quit altogether, have a closet full of stuff they don't need. Used to be that people would sit on those things, but in this economy, they want their money out. Either way, it means a glut of supply, which means I get it cheap, and I have room enough to store it while I wait for some new hobbyist to come along, so why not?"

Louis nodded thoughtfully.

"But it ain't just this reenacting business," Gary continued, "It's really any hobby. This is just the one I know the most about. I don't think art supplies would be a good investment, on account of they don't do well used. But I could sell you a mess a' athletic equipment from the stalls across the way here. An' once I learn a bit more on storin' an' pricing, I think I might get a good thing goin' on musical instruments."

"Back to what you was sayin' though, 'bout people like me wanna replace what they bought early on."

"Yeh," Gary confirmed, "Upgraders. You bet."

"Then you know I already upgraded, so this stuff won't be good enough for me," Louis said. "Why you have me drive out?"

"I see where you're goin'," Gary nodded. "You want somethin' more unique. Not just period appropriate. Somethin' more like a conversation piece."

"Yeah," Louis said, "Exactly."

"That'll be the 'Fine Merchandise Tub,'" Gary answered matter-of-factly. "That stays in the house. If you would care to follow me." He pulled the chain on the overhead bulb and disappeared back into the main space of the stable.

"Hang on," Louis said, his eyes struggling to adjust to the dim stall. He shuffled tentatively toward the jingling of Marlow's tags. Without warning, the sound stopped and Louis' knee struck something soft and warm. The obstacle moved suddenly and the tags jingled away furiously, as Louis fell face first into the trouser pile.

"Watch your step in there," Gary said disinterestedly from the outer door.

The Beard

Louis disentangled himself from the musty smell of strangers' pants and half crawled to the door of the stall. He pulled himself up as he walked into the light and stopped at the door to knock the dust from his knees.

"You two done in there?" Gary asked while he turned to reapply the padlock, "Got everything you come in with? Your dignity, for instance?"

"Yeh," Louis said, "We're good."

The men fell into line with Marlow trotting in between and again passed silently through the auto carcasses. The steady breeze became cooler, and cicadas screamed from the trees along the drive, as the sky over the house began to darken. Gary pulled the mass of keys from his pocket and began flipping through them well before they had reached the grease-stained backdoor of the small house. "Sorry for all the security," he mumbled as he unlocked the deadbolt, "But you can't be too careful these days."

Gary held the door for Marlow and Louis to enter a small, open kitchen. Formica countertops ran the perimeter of the room, interrupted by yellowing appliances and a steel drop sink, above which the luggage rack from the top of a Volkswagen had been wired to the ceiling and repurposed as a hanging pot rack. Peeling floral-print wallpaper peeked from beneath composite wood cabinets, all of which had had their doors removed. A sturdy wooden table and two metal folding chairs stood in the center of the room. On the table, the transmission from a 2004 Honda Civic sat on a torn pillowcase like a filthy centerpiece.

"Grab a seat and pardon the mess," Gary instructed as he crossed the room and exited deeper into the house. Marlow crawled under the table while Louis pulled a chair to one end. After some distant clattering, Gary returned with a large, green plastic tub. A strip of silver duct tape on one side bore the words "Fine Merchandise" scrawled in Sharpie. He deposited the trove at Louis' feet and positioned himself in the remaining chair opposite.

Louis quietly withdrew items from the tub: a touch lamp with a glass paneled shade painted with Western themes, a few flow blue cups wrapped in newspaper, two collectible plates, and a stack of three glass ashtrays stolen from as many casinos. Gary leaned back in his chair and said, "Keep diggin'. You'll want the bulk items, further down." Louis gently removed a brightly painted decanter shaped like a grinning dachshund hiking its leg with four deep depressions in its back to accommodate shot glasses. "Yeh," Gary chuckled softly, "That was a find: I might not part with that one."

Louis leaned further into the tub and came back with a freezer bag full of defunct fountain pens, which he placed on the floor with the larger items. Another freezer bag, this one full of coins, he placed on the table. "There'll be a stamp album down there too," Gary said. "Philatelists, numismatists: I got 'em all covered." Sorting in this manner, Louis concluded with a table collection that included the bag of coins, a second bag full of buttons, and a small tin containing several insignia patches. He quickly inspected all three before gently pouring the buttons and insignia onto the table. "What about this one?" Gary asked, nudging a cigar box on the floor with his toe.

"That's cigarette lighters," Louis said. "I'm still thinking Civil War."

"Yeah, but they're pretty old though. Some cool stuff in there. You see the pistol lighter?"

"I did," Louis replied flatly, still sorting through buttons "But I don't have room to buy everything. Think about selling those online."

"Internet ain't really my style," Gary sniffed. "I prefer transactions like this here: face to face."

"Well," Louis said looking up, "You may end up feelin' different 'bout *this* transaction. Not seein' much here, man."

"Are you serious?" Gary growled.

"Yeah," Louis nodded, "I am. There's a couple dug buttons: rough shape, but I might pay ten bucks apiece for 'em. These others are all reproductions. Thinkin' seventy-five cents each, and I counted twenty in the bag there."

"There's more than twenty," Gary snapped.

70

The Beard

"Not if you don't count World War reproductions," Louis explained, pulling one out of pile. "Look here, Gary, this one got a swastika imprint. That sure ain't Civil War. Have you even gone through these?"

"Lemme see that," Gary said snatching it out of Louis' hand. He examined the piece of brass before tossing it off to the corner of the room. "I don't truck in Nazi crap."

Louis continued, "So two dug buttons at ten each, plus fifteen for the repros, and I'll take these five insignia, but those are worth maybe a buck fifty a pop. An' that's $32.50 so far."

"You're wasting my time at $32.50," Gary said, "You should take another look."

"I'm not quite done," Louis said reaching to the floor. "There's this earthenware bottle. It's new but I like it. Add that to the pile, I'd take the final tally to fifty."

"Total?" Gary asked. "But how 'bout that compass in there? Don't you try tellin' me *that's* a reproduction."

"I didn't see that go by," Louis said.

"Well shoot," Gary answered climbing off his chair to reach into the bottom of the tub, "That's the kind of thing what I was thinkin' of when I told you to come out here. Looks like you missed a couple a' things down there." He straightened up and placed two lead balls on the edge of the table before handing Louis a small brass disc, a little over two inches in diameter.

"Those musket balls are nice, might do something with those for five dollars."

"Y'might," Gary said, "But first you look at what's in your hand there. Now, what'll you give me for that?"

Louis took his time studying the disk. He gently pulled off the thin, bent lid and peered at the compass face underneath. After lightly shaking it, he turned it over, looked at it quickly, replaced the lid and set it on the table. "I'll go with nothin'," he said, "That one I don't want."

Clifford

"And what's wrong with that, now?" Gary demanded. "An original antique compass. And you said you want a conversation piece, well, that's what that is!"

"First off," Louis answered loudly, "It's beat to hell: you've got pocket wear on the side, two serious scratches on the back, and that dent on the lid, I would swear it was folded in half at some point. On top of that it doesn't function…"

"The hell you say!" Gary interrupted, pulling the lid off and turning the compass on the tabletop. "Look at that," he said, pointing at the needle, "Points in one direction, just like it should."

"But which direction?" Louis gestured past the needle to the waning light coming through the windows. "Unless the sun is setting in the North, this is all messed up. I don't figure it's even scientifically possible for a compass to point full West, so this is just wrong beyond all reason. Plus, again, it's from the wrong period."

"It's 19th Century!" Gary wailed.

"It's twenty years late!" Louis insisted, flipping the compass over to reveal an inscription on the back. "Says right here: 'Henry S. Strafford 1880'. I can't use that. But that ain't even the point: in this condition, I doubt you get a dime for it from anyone else."

Gary deflated back into his chair and glowered through his thick lenses for a long moment. "So. What are we up to now, fifty?"

"Fifty-five," Louis answered, "With the musket balls."

"Gonna make yourself some nice earrings with those?" Gary sneered.

Louis countered firmly, "Fifty-five for the lot."

"Gimme three twenties," Gary said, "And I'll throw in that compass you like so much."

"Fine," Louis shrugged, "But I'm only doin' this so's I don't have to watch you count change." Gary waved off the comment while Louis dug out his wallet. Attempting sincerity, Louis held out the bills and offered, "Nice little place you got here."

The Beard

"Nah," Gary said, setting the money on the table and reaching into a nearby drawer, "Kind of a crap hole if we're honest with ourselves. Like livin' in my workshop these days." He pulled out a plastic bag and handed it to Louis, who began packing up his purchases. "Been thinkin' a' buildin' a new place on the property."

"But I thought you grew up here," Louis said.

"I did," Gary answered, "Then I got bigger. An' I got more stuff. An' the house is the same size as always. Still, I don't need anything too fancy. Thinkin' I might look into one of them modular homes, maybe save some money."

"Just make sure the city don't screw you," Louis warned, "You raise your property value, they'll reassess your taxes."

"Forgot about that," Gary muttered. "Been meanin' to get to the courthouse an' ask about permits and such, I'll have to check on that too." Louis knotted the handles of the bag and stood up. "You got everything?" Gary asked. Marlow crawled out from under the table and stretched his nose to sniff the dachshund decanter. Gary yelled, "Don't you even think about it!" Marlow yawned and sauntered to the door.

Louis patted down his pockets to check for his wallet and keys and replied, "Yeh. We're good."

"In that case," Gary said, walking around Marlow to yank the door open, "A pleasure as always, gentlemen, and safe travels."

Louis nodded and followed the dog into the early evening.

Day 12

Jared stepped cautiously through a waist high plastic gate. The octagonal brown floor tiles gleamed darkly under a combination of rainwater and their own sweat that produced a petroleum-jelly-like sheen across the breadth of the Arlington Metro station.

"You need to wait!" Kristin yelled from behind him. Jared paused while she skidded through the gate and then baby-stepped to his position near the base of the escalators. "You don't know where we're going yet."

"Sure, I do," Jared stated, "We're going up."

"Right," Kristin humored him as she took off her backpack to stow her fare card, "But up to where?"

"Up, up," he said dumbly, "To the Women's Memorial, the black horseshoe or whatever."

"But why would we do that? It looks like we come back this direction anyways," she said.

"Yes, but I thought we had to start where it starts," Jared answered. "That's what you kept saying last time."

"Last time was a really nice day," Kristin said patiently. She replaced her pack and tip-toed around to examine Jared's cheek, "As where today is shitty. I can't use the picture on my phone in the rain, and I don't feel like standing in it to figure out your face, so we should check what we can before we go any farther." Jared stood quietly, awaiting further instruction. "So, it looks like," Kristin continued, "We would come back this direction and take a left onto some sort of loop. And then it gets really small."

"Yeah," Jared said, "What's up with that? I noticed the blonde is really fat on both my sideburns, but then I can hardly see it in between."

Kristin shrugged, "Not sure. Maybe we'll find out: there were lots of things last time that didn't make sense until we got up close."

The Beard

"True," Jared said thoughtfully. "So we go up and look for a loop thing on the left."

"No," Kristin corrected him, "Because we're going toward the horseshoe, so the loop will be on the right."

"Right," Jared nodded, continuing to the escalator.

"And don't forget your hood," Kristin called, shuffling along behind him.

Jared pulled up the hood of his sweatshirt and tucked his hands in his pockets while the escalator carried him from the cover of the tunnel through the translucent curtain of water falling beyond. At the top, he stepped over a puddle to pause near the blocks-long hedgerow. Somewhere out of view, Jared heard tires hissing over wet pavement like the sound of so many slot cars. When he was sure that Kristin was within sight of him, he lowered his head and continued down the wet sidewalk, keeping his eyes trained on the ground beside it. The pair continued single file for more than a hundred yards before a break in the hedges opened to a crosswalk with a trail veering off to the right.

Jared glanced up briefly to confirm that Kristin's pink hoodie was still in his periphery before following the trail downhill. Without a word or a thought, he walked several yards between a roadway and a chain link fence, beyond which lie fields of identical white headstones. Both of those features gradually pulled away from the trail as he approached the bottom of the hill. Kristin's voice cut through the patter of rain on his hood, "Hold on! You're going the wrong way!"

Jared stopped and turned to discover Kristin standing halfway up the trail. As he approached, she explained, "The angle we're walking, that was a line of red hair. The blonde trail should have looped around."

"A red line," Jared said. "That's a cross street, right?" He glanced around for an alternate route before eyeing the nearby roadway. "To loop clear around, that's the on-ramp to the highway."

"That looks right," Kristin sighed.

Clifford

"That does not look safe for walking," Jared stated. "I guess… Do we go home and get the car, if we're serious?"

Kristin nodded quietly. After a moment of somber reflection, she exclaimed, "Goddammit!"

"What?" Jared asked, "It's only 9:30… we come back and drive it this afternoon, no big deal."

"It's not that," Kristin sulked, "I got up early and made us lunches again. I'm tired of throwing out perfectly good sandwiches."

"You're pissed that you don't get to eat in the rain?"

Kristin narrowed her eyes and shook her head at him. "Rain, shine, here, or in the car," she said softly, "Your lunch today is that goddamn sandwich."

Raindrops fell hard against the uncovered window of their warm, dry living room. With her hair still damp, Kristin turned on the floor lamp next to the couch and resumed her work on the laptop set on the coffee table in front of her. On the screen, she zoomed in and out of an aerial view of Arlington, pausing occasionally to consult a piece of paper that lie on the table, and to say softly to it and her both, "Yeah… yeah, that's what I thought." She retrieved her sandwich from a plate on the couch beside her and took a bite as she opened a new tab.

Kristin scrolled through a list of short videos while she chewed. She eventually selected the title *Baby Panda Sneezing*. As the prone creature in the video lifted off the floor, Kristin chortled, her mouth still full of food.

From the other side of the wall came the noise of the front door latching followed by the rustle and thump of Jared removing his hoodie and sneakers.

Kristin quickly swallowed and minimized the video before calling, "Hey c'mere, I think I found something."

The Beard

Jared took his time coming around the corner, water still dripping from his hair and beard. "What's so funny?" he asked. "I could hear you laughing from outside."

"Nothing," she said, "Not important." Kristin moved her plate from the sofa to the table and patted the space next to her. "Come sit, I have to show you something."

Maneuvering around the furniture, Jared said, "Well, the car has a full tank, and I moved it around front. Been awhile since I've had it out so I went ahead and checked the oil. The level is fine, but when's the last time you had that changed?" Kristin shrugged and Jared continued, "I noticed too that there's a new scratch on the driver's door...,"

"Can I please just show you what I found?" Kristin interrupted. Jared raised his hands in surrender. "Good," she nodded, picking her phone and the piece of paper off the table. "Before you left, I took more pictures of your face."

"Yes, I recall," Jared acknowledged.

"The first thing I did after that was to blow up the pictures and then copy the shape of the entire blond line onto this sheet of paper. Just to put it in two dimensions without your chin in the mix."

"Yeah," he nodded thoughtfully. "Drawn out like that, it's a lot straighter in the middle than I realized."

"And next," Kristin continued, setting the laptop in between them, "I compared it to the map of where we were this morning."

Jared looked back and forth between the paper and the screen. "Okay. I recognize the exit to Jefferson Davis Highway," he said, "But I don't see a road off the South like you have on the paper here."

"Not from this view," Kristin confirmed, "But you see just past Memorial Ave? That's where the blonde part gets skinny. So I thought if I made the road on the screen a bit skinnier..." She zoomed out on the laptop several times.

"Then the line on the page looks kind of like I-95," Jared finished.

"No, it looks *exactly* like I-95," Kristin corrected, "Every inch of it."

Jared muttered, "But if it changed scale that much, the line would cover a hundred miles."

"And what is a hundred miles south of the cemetery?" Kristin prodded.

"Richmond," Jared answered. "Wait, so we're supposed to drive clear to Richmond tonight? And where in Richmond? Can you even tell from that far out?"

"No you can't," Kristin said. "Which is probably why the lines get so large again on your other sideburn."

"Oh, it zooms back in then, to match the streets where we're going. Y'know, we could just skip the drive and match up the lines with the street view on the map."

"And that brings us to the last thing I found," Kristin stated as she zoomed in repeatedly over a spot on the map near the center of Richmond. As the colors briefly pixilated and snapped into focus, a large gray box appeared that covered an entire neighborhood. Kristin switched to satellite imagery and the box remained, blotting out lighter grays and greens and now featuring the cold label 'Imagery Not Available.'

"Then I guess we're driving to Richmond," Jared conceded.

"Not tonight though," Kristin said as she put the computer back on the table. "If we can't tell where we're going, I don't want to find out in the dark and the rain."

Jared sighed, "Looks like I'll be taking the car back to the lot." He stood slowly and shook his head as he moved back around the couch.

"Oh, it's not so bad," Kristin cooed. She picked up the laptop and pointed the screen in his direction. "Here, I found something to make you feel better." She pulled up the panda video and hit play, laughing along with the audio.

Jared grinned quizzically, "Had you not seen that?"

"No... you have?"

"Sure," he shrugged, "I thought everyone had."

78

Day 13

"You're sure it's 78?"

"Yeah." Kristin retrieved a few sheets of loose paper off the dashboard in front of her. "Says right here, Exit 78."

"But how are you sure?" Jared asked while he concentrated on the tree lined 6-lane Highway in front of him.

"Because the map still works here," Kristin explained. "Last night I compared the photos of the blown up parts of your beard to the parts of the online map that still load. We take 95 into Richmond, then just after the part on your cheek that looks like a witch-hat..."

"That red and yellow triangle," Jared confirmed.

"Right," Kristin said, "The witch-hat. So past the bottom of that we take a sharp right, which on the map would be North Boulevard. And to get to North Boulevard we need Exit 78: I wrote it all down..."

"As long you're sure." Jared signaled a lane change.

"I am," Kristin nodded confidently, "I have street names up to Ellen Road, and then we count cross streets from the red hair for the rest."

Jared slowed as he pulled onto the exit ramp, curving past a radio tower with rusted, tin, out-buildings at its base. The tall weeds along the shoulder parted briefly for a carefully landscaped embankment surrounding an underpass. Sunlight poured through the windshield as the pair emerged on the other side, and Jared resumed easing onto the brake pedal.

"You know the speed limit is still 35 through here, yeah?" Kristin asked.

"But you said we're turning right, right?"

"Right," she nodded.

Jared continued decelerating to a crawl as a pickup hugged his rear bumper, "'Right' as in right, or 'right' as in correct?"

Clifford

"Either," Kristin railed in exasperation, "Or both. Just get in the goddamn right lane and go!"

Jared jerked the car forward through the turn and allowed the speedometer to level off at 36. "You need to calm down a bit," he said firmly.

"You need to stop driving like a confused retiree on her way home from church," Kristin shot back.

They coasted wordlessly through the intersection with Ellen Road and past a baseball stadium before Jared finally replied, "I'm sorry. But this is maybe the second time I've driven all year, and I don't know where it is we're going."

Kristin calmly replied, "The next left and then the second right. That's where we're going."

"Yeah, but where does that take us?"

"Dunno," Kristin shrugged, "Does that bother you?"

"A little bit, yeah. It does. Doesn't it bother you?"

Kristin shifted in her seat and pointed past a gravel lot on her side, "Speed limit is 25, sweetie. And be ready for that left up here."

Jared followed the yellow center line and pulled onto the narrow street between a repurposed factory and a car dealership. "Not going to answer then?" he asked.

"I think you're over-thinking this," Kristin said. "I just want to follow things through. And when we're done, we know our way back to the highway. So we see where it leads, and go home, and that's all."

The vehicle jogged across overgrown railroad tracks before the street widened into a tree-lined boulevard. On the right, small grassy hills surrounded by an ornate iron fence gradually leveled into a pair of football fields, the four uprights jutting toward large, slow moving clouds. Across the next intersection, the neighborhood's character changed again: freshly painted wrought iron transitioned into rusted chain-link and barbed wire, rolling hills gave ground to expansive parking lots, the uprights were traded for telephone poles.

The Beard

Jared flipped his turn signal approaching a red light. "You said the second right?"

"Yes," Kristin answered quietly. "And after that, the second right again."

"So we're driving in a circle," Jared observed, rolling through the turn.

"Not a full circle," Kristin corrected, "But sort of around something."

Jared dutifully took the first of their turns onto a six-lane road lined with two story shops. The windows were dark and the sidewalks and parking lots empty.

"I'm kind of glad we had to do this on a Sunday morning," Kristin observed, "Seems like this would be a totally different experience on a weekday."

"That's an odd mural," Jared said absently. "Is that supposed to be birds or squirrels, you think?"

Kristin calmly reached over and tugged at the steering wheel. "You're drifting, sweetie," she said. "Even if we're the only car here, there are still rules. Also, we should be in the right lane. Also, they're birds. Clearly."

Jared said, "The second right again?"

"Not yet. Soon. Just past this stop light."

"At the chicken place?"

"Hmm... not quite." Kristin scrutinized her hand-drawn map. "A bit past that I think."

Jared nodded, flicked his turn signal and moved over coming through the stoplight. He slowed on the opposite side of the fast-food chicken drive-thru and idled past a much longer building with a gray façade. Above small front doors, an outsized central gable featured an equally overstated arched window framed by the words, "Commonwealth of Virginia."

"Anywhere up here, look for a chance to turn," Kristin motioned. The turn signal ticked again as Jared eased into a driveway at the far corner of the building. "And now you can park. Any time," Kristin concluded.

Clifford

"How about I park by that 'No Trespassing' sign we just passed?" Jared asked.

"Okay, so park in the back, if you're worried," Kristin instructed. "Not like anyone is here today anyways."

Jared pulled around and into a spot near the building, adjacent to a large, paved, lot peppered with islands of grass and small trees. He cut the engine, threw off his seat belt and leaned on the driver's side door. It opened with a long moan.

Jared climbed out into the bright mid-morning. A warm breeze forewarned of the muggy afternoon to come, but for that moment was still content to faintly rustle nearby leaves and press billowing clouds across a temperate sky. Squinting and stretching, Jared slammed the car door and paused to run his hand across a deep white scratch in the dusty black paint. The vehicle was hardly showroom quality to begin with: his uncle had given him the '99 Jetta as a graduation present in 2005. It had been years since the car had passed the hundred-thousand mile mark, and it was pleasantly surprising that it hadn't seen more damage in a decade. Surprising, but no accident: as with everything Jared owned, the car was road weary but well maintained. As seldom as Jared drove, he couldn't practically justify buying a new (or even less used) replacement, and large gifts were rare enough in his life that he felt that trading up would be ungrateful.

"I really think it'll buff out," Kristin called over the top of the car.

"Not so sure…" Jared mumbled.

"I swear it didn't happen while I was driving," she added.

Jared looked over and noted the concern on her face: even he knew that his attachment to the car was silly, but he also knew that she understood, and she didn't judge it. "I believe you," he said, forcing a smile. "So," he continued more enthusiastically, walking around to Kristin's side, "Where to now? Where's the buried treasure?"

"We're close," Kristin said, looking from the hand-drawn map in her hand to Jared's left cheek. "Like real close." She turned to

82

face the back of the long building and pointed without looking up from her paper. "The online map was blacked out to Monument Ave., but I think the last light was North Allison. That puts us a little more than halfway to Strawberry Street, and that means..." She grabbed Jared's shoulder and turned him away from the building, "A few yards this way."

Kristin led Jared by the hand to a small, slightly elevated concrete oval at the end of a row of empty parking spaces. She took one exaggerated step to the middle of the tiny island and stopped. "Then it's that building?" Jared asked, indicating a modern ten-story office building in front of them, "Or this one," he pointed back to the older, stouter building where they had parked.

"That's just it," Kristin said, "It doesn't look like either building. It looks like it should be right here, this spot."

"But that doesn't make any sense," Jared said, looking around. "No historical markers, no signs, just a parking lot... not even signs for the building the parking lot goes to."

"The one out front said 'Commonwealth of Virginia.'"

"Yeah, but what agency? What department?"

"Well... This is where the trail ends," Kristin stated with certainty, "I agree we should look around while we're here, but it won't change where the map leads."

Jared stared at the office building, before turning and walking at a brisk pace to the building nearest the car. He had walked more than half the length of the structure before Kristin sighed and stepped off the island in pursuit. As he disappeared around the end of the driveway, she considered running to catch up, but chose instead to maintain her measured pace and give him a chance to work out his curiosity. She eventually found him cupping his hands to the glass front door, straining to see past the glare from the climbing sun. "Find something?" Kristin asked patiently.

"Found nothing," Jared said without lowering his hands. "Like actual nothing. A couple boxes in the corner, but otherwise the place looks cleaned out."

"You think it's the other building then?"

Clifford

Jared turned and stood thoughtfully with his hands in his pockets. "It couldn't be though, could it? The other building is so new, I don't see how it could be related to Henry Sullivan Strafford."

"Is that a prerequisite?" Kristin countered. "Who says it has to be? Besides," she tapped a knuckle against the aluminum frame of the door next to them, "This place isn't that old either. This looks like it's from the '70's."

"Follow me," Jared sighed, hiking back to the driveway. He stopped in a handicapped parking space behind the façade and pointed to one of several large indentations in the long brick wall. "You can tell where these used to be windows," he explained. "They probably bricked them up when they put in A/C. So this place definitely predates modern ventilation and, given the size of the windows, maybe electric lighting. As for the Strafford requirement, if you have another theory I'm open to it. But the cemetery just lined up so perfectly that I know we found what we were supposed to find there. And this…" Jared trailed off for a moment and looked past a low hedgerow to the modern office building, then back to the raised concrete pad in the parking lot. "What the hell is this?"

Kristin pulled her phone from her back pocket and tapped at the screen several times before stating, "DMV headquarters is what we're seeing. That's what that new building is," she held up her phone for Jared to see. "The map is loading now."

"Perfect," Jared blinked. "So you're saying that if we had waited until next week, we could've stayed home and seen exactly the same thing online."

"Maybe," Kristin said lowering her hand, "Or maybe that wasn't an accident. Maybe if we'd waited until next week, the maps wouldn't have loaded until after next week."

Jared ran a hand through his hair before partially deflating with a heavy exhalation. "It's fucked up. This whole thing is just really fucking weird."

"Yup," Kristin said, "That ain't news."

The Beard

Jared shook his head, "And I feel like we've reached a point where calling it coincidence would make it even weirder. But that must mean we're missing something here... what are we missing?"

"Lunch," Kristin answered, returning to the map on her phone, "If you gimme a second, I'll find us something besides tacos."

"So that's it?" Jared asked. "We just eat and leave, with no answers?"

Kristin replied calmly, "I don't see any answers in this parking lot. So we eat, we go home, we keep digging from there. Then maybe we find something eventually. In the meantime you shave, and we try again."

Third Growth

Day 3

The white glare of the computer screen illuminated the corner of the kitchen and shimmered across Jared's stubble. Each filament on his face glistened colorfully, and the skin underneath reddened, as he thoughtfully rubbed the fingers of his right hand across his chin and toward his left temple. He paused, tapped the touchpad of the laptop on the small table in front of him, and resumed rubbing the itchiest part of his face.

The drive back from Richmond had been uneventful. Following a heavy meal, Kristin had fallen asleep, and Jared had used the time to start getting his head around the problem before and behind them. He resolved that if one map had been a continuation of the other, then one destination must directly relate to the other, which meant that his instinct of tying the parking lot to Henry Sullivan Strafford must be sound. What he couldn't decide was how to go about connecting the two maps. If Kristin's suggestion was correct, and easy answers could just vanish from the internet while they were looking, that might explain why Jared hadn't had any luck searching online for Strafford. But he believed that finding information on a fixed point might be easier than tracking a person. He also felt that he had given up too easily before, and he saw room for a more disciplined approach to the problem.

The surest way to do this, to his mind, was to build the search into his daily routine, and it just so happened that he had a few minutes each morning which he no longer needed for shaving. Unlike shaving, his new activity could be coupled with breakfast for a grand total of fifteen minutes every day before work. But, as with any change in Jared's routine, he had to be sensitive to the fact that it was not only his day that would be affected: there had been some negotiation with Kristin over space, time, and resources, which had resulted in him using her laptop in the kitchen while she watched TV in the living room.

Jared moved his right hand to take a bite of cereal, tapped the touchpad while he chewed, and went back to rubbing his face.

Kristin's voice floated from the arched doorway and broke against his concentration, "How you doin' in here?"

"I'm alright," Jared said, still focused on the screen, "I think I figured some things out."

"That's good," Kristin said. "I just want to make sure you don't lose track of time."

Jared's eyes darted to the clock at the corner of the screen: 7:20 AM. "I'm not late yet," he observed.

"No," Kristin agreed, "But I have to leave at 8:30, and I didn't want to miss you while I'm getting ready."

"Sure," Jared said, "I'll just bookmark a couple things before I take off."

"I can wait, then." Kristin stayed in the doorway, arms at her sides, and shifted her weight from foot to foot while Jared pushed his cereal bowl aside and began closing tabs. Finally she asked, "Did you find anything?"

Jared paused for a beat, his face brightening, "You want me to show you? Real quick?"

"Sure," Kristin shrugged, "No rush."

Jared opened a new window and ticked through his bookmarks, "What I found is what that building is, or what it was. And what it used to be before that." He maximized a recent article about Richmond real estate developments. "According to this, it was the Virginia Department of Taxation until they moved up the road in 2009. Prior to that it was a warehouse for a mail order company, but before that…" Jared pulled up an image of an old, color-illustrated advertisement featuring a picture of the building in its original glory: tall panes, red peaked roofs, and clerestory windows ran its length, while horse drawn carriages raced electric street cars outside. He triumphantly concluded, "The Stephen Putney Shoe Company, which built the place in 1905."

90

The Beard

Kristin squinted at the picture, "Okay, and before that?"

"Nothing," Jared said. "The building dates to 1905, that's when they built it."

"But we weren't led to the building," Kristin reminded him. "And if you're trying to connect to Henry Strafford, he would've been dead by 1905, a couple of times at least."

"This building is the only thing that makes sense," Jared insisted, "And I was thinking about the Strafford thing: if he could die in 1898 and again in 1901, then how can we say he wasn't still alive in 1905?"

Kristin nodded thoughtfully. "Fun theory," she conceded, "But I'd still like to know what was there when we *know* he was alive. Lemme try something," she said, leaning over him. She opened a new tab and typed 'Richmond 1901 map' into the search engine. Clicking on the top result, she was presented with a series of thumbnail images of various parts of the city. Scrolling quickly she observed, "That one looks close to the shape of our route, if you close off that one corner." She clicked on the thumbnail and loaded the full size image of a trapezoidal section of downtown. "Looks like the top street was railroad tracks back then, but you see there?" Kristin pointed at the street names, "We came in on North Boulevard and down Hermitage on the right, to end up on Broad Street here."

Jared blinked at her finger and then at the image beyond, "So according to this, that entire loop we drove was the boundary of the old fairgrounds?"

"Looks like," Kristin said, taking a step back, "And the exact spot where we stopped in the parking lot?"

Jared zoomed in on the map over a small rectangle with a single word stretched diagonally across it. "Auditorium," he read aloud. He shook his head slowly, "I've been at this for three mornings. That took you ten seconds to find."

"Don't feel bad sweetie," she said, placing a hand on his shoulder, "I'm that awesome. And on the bright side: now we know that the exact spot could totally be related to Strafford. So you were right, plus you get me, and again I'm that awesome, so you just have it all."

"Yeah," Jared nodded, "Damn straight I was right. But now, how do I place Henry Strafford in the Richmond Fairgrounds?"

"I'm sure you'll think of something," Kristin encouraged him. "Just do it somewhere else."

Day 6

A thin line of yellow-tinged, blue smoke snaked over a discolored steering wheel that only gleamed at ten and two, then crawled over a dusty dashboard, before breaking against the windshield to hang directionless in the air. The broad white cloud that Louis exhaled dissipated the side-stream and ushered the whole mass toward his open window. On the other side of the glass, about ten yards away, two men wearing orange vests and holding hard hats climbed out of a sedan. As they crossed in front of Louis' truck, one nodded a vague greeting. The other stared in front of himself without acknowledgement, same as Louis. No one wanted to be rude, but it was understood that a man hanging back intended to be left alone.

Louis took another long drag. The tip of his cigarette sizzled, glowed, and cast its toxic tendril over the console.

Ordinarily, the only time Louis spent alone was time spent driving, whether that meant driving his truck or driving whatever equipment his work required. He had always made a point to arrive at job sites a half hour before his shift and had traditionally used that time to catch up with coworkers before they dispersed for the workday: get a read on who was in a foul mood, who was hung over, who was making plans to go out that night... But ever since Louis had moved out of his house, the tone of these morning conversations had shifted. He didn't feel as though he was doing anything differently. He suspected that may have been part of the problem.

Plenty of Louis' coworkers were divorced, so he had a pretty good idea of how they'd handled it, which was probably how they expected him to handle it: anger over what a bitch his ex-wife was being, sadness at living apart from his children, happiness for a rediscovered sense of freedom, or indignation over how much of his pay would now be going to his bitch-ex-wife. Or to his lawyer.

Clifford

Or to his bitch-ex-wife's lawyer. Any combination of those emotions would have likely been acceptable. But Louis didn't feel those things. He didn't really feel anything. He viewed his circumstances as simple facts: he'd been married and soon would not be. He'd had kids, and he still would.

And yet, every morning, when his colleagues asked generally how he was doing, he felt like the question was loaded. Even after he'd offered an appropriately noncommittal response and had seen the relief on their face at having avoided a discussion of his feelings, he still felt the question hanging in the air. Even so, most mornings he'd had enough energy to ignore the awkward sense that this left with him and could spend that extra half hour as normal. But more and more in the past few weeks, Louis had parked his truck, cut the ignition, and discovered that he just didn't have it in him to bullshit. So instead he sat by himself and chain smoked with the window rolled down until a few minutes before he had to climb into another vehicle to sit by himself in the open air.

At 8 minutes before nine o'clock, Louis gave the ignition a quarter turn, rolled up his window, and climbed out of his pickup, hat in hand. He walked past a short line of cars parked along a grassy ditch and hiked the center of a gravel roadway around a bend with an elevated shoulder. On the other side, still a hundred yards distant, Louis observed a burst of activity that was uncharacteristic for the start of a day. All the men who had passed Louis' truck now stood in two roughly equal groups: one batch milled around talking while the other scurried about picking up cones, tearing down signs, and working to haul large equipment onto larger flatbeds. Halfway in between the teams stood a man in a white hard hat, apparently absorbed in his clipboard. Louis stopped, blinked against the sun, and tried to work out what he was seeing. After a few seconds he gave up and moved on, approaching the man in the middle. "Mornin', Matt!" he called, "What brings you out today?"

"Oh, there you are," the man answered without looking up. "I'm surprised, Louis: I really thought you'd get in earlier."

94

The Beard

"I been around," Louis said, "And it's still a few minutes early yet."

"But then, a few minutes too late," Matt said, finally making eye contact through small, wire framed glasses.

In a tone still more curious than concerned, Louis asked, "What's goin' on?"

"Shifting priorities," Matt answered. "We're packing it up here, calling it good."

"We're only half way to the junction."

"Exactly," Matt nodded. "That entire half is paved. The idea was to grade and raise the road for drainage. Paving from that point to the junction was always more like a 'While you're at it' kind of deal."

"So we don't wanna go the extra mile," Louis said.

"An extra mile, we might have," Matt said thoughtfully. "But that's seven extra miles, on a secondary county road... We're already behind on a couple other projects, and we stand to lose more on those than we hoped to make on this last stretch. So the equipment and half the men from this project will be helping to close out a state contract out on Route 22."

"And the other half the men from this project?" Louis asked suspiciously.

"Will not be needed on 22," Matt stated. "I want to be fair about it. I've been reassigning on a first-come-first-served basis. Honestly Louis, I heard how things are for you right now, and I kinda hoped you would get here early enough that I could bring you along. But Walter beat you by three minutes, and like I said, I have to be fair."

"I see," Louis said slowly. "So, Walter is going to the other project. So, what do I do, then?"

"Same as everyone else, Louis: you do whatever it is you do when you're laid off. Didn't you used to tend bar over at John's place?"

"Yeah," Louis said, "But only in the winter when things slow up here. Not sure if he'll have need for me in the spring."

Clifford

"Winter, spring... Don't see why that should matter in a tavern. Just be glad you have a backup. And of course we'll call if something opens up."

Matt returned his gaze to his clipboard, but all the same, Louis nodded as he walked away. "Louis!" Derek called out from the group of active working men. Jogging over, he lowered his voice, "Where the hell were you, man?"

Louis stopped and shrugged, "I was around. You know, over in my truck."

Derek shook his head, "You picked a hell of a day t'come late."

"I wasn't late," Louis corrected flatly, "I'm still five minutes early."

"You know what I mean. Tried savin' you a spot, but Matt said it wouldn't be fair."

Louis caught himself becoming incensed by the whole situation. After a moment's reflection he conceded, "It really wouldn't 'a been fair, if you think about it."

"Well," Derek said, despondent, "I suppose not. You goin' t'work at John's place then?"

"Gonna try," Louis repeated, "But I don't know if he'll need me in spring time."

"Season don't matter in a bar," Derek waved dismissively, "It won't pay the same, but at least you have a plan."

After driving ten miles over the speed limit for forty-five minutes, Louis pulled into a gravel lot situated off of a two- lane highway. Only two cars were parked there, outside of a squat, peeling, red, clapboard building. Above the glass door and solitary pair of windows, an old wooden sign announced the establishment as "*Martini's*." It was very unlikely that a martini had ever been ordered there.

The Beard

Louis stopped inside the door to allow his eyes to adjust to the darkness. No lights were turned on in the large room this early in the day; instead, the blinds had been raised to catch what scant sunshine could force its way through the thick yellow film of nicotine that coated the windows, the walls, and every last acoustic tile in the drop ceiling. A layer of dust clung to every surface save one: a mahogany bar that gleamed across the length of the wall nearest to where Louis stood. After a few seconds, Louis was approached by the next brightest object in view: a pale, overweight man with flowing white hair and a large, soft beard.

"Well, look who it is!" The man beamed in a booming baritone. "You playin' hookie, or you knock off way early?"

"Hi Michael," Louis answered, less enthusiastically. "Say, is John around?"

"Sure," Michael said, "He's in the back, I'll go get him. Somethin' t'drink while you wait?"

Louis started to shake his head but reconsidered. "Y'know… what the hell, gimme a beer."

"You're a Budweiser man, yeah?"

"Not yet ten in the morning," Louis observed. "Better make it Bud Light."

"Good thinking," Michael nodded, filling a glass from a tap halfway down the bar. Louis walked over and took a seat on the stool opposite Michael. "There you are, sir," Michael stated, "And I will be right back with the boss."

As the large man left his post with surprising agility, Louis picked up his beverage and turned to face the center of the room. The morning sun gradually brightened the seating area, and every imperfection became sharper: cigarette burns in the faux leather booths vied for attention with ancient stains on the threadbare carpet that extended clear to the water damage that ran up the far corner. Louis always marveled at how different the place looked in daytime. At night, with a houseful of people talking and listening to music under strategically placed track lighting, the shabbiness completely disappeared and what looked neglected at 9:30 in the

97

morning seemed cozy and welcoming less than 12 hours later. Louis reflected, as he sometimes did, on whether or not he'd be happier here in the evening had he never observed the place during the day. Was a person better off, he wondered, seeing things as they actually are or seeing them only as they are intended to be seen?

A familiar baritone startled Louis nearly off his seat, "John says he'll be out in five. Or he says if you wanna talk in private, you can go on back."

"Jesus, Michael," Louis said, catching his balance and turning back to the bar, "Why you sneakin' up like that?"

"Oh," Michael said sheepishly, "Sorry. People say I do sometimes, but I swear it ain't on purpose."

Louis stood up and used his free hand to pluck a small napkin off the bar. "Need to put a bell on you ol' man." Michael replied with a booming laugh that followed Louis around the end of the bar and into a dark service hallway. At the end of the hall, beyond two restrooms, Louis wrapped his knuckles against a closed plywood door and pushed it open without waiting for a response. Fluorescent lights screamed into every inch of the closet-sized room.

Opposite the door, a slight man with a receding hairline sat behind a beaten metal desk. "By all means, do come in," he said, squinting at a small computer monitor.

"Hi John," Louis said, as pleasantly as he could manage. He slid into a folding chair near the open door and placed his beer with the napkin underneath it on the corner of the desk. "You shaved your whiskers there: lookin' professional."

"Heaven forbid," John answered wryly. "I just couldn't stand how half-assed I looked next to Michael. And anyway, back when I grew the moustache I was trying to look older." He paused to run a hand over his thinning mane, "I think I'm over that now. But brass tacks. You poppin' in this time of day is a little ominous. Don't leave a man my age in suspense."

The Beard

"No emergency," Louis reassured him, "In fact, I'd call it good news. See, I found out this morning that I'm available to work for you through what's left of the summer rush."

John smiled, "That's nice how you did that right there. I'll assume you mean you're laid off and not fired. But you gotta stay positive... especially when your cause is hopeless."

"It's not our usual arrangement," Louis said dismissively, "But I don't think it's hopeless."

"That's because you're not the one who'd be paying you for three extra months."

"You know you get return on that investment," Louis said confidently. "Many hands make light work."

"Yes," John said patiently, "And you're a hard worker, and I like having someone of your stature to keep rough customers in line, and God knows you'll volunteer for more heavy lifting than Michael will. But it's summertime, and you don't work here in summertime. Michael works the warm months when no one needs a Santa Clause. Then around the holidays, he gets his call from the shopping center just in time for your paving to let up. That's the deal. It's a ecosystem."

"But summers are busier," Louis argued, "Ideally, couldn't you do with extra help?"

"Ideally, sure: Ideally I'd pay a full staff to serve drinks here and still have enough cash left over t'have drinks served to me outta' coconuts on a beach somewheres. But we're not workin' from ideal. I can afford to pay one bartender at a time, and as much as I like you Louis, you have to wait your turn, because I can't see my way to firing Santa Claus. I mean, you hear how fucked up that sounds, just sayin' it out loud."

Louis grinned bitterly, in spite of himself. "So, what do *I* do, then?"

John shrugged, "You'll prob'ly get more paving work before the leaves turn. Either way, you should qualify for unemployment. Which I know isn't much..."

"Yeah," Louis said, "But what do I *do*?"

Clifford

"Whatever you want," John said. "And whatever that is, you're welcome to do it here. But you'd have to pay me for drinks instead of the other way around."

Louis shook his head slowly, "Somehow I think that's a bad idea."

"And the fact you realize that," John replied sincerely, "Is the reason I'm sure you'll be fine."

Louis drove the twenty minutes home in a daze. He knew that he needed to figure out a plan, really should have already had a plan for this eventuality. On the other hand, it was doubtful that anyone expected him to spring immediately into action. He could probably take a couple days to absorb his situation before he made any decisions, but his lack of obligations was accompanied by a nervous sense of urgency, and something about procrastinating didn't feel right. He would file for unemployment pretty quickly.

Beyond that, for his own part, Louis was already living on the cheap, but he thought he should probably touch base with Carolyn in the not too distant future. He could still be sure that bills got paid for the house, but she would need to know that his resources would be limited for a bit. She might even have some ideas of what he should do. Then again, she might express those ideas as orders or abject criticisms of what he wasn't doing. Either way, he wasn't looking forward to it.

Louis turned off of the gravel road, bumped a quarter mile up a rough dirt track that had been cut into the woods, and parked his truck on a narrow gravel strip in a quarter-acre clearing. In front of the vehicle was a small and boxy trailer with a pair of proportionately small and boxy aluminum fins hanging off the back. On the passenger side, a chain link fence enclosed a 15-foot length of well-trod grass with a massive dog house and a casserole dish full of water at one end. As he stepped down from the pickup, the doghouse rocked side-to-side. Without a word, he walked to the opposite end of the fence and opened a gate before moving back around the vehicle to open the door of the trailer. Louis stood aside, and after a few seconds, Marlow strolled past him and stepped easily over the stairs and across the threshold. Louis did the same and closed an attached screen door behind them.

In the stifling dimness, Louis reached to his right to turn on an oscillating desk fan that sat on the kitchen table, took three slow strides to the other end of the space, and turned to sit on a twin-size sofa-bed. Without removing his boots, he lay down on his side and scooted back against the wall. Marlow stretched and yawned in the middle of the room before climbing lazily onto the open side of the bed. Louis pulled his arm up to rub the top of Marlow's head while he stared vacantly at a shimmering stream of dust particles that flowed across the thin beam of light admitted by the small window over the sink.

Softly, Louis asked, "So, what the hell *do* I do?"

Day 8

"Stop squirming, for Chrissake." Kristin renewed her grip on Jared's chin. "The lighting in this room is for shit, I don't need you moving things on me." She squinted into the hair halfway down his cheek before consulting the laptop on the living room coffee table.

Jared swallowed before he answered, "I'm not squirming, I'm chewing. And you should take that as a compliment. I'm really into your spaghetti."

"You're taking forever to eat, as usual. I should really just use pictures for this part."

"I'm savoring," he chided, "And I thought you'd prefer the intimacy of doing things this way."

"I prefer that things hold still," Kristin stated. She gave Jared's face one more hard look and adjusted the zoom level on the map she had pulled up on the computer. Satisfied with the scale, she turned her attention to a ruled notepad and scribbled, 'Stay on 95S through Richmond.'

"So, was I right?" Jared asked, winding another mouthful of noodles around his fork, "Do we pick up the trail at the tax building?"

"Not exactly," Kristin replied, "I found the witch's hat in your sideburns, and the rectangle below that looked like the old fairgrounds, but they're both really small this time so I wanted to be sure. It looks like we can stay on the interstate without going clear back to the tax building, so that's what I'm working out now."

Jared responded by taking another bite and training his eyes to the muted television.

"It's kind of a pain really," Kristin continued, "The landmarks shrinking like that. And then the route gets even smaller again than last time. If it keeps up this way, I'm a little concerned it won't be legible."

The Beard

Jared cheeked his food, "I don't think that'll happen. We just have further to go this time."

"Well, sure," Kristin said, "This time. But how far will we have to go next time? I think I'd just feel better if there was more of a pattern to our destinations, something extra to know what we're looking for."

"Like a context?" Jared asked before swallowing.

"Yeah," she nodded, "Like who was Henry Strafford? What kind of things did he do? Some kind of story to follow."

"But it works the other way," Jared argued. "The whole point in following it is to give us something to contextualize."

"All the same, it would help us to know."

"I'm not sure it would," Jared said thoughtfully. "But I can tell you the context of the last place we went, and you can tell me if knowing that would've made any difference."

"What are you talking about?"

He set down his fork and slid closer to the laptop, "Here, let me show you what I found." He switched to his desktop, and opened the browser. While his home page loaded, he explained, "When you came up with that map last week, I couldn't shake the feeling that the fairgrounds have to be connected to Henry Strafford somehow."

"Maybe he liked the fair," Kristin suggested, "Didn't everyone? They didn't have much else to do in those days."

Jared ignored the comment and pulled up one of his bookmarks. "And I was thinking: if we know he died in 1901 at the latest, then whatever the connection is, had to be before that. But the biggest question, to me anyways, is if he didn't die in 1898, then where was he from then until 1901, and why did anyone think he was dead?"

Kristin shook her head, "I'm not sure I follow. Do you mean that you found out he died in 1898 or that he disappeared until 1901?"

"Neither," Jared answered confidently.

"And what does that have to do with the fairgrounds?"

"Nothing," he said undeterred. "Just that I thought I should focus between the two deaths. Just a feeling I had. So," he went on, "to figure out what the fairgrounds were about, I decided to start with what was happening in Richmond in the months after Henry died or not, in February 1898. As it turns out, the Richmond historical newspapers are free online, so I went to a couple months after the sinking of the USS Maine, and the first issue I clicked on was this," Jared scrolled down over a newspaper image on the computer, through a masthead for *The Times* of Richmond, Virginia with dated Sunday, April 24, 1898. The upper left of the front page bore a bold headline with a series of subheadings:

Richmond Is Chosen.

Troops to Be Mobilized in This City.

WAS DONE QUICKLY.

The Victory Gained After Three Days Work.

At Exposition Grounds.

Soldiers Will Assemble There This Week.

The top center of the page featured a crowded illustration captioned, 'WHERE THE TROOPS WILL MOBILIZE IN THIS CITY – The Broad Street Park, Showing Contemplated Improvements.'

"So the Broad Street Park is the same as the Exposition Grounds?" Kristin asked.

The Beard

"By which they mean the State Fairgrounds on West Broad Street, which is what we drove in on. And that," Jared said, indicating a long building with a peaked roof on the right side of the illustration, "is the Auditorium from your map."

Jared paused to take another bite while Kristin sat quietly, examining the image on the screen. Eventually she asked, "So why were troops mobilizing in Richmond?"

"Spanish American War." Jared answered simply.

"That the one with the Alamo?"

"No," Jared said. "That was Mexican American. The Spanish American happened when the US got involved with the Cuban War of Independence. Part of our strategy to put pressure on Spain was to park the warship USS Maine in Havana Harbor."

"Where it sank," Kristin ventured.

"Where it exploded," Jared corrected. "And no one knows why it exploded. It was probably an accident, but a lot of Americans at the time blamed Spanish sabotage, which was a catalyst for public outcry that ended in a war with Spain over their colonies. Which meant that we had to raise a ton of troops to deploy very quickly, and one of the places we mustered those troops was…"

"The Richmond Exposition Grounds," Kristin finished.

"Exactly. And about a week-"

"Hang on," Kristin interrupted holding up one hand. "Let me absorb all this for a second. My history classes were for shit."

"Don't feel bad," Jared said, twirling his fork in his noodles, "Had to troll a couple months' worth of newspapers and half of Wikipedia myself."

"Okay," Kristin said after a long moment of silence, "Continue. What did all that have to do with Henry Strafford?"

Jared finished chewing and moved back to the laptop. "After I landed on the headline about the fairgrounds, I started picking through one day at a time to see what happened next. And in the week after the announcement I just showed you, I found this." He pulled up a second bookmark. As the website loaded, it gradually unveiled a hand drawn portrait about two thirds of the way down the front page of another newspaper. The face staring sideways back at them was the familiar profile of a very bearded man, sketched from the same angle as the medallion on the Arlington headstone. Below the picture, a caption read, 'Maj. Henry S. Strafford.' In the column above, one of the many subheadings announced, 'Major Strafford to Arrive This Week.' Jared said, "He showed up the day after that, apparently to oversee an Army hospital or something. Something about checking the fitness of soldiers before they left for Cuba."

"So he was a doctor?" Kristin asked.

"I have no idea," Jared said, "They only ever mention him as a Major. But the point is, if we had known all that, would it really have helped us find modern street directions? Wouldn't we still have had to go through mapping our route anyways?"

Turning back to Jared, Kristin asked, "When were you planning to tell me about all this?"

"Sometime around now," Jared said, nonchalant. "I just found that last page this morning when you were in the bathroom, and I didn't want to interrupt."

Kristin eyed him suspiciously, "I guess I'll allow it this time." She broke her stare and switched back to her desktop. "Now finish your chewing, this doesn't have to take all night."

While Jared swept the last of his noodles off the plate, Kristin squinted at his jaw line and traced in the air with her finger. To herself she mumbled, "A bump to the right and a hook to the left, then a diagonal to the chin." She turned back to the computer and traced a line in the thin layer of dust on the screen, repeating, "Bump on the right, hook to the left and diagonal..." On the notepad she scribbled, 'Exit onto I-85 S.' As Jared swallowed, she slid across the couch and leaned around to examine the next turn on his chin. "Oh," she said at regular volume, "Oh, I didn't think about that."

"What?" Jared asked, keeping his face elevated. "Did it stop or something?"

"Not on purpose," Kristin said. "It's the tomato sauce."
106

The Beard

Jared used to back of his hand to wipe his mouth. "Sorry," he said, "How about now?"

"Hmm... Nope," Kristin answered, "All brown and red: everything looks like a cross street now."

"Do I wash my face?" Jared asked.

"Meh," Kristin intoned tentatively, "If I'm being honest, I was bored with figuring out the other side in this light. Probably easiest to wait until tomorrow and snap a few pictures before you leave for work." She slid back and started to close various programs on the laptop, then paused and turned to Jared with an expression of sudden inspiration, "Or," she said enthusiastically, "If you're done looking at newspapers in the mornings, I can take the photos on *your* phone, and you can help find the route."

"You know I guess I could," Jared acknowledged. "I really only have fifteen minutes each morning, though. But I could do it during my lunch breaks, that might work better. And it would leave mornings open for whatever the next mystery turns out to be."

"Are you sure?" Kristin asked. "You'd be losing your lunches with your friends."

Jared nodded thoughtfully, his eyes still on the television. "Can I tell you a secret? I don't think I like my friends."

Day 10

Louis wrapped his meaty knuckles just over the deadbolt of the blue front door. He shifted his weight nervously, his baseball cap nearly scraping the ceiling of the small porch while he watched the small, divided windows and waited for the tan blinds to lift. Marlow sat smiling at the top of the concrete stairs behind him.

After what was probably seconds but felt like minutes, Louis tried knocking again. It was a strange thing, he reflected, knocking on the door of your own house, stranger still to worry over who would answer and how they might regard you. He still had his keys, but he forced himself to leave them in his pocket: he felt it was important to demonstrate to Carolyn that he respected her privacy, especially now, since she'd just begun dating Sean. Louis didn't like that she was seeing someone and didn't think he should be expected to like it. But he knew he was still required to respect it, so he'd made that easier on himself by waiting to stop by until Sean's car was absent from the driveway.

Two days earlier, when Louis had had his latest epiphany, it was all he could do to not pick up the phone straight away, but his previous call to update Carolyn on his work situation had not gone especially well, and as thrilled as he was about his new plan, he knew it might sound a little crazy at first, so Louis had taken his time and had carefully plotted his sales pitch to ensure the most productive setting possible. Everyone would be up and moving by 8 AM on a Friday, but there would still be twenty minutes before the kids had to be loaded up and taken to Carolyn's mother's house.

Near the level of Louis' ribs, the blinds parted around a pair of large blue eyes. The gap closed just as quickly, and the deadbolt clacked open. A slender boy of 10 years levered his full weight against the door, and the weather stripping on the threshold let go with the sucking sound of a hundred Tupperware containers. Louis beamed, "Hi Tanner."

"Hey dad," the boy replied brightly as he stepped forward to give Louis a hug. The large man reached down and patted the boy's back between the shoulder blades. From the dimness of the home's interior, a young girl's squeal preceded the girl herself: a stringy eight-year-old with a tightly pulled brown ponytail flew past the father/son moment and directly to the top of the porch stairs.

"Marlow!" she yelled, throwing her arms around the dog's neck. Marlow, unmoved, turned his gaze lazily upward to Louis.

From the doorway, a woman's stern voice intoned, "Madison, you know the rule. Stop hanging all over that poor dog and come back up on the porch."

"It's alright," Louis said to Carolyn, "Marlow's a big guy, he can take it."

Carolyn answered Louis with a look before repeating, "Madison, you know the rule."

With melodramatic exasperation, the girl huffed, "Fiiine." She dropped her arms and stomped back toward the door.

"You hug your dad yet?" Carolyn inquired.

Tanner took two steps back so the girl could turn and toss her arms around Louis as she passed. He patted her on the head and released her to her mother's side.

"So, Louis," Carolyn said finally, "What brings you by this early?"

"Would you maybe want to talk inside?" Louis asked.

"We can if you want, but he can't," Carolyn said, nodding to Marlow. "And as I'd guess it's too hot for you to leave him in the truck, I don't mind talking here."

"Oh, sure... that... that works fine then... here is fine..." he fumbled, trying to remember how he'd hoped to begin his presentation. "Reason I come by today. I've got some extra time on my hands right now, and I've been thinkin' on what I might do with that. An' I've been thinkin' that I always wish I could spend more time with the kids. An' this bein' their summer vacation and all..."

Tanner and Madison watched Carolyn expectantly as she nodded along with his words. "That's a nice idea," she said carefully. "I think my mom might be ready for a break, so long as you make arrangements for your dog. And if the kids get bored at your place, I don't mind you watching them here, either." Madison beamed at Louis while her mother spoke.

"Well that's the thing, I thought about that," Louis jumped in enthusiastically, "about them getting' bored, I mean. So, I thought, 'What could we do that wouldn't be boring?' An' then it hit me: we could take a road trip. An' the least boring place that I can think of? Wanna guess?"

The children stared raptly, silently shaking their heads, unwilling to jinx his next statement with speculation. Carolyn shook her head as well, but with a very different expression on her face. She started, "Louis, please don't-"

"Disneyland!" he announced.

The porch nearly lifted off its cinderblock foundation as both children jumped and screamed with pure joy. Through the din, Louis bellowed to Carolyn, "I know it's a big trip, but we can work out the details, and who knows when I'll have this much time again? An' there's so much t'see between here and California."

Carolyn stood perfectly still, jaw set and eyes seething. Over the deafening childhood elation, she projected with forced patience, "Alright guys, I know it's exciting. But today you still have to go to Grandma's. Go get your stuff together."

The pair of them calmed down just long enough to give Louis a bear hug before they bounced back through the open front door. Carolyn called into the house, "And Madison! Don't forget to wash up! Hands and face, you know the rule!" She pulled the door nearly all the way shut before calmly returning her attention to the man and his dog. "So, Louis," she said with something akin to amazement, "What the fuck?"

The Beard

"I know what yer thinkin,'" Louis said excitedly, having anticipated some light resistance.

"I doubt that," Carolyn said, folding her arms.

"I've got it all worked out," he continued, "I filed for unemployment like you told me, but I'm pacing out my savings until that starts coming in, and it looks like I'll have a little to spare. And I planned on kickin' some of that over to you and the kids, but that still works out since I'll be the one buyin' their groceries while we travel. Tickets to the park are kinda spendy, but campgrounds are always cheap, and gas been goin' down, so I stick to the budget, I really think I can swing this. Plus, I haven't given up on the paving work coming back, but Derek said not for a few weeks at least, so I have the time right now."

"This isn't about your time," Carolyn answered firmly. "Or even your money. California is what, a three, maybe four day drive each way? I swear to God, Louis, I've told you a hundred times that school starts next week."

Louis shrugged, "Couple thousand miles. If we're pressed for time, I could make it in two days."

"You think you can keep an eight-and-ten-year-old in your truck for twelve hours at a time without a bunch of stops? Oh, and even though this isn't about your money, since you brought it up: yeah, I do think it's a horrible idea to plan a cross country trip when you're broke. I mean, what's your budget if Tanner breaks an arm in Oklahoma, or you get a flat tire in Nevada? And I wasn't expecting you to help with the kids' back-to-school expenses, but somehow you can swing the happiest vacation on earth?"

"Alright," Louis said, raising his hands in surrender, "Don't need to get worked up now. I didn't remember school starting, I apologize for that. Now, that in mind, we leave out the cross-country adventure part, I can always swap out Disneyland for Disneyworld. We can make Orlando in a day and a half, each way."

"Jesus, Louis," Carolyn sighed. "It's like you only hear every third word out of my mouth. And none of what I'm saying should even be a conversation: I'm sick of arguing with you over common sense."

Louis stood motionless, chastised but otherwise unresponsive.

"When we were dating," Carolyn explained, "I used to tell my friends what a sweet dreamer you were. And then we got married, and I started thinking, 'Poor Louis can't see what everyone else sees.' Later on, I figured, 'That dumb bastard just never gets the point.' But now... I swear t'God it feels like you're doing it on purpose."

"Doing what?" Louis asked without thinking.

"Doing this!" Carolyn shouted. "You get all wrapped up in some bullshit pipe dream, then come over here and drag us all with you, no matter how ridiculous it is. Today it's Disneyland, but last year it was some make-believe farm, and let's not forget about that goddamn dog."

"Whoa now," Louis argued, "The farm was not a pipe dream. If the bank had approved the loan to expand my property, then... y'know... theoretically, the kids coulda both had ponies- I didn't make that shit up! And nobody has a problem with Marlow but you. The kids love that dog!"

"That just makes it worse! Because again," Carolyn cupped her hands on either side of her mouth to yell, "Your daughter is fucking allergic!"

Louis waved his hand dismissively, "My kid can handle a runny nose. She'll grow out of it if you give her a chance."

"Not how it works," Carolyn stated steadfastly, "That is not how 'allergic' works. And it's not a runny nose: it is hives and swollen eyes and itching and crying and being told over and over again that she can't play with the puppy like her brother does, even though her dad keeps telling her she can. But you wouldn't know that because, like always, you just show up, light a bunch of exciting fireworks, and put it on me to dump water on them before somebody loses an eye."

The Beard

The two adults stood and stared each other down for a long moment before Louis said softly, "I wasn't suggesting we take the dog to Disney."

Carolyn threw her hands up in exasperation, "You know what?" she yelled, "You take the dog to fucking Disney! Take the fucking dog any-fucking-where you please, because the kids are staying here, where I know they'll be safe and get fed and be in fucking school next week!" She dropped her arms and turned back to the house. As she crossed into the dark interior, she paused and said over her shoulder, "I don't want to hate you Louis, but it's bullshit. You already made me break *your* heart, stop making me break theirs. Bull-shit."

With that the blue door slammed shut, and the tan blinds clattered against the small, divided windows.

Day 11

Thick swaths of North Carolina forest pulled back to make way for a clover-leaf interchange. On the opposite side, a narrow field quickly appeared and then vanished as the trees returned to the shoulder, periodically blocking the sinking sun. Kristin took it all in with a sigh. She had been bored out of her mind for 80 miles, at least.

With a grunt, she reached over and turned off the radio. "Fifth time I've heard that song," she announced tersely.

"Not much longer," Jared said, "Just sit back, find something to focus on. Enjoy the scenery, take a nap maybe."

"I did that," Kristin replied, "For like two hours. I'm rested. And I'm hungry. And I have to pee."

"Then focus on not peeing," he said. "I would stop, but we're really close."

"Still, you coulda warned me we'd be in the car this long. I coulda brought a book on tape or something."

"I'm glad you didn't," Jared said, wrinkling his nose, "I don't think I could stand eight hours of a grown man reading one of your lady books. The voices they do... Every female character sounds like Scarlett O'Hara. It's ridiculous."

Kristin shot back, "Well, now you don't have to listen to that, which means you're available to listen to me. And what I want to talk about is how hungry I am. And how bad I have to pee. And that it still bothers me that you won't tell me where we're going."

"It's a surprise," Jared said laboriously, "And we're close. This destination is tough to miss, I am absolutely sure of it this time."

"Wait," Kristin said as the vehicle glided to the right, "Did you mean to take the exit right here?"

"Exit 50B," Jared stated, "What's the paper say?"

The Beard

Kristin consulted a ruled page resting on the dashboard. "50B. But then it just says 'Follow signs,' and I don't know what signs you mean."

"Good," Jared said, "It's a surprise."

Jared proceeded quickly past the standard off-ramp fare of gas stations and hotels, making his way through the outskirts of Asheville. Passing a Tudor style hotel, he turned onto a non-descript side street. The few outlying buildings were replaced by the cover of gracefully arcing trees and a wide, landscaped median. The street funneled through a thick, brick entry gate and resumed as a tree-lined lane parallel to a narrow stream. The light and shadow admitted through the tunnel of foliage extended to the horizon. Kristin asked, "Where the hell are we?"

"The Biltmore Estate," Jared said, squinting against the afternoon light that strobed through the trees. "It was the country estate of the Vanderbilt family: pretty much an 8,000-acre park with a giant-ass house in the middle."

"That's where our map leads? To this park?"

"To the house," Jared corrected. "Lord knows why."

"Any chance I can find a restroom before we find out?"

"Yes," Jared nodded, "That's the other part of the surprise: the house closes in 20 minutes."

Kristin looked at him incredulously. "You're not talking about breaking in, are you?"

"No," Jared continued proudly, "We are not going to the house tonight. We are going to the estate's village hotel. I knew we'd get in late, so I made arrangements. And I packed a bag for us while you were in the shower this morning."

"So, this is a surprise weekend getaway?" Kristin asked.

"If that's what you want to call it."

Kristin's mind raced to commit every detail to memory, to process exactly how she would retell this moment to her coworkers in the coming week. "Yes," she answered finally, her eyes filling with tears, "Yes, that is what I want to call it."

Clifford

Less than an hour later, Jared stood in front of a mirror framed in dark-stained wood. On the granite countertop below, he carefully unpacked a nylon toiletry bag. As he worked, he ran a mental inventory: toothpaste, two toothbrushes, the moisturizing lotion and mascara from Kristin's shelf in the medicine cabinet... He had tried to be attentive in his packing that morning, but had necessarily raided the bathroom in a hurry whilst Kristin assumed he was taking a piss and it was very important to him that he'd covered every detail: he was hoping the trip would go well enough to demonstrate his reliability and commitment to this whole venture.

It was not unlikely, Jared thought, that whatever the map led to the next day would be just one more waypoint, in which case there would be further to go and more travel arrangements to be made. Jared privately conceded that, as a rule, he put more than his share of routine tasks on Kristin, and if he hoped to maintain her enthusiasm toward following these maps, he needed to show her that he could pull his weight.

From the bottom of the small bag, Jared retrieved a cordless beard trimmer. He adjusted the plastic combs to the top of the blades, pulled the stopper on the sink, and opened the faucet. The sound of warm water filling the basin masked the hum of the trimmer that quickly traversed his face. Jared leaned in close to the mirror to relegate as much hair as possible to the still empty countertop beside the fixture.

Up to that point, he considered his small gamble a success. He had worried that Kristin might resist being left out of the planning, or that she might be incensed at having been denied the anticipation of their first overnight road trip, but the moment Jared had realized where they were going, he had known this was meant to be. And apart from the kind of passive complaint one would expect after 8 hours in a Volkswagen, she had seemed very amenable to a surprise. It didn't hurt that they had landed in a nice hotel. There were more luxurious options in the area but again, given that the next leg of their journey might require going even further afield, Jared wanted to pull out only the affordable stops.

116

The Beard

He closed the faucet and examined his face in the mirror. Satisfied at having reduced the weeks' worth of hair to an angry bristle, he blew the stubble from the blades of the trimmer and exchanged it for a safety razor on the opposite end of the counter. As he scraped a path from his sideburns to his chin, the door behind him opened a few inches. Kristin's dull blonde hair appeared through the crack ahead of her profile. From over the shoulder of Jared's reflection she asked, "You brought your shaving gear with you?"

"Yep," Jared said without pausing. "I wanted to keep the beard until we got here, just in case I messed up an exit or something. But I know you like me better when I'm shaved."

"It's not that I like that better *per se*," she said thoughtfully, "I like both, and after a couple weeks I start to miss smooth Jared."

"Either way," he answered her reflection, "I thought I could make the effort."

Kristin extended one bare arm around the door to drop a white bra near his feet. "Just don't take too long with your effort," she said mischievously before withdrawing from the room, "I have plans for smooth Jared."

He suppressed a grin to give the razor a quick pass near the corners of his mouth. As he opened the sink drain, Kristin called from the adjacent room, "On second thought, take all the time you need to clean up in there. Nothing romantic about a hairy bathroom."

Fourth Growth

Day 1

A short, white shuttle bus lurched into action and pulled a tight loop around the hotel driveway, navigating the web of manicured roads that had been laid haphazardly amongst recently constructed shops. Seated in the back of the bus, tucked away from the tall, tinted windows, Kristin leaned her head on Jared's shoulder as centrifugal force dragged them around another corner. "Good morning everyone!" the driver called cheerfully as he pulled them onto a loosely wooded two-lane road. "Welcome to Biltmore Estate! Originally built by George Biltmore, with more than 135,000 square feet, Biltmore House is the nation's largest single-family dwelling."

Kristin addressed Jared softly, "How have I not heard of this place?"

Jared matched her volume, "No reason you would, I guess. It isn't exactly next door to us."

At the opposite end of the vehicle, past three families, two strollers, and a few elderly couples, the driver continued, "Completed in 1895..."

Kristin resumed their hushed conversation, "Can't really hear so well this far back."

"This might be a good opportunity to talk about where we're going."

"What do you mean? Don't they just drop us at the tour?"

"Sort of," Jared said. "They drop us at the entrance. A guided tour would've cost extra. As would a special tour, an audio tour, private tours... "

"And you went cheap," Kristin finished.

"I thought a self-guided experience might be better for what we want to do. But I'm okay with cheap, I'll own that."

"So, we're wandering around on our own then?" Kristin clarified.

Clifford

"No," Jared said, "Other people *wander*. You and me will know exactly where we're going." He pulled a folded piece of paper and his phone out of his hip pocket and continued, "You know how the last map had three different scales?"

"Yeah," Kristin said, "One for where we started, then pulled back for the interstate, and zoomed in again for the end."

"Well this one," Jared said, swiping through close ups of his face on his phone, "Had four. One for the tax building in Richmond, a second for the interstate, a third from Asheville to the Approach Road, and then this," he stopped on a picture of a half-inch wide blond band taking square corners from his cheek bone to his jawline. "And here," he unfolded the paper, "I outlined an aerial view of the house and drew the blonde part over it. It fits perfectly if we hang a left at the main entrance and go clear to the end of the South wing."

"Shit," Kristin mumbled, "Good work." After some study she questioned, "Are you sure about this? Compared to the scale before it, that house would have to be freakin' massive."

As if on cue, the shuttle slowed briefly and jerked to the right. Around a wooded corner, a close shorn lawn nearly twice the length of a football field embraced a large central fountain. At the far end stood a chateauesque stone monolith, whose peaked roofs sent more than a dozen slender chimneys reaching into the summer sky. As the vehicle approached the structure, the general impact of its sheer size was replaced by innumerable overwhelming details: open arches transitioned to large arched windows at the ground level, all of which supported gothic lacework and small, but varied, spires running the leading edge of steep rows of gray roof tiles. Atop the second of four enormous forward gables, gargoyles lunged past grotesques, forever screeching their silent warning against the encroaching Smoky Mountains and above an arched double-door that stood open to its guests like a gaping maw.

The shuttle neared a milling crowd at the front of the building, and the driver slowed, silent now as his cargo stared out the

The Beard

passenger side windows, still too awestricken to raise their cameras. "Imposing," Kristin said quietly.

"Maybe a little ostentatious," Jared replied.

"You really can find fault with anything, can't you?"

The vehicle pulled left, parallel with the house, and slowed to a stop before reaching the entryway. Jared and Kristin remained seated while the passengers in front of them began preparing to disembark, and a portion of the crowd outside broke away and patiently queued to replace them.

Jared and Kristin inched to the exit while their improvised carpool paused to individually thank the driver before wrestling their gear onto the pavement. Following the custom, Jared mumbled, "Very informative, thank you," and led Kristin into the late morning glare. They continued past the small crowd and beyond a life-sized lion statue, to stand in the deep shade of the nearest exterior corner.

Kristin asked, "Isn't it open?" She motioned to the crew they'd arrived with, "I don't see anyone going in."

"Timed entry," Jared explained, focusing again on the piece of paper, "We go in another five minutes. And once we're in, you're not allowed to take pictures, so everyone is getting that out of their systems."

"I see," Kristin said, returning her attention to Jared. She casually observed, "You know, we should get you some shorts. Seems way too hot for blue jeans."

"I'm fine," he said dismissively, "But I did pack shorts for you, though," he nodded to Kristin's bare legs.

"Noticed that," she said, slightly perturbed, "Interesting choice by the way, khaki shorts and a tan tank."

"What?" Jared shrugged, "You wear those all the time."

"Not together," she said emphatically, "It's basically a nude-colored jumper."

"I still think it looks fine."

Clifford

"Of course, you do." Kristin paused and decided to let the matter drop. "What are you so focused on? I thought it was just in the door and to the left."

"It is," Jared said absently, "Then forward a ways and a little hitch to the right. But I was thinking we should start by getting to the end of the map: stay ahead of the crowd, find what we need, then go back if you want to tour the house." The group Jared and Kristin had arrived with began packing away their cameras and filtering through the front door. "This will be us," Jared said, folding the paper and pushing it back into his pocket. He pulled two tickets from his wallet and led Kristin around the corner into a dim vestibule.

The couple discovered remnants of their group lined up in the square, stone chamber. As the August sun poured in behind them and washed out the weak light of a handful of wall sconces, a slight breeze invited them toward a large, open door bookended by tall, ornate windows. The herd trudged over plush red carpet, pausing only for a middle-aged gentleman with a maroon necktie to verify the time on their tickets, before it marched slowly up a short staircase and into a brightly lit, oval shaped room ringed by archways. Guided by a string of velvet ropes, the crowd pressed toward an even brighter room on the right.

"So, you said to take a left?" Kristin asked sarcastically.

"Looks like our plan just got adjusted," Jared said, pulling a brochure from a wooden case nearby. "If you can, try to keep tabs on what direction we're facing. If we don't get too turned around, maybe this line will pass what we need to see."

The group slogged gradually through the outer loop of a round conservatory where boxes of colorful flowers lay in geometric patterns surrounded by potted palms, all of which drew the eye upward to a steel framework that supported a glass dome and dripped with iron fixtures. The human chain, speckled with strollers and wheelchairs, snaked through yet another archway, the air heavy and silent but for the distant hum of electric fans and hushed conversations.

124

The Beard

"Whatever we find here," Jared said, "I will say the place is impressive."

"Yeah," Kristin acknowledged, "But we could see a lot more of it if these people would pick up the pace."

Jared leaned over the velvet rope and looked a short distance up the line to a trio of elderly women wearing headphones, fixated on something in the center of the room. "Oh," he said, "So it looks like all the people who paid for the audio tour keep stopping to look at what they're hearing about."

"So, we're basically on their tour, but without the audio."

"Seems about right," Jared said. He fell back into the line as it retreated through a short passage and oozed along the margins of an opulent billiard room, finally emerging from underneath a pipe organ into an unspeakably overstated banquet hall. The casements of the seventy-foot vaulted ceiling bristled with unfamiliar flags, which hung limply above 16th century Flemish tapestries.

"Daaamn," Kristin said, "Check out the triple fireplace down there."

Jared grabbed her hand, "C'mon. We got an opening." As more than half of the audio tour group drifted closer to the velvet rope and looked to the ceiling, the non-headphone-wearing guests pulled to the left and formed a second line that shot double-time to the far end of the room. Approaching the dwarfed exit, progress suddenly halted, and the pair was left to their original pace. "Okay," Jared said, "Now you can look."

"I think I got the gist," Kristin replied, squinting at a carved relief under the organ. "Sweet set-up though." Cutting across the corner of a smaller dining area, the group in front of them stopped then suddenly moved forward, only to stop again.

"This seems different," Jared observed.

"I'm starting to wig out a little," Kristin said. "Is it me or is it getting really warm in here?"

"The windows are open, but you're right. Not much air moving with this many people. What is the damn deal with this line?"

Clifford

The group marched with fits and starts into a long salon where the damn deal became evident. Halfway down the roped path, families and couples were pulled out of the line to pose for a professional photographer. Jared grunted in frustration, "The reason we're not allowed to take pictures is so they can sell us one?"

"Don't worry," Kristin reassured him. "That's something I won't make you buy: I am a sweaty mess. And, you may have noticed, I'm not really dressed for it…"

"Alright," Jared said, "Point taken. Let's just find a way around this." He located a gap between strollers and charged under the delicately upholstered ceilings into an oval shaped room that featured a harpsichord. As the crowd thinned, he turned to check in with Kristin, "Did you want to slow down or-?"

"No," she answered, passing him. "I swear I feel a breeze up ahead." She led the way onto a long, covered porch wedged between large windows and a sweeping view of the mountains. The faintest breeze brushed through the shade and across the beads of sweat at Kristin's hairline. She sighed heavily and stopped to let Jared catch up. "Sorry," she said, "I don't know how a place this big can feel so claustrophobic, but it just hit me all of a sudden."

Jared took a leisurely pace past a young couple leaning on the railing, to a pair of lounge chairs twenty feet away. "It's alright," he said taking a seat. "It's just all the people. We can take break."

Kristin sat forward across from him and peeled her shirt away from her collar bone. "It's getting hot out, too. Earlier might have been better."

"It occurred to me," Jared said, "But they were sold out except in the middle of the day. Now we know why." He paused to appreciate the view. "Maybe if we stay here a bit, the group will pass."

Kristin dismissed the idea, "We'd just catch up with them. How close are we?"

Jared opened his brochure on the chair beside him and unfolded the now damp sheet of paper from his pocket. Examining
126

a floor plan in the brochure he said "We came out of the salon by way of the music room and out a door there, so what we need should be..." he looked back to the paper and pointed behind himself, "Other side of that wall."

"Alright then," Kristin said standing and stretching, "Let's do this."

"You sure? You good?"

"Yeah," Kristin said, "Can I see that for a second?" She snatched the brochure map and studied it quickly before tossing it back into Jared's lap, declaring, "Let's go knock this out." She turned and marched purposefully back to the house. The fresh summer air was quickly subsumed by the building's ambient scent of cologne, body odor, and old money. She cut a tight corner through the music room, briefly through the entrance hall, and around to a long gallery with arm chairs and couches, lined with yet more Flemish tapestries. Jared jogged up behind her as she eyed gaps in the scattered crowd with all the skill of a seasoned running back, sliding between wheelchairs, strollers, and gawkers in headphones, to pass a final handful of tall windows and another pair of cozy fireplaces near the velvet rope.

Jared finally caught up at the end of the gallery, when she slowed to join a group that had bottle-necked in a double door surrounded by portraits. Shuffling into the next room, the pileup sorted itself into a line moving in on the right side, making way for a second line to exit on the left. Moving toward an arched window, the ceiling suddenly lifted away into a shallow vault two stories above, which was covered from end to end by a mural of angels in a cloudy sky. As Jared's eyes adjusted to the room's relatively dim interior, his first impression was of polished wood: on the walls, the floor, the fireplace mantel, and the short spiral staircase that climbed one far corner. It took a moment for him to register what all the wood was for. Thousands upon thousands of books filled hand carved cases from floor to ceiling, many of the volumes only accessible from a balcony that ran the length of three walls.

Clifford

Over the murmuring of passing tourists, Jared heard a woman's voice at the entrance call, "The question was, 'Why do so many of the books look identical?' After George Biltmore read a book, he would often send it to be bound in Moroccan leather, before storing it here." Jared looked over the retreating line of people that stood between him and the red velvet furniture around the fireplace, and spotted a short docent in a maroon neck tie standing next to a massive wooden globe.

Kristin beckoned quietly over her shoulder, "Okay. This looks like the end of it. Where do we need to be?"

Jared discreetly consulted his folded page before muttering in her ear, "We hook to the right just at the end. Looks like the shelves just before the door in that corner," he pointed around her right side to the nearest wall of books, a few feet behind the velvet rope. "I'm not really sure how to get to it."

Kristin gave an exasperated sigh. As they neared the turnaround point near the window, she hissed back to him, "Just block me." Before Jared could answer, she had crouched beside a small metal post in the corner and slipped under the end of the rope barrier. He turned around, stepped backwards, and assumed a wide stance behind her. Facing the center of the room, he stared hard over the crowd and nodded knowingly at the painting over the fireplace. The next couple in line glanced up from their brochure, met his eye, and turned to study the same point he was looking at as they passed him to take the corner and double back. A family of four behind them followed suit.

Behind Jared's calves, Kristin stayed low. Even camouflaged in head-to-toe-tan, standing up would draw the attention of at least the other tourists if not the docent. On top of which, she had no idea if standing would get her any nearer to her goal: with no indication of what to look for or where to go beyond the two-dimensional map Jared grew, she decided there was nothing to lose by starting out safely near the floor.

Kristin used a finger to trace the narrow baseboard below the bottom shelf before moving up to the lowest row of leather-bound

The Beard

volumes. Every second that passed, she felt a vague sense of panic rise closer to the surface. As she struggled to carefully monitor her breathing, she noted a drop of sweat falling from her forehead to form a dark spot on the smooth carpet at her feet. It was only as she shifted her gaze to the third shelf from the floor that she was struck by a sudden realization: the thing she was looking for wanted to be found. She and Jared had not set out looking for a map to follow, it had come to them. And in each of the previous cases, they had not had to wait very long for an explanation to present itself. Kristin couldn't be sure that what they wanted would be easy to access, but whatever it was, she was confident it would make itself known.

A sense of calm washed over Kristin, and every detail took on a new sharpness. In the tiny strip of shadow between the third row of books and the shelf above, a slight movement demanded her attention. She leaned in and squinted. She could just make out the very edge of a yellowed piece of paper protruding from the top of a volume. As she looked, the paper fluttered, and even though Kristin knew from her own discomfort that the air in the room was perfectly still, she found the peculiar motion unsurprising, almost predictable.

Without a second thought, she blotted the sweat from her palms on her shorts, carefully tugged the binding toward her, and delicately dragged the loose paper from its sheath. Kristin's eye was immediately drawn past a handwritten message to the closing line, 'Gratefully yours, Maj. H.S. Strafford." As quickly and quietly as possible, she moved in a crouch back under the rope and rose to her full height behind Jared's shoulder. She reached around his midsection and took the hand-drawn map and brochure from him while muttering, "Found it."

Without turning around, Jared quietly replied, "That was quick." As Kristin followed him to rejoin the flow of people moving toward the door, she carefully slid the brittle note under Jared's map and tucked the set neatly into the brochure. Jared asked over his shoulder, "You ready to finish the tour?"

Clifford

Leaning close, Kristin said softly, "I technically just stole something, so..."

"So back to the shuttle then," he finished, expressionless.

She answered brightly, "Might be best." Approaching the double door, she turned to the docent behind the rope, "Thank you for all that information. This is definitely my favorite room so far." The other woman nodded warmly, and the couple followed on, into another gallery lined with Flemish tapestries.

Day 4

Tim Donaldson pulled the trigger and released a fine blue mist across the top of a display case. He methodically drew his paper towel over the surface, hardly noticing the grainy photographs on the other side of the glass. He had seen them nearly every day for five years now, and he knew from experience that they were unlikely to be seen by anyone but him for months to come. Their constancy bored him, but changing them felt pointless.

For Tim, the next phase of his life could not come soon enough.

As he often did when he felt dissatisfied, Tim reflected on how he had gotten here in the first place. On paper, he had done everything he was supposed to: he had been a devoted student at three of the top schools in his field. He had barreled through an aggressive undergraduate program, had majored in history with a minor in anthropology to finish near the top of his class. For the remainder of his twenties, he had taken a series of internships before pursuing his MA in Museum Studies. Tim had felt confident that his qualifications would put him on the fast-track when he had accepted an entry level position tending a minor historic site for the National Park Service, but then... something had happened that he still struggled to understand.

For the better part of a decade, Tim had watched people with less education and less stellar marks than him, race past to more prominent roles. As a matter of principle, he had resigned from his position and had tested his luck in the private sector, where he had been shocked to discover (repeatedly) an even worse scenario: people with shark smiles and half his intelligence fundraising their way to the top while he languished in nominal, often unnecessary posts. Time and again, Tim had left for greener pastures, until he found himself beaten, watching over this small community museum off of an interstate in Southern Wyoming. The place operated at a loss and likely always would, but it stayed open as an advertisement of the local historical society's pride and a boast of its funding.

The majority of the museum's collection consisted of old photographs, newspapers, and some arrowheads discovered in local backyards. In summary and in total, Tim found the place to be a waste of his talent and the only sort of place that was willing to hire him. This was the paradox he found himself pondering dozens, if not hundreds, of times each week. He rolled his resume over and over in his mind, scoured his decisions point by point, from every job interview to every curatorial judgment, searching for some mistake on his part, some fault he could have corrected. As always, he could find none. He would have been tempted to chalk it up to bad luck, had he not considered a belief in luck to be the last line of defense for the weak. The best he could come up with was a lack of understanding by the people in his industry. No one took history and preservation as seriously as he did, no one could care as much as he cared about the artifacts of their country and their culture.

Tim's position, he believed, was symptomatic of a superficial society that trivialized his discipline through consumerism, and consigned his passion to the same category as so many roadside tourist traps. In a world gone mad full of simple-minded people, Tim concluded that he was the better man for *not* getting ahead. But that did not change his distaste for where he was.

Satisfied with the slightly less streaky display case, Tim moved on to the nearest wall, where he straightened a portrait of one of the town's founders.

On a normal day, Tim felt like a glorified janitor. He would hardly have bothered to even be that, but occasionally a member of the historical society stopped through on their way to somewhere else, and invariably their only comment was an assessment of the museum's cleanliness. So, in service to his patrons, Tim tried to keep things tidy and ready for the visitors who almost never came.

Until very recently, he had given up on finding more worthwhile activities to get his career back on track. But then

The Beard

through sheer serendipity, a ray of hope had cut through his darkness.

Six months earlier, whilst excavating a storage closet in search of WD-40, Tim had come across an unprocessed box of donations from 1992. As much out of boredom as any sense of duty, he had set about cataloging and disposing of the contents. Under the usual faded and unattributed photographs and lacework, Tim had discovered a thin, yellowed manuscript: the memoirs of an early resident of nearby Wheatland, a man named H. Sullivan Strafford. The find would have been remarkable under any circumstance as a contemporaneous account of local historical events, but it had turned out to be so much more than that. Covering the author's experiences from 1880-1899, the story it told was too fantastic to be believed, which was why Tim had not initially believed it. He had instead set himself to authenticating the document's provenance, and afterward had dedicated many of his days to verifying the more plausible of Strafford's claims. Tim was amazed to have discovered evidence from all over the country that supported every sentence he could test.

The only part of the memoir left for him to pick at was the very beginning. Tim was not a superstitious man, and he did not believe it could be true. But if it was…

Tim moved inattentively from the portraits to a long wooden desk near the door; the surface was covered from end to end with Xerox copies of pages in Strafford's handwriting, interspersed with library books about Chinese astrology and pre-Columbian cultures. If the first portion of the memoir proved out, it would change everything for Tim, although he could not yet know how. He might not gain recognition in his chosen field or have the chance to rub his success directly in the faces of the many people who had wronged him, but he expected he would be able to make them pay, even if he couldn't make them sorry.

Tim sat down in a creaky chair behind the desk and reflected on the problem in front of him. He knew what he needed to do, and he was almost certain of where he should go, but that still left the outstanding question of when it would all begin. He started to reach for an astrological chart, but paused with his hand in the air. He considered that a chart was really just a map, and a map was a symbolic representation of space. Maybe searching this way had been the wrong approach. Maybe he should zoom out a little, start with a symbolic representation of time. As Tim's hand lowered absently to the papers in front of him, he gave some thought to the most accepted, ubiquitous, and wholly arbitrary of tools: the calendar. He had already incidentally ruled out the Chinese Lunar calendar, and felt very safe eliminating the Julian and Gregorian calendars as well. He did not know much about the Mayan calendar, though he could be looking for a distant cousin of that. Tim shuffled through pages of Strafford's manuscript, looking for some clue, some passing description that might point him in any direction. His eyes settled once again on a phrase he'd found himself staring at repeatedly over the past several weeks: it began, "He told us that once in every generation..."

Tim set the page aside and rifled through the desk for a pen and a blank sheet of paper. Every generation would be what, 20 years, roughly? And that sentence was written about 1881, and it was now 2015, so 134 years earlier. On the blank page, Tim divided 134 by 20, giving him a result of 6.7. He circled the number, and then paused to think before scratching it out. Not helpful, he decided: in this case, 20 Gregorian years was broad and inaccurate, and he needed something more specific. He went back to the copies and began skimming the first few pages, praying for some sort of divine intervention. Suddenly he saw it: a reference to an earlier event, that one having taken place in the spring of 1824. Jumping back to his pen and paper, he drew a line with 3 dots on it. He'd been searching for point C based solely off of point B, but using point A as a reference should give him the last piece of the puzzle.

Tim jotted numbers frantically across the paper: If end of August 1881 was 2/3 through that year, and he called mid-march the start of spring in 1824, then 1881.66 minus 1824.23 would give

The Beard

him a difference of 57.43 Gregorian years. If that was in the ballpark of three times what he would roughly call a generation, then a generation by whatever calendar this was, had to be about 19.143 years. And if everything played out exactly every 19.143 years, then rounding up to seven generations from his earlier-20-year-guess would total 134.003 Gregorian years. And adding 134.003 years to Stratford's account from 1881.66 meant that the next cycle would begin...

Tim's jaw dropped as he stared at his final number: 2015.663: late August, just a few weeks away. It occurred to him that out there somewhere it had probably started already. He would have to move quickly if he was going to jump in.

A small metal bell above the front door jarred Tim out of his contemplation. A woman in her late 60's wearing thick spectacles and a loose perm walked past his desk and stopped to look broadly into the large, open room. Tim tilted his head forward to regard the stranger over the wire rims of his glasses. "Can I help you with something?" he asked.

"Yes," she said, turning her attention to him. "I'm wondering if you could help me find information about someone who used to live in the area."

"Well, we usually handle this kind of thing by appointment," Tim said curtly, leaning back and crossing his arms. "But since you're already here, I suppose we can discuss it. To start with, you'll want to be more specific: a lot of people used to live in this area."

"My grandfather," the woman explained patiently, beginning to move toward the first row of display cases. "He lived outside Wheatland in the 1920's, and I'd like to learn more about him."

Tim stood and stepped out from behind the desk, subtly blocking her path. "Was he important?" he asked.

"Excuse me?"

Tim clarified sharply, "Did. He. Do. Something. Did he own a business or organize an event? Was he a charter member of a church or social organization, or anything otherwise noteworthy?"

Clifford

"Well, I don't know," she answered, dumbfounded. "I was hoping you could tell me."

"That is not how it works," Tim said imperiously. "It goes without saying that our goal is to focus on artifacts and documents of historical significance to the community. If your grandfather was *somebody*, then he might be in here somewhere. But we could spend all day finding out that he was nobody." Tim raised one hand near her shoulder and moved forward, guiding her back toward the entrance. He continued in a slow, exaggerated tone, "Now, *if* you had called for an appointment, I could have saved you a trip. What *you* want to do is go to the *li-bra-ry* in Wheatland. There they can help you get on the *in-ter-net* to check censuses. And *they* can help you with the vertical files, to find out if your grandfather mattered. If he did, *then* you may call and arrange a time to review the relevant items in our collection." Tim pulled the front door open in what he considered a chivalrous gesture.

As she crossed the threshold, the woman turned. "Y'know," she said over her shoulder "You are as rude and unhelpful as anyone I've ever met. Just a real piece of work."

Tim repaid her with a tight smile and slammed the door in her face. The brass bell overhead shook nearly to the floor.

The *gall* of these people.

Here she was, having violated the society's protocol to interrupt his day, and Tim had been kind enough to set aside his other work and offer her his expert guidance, and *she* was calling *him* rude. If nothing else, the entire episode demonstrated what Tim had felt in his gut for as long as he could remember: that there was no hope of his ever getting ahead in a world full of such horrible ingrates.

As Tim turned back to his desk full of paper, a wave of relief washed over him. Very soon he could make them all pay. It just couldn't come soon enough.

Day 5

In the only unused corner of the small kitchen, at 2:36 in the afternoon, the dusty cuckoo clock's doors remained shuttered, its lonely mechanical occupant dormant, even as its hollow ticking drove false urgency into the heavy silence. On the opposite end of the room, Kristin hunched over her work, squinting intently at a white cardboard frame on the table while she pulled a pencil along the metal edge of a ruler.

In the days following their sojourn to North Carolina, Kristin had been trying to convince herself that the trip had not been wasted. She and Jared had technically found what they were meant to find, but the note she had walked off with had been so vague that she still struggled to see the point. Jared had taken the more positive stance that if they didn't know exactly what it meant, then it could mean anything, and that only meant that they needed more research.

One thing they had agreed on during the long drive home was that the note served as proof that Strafford spent time at Biltmore in 1899, and in a sense, this made it no more or less valuable than any of their discoveries thus far. After all, they knew what had taken the Major to Richmond, but that, in and of itself, didn't explain why they should care. They would, they decided, need to assemble more of the story, need to follow the maps to their conclusion, and then they could see how each of these pieces fit together. Hopefully.

Kristin set aside her pencil and picked up a small utility knife. She carefully adjusted the length of the blade and poked it through a corner of the shape she had drawn on the cardboard. Slowly and deliberately, she held the surface firm with one hand and slid the knife down the line with the other.

Kristin and Jared's drive-time discussion had naturally led to where they might need to go next, and there were significant questions to hash out. For one thing, it seemed reasonable to assume that future destinations would only get further afield, and they agreed that once they were past the Carolinas, trips would become too cumbersome to fit into a weekend. Jared had a few weeks' vacation saved up, and had suggested parsing it out at two or three days a week as needed, which Kristin had admitted was sensible.

At the same time, she was definitely not enamored with the notion of repeatedly driving the earlier portions of the same route again and again. But she chose to keep that to herself: her reluctance was fueled less by a devotion to efficiency than by a sense of urgency that she did not fully understand. There was something in the back of her mind lately, some nagging feeling she had, that this whole adventure was happening under someone else's deadline, and the idea of meting out progress on an open-ended basis had landed as a ball of panic in the pit of Kristin's stomach.

Satisfied with her work, Kristin set the cardboard in a glass picture frame and gently set the brittle paper behind it.

Jared had volunteered to handle travel arrangements, and Kristin had been happy to agree. Although she privately questioned his ability to find the best deals on accommodations, Jared had the map and would be the one driving, and she found the idea of communicating every detail of every stop too tiresome for words. More importantly, though, it was rare that he took a strong interest in anything, let alone something that involved her, and she loved to see him let himself run with it, to become that invested in something they could share.

It was Kristin's hope that ceding those responsibilities to him would help them to keep their momentum. But momentum towards what? It always came back to that, and she had no clue. But somehow the further they got, the less concerned she became with answering the question.

Kristin replaced the plastic backing in the frame and used the handle of the knife to bend the clips back into place. She leaned the object against the wall and sat back to admire her handiwork.

The Beard

Centered in a white matte, a florid script cascaded down a yellowing page behind glare proof glass:

George,

Please accept this volume
with my gratitude for your
warm hospitality and inspirational
conversation.

Gratefully Yours,
Maj. H. S. Strafford

Kristin smiled proudly and reflected: Along with everything else she couldn't know about the future was how many chances she would get to collect souvenirs.

Day 10

Louis believed that he reeked, but he knew that he did not care. He took a long pull from his whisky bottle and fumbled to mash it into the cup holder of his folding camp chair. After the third try, he remembered the outcome of the previous dozen attempts and resigned himself to setting the bottle in the dirt near his feet.

By the time he and Marlow had pulled away from the house twelve days earlier, Louis had realized how badly he'd stepped in it. Carolyn would get over it: she always did, he was the father of her children so what choice did she have? But he knew from experience that it would not happen overnight, and that she would require some space in the meantime. For so much of their lives they'd been locked in a cycle: he would screw up, she would be furious, he would apologize, she would accuse him of trivializing her feelings, and the harder he would try to make up for his actions, the harder she would push him away.

So, Louis thought it would be better for both of them if he kept his distance for a while and allowed her the time and freedom to resent him. He figured he probably had that coming anyhow. But that left the question of what he should do while his family went on about their lives. For several days Louis had tried to be social, but the only people available to spend days with him were other men who were out of work, which had proved to be very depressing; only slightly less depressing, he discovered, than waiting until evening to spend time around friends who still had jobs. It wasn't so much that Louis felt shame around them, but he got the impression that they didn't want to get too close, like his bad luck might be contagious or something.

On the other hand, those who would brave a conversation with Louis had been almost too understanding. That familiar look they gave him, an overt sympathy that belied their gratitude for not being him... the whole exercise felt like a farce. Louis could not

The Beard

tolerate their pity, but did not have the energy to pretend to be fine for their benefit.

Thus, he now found himself, at 1:30 on a cloudy afternoon for the third consecutive day, sitting alone in his small clearing outside Selmer, Tennessee, with a thin film of liquor seeping out of his pores. This last part was not helped by the weather: for weeks, each day had been slightly hotter than the one before, the rising mercury mercilessly dragging the humidity along for the ride. And now, thick clouds had wandered in to tamp down the stifling air where it stood. Louis mumbled to himself, "Somethin' gotta break. An' it gotta break soon." He leaned over again to retrieve his whisky.

As the sky continued to darken, confused cicadas began singing prematurely in the tree line twenty yards distant. Over their rhythmic whine, Louis sensed movement in the brush. For a time, he stared numbly at a large shadow rooting through the vegetation, before lazily settling his gaze near his left foot. In the grass, with the rest of his litter, was his cell phone. He had made a point of keeping it nearby, but it had not rung in four days. As he began to feel sorry for himself, Louis suddenly realized that he couldn't remember when he'd last charged it. For that matter, he couldn't remember when he'd last eaten. He guessed that it must have been recently, since he'd woken up earlier next to an empty Pringles can, but there again, that could've been in his bed for a week without his noticing.

Lost in contemplation, Louis was surprised by a large water droplet on the face of his phone. Looking past it, he watched a second drop break against the brown glass of a discarded beer bottle. He returned his attention to the sparse woods, and noted that at some point a cool breeze had kicked up. The hiss of water against leaves rolled down the hillside and brought with it a deep sense of relief.

Louis drained the last of his whisky and tossed the spent bottle onto the lawn before retrieving his phone and struggling to his feet. "MUR-LOW!" he bellowed, "Hurry up!" As he stumbled to the trailer, he mumbled, "God's way 'a tellin' us to get inside and freshen my drink."

Louis opened the door and stood, swaying on his feet while the clouds opened up and blasted him with cold water. "MUR-LOW!" he reiterated, "Got-Dammit Boy!" The dark shadow burst from the trees and loped at full steam, across the clearing and directly through the door. "Well there he is," Louis slurred, turning to take an exaggerated step over the threshold.

Louis closed the door of the trailer behind them, and the white noise of large drops slapping the ground was consumed by the thunderous pounding of rain against the aluminum roof. The sudden spike in humidity had transformed the stale air of the dim room into an unbearably damp blanket. Louis leaned over to switch on the oscillating fan and turn the small hand crank that opened the plexiglass slats of the nearest window.

Marlow proceeded to shake himself dry at the other end of the space, rocking the trailer on its axles and nearly throwing Louis off his feet. "Oh, Fer Fuck's Sake!" Louis shouted, "What is yer got-damn problem, man!?!" As Louis regained his balance, it occurred to him that the dog had a point: after only a few seconds in the storm, Louis' clothes were soaked through. He mused that if he went back outside for five minutes he could cross laundry and bathing off his to-do list in one go but instead decided it would be wiser to change into something dry. While he was at it, he might find motivation to take an actual indoor shower, with soap even.

Louis kicked off a boot, teetering on one foot as he began peeling his T-shirt away from his torso. The bottom of the garment rolled up, locking into a near tourniquet over his bicep. He attempted to wrench the taut collar over his head, but succeeded only in launching himself sideways against the paperboard counter of the kitchenette, forcing his raised elbow onto a thin shelf above the sink. The surface flipped away from its braces with a dramatic clatter, sending its contents of cooking utensils and knick-knacks across one end of the trailer.

The Beard

Louis pivoted and somehow got his bare foot down without falling clear to the floor. He felt a string of obscenities building inside of him like an epic sneeze, and was surprised when he instead began to weep into his shirt-prison. Losing the drive to fight against the fabric, Louis suddenly thought of a finger trap. He loosened the muscles of his shoulder and slid the shirt to one side before sinking to his knees to blink through his tears at the floor.

"Fucking mess..." Louis sobbed over the mess. Marlow padded softly from the sofa, stopped at the perimeter of the kitchen shrapnel, and concernedly sniffed the air a few feet from Louis' face. Louis used the edge of his meaty hands to begin sweeping small items into a pile. Buttons, pins, badges, and patches, multiple broken pocket watches, and an antique belt buckle that he had spent a pretty penny on because he'd appreciated its patina. Settling absently to sit on his heels, he surveyed the rest of his space. An expensive saber hung from a nail near a clothing rod that supported several uniforms, all swinging freely above multiple pairs of shoes and the reproduction rifle that Louis cleaned regularly.

Louis wondered how in the world he had justified accumulating all this stuff. He had a family, whether or not they wanted him, and he clearly had no job security... what in god's name had he been thinking, dumping good money on this crap? Louis' tears tapered off as he returned to the task in front of him, seeing not prized possessions but humiliating price tags. Here he had a watch that he'd mostly bought for the chain, twenty-five dollars. And over there a dug button that he'd gotten at a 'bargain' for fifteen. And none of it did him any good now, sitting out here, lost in his own property, surrounded by his shabby, pointless things.

And there, that busted-ass compass. It was too poignant a metaphor: the once useful tool that had long forgotten true north, it now gestured into what would be the sunset, its misshapen cover knocked into some unseen cranny. How had he been talked into giving away five bucks for a compass that he didn't even want? That could've been a meal for one of his children. That could've

Clifford

been two gallons of gas. Louis shouted in frustration at the object's smug face, "What the *hell* are you pointing at!?!"

The compass' thin needle shuddered and began to turn clockwise across the dial, slowly for one rotation, it then accelerated to a frantic hum. For five full seconds it spun as a blur, its metal housing vibrating against the nylon floor tiles while the man and his dog both stared in disbelief. Suddenly, abruptly, and just as inexplicably it froze, the needle locked once again on a point just north of due west.

Louis softly iterated what both companions were thinking: "What the hell was that?" Marlow eased tentatively around the pile Louis had gathered and lowered his front half to bring his nose closer to the compass. Louis leaned forward on the palms of his hands, accomplishing the same. Zeroing in from his day-drunk haze, Louis wondered aloud, "What the hell *are* you pointing at?"

The needle moved once more in a single, emphatic track around the cardinal points before defaulting insistently on its preferred orientation.

Had to be a fluke, Louis told himself. The thing just *had* to be busted. Whatever was going on must be arbitrary, if a little unusual. The compass must be pointing at nothing because there was nothing to point at. But then again, that wasn't really true, was it? In a sense, there was always something to point at, would always be something to the west no matter how far west you went. Louis levered himself back onto his rear and sat cross-legged, still regarding the compass. Marlow gave a single wag and approached, inviting Louis to scratch his ears. Louis vaguely obliged the animal while following his train of thought.

What it was pointing at was Arkansas. Then past that, Oklahoma. New Mexico, Nevada, California, then the sea. All just points on a map, most of which he'd never seen. But also places in actual space, all of which he could easily get to. Louis knew that the idea of following an obviously broken compass was silly, impulsive, and probably stupid. But he couldn't keep going as he had been, couldn't continue where he was. If only to preserve what

144

was left of his sanity, he had to go somewhere, even if the destination was arbitrary and a little unusual.

"Somethin' gotta break," Louis sighed, "An' it gotta break soon.

Day 11

For the twentieth time that day, the nation's headlines grumbled at Jared through plexiglass. With as much enthusiasm as he could muster by that point in the morning, he announced, "Next in line please," before cutting the volume of the small speaker in his window. A young man in denim shorts and a tank top crossed half way from the front of the line then stopped to sling a backpack off his shoulder. In the middle of the floor, in front of a string of waiting customers, he dug unhurriedly through his bag.

It never ceased to amaze Jared how someone could spend that long waiting and still not be ready when their turn came. It struck him as peculiarly analogous to Washington: people showed up with a goal in mind and were told to get in line. Then after a while, getting to the front of the line became a goal in itself and by the time they had accomplished that, their own progress had supplanted whatever it was they had come to do in the first place. Jared adjusted the outside speaker of his intercom and said, "Whenever you're ready." The man obliviously continued to rifle through his bag.

When the customer finally stood, white envelope in hand, Jared returned his speaker to its previous, grating strength. "HI," the man shouted over the television, "I'D LIKE TO MAKE A DEPOSIT." Jared gave the intercom a tweak to compensate for the customer compensating for the news. At least this transaction would be brief. Jared's lunchtime was coming up soon, and he had plans for every second of it. For the previous two weeks, he had spent his break happily and quietly picking through maps, comparing hotels, and reworking meal and fuel options for the road from Arlington to Asheville.

In retrospect, handling logistics for the next leg wasn't especially convenient for Jared. The website blockers on the bank computers forced him to drag Kristin's laptop to and from work, and making arrangements without distractions meant giving up his only chance to get out of the building each day. But he'd hoped that by ironing out the wrinkles on his own, he might avoid burdening Kristin, which could help him to keep her invested in something they could share. And he'd found the planning, setting, and readjusting of their steps weirdly relaxing, so while much of it was redundant until they had the next map, he kept coming back to it all the same.

Jared finished the transaction in front of him placing the customer's receipt in the tray with a flourish. By the time the man finished burying the slip of paper deep in his bag Jared had already put out a sign directing customers to the next teller. Jared retrieved a nylon satchel from next to his chair, and retreated to the end of the row of teller windows, through an access door into the lobby. He moved efficiently to a pair of inexpensive waiting room chairs set around a low coffee table near the door. There, he seated himself and emptied his satchel of a laptop, a pair of foam ear buds, and an apple. He was already chewing a bite and waiting on his computer to start by the time his last customer walked past to the exit.

Jared had noticed that the employee break room was a draw for employees on break, and while he had nothing against his coworkers, he found their constant conversation distracting. As for the lobby, though: Jared had years of practice tuning out the relentless news noise, but, for the uninitiated, the customer lounge did not invite lounging customers. To take the edge off the sound and to signal the world that he wasn't going to listen to it, Jared pressed his headphones into his ears and tucked their disconnected cord into his pocket.

Through this muffled backdrop a familiar voice wafted, "Look up, Asshole."

Jared looked up. Slightly bewildered, it took a moment for him to register Kevin's perturbed glare. Removing his headphones to set them on his keyboard, he said pleasantly, "Hey. So what's goin' on?"

Clifford

"Came to check on you," Kevin answered tersely, "It's been a while."

"Yeah," Jared confirmed, "Did you not get my text?"

"Oh, I got it," Kevin said, "Today's text, and all of them from last week, and from the week before that. Should I even bother stopping to get you anymore?"

Jared answered slowly, incredulous, "Not if I text you to say I'm not coming. No."

"But it's been, like, ten workdays in a row," Kevin argued. "And it's not like you're out of town or something. I mean, what are you even doing?"

"I've been busy," Jared shrugged.

"Busy with what?"

"Personal stuff," Jared said, "Does it matter?"

Kevin crossed his arms exasperatedly, "I think you at least owe me an explanation, is all."

Confused, Jared squinted and shook his head, "Why? Why do you care what I'm doing? Just go eat lunch for chrissakes. Why would you come in after I cancelled?"

"Because," Kevin said, "You're the broken window, and you're starting to snowball."

"That's too many metaphors. I don't follow…"

Kevin sighed and uncrossed his arms to lean in and lower his volume, "After a couple days of you being 'Too Busy' for us, Anthony decided that *he* was too busy. And if Anthony doesn't come out, then Chris doesn't think *he* should. So now it's just me and Roger, and that kid by himself drives me nuts."

"I see," Jared said thoughtfully.

"Yeah," Kevin said, straightening his posture, "So I invite you into our group, and now you're patient zero. Now, let's get your stuff and get going: Roger's fat ass is waiting out front."

"Umm, no," Jared said, perplexed. "Nice as that sounds, it doesn't change the fact I have other things to do. Sorry, but I can't help you."

The Beard

Kevin shook his head in amazement, "That's messed up dude. You have *no* loyalty."

"To you? No, I don't," Jared stated plainly.

"After all this time," Kevin said, gesturing melodramatically, "I brought you into our group, I went out of my way to take you along…"

"Yeah," Jared answered. His voice began to escalate in spite of himself. "Taking me along like a poodle. Going wherever you want when you want, so you can feel special for having a captive audience that you think somehow owes you something. It is a pain in my ass, and I have better shit to do with my time than laugh at you guys' stupid inside jokes."

"*Fuck* you, dude!" Kevin shot back.

"Screw you *and* your fat Roger!"

These last words echoed into empty silence. Jared blinked against the abrupt quiet then looked sheepishly across the faces of the dozens of customers and handful of employees staring back at him. Beyond the long line of people, teller windows, and judgement, a tall, slender man with a light suit, dark complexion, and pencil mustache was peering intensely over wire frames. The man hand held aloft a chunky universal remote, his thumb still hovering over the mute button.

Seething, Kevin shook his head and marched to the exit, forcefully throwing the glass door open as he left.

Jared mumbled, "Oh, Mr. Sherman, I…"

Without a word, Mr. Sherman beckoned Jared with one long finger of his free hand before flicking the button a second time and briskly retreating down a beige hallway. As though the man had called 'Action' on the scene, the midday monotony resumed with the anchor's voice, the collected assembly going disinterestedly back to their business on cue.

Jared left his things and, with a sinking feeling, followed the other man to the end of the short hallway. Past a pair of restrooms, he paused briefly at an open plywood door.

Clifford

Without realizing it, when Jared had been young, he had conjured an image of what he expected a bank manager's office to look like. He didn't know where it had come from: maybe Mr. Potter's office in *It's a Wonderful Life* or something. All he knew for sure was how disappointed he still felt every time he had to confront how inaccurate that idea was.

"Come in," Mr. Sherman called sternly, "Have a seat."

Jared took a deep breath and stepped into the windowless plaster box, to sit rigidly in one of two small chairs near the door. Jared's steely boss stood stiff as a board with his arms crossed in front of him, on the other side of a tidy metal desk. Jared shifted nervously in his seat, not comfortable with Mr. Sherman's deliberate silence, but not wanting to be the first to speak.

The older man finally initiated, "Care to tell me what I just witnessed?"

"That wasn't a customer," Jared quickly reassured him, "That was a personal thing, it should never have come into the building, and I promise it will never happen again."

"It happened in front of customers," Mr. Sherman reminded him.

"Yes," Jared acknowledged, "Which should never have happened. I am sorry for that. I'm happy to apologize to anyone you like and, really, it won't happen again."

The manager allowed his arms to drop and his composure to slip, shouting, "That happening once is unacceptable!"

Jared jumped and then sank in his uncomfortable chair.

Mr. Sherman shook his head and added forcefully, "I know you are better than this, Jared." As deliberately as nearly everything else he did, the man finally sat down and folded his hands on the desktop. He stared back at Jared for an excruciatingly long moment before continuing drily, "You say it was a 'personal thing.'"

"Yes," Jared confirmed.

"You've been bringing in a number of 'personal things' lately."

The Beard

"Well I- ," Jared started before thinking better of confessing anything specific, "I'm not sure what you mean."

"Your personal computer," Mr. Sherman stated off-handedly. "Your personal break-time on your personal phone calls and whatever personal projects go with those. You're allowed to have a life outside this bank, but you need to work harder at keeping it outside this bank."

"Understood, sir."

"Because when you blur those lines, when you let these 'personal things' of yours pile up, eventually one of them ends up screaming in my lobby." Jared sat quietly, not sure how to respond, if he was even supposed to. After another mean pause, Mr. Sherman continued, "When was the last time you took time off?"

"I'm not sure," Jared said.

"I looked it up the other day," Mr. Sherman clarified, "I had been planning to talk to you about it. Your last vacation day was in 2008. That is now seven years ago."

"Wow," Jared said, feeling at the same time proud and depressed.

"Yes, exactly: Wow. So I shouldn't wonder that you haven't had enough personal time to resolve your personal issues. Not to mention, having saved up your maximum three weeks' vacation, you've been losing leave for years now."

"I had no idea," Jared said.

"I assumed as much," Mr. Sherman answered. "And I *had* planned to suggest that you take a few days for yourself every now and then."

"You know, I was looking at doing some traveling in the next few months-"

Mr. Sherman continued unabated in his even tone, "In light of what just happened, I think you should use as much of it as possible as soon as you possibly can."

"What do you mean?"

Clifford

"I mean that after that display, I don't want to see your face in my bank for a couple weeks. You have the time. It's time you use it."

"So it's... Is that punishment, then?" Jared asked.

"Not officially," Mr. Sherman said carefully, "Although I won't squash that rumor if it circulates. No, at this point you are being encouraged to take full advantage of your accrued benefits. Now, if you can't see your way to doing that..."

"I understand," Jared said. He took a few seconds to absorb what he was hearing. "If it's okay though, I would like a couple days before I start into my... benefits."

"You're not really in a position to negotiate." Mr. Sherman leaned back in his seat and sighed, "Then again, if you did work out the week, it would give me time to rearrange people's schedules. I could see a case for that, but no longer than that."

"Okay," Jared said, trying to not sound too relieved, "Thank you. And I'm sorry for putting you in this position."

"You've been with us a long time," Mr. Sherman said, not standing, but with an air of finality. "And I know you are a better employee than this. I'd like us to get back to *that* place."

"We will," Jared said, getting up and backing toward the door, "No more distractions, I promise." Jared returned to the customer area only long enough to scoop up his things. Returning to his workspace, he dumped them onto his desk, took a deep breath, and exhaled slowly.

At the window next to Jared's, a young woman quickly put a hand over her microphone and asked him, "Are you alright? What did he say?"

"Said he's going to take a few days to decide my fate," Jared answered, "But he's leaning toward suspending me for a few weeks."

"Jesus, a few weeks? That's harsh. It was loud, but..."

"You know Sherman," Jared sighed. "He runs a tight ship."

Fifth Growth

Day 3

"Did you turn off the air conditioner?" Kristin called from inside the front door.

"Yeah," Jared yelled back from the kitchen, "Just got it."

"And you unplugged the coffee pot, and the TV, and the alarm clock?"

Jared walked casually up the hallway and replied, "Check, check, and check. Not sure I see the need, though: they don't draw that much power."

"Yes," Kristin answered with all the patience of a woman explaining basic arithmetic to a five-year-old, "But how do you think our neighbors would like it, if our alarm clock was going non-stop for three weeks? And what if there's a power surge or something while we're gone?"

Jared looked incredulous, "What if there's a power surge while we're here? How would that be better?"

Choosing not to dignify the follow up, Kristin asked, "Did you get everything you need out of the bathroom?"

"Done," Jared answered. Gesturing at two suitcases and three stuffed tote bags next to the door he said, "Since we've packed everything but the furniture here, I don't know what's left to miss."

"We don't know where we're going," Kristin reminded him. "It pays to be prepared. But why am I telling you that? You were a Boy Scout."

"For like, a minute," Jared said, standing expectantly beside the luggage.

"So…" Kristin said, "Not long enough to get the merit badge for carrying shit to the car?"

"Oh," Jared said, "Right. Got it."

"Chop-chop, buddy," Kristin said. "I left something upstairs, but I'll be out in sec." Kristin climbed halfway up the staircase while Jared picked up the tote bags. He let the front door close behind him, and she jogged back down to the kitchen. As she had suspected, the coffee pot was still plugged into the wall. She corrected the problem and moved on to the thermostat.

Jared's announcement about his job two days earlier had been jarring, to say the least. It wasn't at all like him to be involved in an altercation of any description, let alone at his work, a place so sacred that not even Kristin was allowed to stop by unless she had actual banking to do. But it took no time at all for the shock to wear off. The second he had said he would be available, and for nearly three weeks at that, Kristin had come out with a plan.

She had presented it as making lemonade out of lemons, but the truth was that she had been wistfully considering it all week. Jared was already on the cusp of having another map to follow. If he were to stay up, draw that out, and shave it that night (which he had), and if they left on Saturday morning, they could reach their first destination on Sunday afternoon and have a new map to work from by Friday. Growing maps as they moved along, they could clear three of them by the time Jared used up his leave. And since the destinations seemed to be getting further apart, and they'd have ten days to explore between each, that approach to that much time might be enough for them to cover serious ground.

And if that wasn't enough for them to reach their final destination… Well, Kristin wasn't sure about that part yet. But she had more than three weeks to figure it out, and in any case, they would be moving, it would be progress, and she still couldn't shake the nagging feeling that that was important.

Having confirmed the air conditioning and unplugged the television, Kristin paused by the couch to retrieve her pink backpack and walked to the door which was now clear of baggage. She surveyed her tiny kingdom: all quiet, all still, already awaiting her return. Quietly, she said, "Bye house," before stepping onto the porch.

Jared stood just outside with keys in hand. He waited patiently while Kristin pulled the door shut, then pushed it to test the latch. Somewhere in the distance a lawnmower hummed, faint enough

156

that unseen sparrows could still be heard waking in the trees. "We ready?" Jared asked.

Kristin nodded and took a step back so she could watch while he locked the doorknob. "Deadbolt," she reminded him.

"I know, I'm getting to it," he answered, swapping keys and moving to the other lock.

"So where are we going?" Kristin asked abruptly.

"Asheville by evening," Jared answered.

"Well yeah," Kristin said, "But what about tomorrow? I got so busy packing, I forgot to ask where the map ended."

Jared palmed his keys and stepped back from the door, giving Kristin room to test it one last time. "Selmer, Tennessee," he said, "Or technically a few miles past it, but the hotel I have us at is Selmer."

"Selma?" She asked over her shoulder as she pressed on the portal. "I thought that was in Alabama."

"No," Jared clarified, "Selm-er. A little bit smaller and one state off."

"Alright," she said taking his hand. "Then away we go to Selmer."

Jared smiled, and they strolled side-by-side down the front steps.

Day 4

"Alright Marlow, git on up!" The dog paused to look inquiringly at Louis, then gave a half-hearted hop into the cab of the truck. Louis climbed in after him, closed the door and sat for a few seconds before getting back out and calling, "Okay buddy, not yet. Git on out." Marlow appeared unsurprised as he disembarked and wandered toward the rear of the vehicle. Louis walked past the dog and kneeled to examine the trailer hitch. As he suspected, the connector for the brake lights dangled by the dirt, unfastened. He affixed the cable on the trailer to its mate on the truck and walked back to the driver's door. "Alright Marlow, git on up!" he called. Marlow approached and began to crouch for another leap, then hesitated. After a moment, Louis said, "Y'know what? Hold up, boy. Gotta check somethin' quick." The dog turned and sauntered off to hike his leg on the corner post of his chain-link enclosure.

Louis had been leading this dance for more than two hours and was beginning to wonder if it hadn't gotten late enough to justify delaying their departure until the following day. But he couldn't let himself do that, just couldn't. For five days, he had found reasons to push this trip back, each of which was legitimate on its own, but which taken together were shameless procrastination. And as odd as this jaunt had seemed on impulse, it became even stranger when treated as something that might be intentional or well planned.

He unlocked the door of the trailer and stepped inside. Reaching to the center of the ceiling, he turned a hand crank to lower a small plastic cover over the ventilation fan.

After he had determined that this journey was necessary, Louis had devoted two days to drying out: it was hardly his first time, and experience had taught him that two days was a safe bet to wrap up a bender. The first of those was the predictable-unholy-hangover, but the second was about cleaning up. Traditionally, that had only meant cleaning up his physical environment and maybe

The Beard

apologizing to anyone he'd offended in the course of things. But this time around, his clean-up day had required more thought. He had asked himself a hundred times whether this plan still seemed like a good idea when he was sober, and every time he had come to the same conclusion: good or bad, the plan was his only idea. And, as always, an idea that runs unopposed wins by default.

This had naturally brought him to the next phase of realizing his only available strategy: figuring out what he would need. This had occupied all of day three. It was helpful that his normal life was portable and self-contained, but he didn't want to hit the road without adequate supplies, which led to his fourth day: procurement. On the morning of day five, Louis had realized that he should probably check his post office box and have his mail held for a month or so. After squaring that away, he had looked up an RV park eight hours west of Selmer and called ahead for a reservation.

It was while he was making advance arrangements with the park manager, a step very unlike him, that Louis realized that he was grasping for excuses to not leave immediately. But he knew himself pretty well, and he knew absolutely that if he didn't get out soon, he'd settle right back into his unhealthiest patterns. It was now or never.

Satisfied that the interior of the rig was buttoned up, Louis re-locked the trailer and climbed back into the truck. Taped to the dashboard, a three-year-old Polaroid of Carolyn and the kids was beginning to yellow at the edges, the product of consistent sunlight, dust, and smoke. Louis removed the old compass from his hip pocket and placed it delicately against the inside of the windshield above the photograph, leaned upright against its bent cover.

"There," Louis muttered to himself, "Should be the last of it." He turned the keys in the ignition and leaned out to pull his door closed. From the ground outside the cab, Marlow stared impatiently. "Oh shit," Louis said, "Sorry boy." Louis de-boarded and enthusiastically said, "Alright Marlow, git…" Not waiting for the conclusion, the dog jumped onto the bench seat and climbed over the cup holder to look out the passenger window.

Less than two miles from his wooded acre, Louis got a nagging feeling. He struggled to remember, in no particular sequence, what it was that he could possibly have forgotten. He had handled the mail, he'd left Carolyn a voicemail since she still wasn't taking his calls, the trailer was buttoned down and stuffed to the gills with groceries... but there was something, he was sure, just something *off*. Louis spent a moment taking stock of his environs: contented dog, side mirror extensions on, phone charging in the armrest, compass pointing north-

Louis slammed on the brakes, causing the trailer to drift across the gravel road. Remembering himself, he lifted his foot and corrected the angle of the truck before the rig completely fishtailed, then coasted to a gentler stop along the shoulder. Marlow stared at him, offended at his having suddenly lost his mind.

Louis looked around the vehicle and glanced up at the sun, still fairly high to the southwest. He decided he was certain: the compass (which through everything had somehow remained in position on the dash board) had moved from its westward orientation to indicate almost full north. Which it should have been doing all along. Had it somehow unbroken itself? He set the small item in his large palm. So now what?

Louis had reservations: not just reservations about taking this trip, actual reservations at a camp ground in Arkansas. But they hadn't taken down his credit card, and it wasn't like he'd ever speak to them again if he didn't show. He could still ditch out and change directions. But then he wouldn't be going on the great Western adventure he had expected. Then again, was that the whole point, to go west? Or was the point to find out what lay beyond the compass needle? Louis decided that there was no real point to either. Unless there *was* a point, and he just didn't know what it was yet. But there was only one way to find that out for sure.

Louis put the compass back and eased the truck onto the road. He would go north, apparently. It wouldn't require a major

The Beard

adjustment this early in the trip: he would just hook up with Highway 45 instead of 64, no harm, no foul.

As Louis got back up to speed, he decided that he felt good about the decision. If anything, the sudden shift in plans was liberating: if he didn't know what direction the compass would take him, then he couldn't make arrangements along the way, which meant that he couldn't fault himself for not having been more prepared to go to places that he could not have predicted. With every yard he covered, Louis found himself getting more excited, more intrigued by the prospect and potential of the unknown.

Just over halfway to the junction with the interstate, Louis slowed behind a black Volkswagen going fifteen miles per hour. As he moved up to crowd the other car's bumper, he noted its Virginia plates. It was a safe bet on this narrow back road that any vehicle he didn't recognize didn't belong. Out-of-state plates on top of that... lost, for sure. A pale arm reached out of the Jetta's window to wave Louis around.

Louis mumbled to himself, "Gonna move over for me then?" He began to pull a bit to the left, and realized two things: first, the guy was not giving him room to maneuver, and second, based on the deep scratch across the Jetta's front fender, the guy likely didn't know he needed to. "Alright then, man," Louis said, "We'll try it this way." Louis slid the truck back behind the other car, pressed forward to within inches of the trunk lid, and laid hard into his horn.

He might not know where he was going, but damned if Louis was going to take all year to get there.

Over the angry drone of the horn behind them, Kristin yelled, "Just pull over!"

"I already waved him around," Jared shouted back, watching the square grill of the pickup fill his rearview, "He has plenty of room."

Clifford

"He doesn't think so!" Kristin insisted, "Fucking pull over and let him by!"

Indignant, Jared eased onto the narrow shoulder and braked. As the rear vehicle accelerated past him, he caught a brief glimpse of a massive dog's smile in the passenger window, and just above that, an equally massive middle finger extended in his direction. "Fuck you hillbilly!" he called at a small trailer with aluminum tailfins as it bounced over a rise and out of sight.

Jared's rage dissipated with the cloud of gravel dust, leaving a heavy silence in its wake.

With deliberate calm, Kristin suggested, "Maybe it was time to stop anyways. We've definitely been on this road for more than two miles."

"Yes," Jared admitted sullenly, "More like five miles at this point. But I swear I didn't see any turnoff on the right. A couple driveways maybe, but that doesn't seem right. Guess we should back up a few miles and take another look."

"Or we can keep going straight to the next intersection and find our hotel from there, try again tomorrow when we're fresh," Kristin offered.

"No," Jared said, putting the car in gear and cranking into a U-turn, "We're all the way out here, we're finishing the map."

After three quiet miles, Kristin said, "Wait. There, on the left." She pointed to a rutted dirt lane running between a stand of trees and a small open field.

"I don't think that's a road," Jared said, slowing to a stop. "An access road maybe, for a tractor or something."

"You don't think that counts?" Kristin asked. "It's the only option for a mile in either direction."

Jared considered this for a minute before whining, "I don't know. I don't want to bottom out the car and then find out we're wrong. Maybe we should go to the hotel."

Finally letting her frustration show, Kristin exclaimed, "Maybe you should stop being a baby. You don't want to risk your precious undercarriage? Fine." She unfastened her seat belt, grabbed a piece

162

The Beard

of paper off the dash, and threw open her door. "Your directions say it's about a quarter mile. So, you sit tight there, Sally, and I'll go look into it." She climbed out and slammed her door behind her.

"Hang on," Jared said to the now empty car. He pulled further onto the shoulder, cut the ignition and jogged out to catch up. Without another word between them, the couple walked side by side along the edge of the field. After a hundred yards, the bare earth was covered by a layer of thick brush, which immediately disappeared into forest land. The shallow wheel ruts in the road became slightly more pronounced, the crown in between punctuated by weeds.

"At least we can tell there's something back here now," Kristin observed as they crossed into the dense shade of the trees.

"What makes you say that?" Jared asked.

"Look at the branches," Kristin said, "They're pruned back over the road."

"I'll be damned," Jared breathed, "That's like what, a fifteen-foot clearance or something? Maybe they're hauling equipment back here?"

"Have to wait and see," Kristin said.

Coming out of a gentle curve, the dirt lane emptied dramatically into a carefully landscaped clearing. Surrounded by trees on all sides, the short lawn was interrupted only by an aluminum shed at the far end, a chain link enclosure surrounding a doghouse near the center, and a long adjacent patch of dead grass headed by a solitary wooden post featuring a covered electrical outlet and a narrow vertical pipe with spigot.

Kristin turned the directions over to look at a hand drawn map on the back. "I feel like this has to be the end of it. But I don't see anything on hear about a clearing, it just sort of ends. Was there a ring of black hair around it?"

"Not sure," Jared answered, "Or I don't remember. I was in kind of hurry this time."

Taking stock of her surroundings, Kristin said, "We should do some kind of grid search, see if there's anything here while we're here. I'll walk the perimeter and work my way inward. And you can start in the middle and work your way out."

With tacit consent, Jared proceeded to the middle of the clearing with Kristin along the tree line. Both stared carefully at the ground in front of them, scouring for any wayward clue. Kristin called out, "Shed's locked!"

"Dog's not home!" Jared replied. After twenty minutes of pacing off their assigned routes, the pair met up twenty yards in front of the dead patch.

"Nothing," Kristin announced. "Why am I not surprised?"

"On top of kenneling a dog, somebody's been out here lately." Jared nudged an errant beer bottle with his toe, "The empties seem pretty fresh. And numerous."

"Could be teenagers," Kristin said, "Or maybe not. You know, there was nothing obvious in Richmond, and that turned out to be something. So maybe we just dig a little deeper."

"Still," Jared sighed in disappointment, "It would be nice to have an easy answer for once, instead of more questions. *Somebody* is using this place for *something*: it couldn't hurt to know what."

Kristin rubbed Jared's arm reassuringly, "Well, we still have until Friday to find out."

Day 7

Louis leaned on the steering wheel, pulled slowly through the corner, and checked his rearview. Satisfied that he would not be in anyone's way, he allowed the pickup to coast down a gradual incline that overlooked a stretch of the Missouri River and a slice of a picturesque park on its bank. He carefully covered the brake pedal and glanced at the compass: still showing east, no... southeast... sort of... it had to be close by now.

In the previous days, after a couple minor course adjustments, Louis had found himself on Interstate 55. In the interest of getting a space to park for the night, he had stopped North of Cape Girardeau. Having lighted on a pleasant campground, he had spent a lazy Monday getting to know his neighbors-of-the-moment before getting an early start on Tuesday.

After three more hours on the road, he had noticed, to his frustration, that the compass had at some point changed direction again. Throughout nearly an hour of backtracking, he had caught the needle spinning from south to west and back to north, and had taken that to mean he'd missed an interchange with Interstate 275. The afternoon had proceeded apace: driving until he'd gone too far, then doubling back only to double back again. Louis had circled the drain in this fashion until he had gotten completely fed up and had instead followed signs to a campground west of St. Louis.

But now it was a new day. Once he was rested, it had occurred to Louis that the more he had looped around, the smaller the loops had become, so by this point he had to be within a few miles of the center of the spiral. And so, with that in mind, he had paid for a second night, unhitched his truck from the trailer, and had taken Marlow for a driving tour of historic St. Charles, Missouri. For the better part of an hour, they had driven the red brick roads, had circled blocks of restored brick buildings filled with quaint antique shops, candle makers, souvenirs, and similar.

Clifford

Louis paused at a stop sign to check above the dash. Marlow lifted his head from the bench seat to look at him quizzically. "Don't worry boy," Louis said while he signaled another right turn, "You're not alone: I'm sure I'm confusing the locals plenty too."

In truth, though, Louis had noticed that the locals didn't seem to think anything of the clearly lost guy with the out of state plates. In a neighborhood as proudly touristy as this strip of old Americana, people were probably used to it, which was itself a feeling that Louis was not used to. It had never occurred to him before that, having lived his whole life in one place, having never travelled more than one state in any direction, this sensation of being a stranger would be very strange to him. He still hadn't decided whether or not he liked it, whether it was liberating or unsettling. But then, he saw no reason that it couldn't be both.

Louis looked again to his mirror and slowed to a crawl. The needle had shifted to almost full east, into the riverfront park. He could see roads running through, but no vehicle entries or parking spaces. "Alright boy," he said, signaling another right, to pull into a gravel lot behind a tavern. "You ready to go for a walk?" Marlow thumped his tail twice against the seat back and pushed himself into a sitting position. After collecting his cigarettes, the compass, and a small strap leash from the dash, Louis climbed down into the sunlight, allowing the dog to follow suit before he slammed the truck door. With the leash bunched up in his hip pocket, he led the way across the road, through a short iron gate and into the narrow park.

He knew that he should probably clip the lead to Marlow's collar and that someone might call out his decision not to, but Marlow had never responded well to the leash. It was a trait that Louis understood and quite respected, so he was willing to exchange a small amount of trust for the right to keep his hands free to monitor the compass. With his baseball cap blocking his periphery and his eyes on the small metal object in his palm, Louis wandered blindly over pavement and red brick, veering right at a large bronze memorial that he didn't bother to notice, and onto a

The Beard

broad gravel path. After a few hundred yards, the needled jerked suddenly to his left, leading him into a cut in a stand of trees.

It was only when he heard the hollow clop of wooden planks under his feet that Louis bothered to stop and look up. He found himself on a densely shaded foot bridge, spanning a narrow creek. He walked to the side, lit a cigarette, and stared upstream at the sparkling water as it tumbled over rounded stones and beneath a fallen bough. Just feet from either side of him, the summer sun beat down on short grass and concrete, but within this brief respite Louis could imagine the wilderness that had once dominated the place, and that he hoped still did somewhere. Marlow joined him, standing on his hind legs with his front paws braced against the handrail. "Like a Robert Frost poem," Louis breathed. He checked behind them to take in the view downstream: plastic bags fought with paper cups and fast food wrappers for an unseen right-of-way. Turning back deliberately he repeated, "Fuckin' Robert Frost."

At length, Louis reached over to flick his filter into the downstream pile before returning to the task at hand. Marlow followed the man following the magnet across a narrow parking lot, past a small black obelisk, and toward the edge of the river. A hundred feet out from the bank, a pier with a tethered spud barge sat connected to the park by caged-in concrete walkways at either end. At the head of the nearer of the two, a rusted steel door swung freely on it hinges, its shiny chain and padlock dangling limply on the ground.

Louis looked up, then back down, then at Marlow. "If we wind up havin' t'swim, I'm out," he said. "Or maybe I just ride you across, like the dolphin show at Sea World." The dog, loathe to dignify the remark, strolled lazily past his master and out to the pier. Louis continued to balance the compass at a slight angle on his palm in a slow-motion pursuit. As he crossed onto the large concrete slab, the tip of the needle glided gently to his left then abruptly dropped towards him.

Louis held the object upright and turned it slowly in front of his face. The needle swung slack across the dial at the bottom of

167

the casing, now answering only to gravity. He gave it a sharp shake before asking, "This it then? What all the fuss was about?" Marlow whined insistently from Louis' left, causing him to lower his hand and look around. A low railing surrounded the pier, a few feet beyond which the rusted hulk of the barge stood well above their heads with its corner pilings towering further still. Attached to the railing at about the halfway point, Marlow had discovered a large white sign, posted under Plexiglas in a bolted frame. At the top, a drawing of a paddlewheel boat in flames sat beside a grainy black-and-white photo of a lanky man standing on the river bank, wearing a long beard and a thousand-yard stare. Below these was an excessive explanation in printed script.

Louis approached the marker with an unsettled feeling building in the pit of his stomach as he read:

304 feet from this spot, the steamer, *City of New Madrid,* met her fate. Constructed in 1879, this 290-foot side-wheeler served landings on the lower Missouri between Saint Louis and Kansas City.

After colliding with the railroad bridge on the evening of October 10, 1892, *City of New Madrid* began taking on water while being moved by the 201-foot stern-wheel coal tow, *Turner.* A fire, thought to have begun in the latter, claimed both vessels during the night.

While all of *City of New Madrid*'s passengers had been safely evacuated, no fewer than eight crewmen from both vessels credited a good Samaritan named Henry S. Strafford with saving them from the burning wreckage. By dawn, only Jacob Franck, engineer of the *Turner*, was unaccounted for.

This marker dedicated on behalf of the survivors' descendants on May 26, 2004.
National Society Colonial Dames Seventeenth Century.

Louis turned over the compass in his hand. Not needing to look at it, he ran his thumb across the worn inscription on the back while rolling it through his brain:

Henry S Strafford
1880

The Beard

"So twelve years later," Louis reasoned with his dog, "and he was here. And now… we're here and… What the hell?"

"Well you are a lucky guy!" a man's exuberant voice proclaimed.

Louis and Marlow turned in tandem to discover a heavyset man in a bright red shirt standing at the end of the pier. "Excuse me?" Louis asked on their behalf.

"Said you're lucky," the man repeated as he approached. "I live not too far from here. I walk Bishop's Landing every day. Yeh, every day for the last ten years, and this is the first time I've ever seen the pier open."

"What… Why?" Louis asked, still trying to work out the purpose of the conversation.

"Oh, I don't know," the man went on, "Just something I do. Something calming about the water, sound of the birds maybe, or… Oh, you mean why the pier's not open?"

"Sure," Louis surrendered, "That's what I meant."

The man walked up to Marlow and extended his right hand, palm down, for the dog's inspection. "You're a big boy, aren't you?" he cooed. As the dog sniffed the man's hand and stepped closer, the man returned the favor by checking the tag on the dog's collar. "So, Marlow is it?" He flipped the bone-shaped metal in his fingers, "Which would make your friend… Loo-ee from Tennessee?"

"Lou-isss," Louis stated emphatically. "And you are?"

The man stood and offered his right hand to Louis, "I'm sorry, that's rude of me," he said, "Carl. Is my name."

Louis obliged with a brief handshake, not wanting to be impolite but also not sure what difference it would make if he were. "Nice to meet you Carl. So you were saying? About the pier?"

"Oh right," he nodded, "Why they keep it closed. I couldn't say. Liability maybe? Maybe they worry some teenagers will get drunk out here and fall in? Not sure, really."

Clifford

"But you said ten years and you haven't seen this open." Louis pointed to the plaque, "So how did that get out here?"

"Well, how about that," Carl wondered, "I had no idea that was here. Oh, that explains it: 2004 would be eleven years ago." With a chuckle he added, "Splitting hairs I guess, but what an odd place for a historical marker."

Louis stared out over the water while Carl began absently reading the plaque aloud. "Hey Carl," he interrupted, "Does something seem off to you? Like the river is flowing backwards or something?"

"Oh that," Carl said, "The river bends northward here. I can see where that might feel odd if you like your water ways feeding the Gulf."

Louis nodded and instinctively checked the broken compass. Awakened once more, the needle firmly gestured downstream. Under his breath, Louis muttered, "Well shit." He snapped the fingers of his free hand to get Marlow's attention and moved back toward the walkway without comment.

Carl politely asked, "Oh, you got a pocket watch?"

"No," Louis answered without slowing, "But it does tell me it's time to go."

Day 8

Kristin straightened her posture and pressed her bare shoulders against the oversized glazed bricks that ran the length of the dim interior hallway. The A/C in the county courthouse was turned up more than enough, as had been the small air conditioner in their hotel room, but she and Jared had been spending more time outdoors than they'd anticipated, and the resulting sunburn held the heat close everywhere she went. The cool surface against Kristin's skin was a welcome relief.

Having five full days to search for clues with no notion of where to start had thrown Jared and Kristin off balance. On the first day, Jared had immediately defaulted to his previous strategy, scouring search engines for anything regional from the 1890's, but he'd had very little luck and none at all in relation to Henry Strafford. After that, Kristin had begun speaking to locals about the clearing in the woods, from the hotel clerk to patrons at a nearby lunch place, to the cashier at the thrift shop. For the most part that had yielded only confused looks, but Kristin had expected as much: she'd really only pushed that approach to avoid a second consecutive day of sitting in the hotel watching Jared become irate with the internet.

But one of the diners they'd spoken to had, in passing, made a viable suggestion. If they were curious about the historical significance of a property, he'd said, they should try the Register of Deeds at the courthouse just down the street. And the following morning they had attempted exactly that, only to find that all the county offices were closed on Wednesdays. For lack of a better alternative, they'd purchased supplies for a picnic and returned to the clearing in the woods to wait for someone, anyone, to turn up.

No one had, so Jared and Kristin had spent the better part of the afternoon and early evening taking advantage of the quiet to work out the best way to proceed. Jared had advocated an adaptable strategy, some sort of repeatable process that could be applied to future destinations, as he was wont to do. But Kristin felt that if there was anything to be learned from the days' worth of dead ends, it was that their attempts to repeat things that worked once, under new and varied circum-stances, were futile. She argued that there was more value in flexibility, even though it did not come naturally to him. She had encouraged him to do more thinking on his feet, to engage more with what was in front of them instead of getting lost in how things should be. Jared had conceded the point, which meant that their agreed upon strategy was to avoid strategizing any further.

In this way, they had returned to the hotel with nothing but the sunburn on Kristin's shoulders and another on Jared's forehead. Kristin peeled herself from the now warm wall, shuffled sideways a few inches, and replanted. "Hey," Jared said, approaching from a restroom down the hall. "Getting comfortable there?"

"Don't knock it 'till you try it," Kristin said. "No, seriously, try it on your face, it feels great."

Jared looked at her quizzically, "I think I would look fucking nuts doing that. Plus, I'm not sure how hygienic that would be. How often do you guess they clean the walls?"

"I am choosing to not think about that," Kristin replied.

"My loss, then," Jared said. "No rush, but I'm ready when you are."

Kristin sighed and slowly pulled herself forward into the hallway. "You know where we're going?"

"Room 105," Jared confirmed, "Which is on this floor, so it can't be too tough to find." The pair walked slowly, reviewing room numbers and eventually turning into an office circumscribed by the same glazed brickwork as the hall.

A woman with short grey hair and round glasses looked up from a desktop computer to greet them. "Mornin'," she said politely, "Can I help you two find something?"

Kristin took a cursory look around: the office was empty but for the three of them, a couple computers, and a heavy grey vault

The Beard

door that stood open on one side of the room. "Yeah," she answered brightly, "We're looking for some deeds."

"Okay, we got some of those," the woman said drily. "You wanna be more specific?"

Kristin replied, "It's a clearing in the woods a few miles north, maybe more northeast of town. We want to know what it was and whose it was, back in the 1890's. Probably between 1898 and 1901."

The woman blinked at them, dumbfounded. "A spot in the woods, more than a hundred years ago. I don't guess this spot has an address?"

Kristin offered, "It's near a gravel road, but I didn't see any signs. No address comes up with any online maps either."

She replied sternly "And you know who owns it now?"

"We were hoping you could tell us," Kristin said.

The woman leaned back in her chair and took off her glasses to rub her eye in frustration. "Not much to go on. I can help get you started, but you should know that it will be a whole thing. And based on what you've said, I wouldn't get my hopes up."

Kristin nodded along, "Now when you say 'a whole thing…'"

"I mean a Whole. Thing. First you want to find a parcel number to work out the current owner. From there you have to find record of… Actually, what are you hoping to use this for? If you don't mind my asking."

Kristin answered, "We're trying to find out if a specific man was tied to that property around 1900, but before 1901."

The woman looked supremely relieved, "So you have the name of a person? Oh, thank goodness." She rose nimbly from her seat and breezed past the couple toward the vault door. Gesturing to a pair of chairs at a long wooden table she said, "If you'd like to take a seat, I'll be right back."

Jared and Kristin obliged. Following a clatter from inside the vault, the woman emerged holding an extremely thick, oversized volume with scuffed white canvas covers bound in brown leather. Dropping the book heavily in front of the couple she continued,

Clifford

"The index for that period is organized according to grantor and grantee, so you understand that finding a person in the deeds is a lot simpler than finding a place. You looking for your ancestor or something?"

Kristin shrugged, "Or something."

The woman nodded knowingly, "Fair enough. And the name?"

"Henry Strafford," Kristin stated.

"That'll do," the woman said, taking a position across the table and opening the book to its middle in front of them. Thumbing a series of lettered tabs along the edge of the yellowed pages, she carefully turned to the beginning of the 'S's. "Now, as you can see, the index is organized roughly by the last name of the individuals involved in the transaction." She pointed to a handwritten heading above many lines of names in the same clean and somewhat elaborate script. "See, here it tells you what book the deed is in, and what years that book covers. But beyond that, these were entered in the order received, so you'll want to find the book that covers your time period, and then go through line-by-line to find your guy. Make sense?"

"Yeah," Kristin said, "I think so."

"Good," the woman said. She backed away and called out, "Can I help you?"

Slightly startled, Jared and Kristin looked to the entrance and discovered a wiry gentleman with thick glasses, dressed head-to-toe in dark denim. "No rush, Pam," he answered. "Just come by to say hello."

Pam looked at him over her frames, "Come all the way in town to say hello?"

"Not exactly," the man answered, undeterred, "Lookin' at makin' some improvements on m'property, want to know what that does to m' tax burden."

Pam replied sternly, "I know that you know that's the Assessor's office downstairs."

"Yeeeah, I know," he said sheepishly, "But I always get the feeling they don't like me down there."

174

The Beard

"So, you're procrastinating?"

"Nah," he said, affronted, "I just thought it'd be nice to start the morning with *your* friendly face. Help me buttress for the bad news."

"Well, obviously I'm busy right now, Gary. You can go or you can wait, but it might be awhile." Pam turned deliberately back to the tome on the table. Gently turning the pages of the index a few at a time, she adopted a matronly tone, "So let's just get you to the right years here, and see if we find your man." Refusing to take the hint, Gary shuffled his feet awkwardly in the corner.

On the table in front of Jared and Kristin, Pam continued turning several pages at a time, and arbitrarily opened the worn volume to a page that bore the heading: Book 'Y' 1899 To 1900. Beginning three lines from the top in the left-hand column, a series of entries for Strafford, H.S. marched clear to the bottom of the smooth, oversized paper. "Oh, there he is," Kristin said, unsurprised.

Pam scooted around the end of the table to take a closer look. "Well, I'll say there he is," she said, "Looks like he was busy too."

Kristin asked, "So each of these entries is a different deed?"

"A different transaction," Pam affirmed. "You see at the top of the next column, where they wrote 'From'? That means that for each of these entries, your H.S. Strafford was buying land from the person named in this third column."

"So," Kristin said, "At some time in 1899, Henry Strafford was buying up a ton of property."

"Or early 1900," Pam nodded, "That's correct."

Gary ceased his scuffling and wondered aloud, "Henry Strafford... now, why do I know that name?"

Kristin picked up, "Can we see those transactions?"

"Sure," Pam said brightly, "And it looks like they're all in the same book."

Gary interrupted jarringly, "Henry *S.* Strafford?!?"

All three of the others looked to him, confused. Jared answered, "Yes. That's who we've been looking for."

Clifford

Excited now, Gary asked, "What if I told you I had his compass? Like a compass from the 1800s with his name engraved on it, how much would you pay to own that?"

Caught off guard, Jared turned to Kristin. Without hesitation, she subtly held up two fingers between them, and Jared muttered, "If you say so." Looking back to Gary he stated, "Give you two hundred for it."

The blood drained from Gary's face, then immediately returned, flushing to a violent red. His neck nearly purple, he sputtered, "God! Dammit!"

Pam scolded, "Gary, language!"

"Hold on though," Kristin interjected, "Let's talk this through. Can you do two twenty-five?"

Through his apoplexy Gary forced, "Why, that's even worse!"

"I don't get it," Kristin replied. "You won't sell it then?"

"No!" Gary said, "I don't *have* a damned compass to sell you!"

Pam demanded, "Do I even need to ask at this point, for you to leave? What has gotten into you?"

Shaking his head and storming toward the hallway Gary answered, "Screw that giant cheapskate *and* his sixteen-hand dog!"

Day 9

Outside Louis' window new, single-story, ranch-style homes with expansive lawns marched past an open field. Across the road, a dark red barn, seemingly and literally from a bygone era, looked on in isolation. Each side held its own under clear blue skies where dense clouds passed as infrequently as oncoming vehicles below. "You figure they still market this as a 'Country Road?" Louis asked Marlow, who continued to nap on the other end of the bench seat. "I dunno," he mused softly, "I think we're gettin' to the outskirts of somethin'. Maybe Kee-o-Kuk? Kay-oo-kook? However you say it… seems like we're close."

Slightly lost though he was, Louis was proud of his newfound navigational skills. Now that he had an idea of what to expect, he had begun to notice the more minor fluctuations in his compass, to note where he was meant to go before he passed it. He hadn't been forced to double back for more than 60 miles. It also didn't hurt that the further he got from St. Louis, the fewer exits there had been to choose from.

The houses and fields became increasingly sporadic before they finally gave way to dense trees on all sides. Slowing his rig to cross a rail bed, Louis took the opportunity to consult the compass again. The needle nudged gradually from East to Northeast, following the road around a cluster of corrugated steel outbuildings in a gravel lot carved from the forest. "Roger that," Louis grumbled, goosing the accelerator past a fork in the road and up a low rise. In short order, he found himself in a strictly residential neighborhood. Past comparably time-worn homes on evenly spaced lots, the needle pressed ever further to the North, then jumped to the Northwest at an intersection.

Louis slowed to follow, with a wide turn onto a narrow street pocked with asphalt patches. Across from a stop sign at the end of a non-descript block, a large monument, comprised of concrete arches, rose inexplicably from a manicured lawn. With mild apprehension, Louis checked back with the compass. He sighed, released the brake and idled to an access road behind the memorial. On the triangular corner a sign announced, 'Oakland Cemetery Entrance. Visiting Hours Dawn to Dusk.' A separate sign below read, 'No Pets Allowed.' Louis answered, "Weeeelllll Sheeit."

He changed course abruptly, albeit slowly, jarring Marlow out of his slumber as he pulled back to the street to park at the curb in front of a two story house. Not taking the time to consider any alternatives, Louis cut the engine, grabbed his cigarettes and compass, got out of the truck and called Marlow down. The dog groggily complied and followed him back to the trailer. Louis took care to crank open all the windows, turn on the oscillating fan, and put down a casserole dish full of the bottled water he had stored under the table. Having thus prepared, he didn't want to take too long getting underway: he wasn't sure how far he would have to walk, and the Shasta wasn't going to get any cooler while he waited.

Louis pulled his cap low over his eyes, crossed the street, and moved quickly past what he now saw was a veterans' memorial. He cut through and made his way back to the access road as directly as possible. Louis knew he *could* cut through the cemetery: that was, after all, the only way to reach half the graves, but he wasn't entirely clear on whether he should, on the etiquette of that. Something about traipsing over people just felt improper. That was one of many reasons Louis had not spent much time in graveyards.

The primary reason was dumb luck: he had not had to bury anyone, and so had no dead people to visit. But beyond that, or perhaps because of it, he never really saw the point in collecting and marking the dead. As the cracked road narrowed and wound across a rolling lawn, dotted at regular intervals with waist high stones, Louis reflected that he could understand the attraction it had for other people, the security of always knowing where their loved ones were, in a sense they would never even need to say goodbye, not completely. But was that healthy? Louis wondered. And was

The Beard

the desire to memorialize driven by survivors, or was it an excuse to make soon-to-be-deceased people feel better on their way out with some macabre hail-Mary at immortality?

Louis followed the compass, which followed the road, around a bend and over a ridge. On the downhill slope that unfolded in front of him, older, darker stones jutted at odd angles from the hillside like so many broken teeth. Some had turned nearly on their side, supplanted by roots and erosion, while others lay in fragments near obelisks that had fallen from their bases like dead trees, the victims of high winds, or maybe vandalism, or just the simple, ceaseless passage of time. This, Louis thought to himself, was why he could not, in good conscience, invest in a burial plot. If the plan was to immortalize one's self, how could he ignore the shelf-life of headstones? To be covered in dirt having known that *he* would become dirt, pretending that a single stone among many but placed over the top of *his* dirt wouldn't eventually do the same... Postponement of the inevitable was hardly a legacy.

But far from feeling intimidated by his impermanence, Louis found a deep sense of calm in conceiving of a deterioration shared by rocks, trees, and people alike. To see the earth reclaim these souls clear to the extent of absorbing their memorials, to know that the universe in its unending course had the capacity and desire, even if absent the intent, to right itself and to take its inhabitants along... That, in Louis' view, was to know an actual legacy and the truest continuity: Dust, to dust, to dust all over again.

But to get a headstone or not get a headstone... Based on his experience in life, Louis didn't guess that his treatment in death would be his decision either way. And if planting a rock in a field made his kids feel better, that was fine. It would be their money paying for it anyhow.

Having reached the bottom of the hill and followed the crumbling road past a fork and into a small circle around a mausoleum, Louis discovered a third option to consider. Ten yards in front of him, a twenty-by-twenty-foot section of the hillside had been cut away and reinforced with a rough stone wall, creating an

Clifford

alcove surrounded by low stone benches. At the center of the space, on a five-foot pedestal, lay a life-sized marble statue of a woman in repose, with one arm extended over her head and the other holding an infant, a cherubic boy who seemed to glow in the morning light. Both figures reclined on a long stone cushion sculpted to look like silk, their eyes closed in perpetually peaceful slumber. Louis decided that if he ever won the lottery, then a marker like that could be worth the cost: remains and memorials might be transitory, but both should be outlived by the fame of 'That-Guy-with-that-Super-Fancy-Sculpture.' It had worked for the pharaohs, but did it work for whoever this was? She wasn't famous enough for Louis to have heard of her. But he had to allow that he wasn't from here, and he didn't get out much.

Louis shook off his morbid curiosity and held up the compass: the needle pointed insistently eastward to the statue of the woman and child before flopping, exhausted, to point at the bottom of its case once again. Louis heard a thick slapping sound. And another. And still more in quick succession. Returning his gaze to the statue, he observed a single drop of water tracing a path through the dust on the woman's cheek to settle on the little boy's hair. It was only then that he noticed dark spots appearing on the pavers around him, felt a fat drop breaking on the bill of his baseball cap. Through an opening in the foliage overhead, he spotted the culprit: a single cloud bowing low and well clear of the sun.

As Louis approached the monument, the undeterred daylight sparkled through the rain, and the marble stood in ever sharper contrast to the wet limestone wall and the mottled grass beyond. Louis stepped reverently from the shady road onto a granite walkway, hoping to look these figures, whoever they were, in the eyes.

But there were no eyes. There were no eyelids. There were virtually no features whatsoever. From a closer vantage, myriad imperfections came into focus. The once exquisite craftsmanship had fallen as much a victim to the elements as had the crumbling street he'd walked in on. The figures' clothing was a spider web of

180

cracks and fissures, the cushions were dull and deeply pocked, and all the detail in the faces and hands, from nostrils to fingernails to the grooves between the fingers, and the edges of the ears, had worn to a mere suggestion of the original subjects. A petrified log with bumps and depressions was all that really remained.

With an uneasy feeling, Louis took a step back and looked to the base. Protected by the ledge of the cushion, a pair of side panels bore the still legible inscription:

Lucinda M. Strafford Beloved Daughter and Mother	Hugh T. Strafford Son of Lucinda Strafford
Born March 10, 1869	Born June 8, 1890
Died May 16, 1891	Died May 16, 1891

So mother and son Strafford had died the same day. Louis toyed with the compass in his hand. Glancing around to confirm he was still alone, Louis softly asked, "So who were they to you? Was she *your* beloved daughter?" No reply was forthcoming. But the picture of Henry that Louis had seen in St. Charles had been taken less than eighteen months after these two had died, and while the age of the man in the photo was tough to determine, he was clearly too old for Lucinda to have been his 'Beloved Mother.'

Louis looked back to the compass and found it had regained its vigor, now pointing due west. "No," he said, shaking his head, "We're not done here. You drag my ass up and down the Mississippi, I deserve some explanation..." But where would that come from? He knew there would be no more to see here, and even if there was, he wouldn't leave Marlow closed up for much longer.

Clifford

The rain had passed quickly and was only enough to keep the dust down: it was still at least eighty five degrees out.

Louis wracked his brain and came back empty. The obvious first step would be to find an RV park close by where he could regroup. After that, he had no idea where to start. But he couldn't keep rushing from one meaningless place to another that meant even less. If he was going to do this, he should do it right. And that would require that he get organized, even start planning ahead.

It was that idea that finally left Louis tired and beaten. Doing his best to suppress his misgivings, he touched the bill of his cap and nodded farewell to the woman and child, before starting his hike back up the hill.

The Beard

Day 10

"What are you doing?" Kristin asked half-accusingly from the bathroom doorway, a towel wrapped loosely around her hair.

Jared continued transferring tightly rolled T-shirts from a small pyramid on the faded floral comforter, into a large red duffle. "Just what it looks like," he said. "I'm packing. Oh, I forgot to mention I was opening the curtains: are you dressed back there?"

Ignoring the question, Kristin pulled the towel off her head, dabbed a stray drop above her neckline, and chucked the wet fabric into the dark powder room behind her. "Why are you doing that?" she demanded. "I already packed last night. All you had to do was add your toothbrush, it was ready to go."

"Yeah, well, kind of..." Jared said tentatively. "Every-thing was in the bag, but it was all mixed together, and I thought I'd help, y'know, tidy it up."

Kristin approached the bedside and explained impatiently, "I have a system, Jared. I put everything in the order we would need it so we wouldn't have to dig. Now you have all the shirts on top of all the socks... What are you gonna do when you need socks tomorrow?"

"Reach under the shirts," Jared answered simply, "Which won't be wrinkled now because I put them on top."

Kristin reached past his arm into the duffle, removed a pair of neatly folded boxer shorts, and unrolled it in front of her. Looking Jared directly in the eye, she wadded up the garment and jammed it back into the bag. "Wrinkled," she chided, "Who are you trying to impress?" She walked around the bed and sat down in a chair by the window to put on her shoes. Jared quietly removed the balled-up drawers, shook them out and refolded them. "For real though," Kristin said, "When you finish with your stuff, please just leave my bag as it is. We have to check out soon, and you still have to shave."

Clifford

"Not shaving today," Jared said while he zipped up his bag. "The end of this next map is a new kind of weird, so I want to keep the original until tonight."

"Oh, you mean the phallic looking thing by your side-burns," Kristin said. "Those should all be cross streets. Are we sure about Little Rock, at least?"

"Yeah, definitely North Little Rock," Jared said. "That part I'm clear on, for sure. And we have the hotel reserved?"

Kristin stood and pushed her damp hair back over her shoulders, "Check. Done. Listen, even if you don't shave, please don't repack my stuff. I like how I have it. You're allowed to disagree." She collected a pair of card keys from beside the TV and continued, "If you want to pull the car around, I can run these to the front desk."

Jared nodded his assent and collected their bags.

Even with the sun well below its zenith, the small black car belched a cloud of hot air in Jared's face when he opened the door. He counted to five to let the unpleasantness dissipate, then climbed in, started the car, and rolled all the windows open. By the time Kristin walked out the front of the motel to meet him, the air conditioner had just begun cranking out cold. She opened the door, flopped into her seat, and immediately leapt halfway out again.

"Hot damn!" She shouted, pulling the seatbelt out from under her, "I just about branded my ass with that buckle!" Jared chuckled under his breath, enjoying the show, but not wanting to make light of her ass. "Don't think I don't see you smirking," she said, pulling the strap across her body. Jared put the car in gear and pulled away without apology. As they slowed at a stoplight partway through town, Kristin asked, "So, how far to Little Rock?"

"North Little Rock," Jared corrected. "About four hours, not a bad day's drive. You know," he said after a thoughtful pause, "We have enough time left right now to go back out to that clearing if you want. See if there's any clues we missed."

"I don't see the point," Kristin shrugged. "It would be a better use of our time to get where we're going so you can shave. I know

184

we're only halfway through the trip, but your face is on a tighter timetable than you seem to realize, if we plan to get through another map after this."

"Yeah," Jared sighed as he pulled forward to the next intersection, "I know it is, I just…" he trailed off.

"Boy, it is really bothering you, isn't it? Not knowing who owns that clearing now?"

"I know it probably doesn't matter," Jared conceded, "But I feel like knowing can't hurt us. And we're all the way out here. And I really think we should have followed up about that at the courthouse-,"

"How did I know you were going to bring that up?" Kristin asked, her tone taking an edge of frustration. "You were in the same room I was in, with the same people, and we'd just had a conversation about how you were going to be more flexible, get more involved, ask more questions in the moment-,"

"I remember," Jared interrupted. "We were both there, but then things got weird after that crazy guy left, and we both got distracted… I'm not just blaming you for not asking."

"But you sort of are," Kristin argued. "I didn't ask who owns the land because I don't really care who owns it. And if you do care about that and you didn't speak up, then you're leaving it on me to read your mind and speak for you. Which is kind of bullshit."

"It's not mind reading," Jared snapped, "I thought it was pretty obvious that I wanted to know. But you don't?"

"No, I do not," Kristin confirmed. "We already got copies of all those deeds. We know that Strafford bought more than 5,000 acres in 1900. We already knew that he died in 1901, and now we know that the land went back to the state because he had no family. So, we did learn something about him here: that he died alone. And by 1902, he was still dead and the land had nothing to do with him. Why stress over the next 113 years of a spot in the middle of nowhere?"

"I guess-,"

Clifford

"But that isn't even the issue here," Kristin continued. "We agreed on 'flexible' and you went with 'fixated.' We spent a whole day out in the woods and it was a dead end, end of story. And we said creative but instead you clammed up and left the talking to me, as usual. You need to learn to let things go at some point. And when you find yourself waiting for me to bring something up, you need to just say it yourself."

"Alright," Jared conceded, raising one hand from the wheel in defeat, "I get it. And I'll try letting go and... I dunno, try being more vocal or something."

"Oh, you *will* be more vocal," Kristin answered, "Because when we get to Arkansas, I will not be speaking. Not a word."

"Seriously?" Jared asked.

"Don't get too excited," Kristin said, "I'll still be talking to you. Everyone else though, radio silence. If we need direct-ions, or we're doing more research, it's all you. Hell, I'll even make you order for me at restaurants, like it's the olden days. I don't even care. I'm crazy."

Jared laughed, "You really think you can help yourself? You love chiming in."

"Yeah, well," Kristin shrugged, "Maybe I could stand to practice giving up some control. But you need to practice going with the flow."

Jared nodded quietly.

"Seriously," Kristin said in a somber tone, "Be decisive. Speak up for yourself. Wear wrinkled underwear."

Jared nearly offered his tacit acquiescence, but thought better of it. "Don't worry," he stated firmly, "I will."

186

Sixth Growth

Day 2

Louis bounced his truck out of the parking lot without bothering to check for traffic. He drove past the imposing brick tower of a Victorian courthouse, and quickly transitioned to a block of eviscerated buildings with broken and boarded up windows. Louis turned right onto Main Street at a three-story building that boasted new awnings on the ground level, chipped white paint on the floor above, all topped off by a full story of raw, crumbling brick. Aesthetically, this block by itself reminded him of Neapolitan ice cream. More generally, the Keokuk business district appeared as a once grand dame now consigned to a third-rate retirement home: the thought of how stately and active it must have been forty years earlier was at once both lovely and sad. But on the other hand, as it was, Louis had had no problems finding available parking.

After leaving the cemetery and locating a suitable campsite with full hookups, Louis' first order of business had been to figure out his first order of business. To that end, he and Marlow had taken up opposing positions at the small kitchen table, with a pen and blank paper between them, and had brainstormed all the questions he might ask about the grave marker they'd found. At the bottom of the page, he had reframed each of these questions as statements, thereby clarifying the specific information he wanted. This part of the process had, in retrospect, been redundant, so Louis made a mental note to not bother with it in the future. For the current project, though, he would run with what he had.

In a column to the right of each piece of information, he had then written the kind of document that he assumed would answer his questions. And to the right of that, he had written the name of the place where he expected to find said documents. Ultimately, it had been a much shorter list than he'd expected, but thorough enough in his view:

Clifford

1. Lucinda was the beloved daughter of _____.	Birth Certificate	?
2. The father of Hugh was _____.	Birth Certificate	?
3. Lucinda and Hugh had died of _____.	Death Certificate	?
4. The marble statue was paid for by _____.	Cemetery records	Cemetery office
5. This matters to me because _____.	Local history book	Public Library

Since Louis already knew where the cemetery was, he had made that his first stop. In the end, it had been a wash: the only record they had for that section was a map of where the graves were located, and he already knew that part. Then again, they had given him directions to the local library. That had been equally unfruitful. There had been a decent collection of local histories, but none that mentioned the name Strafford, from what anyone could tell. The librarians had done their level best to be helpful, and had referred him to their microfilmed newspapers to try for an obituary, but the only announcement he had found seemed almost intentionally vague, and contained only slightly more information than the marker, namely that the deceased had been "of Fort Madison," and was survived by her parents, "of Keokuk."

The librarian had, however, been able to tell him that the birth and death certificates he wanted would be at the county courthouse, and had given him directions to find that. Except that when he got there, he was told that they did not have those certificates, as the deceased had been, "of Fort Madison," which was a second Lee County seat with a second Lee County courthouse, but he shouldn't actually go to that courthouse, because the second set of Lee County offices were in a building a mile away from the second Lee County courthouse. With those instructions, Louis set off up Main Street yet again.

New facades passed in a blur, interrupted by vacant storefronts that still bore the scars and silhouettes of signs from otherwise

The Beard

forgotten occupants. As he made his way north and out of town, impromptu pocket parks were replaced by sporadic, overgrown lots which increased in frequency until the last scattered businesses, light industrial from the look of them, gave up and returned the land to forest and field.

Based on Louis' day thus far, he wasn't completely sure that this whole exercise wouldn't be futile. In a way, he almost hoped that it would be. While that would mean that he had lost a day, it would also make it easier for him to rationalize blindly following the compass, which would save him the considerable effort of continuing to try to make sense of where he was.

But for reasons Louis did not know, he felt a sense of obligation to do this thing right. Perhaps it was something environmental: he'd never been this far from home and didn't want to waste what opportunities the trip presented. More likely though, it stemmed from a sense of purpose that was as yet unfamiliar to him: sure, he could follow along through this whole adventure, just like he followed along every day back home. Or he could *participate* in it.

And for once in his life, *he* wanted to direct things, to believe against all prior evidence that the compass or God or fate or the universe might actually have chosen *Louis Francis Kessler* to do something worthwhile. Louis felt a brief twinge of guilt at the immodesty of the idea, then decided that he didn't care: It felt good to be self-important. And Lord knew he'd had few enough chances to enjoy a delusion of grandeur.

A few miles off the interstate, Louis coasted down a steep grade, into the residential equivalent of the business district he had left behind. Meticulously maintained homes alternated with peeling paint and rotting porches, tied together with the common thread of expansive lawns, all brown and parched after so much summer. He turned, as instructed, at a small cemetery (he was beginning to suspect that the dead out-numbered the living in this state), and onto what he had been led to believe would be a major road, but

Clifford

Louis wasn't so sure. There was more traffic here than there had been in Keokuk, but no sign of a destination for any of it.

Beyond an odd mix of tired looking businesses and single-family homes, Louis at least discovered his own destination: a single story, brown brick building that occupied a full block, like a burnt pancake set across from a sweeping view of the Mississippi River. The interior delivered all that the exterior had promised: fluorescent lights blazing from an acoustic-foam drop-ceiling over cheap nylon floor tiles. An open aisle ran the length of the building between inexpensive countertops, which were in turn divided by beige cubicle walls. In a word, it was 'utilitarian'. In two words it was 'adequately functional'.

Louis was greeted at the nearest of these counters by a heavyset woman with shoulder-length silver hair and small, square-framed glasses. "Can I help you?"

"I hope so," Louis said politely. "I was told to come here to find a death certificate."

"We have some of those," the woman replied brightly, "What year were you looking for?"

"They would have died in 1891," Louis answered.

"Oh, that long ago," she nodded. "That should be in the vault, if you'd like to come around the counter here." Louis followed the woman through two rows of metal desks, to an open vault door hung incongruously in dated, plywood-paneled walls. The claustrophobic space beyond was lined floor to ceiling with oversized volumes laid sideways on racks and rollers. A large island, waist high, housed more of the same racks under a Formica tabletop. On a tall metal stool at one end of the island, a nine-year-old blonde boy with a sallow complexion scribbled quietly in some kind of workbook. "So, you caught the genealogy bug or something?" the woman asked.

"Nah," Louis said, "Just found an interesting tombstone, thought I'd like to know more about it."

"I see," the woman said. "Well, I applaud your curiosity. Y'know, not enough people make the extra effort over those sorts

192

of things, I don' think. Seem t'think if it ain't on the internet already, it ain't worth knowin'. 'S tragic. Just curious: which cemetery was this headstone in?"

"Oakland, down in Keokuk."

The woman concernedly asked, "They died in Keokuk?"

"No," Louis answered a bit impatiently, "They're buried in Keokuk. They died in Fort Madison."

"Oh, good," she said, "Because if they died in Keokuk, you would need to... Never mind. They died here, so you know what you're doing." She walked to the end of the island opposite the boy and leaned to point at the third book from the top. "This is the one you want. Y'mind? I have a bad back, and you look pretty able-bodied."

Louis shrugged, pulled the book from its rollers and set it on the tabletop.

"Ooh," the woman said, "And one-handed." Looking over her glasses she added, "That's nice, that's... That's very nice." After an awkward beat she enthusiastically concluded, "Well okay, I'll leave you to it then! I'll be over at the counter if you have any questions. My name is Fran. If you need anything."

Louis had several questions: What was Fran leaving him to? What book had he just retrieved? What was with the kid they were pretending wasn't there? Was one of them meant to be in charge of the other? But Louis held back his inquiries. Fran made him a little uncomfortable, and he preferred to have faith that he would find what he was meant to find on his own.

Opening the volume in front of him, he discovered he'd been given a death registry, starting from 1880. Each page was a printed ledger with information entered in longhand. He gingerly turned through the still supple leaves, quickly covering the first decade before he found an entry, halfway down a page, for Strafford, Lucinda. A series of adjacent columns populated by scribbles and tally marks identified her as a married white woman, provided her birth date and death date, and showed that she was born in Keokuk but lived in Fort Madison. Columns for 'Occupation' and 'Disease' had been left blank. In the row directly below Lucinda, the entry for Hugh was equally uninformative.

Louis mumbled to himself, "So that's it? Is there a certificate or somethin'?'

A small voice floated through the room, "When did they die?"

Louis nearly jumped out of his shoes, having forgotten that he wasn't alone. He started to sputter an apology for his reaction, but the boy at the end of the island, holding his stare as steady as he held his pencil, interrupted, "Did they die before 1904?"

"Yes," Louis said, unsure of what tone to assume in this situation. He landed on business-like. "Born 1869, died 1891, it was a mother and child. But it doesn't say how they died or who they were."

Turning back to his workbook the boy said, "Certificates started in 1904."

"Okay," Louis said, not taking a hint. "Then this is all they have here?"

The boy sighed and folded his hands on the counter in front of him. "They have a lot here. Does the register say she was married?"

Louis checked for a tally in the 'Married' subsection of a column marked 'Condition.' "It does," he confirmed.

"Then try the book by your left knee." Louis stepped back, leaned over, and found an equally thick volume labeled 'Marriages.' The boy continued drily, "If she was born in 1869, then she wasn't very old when she died, and she couldn't have been married very long. Easiest thing is to start when she died and go backwards."

"You work here or somethin'?" Louis asked sarcastically as he set the new book next to the old.

Unamused, the boy replied, "No, my mom does."

"So that's your mom?"

"Who, Fran?" the boy asked, baffled. "Fran's way too old to be my mom."

Louis nodded quietly. He deemed the assessment harsh, but accurate. He appreciated the young man's demeanor. It was very

194

different from his son's, but the conversation still made him miss his family. "Homework already, huh?" Louis asked jovially. "Seems like school starts earlier every year."

The boy picked up his pencil and turned his attention back to the workbook. Softly he answered, "Yeeeeaaah... I'm not really supposed to be talking to you."

"Oh, right," Louis said, taken aback, "Okay." He returned to the marriage index and searched backward as the boy had instructed. In an entry dated April 27, 1889, one Strafford, Henry S. married a Miller, Lucinda. So there was the answer, or rather one answer. Louis still didn't know how they died, or why they got the fancy tombstone, or why Henry Strafford wasn't listed on the marker, or in the obituary, or anywhere else that Louis had been. He considered directing some of this follow-up to the expert in the room, but the boy was intent on his studies and would clearly not brook further interruption, so Louis closed the books and headed for the door.

"Hey," the small voice said forcefully, "You wanna put those back?" Under his breath the boy added, "Not like *Fran*'s gonna do it."

Louis retraced his steps, and rolled the two books into their respective spaces. Straightening up he said, "Hey, thanks for your help."

The boy grunted in response, and continued scribbling. Louis paused uncomfortably for only a moment before he headed to the door of the vault. It seemed he had gotten all that he was going to get.

Day 5

"We doing this, or what?" Kristin asked.

"Yes," Jared sighed, shifting in his seat. "I'm just working up the motivation to go back out in the heat."

Kristin reached over and turned his keys, silencing the engine and cutting off the cool air from the vents. Almost immediately, the raw sunlight that reflected from the concrete parking lot began to warm the black vehicle. "There," she said, "I helped."

Jared sat, unmoving. Finally he said, "So if you were me, how would you approach this?"

"No," Kristin replied, "We're not playing that game. You're taking the lead on this, I told you. You've already had the last hour of driving around looking at nothing, not to mention five whole days before that. You know, you were the one who was all gung-ho about waiting to shave so we could come straight here, but by the time we get through Memphis all you care about is seeing the Clinton Library."

"We have a whole week for this stop," Jared said defensively, "And the Clinton Library is a fascinating peice of green architecture. And if you want me to take the lead, then you have to follow my timeline, that's how it works."

"I'm fine with that part, but if you're going to procrastinate, you can't expect to not be called out."

"Was it procrastinating when you wanted to go to the purse museum on Tuesday? Or yesterday when you had us at the zoo?" Jared inquired. "I mean, shit, we have a zoo back home."

"I like zoos," Kristin shrugged simply. "And *may-be* after that whole week in Selmer, maybe I've gotten excited about being someplace that has things to do."

"Yeah, well, maybe that's what I've been doing too then," Jared offered.

The Beard

"If that's where you want to leave it…" Kristin said. "But now that we're here, can we get out and do this please? I am seriously sweating in this car."

Jared conceded by pushing open his door. The warm air outside felt ten degrees cooler as the sweat evaporated from his forehead. "This place is just a little intimidating, is all," he said. "It's not that I have to do the talking. It's just… I don't even know who to talk to. And honestly, I hate hospitals."

Climbing out of her side Kristin said, "I can't change where the maps lead. At least this time we know we can find someone to talk to: chatting up some nurse beats wandering around in the woods again like assholes."

"So you think I should talk to a nurse then?"

"Just stop it," Kristin ordered, walking to the front of the car and taking Jared's hand. "When we get inside, I have faith you will figure it out." Kristin took a half step back, forcing Jared to lead her up a tree lined sidewalk and around a low fountain to an imposing brick building. Projecting from a glass entryway, a sturdy metal overhang bore a sign designating the structure the 'Eugene J. Towbin Healthcare Center.' Just inside the sliding glass doors, Kristin dropped Jared's hand, stepped to the right, and stood.

"What?" Jared asked. Kristin shook her head and said nothing. Jared got out of the doorway and took a moment to look around before he noticed that she had moved in the general direction of an information desk with a short line of people at it. "You couldn't even say that?" he asked incredulously. Knowing he would get no response, he walked past her and positioned himself behind an elderly man in a wheelchair pushed by a woman in her 30's. Kristin joined Jared at a half pace behind.

As the pair in front of them moved up, Jared sought to distance himself; he hoped to find the sweet spot where he wouldn't be eavesdropping, but wouldn't lose his place in line. Waiting quietly, he allowed his focus to wander to the sunlit entryway. He still wasn't sure how to frame his question, or even where to start. He also wasn't sure why he was being such a pussy about it. He wasn't

Clifford

going to see any of these people again, and odds were that they would be tolerant if not helpful. But still, imposing on strangers made him nervous for some reason. And then there was the setting. He really did dislike hospitals: something about the neutral colors and the antiseptic smell instantly put him on edge.

Kristin kicked his shoe and jarred him back into the task in front of him. Looking back to the counter, Jared saw that the man in the wheelchair had moved on, and the stern middle-aged woman behind the desk was placing a sign that read 'Will Return.' Without another thought, Jared rushed the counter. "Excuse me, Ma'am," he said, "I'm sorry, just a quick question."

The woman paused halfway out of her seat, apparently unsure of how quick the question might really be. "I couldn't tell if you were in line. How can I help you?"

"I was wondering if you could tell me what used to be here." Jared said.

The woman settled back into her chair and turned the sign around. Coldly she asked, "Come again?"

Jared searched for words that would be specific but not sound ridiculous. "Like a hundred, hundred-twenty years ago on this spot, what was here?"

The woman squinted back at him quizzically. "Are you serious?" She asked. "How would I know that?"

"Well, maybe there's someone on staff," Jared ventured, "Like a history buff who would know that kind of thing. Doesn't everyplace have one of those?"

"Sir," the woman said crossly, "This is a veterans' hospital, not a museum. There are a lot of people here whose questions are higher on my list of priorities."

Jared looked to Kristin. She shrugged. He looked up and noticed a man with a prosthetic leg waiting quietly behind her. "Oh, I'm sorry," Jared said stepping aside and gesturing to him, "Did you want to go in front of us?"

"Thanks," the man said graciously. Leaning in to the woman at the counter he asked something about where to find rehabilitation,

198

The Beard

and she patiently gave him directions. Jared stepped back out of the way and stood awkwardly, unsure whether he had officially been told off or told to wait.

After the man had moved on, the woman projected, "So *now* are you in line?"

"I, uh… Is this… something you can help me with?"

The woman reached under the desk and came back with a small, colorful brochure. She stood up and held it out to Jared. "This might help you," she stated. "I think there are a few sentences in there about the history of the hospital and Fort Roots."

"Fort Roots?" Jared inquired, taking the pamphlet.

"Yes," she said, righting her 'Will Return' sign and moving to the end of the desk. "Fort Roots. Where we're standing."

"I thought this was the 'Edward H.-"

"Eugene J. Towbin Health Center," the woman interrupted, "Yes, it is. They renamed it back in the '90's. Before that it was Fort Logan H. Roots, it's all in the brochure."

Unable to help himself, Jared pressed, "I thought you didn't know what used to be here."

"Not right where we're standing," she said humorlessly as she stepped from behind the desk. "Most of the original buildings are near the Parade Ground." She walked briskly to the nearest corridor and called over her shoulder, "There's a map in the brochure."

Once the woman was well out of earshot, Kristin burst out laughing. Jared asked sourly, "Was that fun for you?"

"Oh," Kristin said, trying to regain her composure, "Oh you are so *bad* at that. How do you manage with bank customers all day long?" She resumed her chortling.

"She's cold as ice," Jared said seriously. "I think you're just amused that you didn't end up having to talk to her."

"No," Kristin forced out, "She was not buying what you got to sell, dude. It was like a verbal crotch kick." Settling herself, Kristin continued, "Besides, none of that would have happened to me, because I wouldn't have come in here to begin with."

"What are you talking about?" Jared asked.

Clifford

Kristin pulled her phone from her pocket and laughed again, "This isn't even where the map goes." She held up the screen to show Jared a photo she had taken the previous weekend. "You see that phallic shape by your sideburns? This building is the tip, but your map runs clear to the base."

Jared squinted at the screen then opened the brochure in his hand to the map that the woman had mentioned. Turning the page on its side he held it up next to Kristin's phone. "I'll be damned, not far from the Parade Ground." Looking back to Kristin's grinning face he asked, "So you just let me lead us the wrong way?"

"Uh huh," she nodded, "To teach you a lesson: you have to stop getting distracted by the tallest building in sight. You know you've been doing that since Richmond."

Jared prepared to argue, but realized that she wasn't wrong. Instead he just mumbled, "Worked out okay so far."

Ignoring the comment Kristin asked, "Does it look very far on your map? It doesn't look too far on mine."

"No," Jared said, "Not really."

"You want to walk then?"

"After you," he said.

Kristin took Jared's free hand with her right and held up her phone with her left. As he followed her back down the driveway, Jared reviewed the rest of the brochure. "It says here," he said, "That before this property was turned over to the VA, it was a military training facility. It says they chose the site for the Fort in 1893."

"So he was around here somewhere after that," Kristin said, still transfixed by her phone. "We're turning right at this intersection."

"What I'm trying to figure out, though," Jared continued, "is the timing. We seem to be tracking him between death dates: we have him in Richmond a few months after the USS Maine sank, and then at Biltmore a few months after that. Selmer wasn't very long after that, and less than a year later he died again. But how much can possibly be left? I mean, how many places could he have been between 1898 and 1901?"

"As many as he wants," Kristin said casually. "If he can die two times on opposite sides of the world, I don't guess there's a limit. Left at the next corner please."

Jared obliged and tucked the folded brochure into his back pocket. "Even so," he resumed, "It was less than three years of his life we're talking about. Don't you think we'll fill out that window pretty soon?" The couple walked down a shady sidewalk past long, red brick buildings with neatly manicured lawns. Kristin slowed in front of a smaller two-story building with an enclosed front porch, and looked up. A slender white marker with a rounded top stood in the lawn next to them:

Fort Logan H Roots
"Hank Strafford House"
COMPLETED IN 1897
AS OFFICERS' QUARTERS
AT A COST OF $3,200

"So, 1897," Kristin observed. "Does that answer your question?"

Jared shook his head, "Well shit."

Day 6

Louis sat on his tailgate with a lit cigarette hanging from his lips, absently unfolding and refolding a mostly blank piece of paper. He figured he should just get on with it, get the day done with, but he was enjoying the fresh air, even if there wasn't much shade. He had backed his truck into an angled space across the street from a small public library, and sat facing the side of a large, art deco building that would've been out of place just about anywhere, but was especially so in a town this size.

He had arrived late on Wednesday with high hopes. Those had immediately been shot straight to shit. After a seven-hour drive west, the compass had finally turned once again. Even with the possibility that they might find themselves in another place that didn't allow dogs, Louis had seen no harm in driving to their destination before they found a campsite: after all, accidentally starting with the end point back in Iowa had enabled him to plan the rest of that stay around their subject.

With this in mind, Louis had followed his guide off I-80 and into York, Nebraska. The town wasn't too much bigger than Selmer but was perfectly rectangular with an even street grid and a tidy commercial center. Louis wondered if this wasn't a function of its being so far from major waterways: his previous run through the river valleys had kept him in towns that were forced into the corridors between channels and bluffs, while the last few hours' worth of road had been mercilessly flat. In any case, the city plan of York made far more sense than did the focus of his visit.

The compass had given up, quite unexpectedly, halfway through a downtown intersection. Louis had parked and popped a leash on Marlow, to take a lap around the surrounding blocks, but he still had no idea what he'd been meant to find. The four corners of the intersection were host to a small garage, a smaller tavern, an office building, and a parking lot, nothing nineteenth century,

The Beard

nothing historical or noteworthy. Louis had begun to get frustrated, but had forced himself back onto the bright side: it was because each stop had been increasingly ambiguous that he had adopted a new approach at the last one. So perhaps the better way to look at this was as an opportunity to test his new model.

So far his process was failing. When he had sat down to brainstorm that evening, Louis had realized that he didn't know what he was asking questions about, let alone what questions to ask. After wracking his brain for an hour, he could only be certain that they would have something to do with Henry Strafford, and would be related to a spot at Lincoln and 8th Streets. But beyond that, there was really no limit to what kind of information he was meant to discover, which meant no limits on where he should look. The best he could think to do was to look in the same types of places that had worked for him in Iowa. It made for a very short checklist, which Louis now nervously played with:

1. Cemetery   Strafford headstones?
2. County Courthouse   Vital Records?
3. Public Library   Newspapers.

Louis had started with the courthouse. In the interest of staying positive, Louis could say of the experience that it had been nearby, easy to find, and very brief. But it had only gone so quickly because they didn't house vital records at the county level, and again, weirdly, there hadn't been birth or death records before 1904, or marriage records before 1909. So he was left with the basic option of asking the state health department to tell him 'no'. They might have had other helpful records for all he knew, but by that point he had felt so foolish for having wasted people's time that he'd moved on.

A walk without much chance of conversation had appealed to him by then, so he had taken a ninety minute constitutional in the town's largest cemetery. Again, it turned up nothing. And, similar to before, he suspected there were probably more nearby cemeteries that he didn't know about. The truth was, he knew that he was grasping at straws, and he didn't want to invest too much time and energy in what would undoubtedly be a dead end.

But Louis had decided he was doing this all the way. He had come up with a system, which had rules that he had promised himself he would follow. And because it had worked once, he had no cause to abandon it until it stopped working, even if it only stopped working due to a self fulfilling prophecy that he himself had also devised.

Louis ashed his cigarette and realized that he only had two small drags left on it. He considered chaining a second before going into the library, but he knew that he was procrastinating: the library was likely where he *would* find something. By all rights he should have started there, but as it was his most obvious answer, were it to fail him he had no alternatives. On the other hand, if he succeeded there, he'd be forced to rerun this whole cycle wherever he wound up next. He sighed to himself and stubbed out his filter. Procrastination had its limits: it was pushing 4:00, the library closed at 5:00, and he saw no need to drag this into tomorrow.

Louis meandered, paper in hand, around the single-story, 1980's vintage, brown brick building. Walking into the library proper, his eyes required much less adjustment than expected. A large skylight and continuous line of transoms lit a wide open space that contained a handful of tables and a smattering of study desks, these last circumscribed by rows of wooden bookshelves that stopped a few feet short of the ceiling. Pulling to his left, Louis approached a long wooden circulation desk manned by a petit woman in her 60's. Before he could speak she asked, "Can I help you?"

"I'm not sure," Louis answered thoughtfully. He consulted his worn sheet of paper, but only as a matter of course, having easily memorized its contents. "I think I need historical newspapers."

"You think?" The woman asked over her glasses. "Is there something specific you're hoping to find in them?"

The Beard

"Specifically…" Louis ventured, "I'm looking for the history of a place near here, or maybe information on a person that used to live here, but probably both. And I think that those things are related somehow, but I can't say for sure without proof."

The woman cocked her head curiously, as though trying to discern if what Louis was saying was some approximation of actual English. Finally she said, "I'm not sure how much help I can be. But before we get you lost in newspapers, there's someone I think you should talk to. Wait here a minute." She moved nimbly to the end of the desk and around the corner into a larger reading area. Before Louis could so much as refold his list, she reappeared in the seat in front of him. Within a few seconds, a gentleman with a neatly trimmed silver beard followed her path at a much more deliberate pace. He used a wooden cane and moved in a way that was not entirely stable, but still dignified. Turning back to what she had been doing before Louis had interrupted the woman said brusquely, "This is the one. Thank you Ben."

"Hi," Ben said warmly, "I'm Ben."

"Louis," Louis answered.

Suddenly aware of the woman at the desk glowering at him, Ben cheerfully suggested, "Why don't we talk over here?" He made his way slowly around the desk and led Louis to a small wooden table where he offered him a seat. "So what is it you were looking for?" he asked, settling into a chair across the table and leaning forward on his cane as though preparing to tell Louis a story. "Jeanne was a little vague about it."

"I'm afraid that's my fault," Louis admitted. "I'm interested in the history of a spot in York-"

"Hang on," Ben interrupted, "Which spot is that?"

"Intersection of Lincoln and 8th," Louis explained.

"And just the general history? What the land was used for and the like?"

"I think so," Louis said. "What it was used for, who owned it, just what was there in the late 1800's, early 1900's…"

"Okay," Ben nodded, "Proceed. Something about a person?"

"Yes," Louis said, "A man named Henry Strafford that I'm pretty sure used to live here. Probably not for very long though."

"And this was around the same time? Late 1800's or early 1900's?"

Louis considered for a moment. He had been giving that some thought. He felt very strongly that he'd been following Strafford's life in reverse: the route from Nebraska to Iowa to Missouri would have made sense even in the olden days. But with only two points in time and space to draw from, Louis could hardly call it a pattern, and there was nothing saying that Strafford hadn't turned around at Saint Charles to end up on some farm in Nebraska. One thing Louis had committed to though, even if his case for it was equally thin, was the idea that nothing he found would predate the compass from 1880. With all that in mind Louis had decided to focus on the period from 1880 – 1910, just throw those dates at the wall to see what stuck. "Yes," he said, "Probably between 1880 and 1910."

"Okay then," Ben said, leaning back to mentally process Louis' request. "Where to start… It's good that you have specific things to look for. One name and one place, that's pretty approachable. But forty years is quite a span, and we're pretty near closing time."

"Also my fault," Louis conceded, "I spent too long walking the cemetery."

"Oh," Ben perked up, "Do you mean Greenwood? So you know when he died, where he's buried?"

"No," Louis said, "But I thought if he had family here, maybe there would be someone with that last name…"

"Ah, that's…" Ben trailed off, deflated, "Not the best way to do that. Well here, let me show you something." The older man levered himself out of his chair and made his way to a computer terminal in one of the study desks. Louis followed and pulled a second chair to sit beside him. Ben pulled up a page titled 'Greenwood Cemetery,' which contained a search field. "Care to do the honors?" he asked. Louis typed Strafford into the basic search. It returned no results. "Hate to say it," Ben said, "But it

206

sounds like *that* could've saved your whole morning. You should always, always, always start at the library." Louis nodded, striving for an appropriate amount of shame. Ben continued, "We also have bound indexes for the other local cemeteries... that actually gives me an idea. Your problem is not a lack of options for finding information on this place and that person. Your problem will be that it's too late in the day to come close to exhausting just the options we have on site here, to say nothing of our online databases and subscriptions. So what I'd like to do is, just to get started, we'll have you look over some indexes and general stuff for the hour today, and then if you come back tomorrow, I'll get you set up with more of our in-house material."

"Sure," Louis said, feeling so out of his depth that he would have approved any strategy presented to him by anyone who happened by.

Ben pulled up a bookmarked website and mumbled as it loaded, "It's too bad you weren't here last week. I'm not really the best at this sort of thing, more of a local history buff. Our resident genealogy buff is on vacation through Thursday. Don't suppose you'll still be around then..."

"No," Louis said, "I'm not local."

Ben laughed, "Kind of guessed that. Nothing bad, just your accent gave you away." Turning back to the computer, he enthusiastically said, "Alright, so what this is..." Louis slid his chair closer, careful to avoid the cane hanging from the crook of Ben's elbow. "The York County Historical Association put together this list of databases and indexes. It's all very general, but it's something we can start with for the next," Ben paused to consult his watch, "Oh shoot, thirty-five minutes. Not enough time for much more than this. But while you do that, I'll go grab a few things: those cemetery indexes I mentioned, a couple of biographical compilations... Just stuff we can get through quickly looking for a name. And then tomorrow we can start with some microfilm and go from there."

Clifford

Ben pulled himself out of his seat and Louis slid closer to the screen. He went carefully through the first index, that of a local mortuary's records, and checked every name that began with the letter 'S', allowing for minor misspellings. By the third index, for an 1890 Gazetteer, Louis lazily hit Ctrl+F and did a whole word search. Ben had not been gone for more than five minutes when Louis got a hit. In his rhythm of clicking and searching, Louis wasn't even sure what the index was for, but there, in a column on the right hand side of the screen, was the listing: 'M = Strafford.'

"How goes it?" Ben interrupted. He stood with his weight balanced on a small metal cart containing binders, books, and his wooden cane across the top.

"I got somethin'," Louis said, "Not sure what it means. Says 'M equals Strafford.'"

"No kidding, that quickly," Ben said, surprised. "Which index was that?"

Louis looked to a link for the main page. "Sedgwick, it says."

"Ah, Sedgwick. *York County Nebraska and its People* by T.E. Sedgwick." Ben leaned forward carefully and pulled a volume from the lower shelf of the cart. He retrieved his cane and shuffled back to the seat next to Louis. Checking the computer for a page number, he opened the book on the desk next to the keyboard. "The 'M' in the index stands for miscellaneous," he said. "This book, and there were a lot of books like this in the early part of the century, is a local history with biographies. A publisher in New York or Chicago, as in this case, would compile the history of a small town like York, and then in the back they would include flattering biographies of a number of the local people, to whom they could then sell the book. They were really selling a sort of way to commission a place in history, and they were quite successful for a time. But if your man is listed as miscellaneous, that means he didn't have a biography: he was mentioned in the story of someone who might pay for it. And that someone is... Right here," Ben said pointing halfway down the page to a heading for a George R. Winfield.

208

The Beard

Ben began to read aloud, "'George R. Winfield is now and has for many years been a representative agriculturalist of York County. Born in Pennsylvania to'... etcetera and so on... 'Through his industry and tenacity his farm has flourished to include...' And then they have his children, political affiliations... oh here we are: 'The Winfield family are members of the Presbyterian Church and takes an active part in the affairs of that organization. Mr. Winfield ably assisted Mr. H.S. Strafford in the considerable effort of funding the construction of the church's current house of worship.'" Ben concluded, "So there he is."

"When was this?" Louis asked.

"The book was published in 1921," Ben said, turning pages toward the front cover, "But I think we can follow it back to when your man was here. It said he was involved in constructing a church, and there should be another section in here about churches."

"Commissioned by the churches?" Louis asked.

Ben chuckled, "If the churches weren't buying copies, their congregants might. You'd be hard pressed to find an unkind word about anyone in these things. So. We want the Presbyterians and specifically the part where they construct a new building. And you said you thought he came here in 1880, just as a jumping off point."

"That's right," Louis confirmed.

Reading aloud once again, Ben continued, "'Fifty years ago there were only four buildings in what is now known as the City of York.' So I guess we skip ahead then... 'July 22, 1871... There being no building in which we could meet,' so still not there... 'In 1872, by the assistance of the Board of Church Erection, we were able to build our first house of worship. It still stands on the corner of Lincoln Avenue and Eighth Street." Ben looked up and blinked, "Well that sounds familiar. Where did you say you got that address from?"

Clifford

Louis moved quickly to find an explanation more plausible than a haunted compass. "Something my great aunt wrote down somewhere. Henry Strafford. Lincoln and Eighth."

"Oh," Ben said, "Intriguing. Let's read on. 'In 1886 Rev. F. N. Riale commenced his ministry with the church. He was so successful that the sickly child soon became too large for its wardrobe, and it was evident that a larger and better one must be provided. Through his leadership, and the efforts of member H.S. Strafford, who had arrived only that year from Wyoming, the necessary funds were raised, and the cornerstone was laid with appropriate ceremonies in 1887. Mr. Strafford departed in summer of that year, while Mr. Riale remained fifteen months and left us in the midst of our building difficulties.' And then it goes on about the next pastor, the new building... Oh here's something," Ben perked up. "In their description of the building dedication: 'Mr. Strafford unfortunately had most of the subscription list in his head rather than on paper, and being several hundred miles away and having his head with him, the list was not available, so that on the morning of the dedication it was found necessary to provide for the entire indebtedness, amounting to $13,000.'"

"So that all means... what?" Louis inquired.

"Quite a lot, actually," Ben answered. "First, this tells us that he was only in York for about a year: part of 1886 and 1887, which eliminates all of the in-house resources I was going to help you with tomorrow. Next it tells us that he came from Wyoming, and if you want more information on him, that will be helpful. And we can say he was a Presbyterian, although I'm not sure he was a good Presbyterian, given that his greatest contribution was taking fundraising pledges from people and not leaving proof of them. So he split town and left the church holding the bag on thirteen grand."

The woman at the front desk called over, "Ben, you wrapping up over there? It's five 'till."

"We're on our way," Ben answered. "Is there any other very quick question I can help you with?"

The Beard

"That's pretty much it for me," Louis said. He glanced needlessly at his piece of paper and asked, "You said there wasn't anything else? No newspapers or anything?"

"Oh there's always something else," Ben said seriously. "But as far as items exclusive to our collection, that period is spotty. The newspapers for example: we have back to 1873, but they jump from '85 to late '87. The only city directory we have for that decade was published while he was here, but it would have been compiled earlier, and the list goes on and on. Your Strafford landed in the middle of a blind spot like he did it on purpose. I'm frankly impressed that we found him at all."

"And here you thought we wouldn't have enough time," Louis joked.

Ben worked his way back to his feet. "We didn't have enough time," he said, transferring his weight back to the cart, "You just had enough luck."

Day 8

Timing was still his biggest issue. Tim Donaldson crossed from his closet to his bed in two strides and tossed three pairs of khaki pants and three button-down shirts in a pile near the headboard. Closer to the foot of the bed, he had stacked his more durable hiking gear. On the floor, he had stowed a compact tent next to a large expedition backpack. He wanted only the necessities for the pack, but not knowing the full range of circumstances he might face, he would keep the headboard pile in the trunk of the car, just in case. Whatever came his way, he would be prepared.

But 'when' was still a concern. Tim had gone over the math a hundred times, had fine-tuned his calendar relative to the historic pattern, and was very confident that events would play out over the next ten to forty days. Assuming that they played out at all.

He wanted to err on the side of caution, to be absolutely sure that he would arrive at his rendezvous before opportunity had passed him by. At the same time, if he had left when leaving had first occurred to him, he would have run out of money and supplies. With that in mind, Tim had waited, planned, and schemed. He had accumulated every useful accessory he could think of. Even knowing that his preparation was based more on stories and hypothetical scenarios than on fact, he had allowed his activities to clutter his modest apartment to such extent that he could not avoid being constantly reminded of how soon he needed to move, or of how much time and material he might still lack.

Tim couldn't imagine how Henry Strafford had done this. What courage must have been necessary to strike out into the wilderness without the GPS unit, or the protein bars, or the rain gear Tim had purchased? In the grand scheme, 1880 was not so very long ago, but the world had been so different, so dangerous. And yet this man had shown the force of will to leave home with no more than a compass, without even knowing, as Tim did, about the man with the map he would find at the other side.

These ideas reinforced Tim's sense of purpose. However much time he had, at a certain point he had to commit, to have faith that he was as prepared as a person could be and to strike westward to meet his destiny. But before he did that, he had a side trip to make: more fact finding that Strafford had not had the luxury to do. It would only be two days out of the way, so Tim had spent the weekend revisiting his strategy and packing. It had actually fit nicely with the end of the work week by allowing him to serve his last day at the museum on a Friday.

Tim had been hired as an 'At Will Employee,' so was not required to give notice, and had never been tempted to give it. Considering how rarely one has the chance at a truly clean slate, Tim had considered taking the opportunity to tell his employers what he really thought of them and their two-bit collection. But the whole point of that would have been to see the look on their faces, and arranging an in-person meeting with the Society's directors would have further affected his timing.

Also, Tim had to entertain that, even if this venture had the potential to make his dreams come true, he might just as easily be chasing a ghost story, might have to come back empty handed. He didn't intend to return to that job either way: it was demeaning and beneath him, and he knew he deserved a better position, which had given him that much more freedom to leave Wheatland in pursuit of any truth behind the memoirs. But if it did turn out that the whole thing was as crazy as it sounded, he would not want the nature of his departure to taint future prospects. He had settled on posting a dispassionate resignation letter on the front door: less courageous than Martin Luther, but it got the job done. Tim wondered how long it would be before anyone found it.

For similar reasons, Tim had settled his next two months' rent in advance. Whatever the future might bring, he could rest assured that he would still have his furniture. But he was still desperate to believe that none of those measures would be necessary, that the

Clifford

stories were true, and that all he had to do was follow in Strafford's footsteps to finally catch his break… whatever that might come to mean.

Tim put two canteens in the pile near the headboard, and two more in the pile near his backpack. He had considered buying larger containers, water cooler bottles maybe. But he shouldn't need to carry extra water until he left the car behind, and once he did that, he couldn't carry the larger bottles anyways. So, while he might not need the canteens for weeks yet, once he did need them, they had to be there and be ready. Which got him thinking…

Tim rummaged through the pile of clothes and miscellany at the headboard to retrieve a Glock and a box of 9mm ammunition. He sighed and deposited the weapon and ammo with his backpack pile. Another example of something Henry Strafford hadn't known he would need. And even though the gun would not be necessary for a few weeks yet, once it was inevitably required, it had to be there and be ready.

Day 9

"So, we start at the library," Louis said, squinting against the glare through the windshield. After seven hours on the road, he had finally found the limit of Nebraska and its incessant flatness. The sea of dark, turned earth had given over to gently rolling hills covered in parched, brown grass with sporadic tufts of brush, all cascading to the shoulders of an unobtrusive asphalt road. The transition was really more an exchange of color for texture: there were finally breaks in the horizon, but all of them were beige. Grateful as Louis was for any change, on a scale of the recent plains to the lush green steepness of his native Tennessee, his current surroundings represented a sort of topographical twilight, made even less impressive by the thick cloud of dust tossed up by his tires.

But, by virtue of the landscape's lack of commitment, one feature truly stood out: the sky, so blue through contrast that it seemed somehow larger than Louis had ever seen it; visible in the entirety of its expanse, yet distant enough to lord over the rising and falling earth. In the absence of buildings, of crops, of livestock, road signs, or side rails, only an occasional fence row hinted at the continued influence of civilization nearby, somewhere... just not here. "So," Louis said, "How far you think we'll end up from the nearest library?"

Louis looked over to check on Marlow. The dog heaved a deep sigh, and did not so much as lift his eyes. For all their virtues, Newfoundlands, Louis was learning, were not engaging conversationalists. Of course, Louis recognized that he was effectively talking to himself, and would even grudgingly admit that he would have done so without the dog as an audience. But after so many hours of watching the road disappear under his hood, a man had to do something to keep himself sane, and having another warm body in the vehicle made that thing feel less crazy.

Clifford

Louis could take comfort in the fact that he wasn't talking to himself or even thinking out loud. He was sharing, just keeping Marlow in the loop.

There was also some legitimacy to his question. The last town the compass had skirted them around was Wheatland, and that had to have been twenty miles ago. And with nothing visible in front of them but broken asphalt winding through yet another rocky rise, Louis chose to focus on what he thought he did know.

"We have to keep this moving," Louis continued, "We've been wasting too much time. It's nice to hang back here and there, see the country an' all, but it needs to be our choice, y'know? If we're takin' a break, we're takin' a break, but if we're lookin' for somethin'… we need to get better at findin' somethin' is all. So, here's what I figure: I figure while we're out here, this is a good time for you an' me to go through what we been doin', vote on what works an' what don't."

Marlow smacked his chops twice and swallowed his saliva in response.

The pair had been conferring intermittently for the last couple hours, but the dialogue had taken on a new intensity since leaving the interstate ten miles earlier, after the compass had suddenly switched again. It was fortunate that Louis had noticed the last few course changes as promptly as he had, but he now had to credit his knowing in advance that Strafford had gone to Nebraska by way of Wyoming. It would have been tempting after that much Nebraska to just tune out until he wound up backtracking as before, but this time he had had a heads up. And that fact reinforced for Louis the practical advantage of continuing to research his destinations: any small clue to the next stop would let him know when and where to focus, which would help him to travel more efficiently. But as for the research itself, there was still a great deal of inefficiency to overcome. Louis needed to prioritize.

"So, what we're doin' now, boy, I think we should keep doin' first. Follow the compass where it goes, is always gonna be step one. 'Cause if we don't do that, we won't know what we're lookin'
216

for at the library. An' I think from now on the library can be step two. Except *you* can't go in the library, so really step two is t'find a campground for you. But then after what we're doin' now, an' the campground, an' the library… shit. Can't really say until we done steps one and three. Maybe that's where we're losin' time: instead 'a runnin' in the wrong direction, we just wait an' do the checklist at the library."

But if he waited to make his list until after the library, then how would he know what to look for at the library? He guessed he could just ask about Strafford and whatever landmark he found. That had worked the last time. Like the old man said, Louis just needed some luck. And he believed that what he had was far more powerful than luck. What Louis had was destiny.

Out of the corner of his eye, Louis saw the compass needle pull sharply south, then back to the west. Slowing to a crawl, he made out a rough access road branching off in front of them, the dirt surface camouflaged as a simple flat spot amongst the dusty hills. "Hmm…," Louis mumbled. "Guess we'll have t'see what the Shasta can take back there." As Louis cautiously turned off the pavement, Marlow finally sat up to survey their surroundings. "Oh, there you are, sleepin' beauty," Louis said as truck, trailer, man and dog jostled slowly along a river bank. "Hope you're rested, 'cause it's lookin' like we might have t'walk pretty soon."

Keeping their pace barely above an idle, Louis noted the compass needle gliding hypnotically with each hairpin turn, until he found that he was navigating the route without looking up to the road. It took more than a mile of moving his hands on the wheel to match the dance of the compass, before the indicator whipped suddenly westward. Louis looked up, saw water, and slammed on the brakes. At their easy pace, the truck and trailer halted quickly; more so than did Marlow, who toppled into the foot space in front of the passenger seat. "Sorry for that," Louis said, shifting into park. "Gotta stay on yer toes though, boy. I always tell ya'."

Louis climbed out of the truck and waved to Marlow, who stood up sheepishly before attempting a nonchalant stretch and stroll over the seat and out the door. Louis waited graciously for the dog to disembark and shake out, before reaching in for his cigarettes and closing up the truck.

Without a leash, Louis and Marlow strolled side by side around the front of the vehicle. A broad river meandered lazily around them, sweeping in from the west and rolling through the rocky silt to the north. But somewhere to the south, Louis heard water rushing, in a way that this stream seemed disinclined to do. The compass confirmed his hunch, directing the pair along the steep bank and down a narrowing outlet. The dead grass and loose stone along the shore leveled off ten feet above the water, and pulled away to accommodate a low, discolored concrete flood wall.

Continuing around the cement wings and rusted guard rail, Louis and Marlow came finally to the source of the sound. A large quantity of water gushed through a narrow channel beyond the wall, fell down a short incline, and roiled in a pool on its way into a gaping hole cut into the bedrock. The margins of the channel were covered in moss and worn smooth by untold years while the tunnel accepted its rushing contents and demanded more.

Louis checked the compass. The needle had gone limp. "So here we are," Louis said, "No marker, no sign, no street address… nor street." He removed his cap to rub his scalp. "Even better'n the last one."

Day 10

Kristin watched a pair of burritos turn, while slices of American cheese softened at the edges and melted over their tops. The faint laughter of a live studio audience floated from the nearby television to mingle with the low hum of the hotel microwave. After more than two weeks on the road, she had decided (and Jared had demurred) that she was sick of eating out all the time. Even if heating frozen burritos wasn't exactly home cooking, it was an opportunity, however small, to bring some warmth and comfort to their transient home. It was in that spirit that Kristin had begun to insist that their clothing should go in the provided dresser drawers, that their mini fridge should be stocked with a few staple items, and that they should eat in at least once a day.

As her meal prep concluded with a hollow 'ding,' she wondered about the cheese. Not the cheese that she had just used, but rather what was left in the refrigerator. She wondered about all the perishables really: would they survive the next leg of the journey, or would she need to find a grocery store again the next day? She retrieved her meal and settled into a small armchair near where Jared sat focused on the laptop, which he had set up on the cheap wooden desk near the window. "So, you know where we're going yet?"

Jared leaned back in his chair and took the last bite of his burritos. Recent time in the sun had finally turned his erstwhile burn to a deep tan. "Not sure exactly," he said, cheeking his food. "I haven't got down to the last leg yet." Swallowing, he offered, "Looks like South Texas by way of Oklahoma City... Not the most direct route, takes us a couple hours out of the way."

"Yeah," Kristin said, "But we're all the way out here, what's a couple hours? We might as well stick to the route if it guarantees we won't miss anything. How long is that, total?"

"Twelve hours, maybe," Jared answered.

Clifford

"Shoot. That might be too long for the milk to keep."

Jared laughed, "Twelve hours in the trunk, in August, in Texas? If you want to bring the milk, you'll be the only one drinking it."

"No, I think we'll just have to find a grocery store down there. But I hate being wasteful."

Jared said, "We're not wasting that much. And I think we have plenty of time for the store." He returned his attention to the computer while Kristin worked on eating her food.

Pausing between bites, Kristin asked, "Speaking of time, did you call Mr. Sherman?"

"Oh," Jared said over his shoulder, "Yeah, while you were in the shower, I did. He said I have a couple sick days I can cash in, so we should be good through the weekend."

"You're sure?" Kristin pressed. "You won't get written up or whatever? You're not on his good side right now."

"Nah," Jared waved dismissively. "He was a little pissed a few weeks ago, but I'm pretty sure he still likes me, overall. Plus, like I told you, if we get tight on time, worst case scenario is that I take unpaid leave."

Leaning back in her chair to tackle her second burrito Kristin said, "I trust you. I just want to make sure our ducks are in a row."

"It's like you keep saying," Jared said as he turned back to the laptop, "We need to stay flexible. Especially now: the last stop took us outside our 1899 to 1901 window, so hopefully, the next one will be something more conclusive. But it might take one stop after that. Best to be prepared either way."

Kristin chewed in silence, staring at the T.V. but not really registering the meaning of the figures moving on the screen. Swallowing the last of her supper, she asked the back of Jared's head, "So how do you feel about doing all the talking for us, after that last experience? If you want me to take the lead again, I'm open to it."

"Was I that bad?" Jared laughed.

The Beard

"No," Kristin clarified, "It's not that. I just want you to know I won't put up a fight if you're not comfortable."

Jared leaned back in his chair and swiveled half way to face her. "Y'know, I've been thinking about that. I can't figure out what I was scared of. I mean sure, I looked like an asshole, but who cares? It's not like I'm ever going back to a V.A. hospital in Arkansas. I'm not arguing for free license to be a dick or anything, but if I do look like a dick, there's basically no consequence."

Kristin nodded, "I'm impressed that you finally figured that out."

"Yeah," Jared agreed with equal surprise. After a pause, he continued tentatively, "Also, I've been getting this feeling lately like... like we're close to something. Like we're finally gaining on him, on Strafford I mean. And I'm ready to... I dunno. Ready to get after it, ready to pounce, I guess. And I don't want to lose that momentum when we're this far in." Leaning back in his chair, Jared took a lighter tone, "But having the freedom to be an asshole, well... that part is just liberating. I think I *want* to do the talking now."

Kristin chided, "My strong, confident asshole-man. It's kind of a hot look."

"Damn right," Jared said firmly.

Kristin stood, reached over Jared and retrieved his paper plate and napkin from the desk. "Tell you what then, tough guy: if you keep doing the talking, I'll keep doing the dishes."

Kristin crossed the room and dropped their plates unceremoniously in the trash.

Seventh Growth

Day 1

Tim trudged through a dry creek bed, stepped briefly onto a flat, blackened boulder, and found a sliver of shade in which to take a long pull from his canteen. Having just rounded a bend in the canyon, he was now surrounded on three sides by limestone. The sandy wash he'd walked in on stretched to the Southeast and disappeared around another corner. Soaring overhead, the canyon rim was worn smooth, streaked purple and black by running water that was no longer anywhere to be found. As they had for eons, the meandering, monolithic walls stood stark and sheer, guarding their occupants from all aggressors, save heat.

With every minute that passed, the sun rose higher over the Eastern wall and dragged the temperatures with it, driving all shade from the wide, exposed floor. Bursts of scrub brush and sparse stands of cottonwood trees provided too little cover for the brown grass that lined the edges of the wash, but was apparently adequate for the occasional chipmunk, some of whom had fearlessly approached Tim before retreating out of discomfort, or boredom, or both.

Tim wished he could have made this hike at a different time of year. It had to be over a hundred degrees already, and he still had a little ways to go before he reached his destination, only after which could he retrace the three and a half miles back out of the canyon. But on the upside, he had not yet run into any other hikers tenacious enough to make the trip today, and he welcomed the solitude.

And, he reminded himself, as uncomfortable as this may be, he should get used to it: this was nothing compared to what he knew would come later.

Tim was amply prepared. He had a map, plenty of water, strong sunscreen, and a large hat. One thing he hadn't bothered to bring was a camera. He believed snapshots, along with souvenirs and independent bits of trivia, to be wholly useless, the stuff of weak-minded people who wanted to brag to their friends about having finally had a worthwhile experience, or of hoarders vainly attempting to recapture a lost feeling that they hadn't given proper shrift in the moment. Tim saw much greater value in memorizing his experiences more holistically. By immediately incorporating new knowledge into his existing world view, he could realize the potential value of an experience on the spot and never revisit anything, ever, which struck him as the most efficient and therefore most effective approach to new things.

On this trip in particular, Tim needed to avoid distractions. He was looking for clues and could not be limited to only what was visible through a camera's view finder. His goal was to simply observe and understand, not to commemorate, and certainly not to share.

Tim replaced the cap on his canteen, used the back of his hand to wipe the sweat from his forehead, and forced himself back into the light and over to the wash. The fine sand gave under his boots as he pushed forward, one foot in front of the other, toward the next bend in the canyon. He had to be getting close. He had already passed a few fine examples, but the furthest of them was what had come to mind when he'd first read Strafford's account. Tim marched out of the turn with his head down. As the canyon widened out before him, he discovered a slender, white-haired man standing to his left under the vanishing shade of a rock shelf, fanning himself and peering through a pair of binoculars at the opposite wall.

Tim cursed his luck: all this way, just to run into someone now... Wordlessly and without regard for the man's view, Tim worked his way to the right, around a small stand of brown shrubs and bare trees to a pathway designated by a low-strung cable. He removed his hat and looked up at the nearby wall. Several feet off the canyon floor, a fifteen-foot-high flat section of rock ran more than 300 feet end to end. Across the entire length of this panel, and well above Tim's head, floated dozens of painted figures, of various sizes if nearly uniform build.

In dark red, brown, and black, most of the simple shapes were mere suggestions of the silhouettes of men. Round, filled-in heads perched atop of thin necks that immediately struck out to broad shoulders. Armless, legless bodies tapered, in some cases over the course of seven feet or more, before fading into the pinkish stone. The majority of the figures were featureless, just dark apparitions emerging from another era, but some had limbs holding spears, a handful of others wore horns or antennae, and a select few bore intricate white designs and oversized, skull-like eyes.

This had to be it, Tim thought: what Strafford had described must have been Barrier Canyon Style painting, but *where* he had described it would have been further South than these painters were thought to have lived. Unless Strafford had been mistaken about the exact location of his discoveries and had actually made them nearby, which was possible. It killed Tim that he couldn't just go to the end himself, just get in his car and drive straight through instead of backtracking hundreds of miles to join up with some jerk. But the description in the memoire was too vague for that. Tim needed that map. And to really play this out, by the end he would need the people who had it as well.

Tim hated needing people.

He walked the length of the massive panel slowly, taking in every scribble of every form. He focused his attention on each individual line, pulled back to consider the subjects in the context of their vignettes, studied the surface on which they were painted, the craggy wall above, and the pile of loose rocks below. Even though the paintings were so out of place, or perhaps because of it, Tim could almost picture the people who had lived here, who had sought shelter and the illusion of security that only high limestone walls can provide. In summary Tim discovered nothing, at least nothing more than he already knew.

Without fully realizing it, Tim stopped walking at the end of the path. In front of him, a triangular section of rock contained the image of six shadowy, limbless people painted in black, congregating around a much larger being that, to Tim, resembled a sarcophagus painted in red. On this central figure, large round eyes stared out from above a stern mouth, depicted as a thick, horizontal line. Tim had seen an incredible number of pictures of this panel and had felt no further need to view it, but he still could not help standing there, transfixed by its unholy gaze.

"Figure it out yet?" a friendly voice asked.

Tim turned to find the old man with the binoculars standing a few feet away. The man was lean and leathery, his posture was strong, but his denim shirt and cargo shorts hung from his wiry frame like a scarecrow. Tim turned back to the paintings and asked, "What's to figure out?"

With a mystic air, the man said, "What it all means. More than a thousand years ago people we know almost nothing about took the time to paint all this stuff, and we still can't figure out why."

"I've read a few theories," Tim shrugged.

"Oh sure," the man said, "That they tell some kind of stories, or they're part of some ritual. Or they're meant to protect the canyon or record shamanistic visions. All those theories... all just conjecture, isn't it? Y'know I been down here a thousand times, and I still can't figure what it *really* means. But maybe that's a good thing. Maybe it's the mystery that makes it so... captivating. Maybe if we're lucky, it doesn't mean anything at all."

Tim reflected that had *he* been down here a thousand times, *he* would have figured out by now what *all* of it meant. Rather than point that out, Tim confidently replied, "It does. Everything means something."

"I suppose..." the man trailed off. After a beat he added, "There's a book I read years ago. I don't even remember the name of it now, but I'll never forget how the guy described this place. He said, 'Beware the horned gods-'"

Tim interrupted, "You mean, 'Beware, traveler, you are approaching the land of the horned gods.' Edward Abbey was the guy. *Desert Solitaire* was the book."

228

The Beard

"So you've read it?" the man asked.

"Obviously," Tim grumbled obviously. "But I think you missed the point of that passage. The more important idea was in the first half of the sentence." Clearing his throat, Tim continued, "'Demonic shapes, they might have meant protection and benevolence to their creators and a threat to strangers: beware traveler...' and so on."

The man stood quietly, visibly nonplussed by Tim's editorial and recitation.

Either unnoticing or uncaring, Tim continued, "So you see: 'what it all means,' all depends whose side you're on." Having concluded his point, Tim pushed past the older man and left the narrow path to retake the sandy wash and hike back toward his car.

Tim chided himself for having invested even that much time and energy in a chat, but every bit as much as he disliked being approached by strangers he thrilled at the chance to correct them. Tim would jump at any opportunity to exercise intellectual dominance: it was the only thing that drew him to conversation as a concept. As a result, the one thing he found less rewarding than explaining facts to ignorant people was being forced to deal with anyone smarter than him. But in Tim's estimation, the latter was extremely rare, assuming it had ever happened at all.

In any case, the preceding conversation had given him exactly nothing to reflect on. Tim might have to leave this place not knowing the *exact* meaning of the *specific* paintings in *this* canyon, but thanks to Strafford, he already knew the meaning of the panel where he was going. It wouldn't be a creation myth or a symbol of protection or any of that nonsense. It would be an instruction manual.

Day 2

The library promised to be a total bust.

The staff had been helpful, to an unreasonable degree given the vagueness of Louis' queries. The collection was organized, and the content covered an impressive scope. But as with all of his destinations, whenever Louis believed he'd worked out a 'best place to start,' or a 'right way to do things,' all evidence of Strafford seemed to evade him. And on top of that, the compass needle hadn't woken up again since the riverbank south of town three days earlier. Louis believed that somewhere out there, Henry Strafford was laughing at him, stringing him along, and enjoying his failures, even tossing up speed bumps to slow the whole process.

Not that it would make sense. Not that any of this did. But Louis chose to personify his recent problems in this way, because he found that concretizing purely circumstantial frustration helped to keep him on task. The practice spoke to his stubbornness, to his defiant nature. In the context of his failed marriage, one of Louis' biggest hurdles had been the fact that he could not hate his family. In his professional life, Louis withered in the face of abstractions like politics and shrinking budgets. Any time Louis had found himself in a difficult position with no one he could punch that would matter, he had failed. But give him a *person* to fight and it was different. He would beat Henry Strafford. He would find the man, for no better reason than it seemed that the man did not want to be found.

Although at this point Louis had to concede that, in the end, he had always found Strafford where Strafford seemingly decided to appear. Still, Louis had clung to the idea that he could control the process when he'd first arrived at the Platte County Library. A librarian had walked him through an inventory of the historical archives and had patiently assisted him in accessing that collection.

The Beard

By the end of two days he had skimmed everything they had, without uncovering a single clue. He had gone home to his trailer full of dog, without any new information or idea of where to go next.

So, he had come back to the library to repeat the process, in the hopes that he had just missed something the first time. There had been quite a lot of information, and he hadn't felt he could responsibly disregard any of it. Even if the historical file was an interview from the 1970's, there might still be a chance that the interviewee mentioned names or places from the 1880's. After all, his last stop had yielded information about 1886 that hadn't been published until 1921.

All of this gave Louis cause for a futile kind of hope, as he stood awkwardly next to an inexplicable grandfather clock opposite the circulation desk. A clean-cut man in his thirties sat across from him, engrossed in a thin computer screen. Louis cleared his throat, a little louder than he had intended, and the man looked up. "Oh, I'm sorry," he said, "I didn't see you there. Did you need help with something?"

"Yes," Louis said. "Is Beth around? She was helping me with a project yesterday."

Transferring his full attention to Louis the man answered, "Beth is not in today. But if you'd like, I can pick up where she left off."

"It's more of double-checking. Beth was helping me with the historic archives."

"So, something in the vertical files. Do you remember which it was in?"

"All of them," Louis said.

The man looked at him dumbly before repeating, "All of them."

"Yes," Louis said, "all of them. I'm looking for the name of a guy, and any reference to a specific place in the 1800's, and it could be anywhere in there."

"And you say Beth helped you with that yesterday?"

Clifford

"For a couple days, yeah," Louis nodded. "Didn't have any luck, but I thought it might be worth trying again. Unless there's some other materials. But Beth said the vertical files would hit the local history highlights."

"In-house highlights, maybe," the man conceded. "But we have several database subscriptions you could try, if you'd-,"

"Nah," Louis interrupted, "I don't guess I'll find him that way. Every other time has been in-house stuff, and I think that's how it's meant to go. Seems to be how he likes it."

"I'm sorry, how who likes it?"

Louis thought about evading the question, but decided it wasn't worth getting that creative. "The guy I'm looking for, y'know, the name of the guy."

"Riiiight," the man squinted at Louis, attempting to diagnose his particular mental illness. "I really think the internet might be a help here, but if you insist..." He shook off his misgivings and continued, "I *could* help you with the vertical files again, or you could try the county courthouse: land records, court records..."

"I dunno," Louis said rubbing his chin. "Just doesn't *feel* right this time. Worth a shot, I guess."

"Oh-kaay," the man said, reverting to trepidation. With sudden enthusiasm, he offered, "Oooh, actually, what you should do if you want in-person-local-history, is go talk to the guy at the historical society museum." Chuckling to himself, the man mumbled, "Yeah, he'd *really* enjoy helping *you*."

Louis noted the sarcasm, but also did not care enough to ask for context, so let it pass. "Where is this, again?"

"It's the Wheatland Historical Society Museum. North of town, off I-25. Joyce could tell you more about it, that's the society's vice president. She's usually here, but I haven't seen her in a few days." He waved off his diversion, "Doesn't matter. The guy who works there, *Doc*-tor Tim Donaldson, he can give you a better idea of Platte County in the 1800's. Maybe help you find

The Beard

your man. If he feels like it," he laughed. "You'll understand when you meet him."

The museum was easy to find, not because it was well marked, or marked at all from what Louis could tell, but because it was the one and only thing across from the gas station by the Super 8. A squat, boxy, single-story building with a brown roof and tan siding, the museum sat in a small gravel lot that ran seamlessly into short brown grass, which then transitioned to a field under the same vast, uninterrupted sky that had held Louis' attention for days. To his eye, the sequence went: Super 8 Hotel, Sinclair Station, then the museum, and beyond that the ends of the earth.

Louis stopped at the glass front door. There was no business name, no posted hours, just a piece of scotch tape at eye level, with a torn strip of white paper still fluttering underneath. He leaned in and cupped his hands around his face to block out the glare of the morning. Inside, a large open room filled with cabinets and display cases stood half dark. Only a few rows of lit fluorescents at the far end belied the presence of people. Skeptical, but not wanting to have wasted the drive, Louis tested the pull handle and found the entrance unlocked.

A small brass bell above the door announced him as he walked into the dim room and took up a position next to a long wooden desk, empty but for an open metal cashbox. A few feet in front of him, the nearest display case stood un-illuminated with the back slid open and a dust rag and bottle of glass cleaner left on top. Deeper into the space, Louis could now see that most of the cases were hanging open, with many of their contents in disarray. From somewhere out of sight came the sudden noise of something metal falling, muffled by the room's thin sheet rock and cheap wood paneling.

"Hello?" Louis called into the vacant space.

Clifford

He was answered by another clatter, and the sound of an older woman cursing. Under the strip of lights at the back of room, a hollow plywood door swung out. Through the opening stumbled a petite woman in her late sixties with dry, bottle blonde hair and a screaming pink tank top. "Sorry, sorry," she called as she righted herself. Louis couldn't tell if she was apologizing to him or to whatever inanimate object she had just tripped over. "On my way, I'll be right with you." She made a show of hustling between cases and cabinets to join Louis at the front of the room. "Now," she said catching her breath and pushing hair out of her eyes, "How can I help you? Are you here to see the museum?"

"Yeah," Louis said, "Kind of. I'm looking for information about a guy who lived here, probably in the 1880's and-,"

The woman interrupted, "Well you've come to the right place. My name is Joyce, I'm-,"

"The Society Vice President?" Louis ventured.

"Sooo," the woman responded melodramatically, "My reputation pre-*cedes* me." She laughed, "Yes, I am the vice president, and I am in charge of this place. Now, before we get to the tour, I should tell you that the museum is free to the public, but we do recommend a donation of five dollars. *Highly* recommend."

Without comment, Louis pulled a bill out of his wallet and started to extend it to Joyce. She waved a hand, "You can just put it in the box on the desk there. And now that I have your money..." Joyce winked. "I should tell you that we are in temporary disarray. You're still free to look around if you like, but I can't promise we'll find anything. At least not quickly."

Louis glanced around for signs of remodeling or similar disruption. Finally, he guessed, "Spring cleaning?"

Joyce laughed, "No silly, we do that in the spring." Propping one elbow on the nearest display case she sighed, "We recently lost our curator. Very sudden, unexpected."

"I'm sorry to hear that," Louis said sympathetically.

"Oh no, he ain't dead or nothin'," Joyce corrected quickly. "He left. Didn't tell anyone why, just left. Still a chunk of his 'Dear

234

The Beard

John' letter stuck to the door, I'll have to get that on my way out. Anyways, like I says, I'm in charge of this place, and now he's gone, and I can't make heads nor tails of where he put everything. I tried askin' him once, how things were organized, but he said he couldn't explain it to me."

"So, he didn't know himself, then."

"Well," Joyce breathed, "His exact words were: 'If you haven't heard of the Chenhall System, there's no point trying to explain all this to you.'"

"Wow," Louis said.

"Exactly," Joyce answered. "Everything is marked, but the tags refer to an inventory I can't find. And I always hated the way he had things displayed, so I'm takin' everything out to put it all back together. Which brings us back to my point: I can't promise we'll find what you're looking for. But," Joyce gestured toward the cashbox, "As you are now a valued donor, I will turn the place upside-down trying."

"This isn't upside-down yet?" Louis asked.

Joyce laughed, "Watch it you. Just 'cause you're a V.I.P. don't mean I won't get the step-stool to come up there an' slap you. Now, you said you were looking for a person and a place. Is that right?"

"Yes," Louis confirmed, "The person is a man named-,"

"Hold yer horses," Joyce interrupted. "What period we talkin' about?"

"Nineteenth century," Louis said, "Probably 1880's, maybe 1870's."

"Ah," Joyce nodded, then with a flourish, "A *very* important time in the *Story of Wheatland*." She walked to the third row of display cases from the door, stood behind it, and waited. Louis followed and stooped over to examine the objects and photographs still carefully arranged along one end of the box. With a tone as exaggerated as her gestures, Joyce continued, "Come join me on a journey to the American Frontier. In a time when our now fertile fields were but barren flats, seven men, nay, seven *visionaries*-,"

Clifford

"Found him," Louis interrupted, pointing through the glass at a large grainy photograph of ten dirty men in front of a canvas tent. "There he is. That's the guy."

Joyce lowered her hands and squinted past Louis' finger, "Really? Already? Which one?"

"In the middle there," Louis said, "Be... fourth from the right. The guy with the big beard and the thousand-yard stare. That's definitely him."

Joyce reached into the case and gingerly removed the picture. She held it up to inspect the back before setting it on the glass between the two of them. "According to the tag, this was part of the crew that dug the Bluegrass Tunnel."

"The what now?"

"Those seven visionaries," Joyce repeated simply, "In 1881, they founded the Wyoming Development Company. The goal was to irrigate the Wheatland Flats, make farmland out of 'em. One of the first things they did was to dig a tunnel from the Laramie River to Bluegrass Creek." Regaining her former steam, Joyce declared, "Completed in the fall of 1883, this 2,380-foot marvel would become the cornerstone of the Wheatland Irrigation District, which is the nation's largest privately-owned irrigation system still today..."

"Wait," Louis interrupted again, "So fall of 1883? And the tunnel is still around?"

Joyce reset to a conversational volume, "Sure is, out on the aptly named Tunnel Road. It's maybe... twenty miles southwest of town? I've seen it on maps, but I've never gone out there."

"Twenty miles," Louis reflected, "Seems about right."

Joyce asked sweetly, "Shall I continue?"

Louis considered this for a moment. As much as Joyce clearly wanted to finish her performance, he felt in his gut that he'd found what he'd come for, and he'd already spent a day more than he'd anticipated in Wheatland. Given that most of the information Louis had come across thus far had been vague, he wasn't expecting to do much better than this. On the other hand, he had found some

236

additional low hanging fruit in Iowa, so that wasn't unprecedented either. He asked, "Do you have any more information about this tunnel?"

"That is entirely possible," Joyce nodded. "I just have no idea what or where it would be. If it exists."

Louis teetered for a moment on the verge of a decision. Suddenly, an easy tie breaker occurred to him. He dug in his pocket, pulled the compass out from under his keys, and lifted the dented cover, only slightly. The needle had remembered itself, and once again pointed insistently westward. Replacing the object in his pocket, Louis said, "Sorry, but I should probably be going. I really only allowed a few minutes to swing by."

Joyce was visibly disappointed. She asked, "Are you sure? We might not find more about the tunnel, but I promise there's plenty more to see here."

Louis nodded politely as he backed toward the exit. "I'm certain that's true, but we gotta leave something for next time." Over the tinkling of the brass bell above the door, he reassured her, "I promise I got my money's worth."

Day 3

In a word, Jared was agitated. Over the preceding weeks, he and Kristin had fallen into a relaxed rhythm: follow a map, spend several days researching the destination and seeing the sights while he grew a new map, and repeat. But the pattern was beginning to wear on him. He had done more touring and vacationing in the last month than in his entire life leading up to that point, and through this he had found his limit on relaxing. It wasn't that he was ready to turn around and get home to his regular routine. On the contrary, he was ready to get to the end of this trail. Every morning when he woke up, he felt a stronger draw westward, felt more compelled to move forward, and correspondingly less concerned with going back.

But, since he couldn't move forward until he knew which way 'forward' was, and that knowledge only came as his beard grew, he continued to suffer this stilting progress: punishment for his uncooperative face. And now after ten days' wait, now that they finally had somewhere definite to go, there were all these hoops they had to jump through. Jared leaned forward to squint through the windshield: nothing but a sparse stand of saplings and yet another cluster of identical white buildings with red roofs, baking under the merciless San Antonio sun. Without looking her way, he asked Kristin, "How fucking big is this place?"

"Don't know," Kristin shrugged. "We're probably a mile from the entrance, so pretty big, I guess. Are we lost?"

Jared pulled away from a stop sign and mumbled, "I'm not sure. We might be."

"Any time you're not sure if you're lost, then you're lost," Kristin stated.

Jared shot back, "Wanna help then? You have the map."

The Beard

Kristin took a sheet of paper from the dash and reminded Jared, "I asked a bunch of times if you wanted my help and all I got was 'Oh I have it memorized. I have it memorized…'"

"Yeah," Jared said, still with an edge in his voice, "Well… I thought an army base would have an organized street grid. This doesn't make any damn sense."

"Then why didn't you ask directions at the visitor center?"

"Because I didn't know I would need them. And besides, directions to where? We still don't know where this ends."

"Lucky for you," Kristin said, pulling a small pamphlet from the backpack at her feet, "I bothered to look around while they were running the background check. You remember, that whole time you were pacing?"

"I wasn't pacing," Jared said.

"Um, yeah you were," Kristin corrected him. "Looked suspicious as shit, too. I mean, why you so nervous about a background check? Is there something I don't know about?" She unfolded the pamphlet and spread out a small map next to Jared's hand-drawn route. "Pull over," she directed, "It's harder to find a moving target."

Jared followed her instructions, signaling and easing to the right beside an open field. He shifted into park and turned on his four way flashers. To her earlier question he replied, "No, I wasn't worried about the background check. I'm just… I don't know. I'm amped up. I want to keep moving, get where we're going. Not stand around waiting for paperwork."

Tracing a diagonal line on the pamphlet with her finger, Kristin said, "Just be glad that they even allow non-military visitors. And that your beard took us to the public entrance. It could've been a lot more complicated than it was."

This had already occurred to Jared, and may have had something to do with his nerves. Even with the on-line maps predictably on the fritz when he needed them, he had been able to tell that this route would take them in the vicinity of Fort Sam Houston. What he had not known prior to their arrival was that they would actually end up inside an active military installation. As Kristin had pointed out, it could have been much more complicated, but she was neglecting how complicated things still could get, depending on their next few moves.

Jared had promised to take the lead, and it was important to him that he do that properly, but what if they had to steal something again as they had in Asheville? What if they found themselves trespassing as they had in Selmer? Doing what they needed to do without knowing what that might entail was pressure enough, and Jared did not think he was wrong to feel apprehensive about the probability of sneaking past armed soldiers. All the same, they needed to go where they were supposed to go, to find what they were meant to find, so the only thing Jared could do was to put the hypothetical out of mind and focus on what was directly in front of him, to push himself to keep on pushing himself.

Jared looked over and realized Kristin was staring at him. Sympathetically, she asked, "You okay?"

Jared shrugged, "Yeah. Why?"

Kristin sat thoughtfully for a second before answering, "You've been wound up all day. And then you were whining for a while, and now you just got really quiet."

"I was thinking…" Jared trailed off, trying to sort his thoughts. Finally he said, "I'm ready. Let's get on with it."

"Okay," Kristin agreed skeptically, "Then you'll want to take a left. Then drive six blocks and take another left. Then three blocks and take a right."

Jared complied without remark. He counted the blocks and counted his breaths, monitoring the speed of the vehicle and the speed of his mind. He had always admired, but had never been, the type of person that took initiative. Jared was impressed by what a challenging balance it required: processing things carefully enough to make clear decisions without sacrificing the momentum necessary to make any decisions at all. Pulling through his final turn, Jared drove that observation from his mind. Now was not the time to look inward. stay sharp, stare forward, keep moving. "So that was our right," he commented, "Where to now?"

"Anywhere you can park," Kristin said. "According to your notes, the path zoomed in here, so it's gotta be close."

"And after we park, which way are we going?" Jared asked.

"That way," Kristin replied, presumably as she indicated a direction.

Not wanting look away from the road, Jared impatiently requested, "Please use words."

"South," Kristin said tersely. "It'd be left up here."

Jared eased to the left and idled toward a corner formed by two long, tall, stone walls. Reminiscent of a castle or an old fort, something about the incongruity of the structure gave the impression of ruins far more ancient than these likely were. A horizontal row of what appeared to be obsolete gun ports on the northern face gave way to an interminable arrangement of arched windows running down its western counterpart. From behind the imposing battlements, a high clock tower of the same material stood sentry. "This is different," Jared muttered.

"It's where we're going," Kristin said. "According to what you drew, we'll walk around the south side and circle back to the north."

Looking away to his right, beyond a static helicopter that had been installed between a pair of palm trees, Jared spotted the glint of many windshields lined up side-by-side. He jerked the car suddenly into a large lot that was less than a third full.

"Shit," Kristin announced, grabbing the armrest, "You could've warned me."

Without answer, Jared parked the car and got out. So now he knew where they were going, and he knew that they were close. But he still didn't know if they could get there. Nor if 'there' would be the end of the trail and, even if they could and it was, whether they would recognize it when they saw it. But he couldn't let himself get bogged down in that, he had to keep moving, have faith. As he marched toward the southern edge of the structure, his vague impression of the old building came into higher relief. A rough cut limestone wall, stained at odd intervals with weeping black suggestive of century old smoke, supported a peaked roof. Even though the aged defenses were so out of place, or perhaps because of it, Jared could almost picture the men who had lived here, who had sought shelter and the illusion of security that only high limestone walls could provide.

At the far end, Jared discovered another corner with another wall, this one two stories high with a combination of gables and windows that appeared to house a long, narrow office building. At roughly half the length of that wall, Jared paused. A tall, arched sally port framed by old metal lamps, protected a blacktop path large enough to drive a truck through. Above the opening's capstone, a large red badge affixed to the wall advertised:

HEADQUARTERS
UNITED STATES ARMY NORTH
(FIFTH ARMY)

Beyond the pair of wrought iron fences that sealed off both ends of the entryway, Jared could see a massive square courtyard with the base of the clock tower at its center.

Kristin called from ten yards back, "You just take off and leave me in the car? Do you even know where you're going?"

"From what you said," Jared answered unabashedly, "It should be through here. But we can't go through here."

"Oh yeah?" She pointed to a white metal sign not five feet from Jared and demanded, "Then why does that say 'Quadrangle *Public* Hours?'" Walking past him, Kristin pressed gently on the middle of the heavy gate. It swung innocuously open. She mumbled to herself, "Dumbass. Want to lead, won't wait for me to follow…"

Jared deflated, but only slightly and only for a moment. He *was* going to lead, from Arkansas forward. He had promised her he would. He had promised himself. And now he would stay out front,

The Beard

if for no better reason than to prove he was capable. Easing the second gate closed behind them, Jared walked confidently around Kristin and into the courtyard. Within the weathered and utilitarian stone enclosure, a perfectly maintained road flowed through meticulous landscaping. The symmetrical lawn on either side served as a bed for large oak trees that lined the path to the clock tower. The square tower itself was flanked by antique cannon and a pair of flagpoles, whose banners fluttered in the same breeze that ruffled the tops of a few tall palms planted beyond.

Jared was meandering distractedly to the right side of the blacktop when something bright caught the corner of his eye. Turning toward the lowest branch of the nearest oak, he found himself staring into the face of a long-tailed bird as big as a turkey and as white as a dove. Perched about four feet off the ground, it maneuvered its long neck to cock its head curiously at him, an action which vibrated an odd crown on top of its head. Jared, stunned, backed away slowly, which gave the bird room to offer a half-hearted flap and leap clumsily to the ground. It slowly high stepped toward him, still staring him straight in the eye. The exceedingly long plumage on its back began to rise and expand gradually outward. Once the feathers had floated free of the dirt behind the bird, it opened its hooked beak and... it screamed. A high pitch shriek: once, twice, three times, after which it shook itself like a wet dog and blasted plumage up and out into a vertical semicircle four times its height.

"What the fuck!?!" Jared screamed back. The bird hopped from one foot to the other, shaking the feathers in a translucent curtain, the thin filaments punctuated by round white spots that resembled flattened cotton balls. Finally breaking eye contact, it strutted regally past Jared, toward a distant fountain in a sunny clearing beyond the trees.

"Oooh," Kristin gushed, "A peacock."

"An albino peacock?" Jared demanded. "What the fuck is the point of an albino peacock?"

Clifford

"That too," Kristin said, "But I was talking about this one." She pointed to another low branch where a second bird with an iridescent blue breast and a luxuriant red and spotted tail continued to relax on its perch. "Oh mi-god," Kristin uttered breathlessly, looking the other way, "They have deer."

Jared looked away from his pale antagonist and surveyed his surroundings more carefully. A group of chickens wandered, clueless, past a flock of geese that floated in the fountain. In the shade of the trees opposite, a herd of small deer nuzzled one another while assorted individual ducks, perfectly white with orange bills, waddled throughout the square. Mostly to himself, he mumbled, "What the Disney hell is this?"

"Hey," Kristin said excitedly, "Do we have anything we can feed them? I think we still have bread in the car, but… do deer eat bread? I never got this close to one before."

Jared walked determinedly out of the shade, across the pavement, and past the cannon to the clock tower. He stopped to examine a pair of bronze plaques to the left of a locked door. Kristin jogged to catch up. "What the hell is your problem?" she demanded.

Ignoring the question, Jared said sternly, "According to the sign, this place opened in 1879 as a supply depot."

Ignoring his ignoring her, Kristin continued, "We just stumbled into a secret petting zoo, which is fucking magical, and instead of letting me enjoy it you're stomping around. I mean, why can't you appreciate shit?"

Looking over at her, Jared shot back, "We're not here for you to play with fucking ducks and chickens. You have had two weeks of 'vacation fun' but," he pointed at the stubble on his cheek, "*This* is why we came here. Now, I am trying to work on *this* like we said we would, and what I would 'appreciate' is if you would try to help, even a little. Or, if you can't do that, then I'd appreciate if you'd stay out of my way."

Kristin pursed her lips, crossed her arms and shook her head before walking slowly back to the shade. Jared was agitated. Jared

The Beard

was frustrated, and Jared had meant every word he'd just said. But even before he'd finished talking, he knew he'd fucked up. For all the quiet effort he'd expended to keep himself on task throughout the day, verbally horsewhipping Kristin to do the same would only accomplish the opposite: on top of paying for his outburst until he apologized, Jared also expected to feel distracted and shamed, which he assumed would be counterproductive, even if it was deserved. He followed Kristin the fifteen yards to the curb and said, much more quietly, "Look I'm sorry. I'm just…"

Jared trailed off and Kristin shrugged and squinted away from him into the distance.

"I'm getting impatient, is all," he finished finally. "I got all fired up to go someplace, ask a bunch of questions, and get some real answers. Then we get here and…" Jared gestured to the open courtyard, vacant but for curious wildlife, "What good is this? I feel like the further we go, the more I should understand, but instead I'm more confused than ever. I'm just sick of it. I want to make sense of it, and it doesn't make any sense."

Still looking away, Kristin said, "So you work on that. I'll just stay here: out of your way."

Knowing that she couldn't see him, Jared cringed. He took a deep breath and spoke softly, "I shouldn't have said that. I know you're not in the way, and you have been super helpful. We wouldn't have even attempted any of this if you hadn't insisted. But I'm trying to be… more assertive? More engaged, maybe. And the point of it all, the point of everything keeps getting fuzzier, and there's nothing I can *actually* do to fix that so I… I don't know. I wanted to yell, and you were the only one here for me to yell at. It's no excuse. If you want, I can go scream at the ducks instead."

"Don't you dare," Kristin said gravely. "They didn't do anything wrong either. And they're army ducks. They're veterans, and you should respect that."

"Then I guess I'll just have to suck it up and be an adult," Jared concluded.

Clifford

Kristin nodded. Finally looking at Jared, she said, "It's good that you're excited. I want you to be excited, just don't be a dick. Or at least don't be a dick to me. You told me it was liberating, being an asshole around people who would never see you again. But I see you. I see you every day, all the time. You don't get to treat me like a problem."

"I agree," Jared said sincerely.

Kristin heaved a sigh, and unfolded her arms. "I can wait a few minutes to say hello to the deer. The map shows us going past the clock, up to that corner."

Jared caught himself about to demand why the hell she had waited so long to tell him. Instead he offered her his arm. "Would you care to show me?"

Day 6

Kristin wrapped her arms around Jared's bicep, both to encourage him to escort her on their promenade and for assurance that she wouldn't be accidentally shoved into the dark water. Following the path as it narrowed to wind around yet another sidewalk café, Jared led at a leisurely pace to accommodate the tourists sporadically milling in front of and behind them. As he pulled her away from a dense pocket of people and up a narrow staircase, Kristin paused, halting his progress halfway across a small, arched bridge.

She quietly steered Jared to the waist-high stone wall and stood, admiring the view of the trail they had traversed. Paved walkways on either side of the narrow stretch of the San Antonio River snaked through ferns, trees, and decorative rocks; they thinned and widened to accommodate small patios, plazas, and tables full of diners under umbrellas, all covered by a lush green canopy, itself enclosed by the distant dome of a clear night sky. The stars that surely shone somewhere beyond were concealed by the brownish-pink glow of the city, brightly lit at the street level just above Kristin's sight line. In their stead, hundreds of small lamps and bursts of isolated rays from the tasteful outdoor sconces and the windows of the many restaurants twinkled in the water that flowed below the couple's feet.

A dank, pungent odor from the water suggested that the scene may have proved less picturesque by daylight, but in *this* moment, on this night, with the lazy channel visible only as a reflection of its sparkling surroundings, the river that lapped at its sculpted stone shores was captivating. A gentle breeze tousled Kristin's hair and replaced the scent of algae and mold with the vague smell of spiced meats and the sound of distant mariachi music. Kristin squeezed Jared's arm, heaved a deep sigh, and moved back from the side of the bridge. Jared guided her down another short flight of steps and onto the less populated walkway on the opposite bank.

Kristin was in a wonderful state of mind. She hadn't discussed Jared's outburst at the Quadrangle three days before, but she hadn't forgotten it either, and pursuant to his complaints, she had become a little self-conscious about filling their calendar with sightseeing. Whether his frustration stemmed from how they were spending their time or their money she wasn't sure, but erring on the side of caution, she had resolved to be less active and more austere. For the first interval since they had pulled out of their driveway, Kristin had not picked up a travel brochure, had not cracked a guide book, had not even so much as asked the hotel receptionist about the local scene. And so, it was without any specific plans that the couple had stumbled into a legitimately romantic evening.

A short drive through downtown had led them to choose a restaurant at random, where they had been surprised to be seated at a candle lit table on a patio one full story below street level, under the trees, next to the river and its attendant path. After a quiet dinner at sunset, as pedestrian traffic seemed to be picking up, they had decided to see where the trail went. That had been almost an hour ago, and still no terminus in sight. Kristin hoped that it would not end for hours more. Although largely lined with hotels and bars, there were also lovely surprises around nearly every corner: quaint stone bridges, fountains, old world architecture, and even with the background noise and the background odor, the air felt perfect after an oppressively hot day. Kristin was cool. She was fed. She was content. And the man she was in love with was as calm he'd been in a week.

In summary, the couple had set out not looking for anything and had found something wonderful in spite of themselves, a polar opposite of their experience of three days earlier. In that case, for all of their trouble, care, and argument, they had been rewarded with nothing but an empty patch of grass near the northwest wall of a courtyard. After returning to the pond and its barnyard congregants, they had come across a museum, nothing especially

The Beard

impressive: it had amounted to series of small rooms featuring artifacts in glass cases topped with posters detailing the origins of Fort Sam Houston and of the US Army in Texas. Jared and Kristin had split up and scoured every display, but found no mention of Henry Strafford.

Jared had, however, come across an item related to the northwest corner of the courtyard: a long poster that detailed the historical highlights of the Quadrangle included a small photo of the Apache leader, Geronimo, with a brief caption explaining that in the year 1886, he and thirty-two warriors had lived in tents in that vicinity as prisoners of the United States government. Kristin considered that even though 1886 was in the right ballpark, they couldn't know for sure that Strafford was in any way connected to that event. After all, according to the sign Geronimo was only there for six weeks, and plenty of other things must have happened in that area outside of that brief period.

But Jared felt otherwise, and she had decided to not mention her misgivings, to give him his moment of victory. And, even though they had been moving around the room in opposite directions and he had been the first to see that sign purely by chance, Kristin had made a point to shower him with praise for his powers of observation and attention to detail. She had chosen this approach, sadly enough, based on an episode that the fort's small menagerie had reminded her of. A few months earlier, one of her coworkers had gotten a puppy, and had naturally become absorbed in housebreaking it. The woman had said in passing that everything she had read on the subject suggested minimal scolding, but excessive praise if the dog did what you wanted.

Not that Kristin thought Jared was in need of training per se. Even when the two of them had moved in together, they had made mutual adjustments, not endeavored to change one another in character or behavior. But now they were in unknown territory: this sudden shift in routine and terrain seemed to have brought with it other, more subtle changes in Jared's disposition, his... energy, somehow. Even now, walking silently along the riverbank, Kristin could sense in him something kinetic just below the surface, a kind of tension that he was hard pressed to restrain. He needed to find a better way to adjust to these new circumstances, and Kristin wanted to find a better approach to help him with that.

Walking up a ramp that led to another set of stairs, Kristin squeezed Jared's arm and pressed gently to the right, forcing him to guide her through a square doorway and onto a path that followed the track of the channel around a bend. The sparkling lights dwindled as the business fronts on the water became less frequent, favoring patios at the street level above. On the water, a low, flat boat with a few tourists seated on benches motored quietly in the opposite direction. "It's like Venice," Kristin breathed.

"Umm..." Jared said plucking absent mindedly at his shirt, clearly prepared to disagree but apparently not wanting to argue.

"You can say it," Kristin assured him, "You don't think it's like Venice."

"I haven't been to Venice, so I can give you the benefit of the doubt," he said quickly. After a peaceful moment he added, "Except it isn't though, not really. There are fewer berets and a lot more sombreros here. And I'm pretty sure the canals in Venice would have to be much bigger."

Kristin rolled her eyes in the dark, "So not like Venice then." Seeking a more positive tone she said, "It feels just as far from home though."

"That is true," Jared conceded, "And who knows how much farther from home we'll get?"

"Will that be a problem, do you think?" Kristin asked.

Slightly annoyed, Jared answered, "No. I don't know. I don't think so. We don't need to worry about that tonight."

Kristin pressed the issue cautiously, "But how much farther do you think we *can* go, before we use up too much time and money?"

"As far as we have to," Jared said, increasingly agitated, "Just let me worry about the rest."

Sensing the bounds of his cooperation, Kristin grudgingly acceded, "It was just a question, I trust you. I'm really curious

250

The Beard

where this will take us, though. We're already further west than I've ever been."

With sudden enthusiasm, Jared said, "I couldn't even guess, but I've been thinking about that too. We know we've been following Strafford backwards through his life, but we don't know where he came from. I doubt that he came up from Mexico, but if he did, we don't have passports, so I'm hoping we start to trend north soon. Something else I was thinking though, since it looks like we'll probably keep drifting to the west: when we reach Nevada, would you want to take a side trip to Vegas?"

"I don't know," Kristin thought out loud, "It could be expensive. And maybe we shouldn't plan on it until we know how far out of the way it will be. Besides, you had a point about getting distracted. Las Vegas is a pretty big distraction, and I don't even like gambling."

Jared halted their progress beside a weathered stone wall, took Kristin's hand and explained in his same brisk pace, "No no, we wouldn't be going to gamble, we..." He glanced around and lowered himself to one knee. "When we get as far as Nevada, would you like to marry me in Vegas?" Following a few seconds of confused silence, he added, "I don't have a ring or anything, but I think I'm supposed to kneel for this, I'm not sure..."

Kristin stared down at him, stunned. Jared, with his mottled beard, still held her hand and knelt on the stone walk, dwarfed by the river behind him as it gently wound between trees and ivy covered buildings, with the San Antonio skyline towering above in the distance. No boats, nor cars, nor people in sight: just the two of them and the soothing sounds of water and muffled revelry. The tableau was sweet and pathetic, impulsive and impressive, and the moment was in every way more perfect than Kristin had imagined it. Fighting back an inexplicable desire to laugh, Kristin discovered she had begun to cry. She took Jared's hand in both of hers and pulled him to her.

As he stood, she stretched to kiss him on the cheek and moved in close to his ear to say, "Yes. I will."

Clifford

The couple held each other in that spot for what could have been seconds or hours. Kristin leaned into Jared's shoulder to dab her tears on his shirt. Without pulling away she asked finally, "Is this why you've been acting so jittery?"

"I didn't think I was acting..." Jared trailed off. He chose a different tack, "I wasn't sure if you would want to."

Kristin laughed, "What I *want*, I... It isn't about what I *want*, Jared. I love you. I love you so I *have* to say yes."

Day 7

There was something different about this one. Not very different, no, that would be too easy: a number of small, subtle differences, each independently meaningless, thus collectively tough to nail down.

Below the photograph of Louis's family, the electric cigarette lighter clicked from its socket. Louis lifted his foot off the gas while he pressed the glowing coil to the tip of his cigarette.

The compass had continued to lead the way, but it seemed more direct this time, more insistent. Before, it had moved in smooth arcs as course changes arose, but now it gave hard, jolting shifts a half mile ahead of the exits. In one case when Louis had missed a turn, the needle had begun to spin like a top with more urgency than it had shown since the first day it had spoken to him. He could entertain that it may have done some of this in the past, and that perhaps he had just become more attentive as the trip drew on, but then there was also this feeling he had. Not ominous or fortuitous, just different.

In keeping with that theme of minor changes, the landscape had also been in slow flux. Driving out of the lush forests of the Mississippi Valley and onto the flatness of the plains had been jarring, as had the transition from the golden summer fields of Nebraska to the arid hills of Wyoming. But on the ride into Montana, the hills had lowered incrementally, the grass had become gradually thicker and taller, and in the last two days the clouds had slowly closed in lower and darker. Louis could certainly tell he was somewhere new, but to pin down any one discrepancy or defining feature was impossible. 'Different' was the best description he could think of.

As sure as Louis was of these differences, he could not seem to help himself from taking the exact same approach as he always had. For the past few miles, since exiting onto a two lane frontage road that ran parallel to the interstate, Louis had conferred with Marlow about what would constitute the most sensible course of action. Similar to their previous meetings, the more Louis had talked, the less committed he had become to any one strategy. Louis recapitulated with his travelling companion that they had tried starting with libraries, attempted to start with cemeteries, and had also ended with vital records and a museum, each of which had worked once. But there was nothing, Louis pointed out, that had worked more than once. The only outlier of sorts was their first stop in Saint Charles, which had been self-explanatory, but what were the odds of that happening again?

In the end, Louis declared, they would have to let the destination decide, to have faith and be ready for anything. The compass-point jumped forty-five degrees to the west, and Louis tapped the brakes and signaled left in response. Thirty yards later, he pulled the rig slowly through a railroad crossing and onto a solitary side street. The compass yanked another twenty five degrees and, halfway through a bend, jolted twenty more to press Louis increasingly south. Not like the delicate dance he had seen previously. As Louis crossed from paved surface to gravel, the thin white pointer seemed to scream at him from its metal casing. He responded to its volume with patience, taking care to not whip the trailer around.

Past a handful of scattered houses and a large gate that hung open, Louis followed the lane for half of a mile between fields surrounded by low wire fencing. At a small turnout more like a recess cut into a field on Louis's left, the compass flopped ninety degrees to full west, then bounced to full east, and then back again for a full rotation. Louis pulled the vehicle over as the indicator continued to spin counter clock-wise, it's pace increasing with each cycle until it became a blur, and the metal casing vibrated against the dashboard.

Louis and Marlow stared as the object fell on its back and convulsed above the digital clock. "Well," Louis said, "What do we do with that?" He cut the engine, opened his door and climbed out:

even if this wasn't the place, it would still do just fine for a break from that nonsense.

Louis reached above his head and stretched, his cigarette still hanging out of his mouth. Behind him, Marlow clamored down from the cab and wandered to the nearby fencerow to hike his leg. "Pretty country," Louis mumbled, staring out across the fields to a hazy bluff peeking out in the distance. "Not much to it, but pretty." Louis stood for a moment, wondering if it was going to rain, wondering how much farther they would go before making camp, and whether they should consider getting lunch somewhere on the way, just in case. He'd seen a sign on the highway for a town called Hardin, they had to be pretty close by now, but he didn't want to backtrack for the interstate. The frontage road they had been on should arrive at the same town eventually, and maybe that would give them some meal options after they found what they were looking for. If the compass chilled out and picked up the trail again. Unless… was this where they were supposed to be going?

Marlow whined from the opposite side of the truck. Louis took his cigarette from his lips to call out to the dog, but then decided to stroll around the hood and investigate. Blocked by the vehicle, Louis discovered Marlow hiking his leg again, this time on a stone marker in the center of the turnout. The granite block was chest high, the size and shape of some of the larger headstones Louis had recently walked amongst. He wondered how he hadn't seen it earlier. A lucky thing he hadn't run into it: it was sturdy enough to do serious damage.

On the opposite side of the stone, Louis discovered a large bronze tablet bolted into the block. It was pocked and discolored, but still legibly read:

FORT CUSTER

Established as a military post November 1877 by order of
President Rutherford B. Hayes and General Phil H. Sheridan.
Garrisoned as one of the important military posts in the
Northwest until abandoned by the Government September, 1897.

Clifford

This Fort was named in honor of General George A. Custer,
who was killed in action with his entire command at the
battle of the Little Big Horn, June 25, 1876.

Dedicated By
Shining Mountain Charter
Daughters of the American Revolution
Billings, Montana
September 21, 1930.

Louis and Marlow stood side by side, processing the information aloud. "So is this our spot? I suppose it has to be the spot. But a fort this time? Does that mean he was he a soldier before he was a ditch digger then? Haven't seen anything military about him, but I guess that could be." Marlow dropped to his rump and scratched his shoulder with his back leg. Louis continued, "D'you think we go lookin' for information 'bout the guy, or 'bout the fort? Or does one lead to the other?" Marlow ceased scratching, looked up at Louis, and whined again. "I know," Louis said, "You vote the same every time. We'll get lunch first."

Marlow jumped up, shook out his coat and trotted back around to the open door of the truck. Before Louis had followed halfway, he became aware of a high-frequency buzzing. Climbing into the truck, he rediscovered the source: the old, pressed tin of the compass continued to bounce across the plastic dashboard. "Goddammit," Louis breathed, "Where's the battery on this thing?" He picked up the vibrating object, now warm to the touch, and leaned over to toss it in the glove compartment in front of the dog. It fell to the bottom of the wedge-shaped box and bounced side to side like a puck on an air hockey table, reverberating in the cramped cab.

The Beard

Taking one last stab, Louis dug around below the bench seat to retrieve a pair of leather work gloves. He plucked the compass from its cradle, bundled it in the gloves, put it back, and slammed the compartment, saying, "Try it now, fucker." Louis and Marlow sat silently eyeing the panel, which emitted a low, muffled hum. Louis muttered, "Good enough. I'll take it," as he started the truck and pulled around the turnout to retrace the lane.

The frontage road that he had assumed would continue to parallel the interstate, began drifting away almost immediately. Just as he was about to lose sight of the highway, Louis reached a T-intersection and stopped. He had discovered over the course of his journey that following a compass pointing every way but north had a disorienting affect, and at this point Louis wasn't at all sure of which way he was going. But then again, as he had hoped to end up in the town of Hardin, and he didn't know which way that was meant to be relative to his direction of travel, he didn't guess that he was really any more lost than he had been. All the same, he knew the interstate would get there. And that was still on his right.

Louis brushed his signal and checked for traffic. Directly across the street, a cluster of a half dozen small white buildings caught his eye: something about them seemed off. It took a few seconds before Louis decided that they looked out of place because there was no road running to them, just a single sidewalk. Continuing to scan left, he noticed that the same was true of a large red building nearby, and that behind the structure sat two railcars without any rails in sight. Next to that was a church steeple, then a couple wood framed cabins and three larger log cabins, all arranged along the same paved walkway and gently rolling lawn like a miniature golf course built life-size.

Just up the road, a large white sign announced, "Historical Museum Visitor Center Entrance."

Louis moved his hand back to the turn signal and stopped. As he had just discovered in Wyoming, these small, local museums could be treasure troves. But that was exactly the problem: he had only just discovered that fact in Wyoming. If the same strategy never worked twice, how could that approach work twice in a row? Then again, there *was* something different about this one, and the museum was right there in front of him. He didn't have a better idea, not even a better idea of which direction to turn to find food. Louis dropped his hand against the switch to signal left. "Quick detour," he told Marlow, "Then lunch, I promise."

Louis rolled past the scattered buildings to an expansive parking lot with only a few cars in it. Still before noon, the day was surprisingly temperate, but with no shade in sight Louis would have to be brief if he was to leave Marlow. A large, notably new visitor center with an asymmetrical peaked roof suggested that this local museum was in a completely different category from the last. He rolled the window down a few inches and cut the engine. The truck fell silent, and the glove compartment continued to hum. "You know I hate to leave you," he said to the dog, "But I won't be long. Just need to rule this place out."

Passing through the front door, Louis was first struck by the cool openness of the space. As his eyes adjusted, he found himself on a quaint old street after sundown: single-story brick and sided facades stood below a high ceiling, itself painted black and invisible but for tastefully concealed lights illuminating the false fronts below. The overall effect was reinforced by a tall street lamp glowing elegantly near the entrance. On the wall nearest the front door, a store display window stood beside a large, open gift shop designed to resemble an old mercantile with a pressed tin ceiling. A man in his early twenties wearing glasses and a beard sat behind a long wooden counter that divided the shop from the 'street.'

"Welcome," the young man said half-heartedly. "Come to look around?"

"I think so," Louis said. "I'm not sure. I really only have a minute, and there is a lot more going on in here than I thought there would be. Maybe I should have guessed that from all that… stuff outside."

"Oh, the village," confirmed the other man. Regarding Louis's incomprehension he explained, "Historic structures that were

258

donated to the society, then moved out to our complex and refurbished. You can tour those too: it's included with the six dollar admission to the gallery here."

"Right," Louis said, digging out his wallet. He paused, "I don't have much time right now, though. I could come back later, but I'm really just looking for information on one thing. Maybe you can tell me if you have anything on it?"

"Doubtful," the young man said skeptically. "Like you said, we have a lot. Unless it's something obvious, I won't pretend I have the answers."

"Fort Custer," Louis clarified.

The man's face lit up, "Something obvious, that's great! Might be our most popular exhibit."

"Would it take long to-"

"No," the young man waved, "That's not so big, if it's all you want to see. It is still six dollars though." Louis handed over a half dozen singles, which the young man put in a cash register. "Care to sign the guest book?" The man asked.

"Not really," Louis replied.

Disarmed but underwhelmed the young man said, "That's fine: not a requirement." He waved past the end of the counter to a large entryway in the next false storefront and said, "If you'd care to join me around the corner here…"

Louis moved as directed and found himself waiting by a heavy iron cage door that stood as a barrier between the shop counter and the dimly lit gallery. The young man swung the bars open and joined him. Louis asked, "They lock you up in there?"

Jokingly the man replied, "Some days it feels like that. Right this way please." He led Louis past assorted displays, professionally arranged and accompanied by a wealth of explanatory signs. Beyond a full-sized teepee and next to an original stage coach, the man stopped and motioned to a set of display cases behind a large table with a scale model. "This is Fort Custer. Take as much time as you like. Or as little, but that six bucks does cover the day."

Clifford

While the young man took his leave, Louis scanned the exhibit. He decided very quickly that the diorama, as thorough as it was, would be useless for what he was trying to find. Moving on to the glass cases, he looked over a trio of uniforms, a set of long rifles and sabers, a pistol and various pocket items, each with an accompanying caption explaining its function and provenance. Louis carefully reviewed each caption for any mention of Henry Strafford. He reflected that not so long ago, he would have instead taken notes on each item so that he could chase replicas for months afterward. It was an odd feeling for Louis, caring less about the stuff than about the story behind it, thinking at all about the man who may have owned it. Something about that felt noble, less superficial than he was used to, but he wondered if that was really the case. After all, Louis hadn't cared about Strafford on his own merits so much as he had about the man's role as focus of a scavenger hunt that he, Louis, was now personally invested in. Maybe it was just a case of Louis requiring something on which to fixate. Maybe he had unwittingly swapped hobbies.

In the final display, beside a winter weather outfit, three grainy photographs hung one above another. The lowest of them depicted two men in greatcoats, proudly facing a line of uniformed soldiers on horseback. The caption explained:

Colonel Nathan Dudley and Lieutenant Henry Strafford
Inspect the Cavalry
October, 1887

Louis leaned in and squinted, close enough that his breath began to fog the glass. He didn't recognize either of the men in the foreground. The officer nearest the camera, a heavyset man with a jovial expression, had a very full beard reminiscent of the other Strafford photos. But then again, so did half the cavalrymen. No, there was no mistaking: Henry Strafford was not in this picture.

Louis's stomach whined, and he thought about Marlow in the truck. He had only been inside for a few minutes, but even with

The Beard

mild weather and the window rolled down, it was August and he was not that kind of dog owner. Besides, staring at a picture wasn't going to change it. Louis straightened his back and walked briskly to the bright gift shop where the young man busied himself organizing children's books on a metal rack. "Excuse me," Louis interrupted.

"You finding everything okay?" the man asked without looking up.

Ignoring the question, Louis asked, "Who handles the captions in your gallery? Like, where does all that information come from?"

The man stopped what he was doing and stood thoughtfully. "That is a really good question," he said. "I think it depends: some donations come in with a story already, for others the historical society does the research... I'm not real sure to be honest."

"I think I found a mistake in one of them," Louis explained, "A guy the caption says is supposed to be in a photo wasn't in the photo."

"Interesting," the man said, turning back to the book shelf. "You should mention that to someone."

"Isn't that what I'm doing?"

"Oh," the man laughed. "No, not me. I'm only here for the summer. Friday is my last day. Between you and me, I'm not real invested in solving your problem. Not to mean I don't care, just that I don't have the information or the authority or anything."

"So you're saying it's above your pay grade."

"Yeah," the man confirmed, "That's a good way of putting it. The museum director will be in at two though. If you want to come back, I'm sure she would love to know more."

Louis thanked the man for his time and moved quickly to the parking lot. He wondered if it was really worth coming back after he had the trailer and the dog settled. His greatest hope when going into the place had been to learn if Strafford was at Fort Custer and in what capacity, and even though the photo caption was wrong, the name 'Lieutenant Henry Strafford' wouldn't have come from thin air. The mere existence of a rank and a date, even attached to the wrong picture, could still be viewed as the confirmation he was looking for.

But if the information was correct in any context, then in some ways it would prompt yet more questions: it would have required that Strafford dig ditches and take up collections as far East as Nebraska, then race westward to join up and earn the rank of lieutenant, before leaving the army to move East again to Iowa. It was certainly possible, if unexpected. But again, everything about this stop had been a little off.

Louis opened the door of the truck, and Marlow lifted his head to glance over. "Told you I wouldn't be long," Louis said, climbing into his seat. "I may have to come back later by myself." Louis reached over to scratch Marlow's ear, "Might be more for me to find. Or not."

He put the key in the ignition and paused. Something was off again, something minor, unimportant. Louis looked around. Nothing was wrong, but something was different: the humming in the glove box had stopped.

Day 8

And again, everything was perfectly still. The sun stared down from a cloudless, windless sky, and the temperature marched quickly from the 60's into the 80's. Some 100 yards distant, at the bottom of the short, steep incline, an overgrown lot stood vacant but for small piles of dirt and broken concrete. Beyond that, a chain link fence topped with barbed wire protected a string of run-down corrugated buildings, though from who or from what was unclear. Tim knew at this point to not expect any movement for another six hours, and even then only from a handful of vehicles at a warehouse far to his left. He was so bored.

Without getting up, Tim wriggled free of his nylon jacket. He folded it carefully in front of him and deposited it on top of a rolled up newspaper, a paperback, and a pair of binoculars that sat in the dry grass next to his camp chair. He would wait another hour before he started on the paper. Then, as he completed each section, he would alternate with twenty minutes of reading the novel. Sometime on Monday afternoon, he had discovered that varying his activities this way made the hours go by quicker. He wasn't sure why: something about the anticipation of the next activity, or the next installment of the same activity, made him feel more active than he really was.

That was important, because Tim had been extremely inactive. For five straight days now, he had taken his perch shortly after sunrise, beside an isolated tree, atop the earthen levee with the Feather River at his back. And he would stay in that position until dusk, rising only to follow the shade around the tree as the sun moved, or to duck down the hill to piss in the bushes. The only thing more sedentary than Tim, it seemed, was the neighborhood in which he found himself. He couldn't even watch the grass grow, as the grass had all died of dehydration. Although, as he often reminded himself, the unchanging scene would make it far easier to identify his quarry when they arrived. Tim supposed he should try to stay positive, given that he had no choice but to sit there.

This was definitely the spot: Yuba City, California, seventy yards west of the levee, just north of the former Dennis tract. If history was any indication, the people Tim was looking for would come through here, and in this exercise, history was Tim's only indication. As sure as he was of the place though, Tim could not be certain of the time, beyond the thirty day window he had determined. And even within those limits, he was forced to make some assumptions: he assumed, for instance, that his travel companions would make their appearance during daylight. This made some sense, as they would have less idea than Tim of what they were looking for and might consequently want to avoid grasping in the dark. Assuming further that Tim had to sleep sometime and couldn't be out all night long, binoculars in hand, naturally led him to assume that there was no point in camping illegally. Rather a happy accident that this combination of assumptions allowed him to retire to a hotel room each evening.

Still, there was no guarantee that they wouldn't come after dark. And if they did that, how would Tim ever be aware of it? He wouldn't: there would be no evidence of them, and he would be back out at sunrise for weeks on end, waiting like an asshole for someone who had been there and gone. For all Tim knew, that had already happened.

But he couldn't allow himself to think that way. He was well past the point of no return on this venture, and he had to either believe in it or scrap the whole thing. There was another three weeks left on the window he'd calculated. After that, even if this was a failure, he'd have done all he could to make a go of it. In the meantime there was nothing to do but to keep *faith*, to *trust*, to have *hope*. People would come because they were meant to come; it would happen while he was there to observe them because he was meant to be a part of this.

Faith. Trust. Hope. Tim hated it, hated all of it.

264

The Beard

This was not who he was, not how he lived his life, waiting with bated breath for the universe to hand him what he wanted. But he had to acknowledge that, like it or not, faith, trust, and hope had been at the core of his decision making for the last few months. How else could he justify obsessively chasing every verifiable detail of a random handwritten manuscript he'd found stuffed in the back of a closet? Or quitting his job and packing up his apartment to pursue what might well be a fiction? How else would he explain the money he'd spent on supplies, the time and energy he'd expended to get to this point?

Then again, he'd been stagnating back in Wyoming. He had hated that job, was sick of that apartment, and was desperate for someplace else to direct his time and energy. If Strafford's story was true, then Tim had confidence in his ability to follow it to the end. At the same time, if it did fall through, he was equally confident in his ability to recoup his losses and make a fresh start. So in truth, if faith had been the foundation of his decisions, but executing on those decisions required only a faith in his ability to control the outcomes, then perhaps this recent, chafing sense of destiny could be reframed as a sort of agency after all. With a wave of relief and security, Tim decided that really there was nothing to do but to keep *control*, to *know*, to have *confidence*.

And to wait.

Tim stood and stretched. He took a moment to pull his cargo shorts away from his crotch before resituating his chair a bit further east and closer to the tree. After shuffling his small pile of belongings in kind, he retook his seat and picked up his newspaper. Before he allowed himself the satisfaction of unfolding it, he took up his binoculars and slowly scanned the empty lot below.

Still nothing. No changes, no movement, and certainly no man with a colorful beard.

Day 10

Kristin decided she should probably stop. Just one more page, though. Then she would totally stop. She clicked the forward arrow with a sigh and pulled up another ten images of diamond rings. The fourth one down was nice, but she wasn't sure if it was nice for her. A little spendy. But all of them were, and she didn't have a clue what their price range would be. On the one hand, she didn't consider herself the kind of person who needed something fancy, but then again, if she was going to wear something for the rest of her life, she didn't want it to make her look cheap. It just had to be right. None of these were right... Was this even her job? Shouldn't Jared be making this decision?

He probably thought so. Kristin suspected that it would be important to him to choose the ring, but that he also didn't actually care what it looked like, which was a little unfair as, again, she would be the one stuck wearing it. She was still juggling a few ideas of how to approach this with him. The obvious choice would be to just talk about it, but then she would give up the surprise of being presented with it. She could, she supposed, be content with the spontaneity of the proposal itself, but the idea of receiving the ring... The image she had in mind precluded discussing engagement rings as though they were dinner options. Except as a last resort, if it looked like he would get it really wrong.

But Kristin believed that it might still be possible to get what she wanted in the way that she wanted if she left the right hints strewn about: a torn add for a jeweler here, an online marketplace page left open there. It could still work, but only if she was clear about what she wanted, and to be that, she first needed to decide what she wanted. With Jared out of the hotel room, it had felt like a good opportunity for her to pursue that. But still, she should probably stop. Right after the next page, she probably should.

The Beard

Jared coming back was only part of the issue. The whole reason he had gone out was to call his boss, cash in the last of his paid leave, and argue for an advance of some of next year's vacation time. If they continued for a couple more weeks, as it increasingly seemed would be necessary, they would cross into unpaid leave, which was hardly a recipe for ring money. It was a catch-22 of a sort: Jared had suggested they stop over in Vegas once they got that far west, but to get that far west with their maps could take a few weeks, by which point they would have to watch their spending. Alternatively, a final destination that didn't require as much time and money wouldn't be as far as Las Vegas, and Kristin wasn't sure how that might affect the terms of Jared's proposal. She had every reason to expect that he would still follow through when they got home, but was almost afraid to ask him: his mood was still a bit touchy for some reason.

In any case, it would likely be months before she could responsibly pester him for the ring she deserved. And if they were married for some time before he could afford it, did she still get to ask for an engagement ring, post-engagement? Yes, Kristin decided, she could and she would. But, for now, she was just teasing herself and inviting a potentially unpleasant conversation. She let the cursor hover over the link to the next page of images. Resolutely, she forced the arrow across the screen and closed the window.

So that was that. Now what?

Kristin had volunteered to map the next leg of their journey. They wouldn't leave for two more days, but they needed to do some advance work before that, and Jared would have to shave that night to stay on track. But as it was only two in the afternoon, Kristin had not yet taken the necessary photos, so that would have to wait for his return. Another option: they still hadn't found a connection between Strafford and Fort Sam Houston. Jared usually handled that, but he hadn't gotten around to it yet. Kristin wasn't sure he wouldn't be territorial about the task, but then, he had been gone for a while, and now she was bored, so really it was his fault.

Clifford

Kristin opened a search engine and stared at it thoughtfully. They had tried searching for every variation of Strafford's name a hundred times to no avail, so the most obvious places to begin would be pointless. But there had to be something else, something they were missing. Some clue or pattern... What did they know about him so far?

Henry Strafford was a soldier: that he was career military might be the only thing they were sure of. So, if he died an officer, then at some point he must have joined the army, and the government would have written that down somewhere. Even if that record didn't address their most recent stop, it might provide insight to the next one, or the one after that.

Kristin typed the words 'United States Army Enlistment' into the search bar. It answered with a page of links about how to join the army. Kristin nodded; she should have expected that. To her original search term she added the word 'Database.' After a moment's consideration she added the word 'Free.' The top ten results provided databases of World War II enlistments. "Okay," she mumbled to the computer screen, "Getting closer." Kristin opened an advanced search for the amended term but excluding the words 'World War.' The top response was titled, *Registers of Enlistments in the U.S. Army, 1798- 1914.* "That's the ticket," Kristin mumbled to the page.

Following links to a collection of images organized by blocks of alphabetical names and years, Kristin once again found herself compulsively clicking from one page to the next, this time shopping for one man amongst an army- *The* Army- reduced to so many lines in a ledger. Across each pair of pages, an embellished script recorded each man's name, his age, date and place of enlistment, place of birth, and occupation. Over and over again, Kristin skimmed the left column and clicked to the next page, settling into a hypnotic rhythm as hundreds of soldiers, now thousands of them, marched down the screen for her review.

This had to be right, Kristin was sure of it. This wasn't some internet search where the universe could choose to omit Henry

268

The Beard

Strafford. This was the official record of what would have been the start of his illustrious career, as permanent and unchanging as the words carved in stone at Arlington. Kristin pressed through the S's, from 1883 into 1884. According to his headstone, Strafford had been born in July of 1860, so she wouldn't expect that he could have enlisted prior to 1878, although he could have lied about his age at some point.

Still, playing the odds meant finishing with this ledger before she tried a different block of years. He had to be in one of these... And there he was. Plain as day: Strafford, Henry was enlisted in December of 1884 at San Antonio by one Lieutenant Hickey. The ledger went on to list that he was twenty-four years old, born in Pittsburgh, and worked as a laborer. Also according to the register, he had brown eyes and hair, fair complexion, and measured five foot nine. In a long column on the right hand side, under the heading 'Remarks' was scribbled the short note, "Apptd Ord Sergt."

There was so much information here, and she had found it. And it still didn't tell her what she wanted to know, gave her nothing about where this was going. Kristin leaned forward and focused on the screen as though more answers would emerge from the page, if she could just stare long enough without blinking. The door closed heavily on the other end of the room. "Hey," Kristin tossed over her shoulder, "C'mere. You need to see this."

Jared mumbled something in the other direction. More audibly he called, "You want to give me a second?"

Kristin looked up. Jared was soaked, his hair and clothes dripping on the carpet, a six-pack of beer under one arm. She asked, "Is everything okay?"

"Raining out," Jared said while he kicked off his shoes and socks, "And Mr. Sherman was in a pissy mood."

Kristin watched him set down the soggy six-pack and peel off his shirt. She noted that beyond the stark tan line on his biceps, his chest now seemed a little tighter than before, his belly slightly less soft, and his ribs more apparent. Above the limit of his beard,

Clifford

Jared's cheek bones were also a touch more angular than they had been. Whether it was the sun or their activity, something about this trip was leaving him lean. Kristin followed up, "Is there going to be a problem?"

"No," he answered quickly, "Just... I have it under control." Kristin looked skeptically from Jared to the beer and back again. Finally he asked, "What?"

"Nothing," she said. "You're just acting weird is all."

"Yeah... Well... I just had an awkward phone call, and I'm drenched."

"Okay," Kristin nodded grudgingly. She patted the corner of the bed nearest her chair and said, "Well, come over here, I need to show you something, and then I need to borrow your face."

Jared crossed the room and settled as suggested. Kristin turned the computer to face him, and he quietly reviewed the image on the screen. "Enlistment register?" he asked softly.

"Yeah," Kristin confirmed. "I figured if he died in the army, he had to have joined it at some point." Reaching over to scroll right, she continued, "Look at all the information here. This is huge: now we know more of what he looked like, we know where he's from, what he did for a living. And it confirms his age when he died. Not sure about this other part, the Apt Oared Surge-"

"Appointed Order of Sergeant, I'm guessing," Jared interrupted in the same low tone. After another pause, he continued thoughtfully, "When we started, I thought we were just supposed to figure out some fact about how he died. But then we kept finding him after the sinking of the Maine: reviewing troops, buying into some land scheme, and I figured he must have been reported dead by mistake, that maybe that was what we were searching for, the source of that mistake, or..." Jared's voice built gradually in volume, tempo and intensity. "Then we did Arkansas and we found him the year before the boat sank, and now we've found him almost fifteen years before, and if we keep working backwards, wherever we go next he won't even be in the army, so whatever we're following can't have anything to do with how he died. We

270

have to be looking for something about his life, maybe something he did or something that happened to him, either way something *before* the start of his career and now we're at the start of his career and-,"

"And all of that means what, exactly?"

"I don't know," Jared answered excitedly, his eyes wider now, "I don't know what it means but it does mean something. It means we reached a benchmark in his life. He was only twenty-four when he enlisted, so whatever we need to find, it can't be much before that. Whatever it is, whatever it means, we're getting close now, I'm sure of it." He turned suddenly toward Kristin and asked, "Where do we go next?"

Kristin answered evenly, "I don't know. But if you shut your face and let me look it, I will find out."

Eighth Growth

Day 2

California was not at all what Louis had expected. He had seen the T.V. shows, seen the movies, seen T.V. shows about the movies, and movies about T.V. shows; yet here it was, the most glamorous state in the union, and not a swimming pool or starlet to be had. He was vaguely familiar with the term, 'wine country,' but felt pretty sure that this was not that either. The area was mostly farms, but those too were not the farms that Louis had come across elsewhere, and again, not what he'd imagined for California. Nebraska, now those had been farms: for hundreds of miles he'd never lost sight of the walls of cornstalks as tall as his truck.

And that was what he'd expected of Nebraska. He'd held no preconceived notions of Wyoming, so was consequently not disappointed by that, and the ranges of central Montana looked like 'Big Sky Country'. After these had given over to crumbling hills and scattered pines, to jutting purple shadows of distant mountains around every bend, he had clipped through the corner of Idaho which looked like... looked like Idaho, he guessed. The part of it he'd seen was the same brand of pretty as Western Montana, which made Louis feel guilty for never having formed a thought of that state apart from potatoes, which he had *not* seen in Idaho. Nevada, on the other hand, was entirely and unmistakably Nevadan.

The compass had routed him some distance from every population center between Bozeman and Reno, and in a way, he was grateful for having seen the 'real' country: unspoiled, unmolested, the way it really was. At the same time, he wondered if it was fair to label the more rural or idyllic portions of his path as 'real.' After all, for the majority of 'real' people living in these states, reality was what went on in the cities and towns where they lived: the very same centers that Louis felt so fortunate to have avoided. Even Louis, whose personal reality was a clearing in the woods in McNairy County, recognized that his was not a lifestyle enjoyed by most people. That was what made it special, the fact that it was uncommon, which could be called less 'real' by extension. Perhaps the better word for this route was natural, not pristine but... original.

That is, until about twenty-five miles back. Ever since Louis had emerged from the wooded foothills north of Oroville, he had been confronted by a constantly shifting mix of agriculture. Rolling pastures flattened into expansive fields, whose organized rows of grain abruptly lowered and solidified into rows of alfalfa, only to spring vertically and harden once more into carefully planted lines of trees whose intended yield Louis could not guess. For some time after crossing what he assumed to be the Sacramento River, these orchards had become even more pronounced, taller and fuller along a wide irrigation canal that ran behind a berm parallel with the two-lane highway. But fronting every inch of it, the shoulder of the road, baked and cracked, belied the region's ongoing drought and drew the eye between the fields and their columns of lush productivity, to evenly spaced paths of desiccated soil that had not felt rain in months.

This land, these farms, were no less engineered and deliberate than a housing development, and the affect made the landscape and everything in it feel fake and superficial. So perhaps a bit like the California Louis had pictured after all. But that assessment wasn't fair either. After all, it wasn't as though corn naturally sprang up across the full length of Nebraska every year, and in Wyoming he had seen firsthand the lengths to which men, including Henry Strafford, had gone to irrigate an arid countryside.

If anything, perhaps the difference between those places and this was the honesty of it all. Maybe by virtue of its blatancy, the California landscape was actually less false than the others. There was no attempt to hide the seams or conceal the intentionality of their crops, few realistic claims to nativism, and no pretense of organic spontaneity: this was a land of transplants, unapologetically shaped with nothing but usefulness in mind. Louis savored that idea for a moment. Over the preceding weeks he had, for the first

276

time in his life, been a tourist, a stranger, and an outsider. Far from being welcomed as exotic, he had gotten the impression at every point along the way that people looked forward to his moving on so they could get back to their business, and he had not blamed them.

But here more than anywhere else, Louis sensed a chance to be a stranger in a land of strange things. It was very inviting, the notion of arriving at a place where he didn't belong but where no other thing belonged any more or less than he. The opportunity to not mean anything to anybody, and that without the world's judgment, struck Louis like a cool breeze cutting through the scorching, cloudless sky. Maybe after he had followed this to its conclusion, after the compass had finally left him alone, maybe he could call a couple realtors and start putting a plan together...

Louis's eyes wandered from the road and rested on the picture of his family attached to the dash. He was doing it again, exactly what Carolyn said he always did, getting grandiose and chasing pipe dreams without considering anyone else. Louis hated that she was always right, but she was. And he hated that he missed her, but he did. He missed all of them. He realized at that moment that it wouldn't matter how far he traveled or how long he stayed: he could never again be a stranger when there were people in the world who knew him so well. He needed to get back to that, back to them. He would follow the compass for this stop, and then he would turn around. No back roads, just a straight line eastward and home.

Marlow whined on the other end of the bench seat, jarring Louis from his revelation. He looked up to the compass and answered, "Still says t'go straight. Dunno what yer bitchin' about." The dog sat up and huffed, flapping his jowls insistently. "I'm serious," Louis said, "You begged to come with me today, you have no right gettin' stir crazy. Settle in, enjoy the scenery."

This leg of the trip had been unusually long, and after a couple frustrating days of dragging the Shasta through mountains and forests, Louis had decided to give himself a break. His campground was within a half day's drive of the coast, so he had decided to

Clifford

ditch the trailer and head out until he reached the ocean, or until the compass gave up or changed directions. Based on his previous stop, he thought he might leave more of his options open by not having the dog with him, but Marlow had been insistent and inconsolable, and in the end, Louis had given in and welcomed him back to his position as copilot. Even as Marlow continued to fidget across the cab, Louis felt that it had been the right call- the clear and temperate morning had turned into an oppressively hot mid-day, and it was just as well that both of them were in the air-conditioned vehicle.

The compass needle wavered briefly to the right and Louis jerked the wheel involuntarily before consulting the road in front of him. His antique nav system appeared to be back to its genteel ways, but he still couldn't drive completely blind. Feathering the brakes, Louis observed a brown sign along the shoulder, posting a white arrow and the words 'Point of Historical Interest.' Might this be the point of Louis's interest? The arrow pointed over a cornfield to a cell tower a couple hundred yards away. He mumbled to himself, "Now, what is this about?"

Slowing the vehicle, he looked to the compass, which again held straight ahead. Louis idled past a crossroads, and the needle slumped heavily to his right, coming to rest in the direction of an embankment, beyond which sat another small orchard: relatively short, but densely planted. He pulled back around to the cross street and scouted a point along the gravel shoulder wide enough to safely disembark. He cut the engine, and the cab of the truck immediately started to warm. The compass, true to form, had followed Louis's movements around the corner and remained fixated on a point in the shade between the trees.

Marlow looked to Louis and began panting. "I know," Louis said. "Best get to it. Don't think it'll cool down any." He reached to the dash for his cigarettes. As he opened the door, he looked down to the dusty ground and the dead grass that carpeted the roadside. As he returned the pack to its home, Louis observed, "We're only here for a day. Suppose we can't be burnin' shit down." Marlow

278

stepped impatiently through Louis's lap and jumped out ahead of him, advancing into the trees and out of sight. "Dammit dog!" Louis called after him. "Them's m'balls! You ain't a Yorkie for chrissake!"

Louis slowly gathered himself and climbed into the relentlessly clear day. From his vantage on the elevated road bed, he could make out the hazy line of distant hills running across the horizon behind the cornfield that surrounded the 'Historical' cell tower. In front of him, lording over the small orchard from the opposite side, the tops of palm trees sat motionless in the still air. For all his philosophizing, all of it together still struck him as a clusterfuck. He picked his way down the short embankment and ducked below the boughs that extended over the space between the first rows of trees.

As Louis pressed further in, dappled shade alternated with glaring sun to disorienting affect. He pulled his cap lower over his eyes and focused on the compass and the task at hand. With each column of shade, the foliage became thicker, but he still couldn't tell what kind of trees these were. He didn't see any fruit, but the perfectly level rows of soft earth that had been scraped from the dead grass to accommodate them suggested that whatever these were intended to grow was worth something to someone. This land had been worked over enough, carefully prepared enough, for Louis to assume that there was nothing left of whatever had been here in Strafford's day.

From the outside, this particular manufactured forest had seemed tiny, but now that he was in it, ducking through row after row, the branches scraping the top of his cap with each burst of daylight, it felt interminable. The shadows became darker, the flashes of sun more jarring, as he navigated entirely from the compass now. While the needle bent and spun, Louis became aware of the sun beating down on his neck and of the crunch of gravel beneath his boots. Looking up, he realized that he had at some point wandered to the limit of the orchard, and now stood on a wide access road facing a perfectly straight irrigation ditch. The compass pointed to his left at an angle back into the trees. He took a large step backwards and the needle went slack.

So, this spot was *the* spot. Louis turned a full circle in place and knelt to examine the ground. As he suspected, there was nothing to see apart from the wide band of packed dust between the orchard and the water, just another random place with nothing to go on. But that had not stopped them before. He anticipated the two usual options: try to track the land or try to track the man, knowing that whichever he chose would lead to the other. Based on experience, it was all but guaranteed that someone around here knew something about this place, but finding that person might be a challenge.

The last town Louis had driven past was Hamilton City, which was more than ten miles away and too small to offer much. Chico was big enough to have some resources... But it was already afternoon, and he was a few hours from his campground. Not to mention that he had the dog with him which... where was that fuzzy bastard, anyways?

From the corner of his eye, Louis sensed movement amongst the trees two rows away. Waiting in a crouch, he watched as Marlow's large head emerged and sniffed at the air. The dog took two steps forward, doubled back, and began to lift his leg. "Hey!" Louis shouted, "That ain't the kind of water that tree needs." Marlow turned to look Louis in the eye while he lowered his hindquarters into a squat. Louis began to object, but stopped himself. "Don't suppose fertilizin' hurts anyone. Hurry it up. Time we get goin'."

Day 3

Jared wrapped the tail of his T-shirt around his hand and gripped the crimped edge of a bottle cap. It gave up with a firm twist and a sharp hiss, and he let it fall to the threadbare, stained carpet. He leaned back in his chair, to such extent that the cheap wooden frame allowed, and enjoyed a long pull from his bottle before placing it on the round, wobbly wood laminate table. He maneuvered his seat nearer to the chipped, hollow core front door, thereby reducing the glare cast on the television by the weak light that filtered through streaked windows and paper-thin drapes. On the screen, a muted daytime court show had just commenced, and beyond this, on the side of the bed nearest the bathroom, Kristin picked up her suitcase, moved it five feet to the left, and dropped it again.

"Hey," Jared said, "Since you're up, would you mind turning the volume on?"

Without facing him, Kristin said tersely, "You have the remote."

Jared reached to the table and mashed the buttons on a thick universal control, already knowing how useless this would be. "Doesn't work," he said, tossing it back with a clatter and retrieving his beer. "I would call the front desk about it, but I'm not real sure they'd give a shit."

Kristin straightened up, took three steps and poked at the front of the dusty television, tweaking the audio into action. Without pause she turned around, moved between Jared and the screen, and began dragging covers off of the bed.

Jared craned his neck to look past her, but quickly grew bored with the effort. "What are you up to anyway?" he asked.

"I," Kristin answered, continuing to separate the sheets from a blanket, "Am getting rid of the comforter." She carefully peeled back the discolored, floral patterned fabric and began to fold it into smaller and smaller squares. Without further provocation she mumbled, "Because it is fucking disgusting. Like everything about this room."

Jared took another drink and tried to focus on the T.V. It was obvious to him that an argument was coming. Kristin would continue to bait him with small jabs until she forced his participation, and he would react because it was the only way to stop her. All of this would happen eventually, and Jared knew that the sooner he let it happen, the sooner he could have it over and done with. But for now, he had to ignore her on principle. If she wanted the fight, he would make her work harder for it than some pissy comments under her breath.

Sensing his resistance, Kristin stiffly carried the folded fabric to the edge of the room near her suitcase and dropped it heavily to the floor. To the corner she loudly observed, "I swear to god this place is gonna' give at least one of us scabies."

"Alright!" Jared said, exasperated, "I fucking get it: you hate the room! What do you want me to do about it? I don't fuckin' work here."

Turning around, Kristin shot back, "You could've let us stay at the last place! It was less than two hours from here-,"

"Yeah," Jared nodded, "And cost two times as much. We don't need to pay a premium to have a hotel in the middle of San Antonio when our next stop is in Austin."

"But this *Mo*-tel isn't even *in* Austin," Kristin pointed out, "And I *would* pay a premium for clean sheets and less spunk on the rugs."

"Is that your hang-up?" Jared demanded, "That you had to downgrade from a Hotel to a Motel?"

"No," Kristin stated, unmoved, "My hang-up is downgrading from a Hotel to a *Shit*-hole!"

"Yeah, well..." Jared trailed off and took another drink. Surveying the stains on the floors he muttered, "Probably not *too* much of that is spunk."

The Beard

Unwilling to let it slide, Kristin said decisively, "Any spunk is too much spunk."

Jared leaned back and pretended to shift his focus to the court show, more willing to sacrifice his pride outright than to stake it on a debate over what constituted acceptable levels of strangers' semen in their accommodations. That, he admitted to himself, was an argument that he could not feel good about winning. On top of which, any continued attempt to extoll the benefits of the room could only end one way, because the room only had one benefit: it was cheap. And if he belabored that point to an extent that suggested cheapness was necessary, he felt it would cause Kristin undue stress.

Jared told himself that there was no need for that, that even if his situation warranted some belt tightening, required some extra caution, he still had everything under control. However true that might be, though, it wouldn't stop Kristin from worrying, and that wouldn't be helpful to either of them. With or without that conversation, the very best thing they could do was keep moving. They had come so far and were getting so close, he could... he could just feel it. Once they found what they were looking for, then they would be free to go work out all the rest. All they had to do to finish this was to tread lightly and stay their course, with no frills.

But Jared hadn't considered that his forced asceticism might cause Kristin as much stress as a conversation about money would have. Maybe there was a balance to strike. He would have to work harder to find it. Jared absent-mindedly tipped the bottle back once more before gently setting it down and using the edge of his hand to brush some kind of black dust from the table top. Kristin stepped into the bathroom and back out, came around the bed with a thin bath towel in her hand, and spread it across the corner of the mattress before sitting down atop of it across from Jared.

He said drily, "If that's how you feel about sitting on it, I'm not sure how you'll do sleeping."

Ignoring the comment, Kristin put a hand on Jared's knee. Nodding to the trio of empties on the table, she said, "You should pace yourself. It's not even seven o'clock, and it's the fourth night in a week. I worry about you."

Jared shrugged. He breathed, "It's under control. Everything is under control. I'm fine."

"Are you though?" Kristin asked concernedly. "I don't want to... I know you're on vacation, but... It isn't just the drinking, is what I mean. The last couple of weeks you've been quiet. Sullen, I guess."

Jared sat thoughtfully before responding, "I don't know. I haven't noticed. I definitely don't feel different. A little tired maybe, we've been living out of a suitcase for a while now, it's not something I'm used to."

"One month tomorrow," Kristin observed.

"Really?" Jared asked. "So maybe I miss my own bed is all. Yeah, that's probably all it is."

Kristin leaned forward, peering intensely into his eyes. In a tone both deliberate and sincere she asked, "Is it time to call it? Are you ready to go home?"

"No!" Jared answered more quickly and loudly than intended. He heard the panic in his voice and forced an odd smile before casually continuing, "We don't have to go back on my account, and not when we're so close. At least, I feel like we're really close, do... Do you think we're close?"

"That wasn't the question," Kristin said, maintaining eye contact, "Are *you* ready to go home yet?"

Jared returned her gaze and took a moment to consider his response. He knew the answer: to keep going was the only answer, really, and it was important, and he was sure, just sure, that it was the right thing for both of them, somehow in both of their best interests, long term. But he recognized now, as he stared into Kristin's dark eyes, that even if he knew what was best, he would have to convince her that it was best. To do that he would have to be careful of how much he presented and of how he presented it. He would have to stay positive, to break things down in a way that was manageable and unintimidating. He would have to keep her looking forward *with* him instead of looking back *at* him.

"Not yet," Jared said brightly. "But it won't be too much longer anyways. I mean, we still have several days to find the next stop and explore the city a little, but before you know it, we'll move on. One more stop, maybe two, and I predict we'll be done. And besides, don't you want to see if we get as far as Las Vegas?"

Kristin's eyes narrowed skeptically as she allowed a faint smile to form at the corners of her mouth. "Of course, I do," she said softly, "I just don't want to break you getting there."

Jared graciously patted the back of her hand and offered, "I'll be alright. I am alright."

Kristin nodded her understanding and kissed Jared's forehead as she stood up. She retrieved the towel from the bed and said, "You know this room is not alright though, right?"

"Yeah, it blows pretty hard," Jared sighed, reclining into the uncomfortable chair again. He tipped back the last of his beer and swallowed before conceding, "I think we're stuck for tonight. Tomorrow afternoon, we can work out something better."

Day 4

Louis wasn't sure he should be there. But no one had stopped him, so maybe it was okay. It didn't matter: he was into it now, either way.

He pinched the bridge of his nose and closed his eyes. He moved on to rubbing his face, removed his ball cap with one meaty hand, and scratched his scalp with the other. Resignedly, he pulled the hat back on and low over his brow. More microfilm, more newspapers, and the beginnings of a migraine: these were his rewards for starting at the library.

Although he hadn't exactly started at *this* library; even after his weeks of trial and error, Louis was still fool enough to hold out for divine inspiration. With no good notion of where to begin, he had tooled around the handful of small towns that littered Glenn County, California. He had considered the courthouse in Willows, but decided he didn't know what he should ask for, let alone who to ask for it. He had tried a few branch locations of the regional library system: exceedingly modest affairs in the county seat and Hamilton City, plus an adorable Carnegie library dropped on the highway at Bayliss.

It hadn't taken much to exhaust their resources, but Louis had made some use of their public computer terminals: a basic search of online maps showed the compass's orchard as having a town name of Jacinto. Jacinto, CA, he had learned, was an unincorporated township and the historic home of a Dr. Hugh Glenn, after whom Glenn County was named. The internet had further explained that Dr. Glenn was a famous farmer who was infamously murdered in 1883. There had been no mention of Henry Strafford, but even that much explanation told Louis who had owned the land at around the time Strafford must have been there: an unlikely clue to flesh out, but the only one Louis had.

The Beard

And so, out of desperation, he had finally found his way back to Chico. The city was on the opposite side of the river and in the wrong county, but it was big enough to host a library or museum where even Louis might find a collection to sink his teeth into. What he had not considered was that the city might be too big for a person to just show up and stumble onto any of those places. After ninety minutes of aimless wandering, he had parked his ride, swallowed his pride, and asked a group of young people in a parking lot if they could point him to the library. Their directions had sent him on foot into the CSU campus, to the largest library he had ever seen.

He allowed that it was possible that he had walked *past* larger without ever knowing it, but his brief stint at college had not included any trips *to* the library. He now wondered how different his life might have been if it had. Probably not very. He still hated classrooms. He wasn't completely sure yet that he didn't hate academic libraries just as much. At a minimum, he felt like he was trespassing. In any case, a place this large must have what he needed, even if he did not know what that was. For lack of a better idea, he had asked the staff to steer him toward their old newspapers.

Louis hadn't been at it for long, and the work was proceeding quickly. Right or wrong, he had begun his search with the assumption that Strafford would have been local in the late 1870's, early 1880's. Since he knew that the man had reached Wyoming by the fall of '83, he decided to start in September of that year and work backwards. The two geographically closest newspapers on microfilm from that time period looked to be *The San Francisco Chronicle* and *The Fresno Republican.* San Francisco was closer, but Louis decided to kick off with Fresno because it looked like there were multi-year gaps in the collection, and he thought he could eliminate it more quickly. On top of that, he had discovered that the Fresno paper was a weekly, so skimming the headlines, while ignoring national and international stories as well as fiction and advertisements, he had cruised through six months' worth in less than an hour.

Louis didn't want to congratulate himself just yet, not before he had found the connection to Strafford, but he tentatively believed that he was getting kind of good at this... now that he was on his last stop, of course. After this was finished, he had been thinking that he might be able to find some use for these newfound, albeit limited, skills: hitting the books, stopping at courthouses, reading more history, it could really help him to develop his re-enactment character. If he still cared about that. He wasn't so sure.

Louis was discovering that having seen a larger chunk of the world had affected his view of it more than he'd expected and much more than he'd wished. Every stranger he'd met, seen, or simply become aware of, every darkened farmhouse he'd driven past, every oncoming vehicle had made his little corner of Tennessee and his group of familiars seem smaller: no less significant per se, not to him, but incredibly isolated and isolating. To see how much of the country had been sitting outside of his view, to recognize all these people who'd been living their whole lives while he wasn't looking... Louis wasn't stupid, he'd understood all of this conceptually, but to witness it firsthand, to experience the actual escape of moving amongst strangers, had made his preferred form of escapism look paltry and obscene. And perhaps it had been.

Perhaps his interest in wearing a bygone army's uniform and surrounding himself with people he'd known all his life had really just been about getting permission to play pretend, about ceding responsibility for his own bad decisions by projecting himself into a personage who'd made their last and worst decisions a century and a half earlier. At the very least, he had to acknowledge that his collection of period-appropriate items had been a distraction and a crutch. Louis resolved that when he got home, he would be *home*: he would lead *his* life, find *his* work, make his own money and raise his own kids. Hell, he didn't even need to wait that long: he could call Carolyn as soon as he reached the truck, set up a time in

The Beard

the next week or so to figure out what they could do, not what Louis might day-dream they would do, but ways they could actually move forward.

Yes, Louis thought, he would do that. From now on he would be grounded, he would live in the actual world, the larger world beyond McNairy County and including it. He would be realistic, decisive, and *present*.

Louis realized that he had been staring blankly at the microfilm reader, reflecting on being present for several minutes without reading anything. He gave himself a light slap on the face, shook his head, and worked to regain his focus. He gave the plastic knob on the reader a slight twist and watched the vertical columns lurch forward and briefly transform into a horizontal blur. He let go suddenly, and the reel responded, halting on the front page of an issue dated Saturday, February 24, 1883. Dwarfed by advertisements for "The Choicest Land," "Provisions," and the "Gregory Spraying Pump!," the lead item at the top of the page bore the relatively small heading, "Murdered His Friend."

Within the first two lines, Louis confirmed that the article was a report of the murder of Dr. Hugh Glenn of Jacinto, CA. The next two paragraphs were a straightforward description of what Louis had seen online: on February 13, 1883, Dr. Hugh Glenn was shot in the head by a former employee named Huram Miller. Miller was, according to the article, "An unfortunate inebriate whom Dr. Glenn had befriended and assisted during a number of years past." He had been employed by Dr. Glenn as a bookkeeper in the weeks before the shooting, but was "Discharged for drunkenness." On the day in question, Dr. Glenn passed his former friend on the porch of the Jacinto Hotel when the latter, "Raised his gun and fired, only a distance of ten feet separating them. The whole charge took effect in the doctor's head, tearing away a portion of the skull about the size of a large hen's egg…"

The article then gave a short mention of the victim's convalescence, followed by the description, "Miller fled but was pursued by R.M. Cocheran and John Marran in a buggy, and **H.S.**

Strafford on a horse, and when they neared him they hallooed to him to surrender, when he drew up his gun as if to shoot, and Cocheran, who had a Henry rifle, then fired one shot at the ground near Miller's feet, and again called on him to surrender. Miller refusing to do this, and still presenting his gun, Cocheran again fired, hitting Miller in the leg, just above the knee..." "Miller then threw away the gun, and was taken into custody and brought to Willows, where his wound- a flesh one- was dressed."

From that point the article devolved into a lecture on the evils of intemperance, followed by the statement, *"The Republican* is not given to reading temperance lectures, but..." There was no more mention of Strafford or of his role at Jacinto. But maybe that was okay. If nothing else, it was what Louis had come for: the place, the man, and the event.

Louis pressed the print button on the microfilm reader, realizing as he did so that he would have absolutely no use for a copy of the article. It wasn't the sort of thing he could justify framing, it would really only be meaningful to him, and it would consequently end up in a drawer somewhere. Still, being at the end of the trail as he was, Louis felt compelled to take some kind of souvenir on principle. Otherwise, what would be the point of the whole journey?

Louis rewound the reel and collected his one-page-trophy. Not wanting to be noticed, but also not wanting to be discourteous, he gave the librarian nearest the exit a small nod and two-point-five seconds of eye contact. Back in the parking lot, Louis left his driver's door hanging open while he leaned over the bench seat, popped open the glove box, and dug out his cell phone. He scrolled down to Carolyn's number, then paused and set down the device while he folded his printed-article-keepsake in half.

Souvenirs aside, he wondered what had been the point of the whole journey. Walking away with some over-exposed print-out couldn't possibly be worth the mileage. So, some soldier-turned-ditch-digger-turned-good-Samaritan who apparently owned a compass had led him all over creation for what then? To be

The Beard

remembered? Memorialized? And what made that guy so damn special, that he thought he deserved a remembrance? The whole conclusion just felt so anticlimactic: Louis had assumed for most of the trip that the end would present him with a full explanation, that he would *see* something, *learn* something, but no, not any of that. So, was he supposed to *do* something?

Fuck it. Louis had done enough.

Thousands of miles over several weeks, and he still had nothing to show for it. He crumpled the article in one hand and threw it into the glove box before slamming the compartment. After reconsidering for a moment, he yanked it back open and violently snatched the metal compass off the dash. Stupid piece of shit that it was, he never should have paid the five dollars for it. At the same time, he knew that, given his decision to follow a broken compass, he couldn't heap too much blame onto an inanimate object. But even as objects go, what a piece of shit: all scratched and gouged, the lid all bent and... where had that lid got to anyways?

Louis tossed the compass onto the seat and stretched his arm into the passenger floor space. In the shadow under the seat, between a fast food wrapper and a fugitive bolt from god knew what, Louis felt the flat metal cap with its deep cleft down the center. With a groan, he pushed himself upright and returned his attention to disposing of the compass. As Louis moved to cover it, the needle twitched reflexively to the North before settling itself to the Southeast.

He stopped and stared. He could *not* keep playing with this damn thing: the entire situation had gotten ridiculous. But southeast... that was the quickest way home. Whatever the compass was pointing to, he would probably drive right past anyways. And he had gotten pretty good at following the thing, so he wouldn't lose but half a day, one day tops.

But he wouldn't hunt for more answers, he promised himself that much. If the trail turned, or it led to some bullshit vacant lot somewhere, that would be that, he wouldn't even stop the truck: he could be finished, and the compass could go out the window. And that was *only* if he, Louis, *decided* to sacrifice the extra day. He sat and thought for a very long moment before he scooped his various possessions off the seat, dumped the compass back onto the dash, and tossed the cell phone into the glove box.

Fuck it. Louis could manage just one more stop.

Day 5

The black Jetta idled between a pair of stout brick columns that anchored a rusting, blocks long chain link fence. It then passed slowly through a once elegant wrought iron gate now peeling in an errant pocket of sunlight, propped open and twisted by a piece of broken concrete. To the left of the vehicle, either a small wooded park or a large wooded lot opened up past the barriers. The trees were old and dense enough to bathe the manicured grass in a deep shade, but were pruned and spaced enough to afford a view of what lie beyond them: a series of squat, single-story buildings with pitched roofs presented as a sprawl of brown brick with long, mint-colored panels, institutional in the spirit of a 1960's middle school.

The road bent gradually between a rusted Victorian fountain and a grand old limestone building. This last structure was strikingly asymmetrical with one long, L-shaped wing opposite a short stub, but it compensated by drawing the eye to a massive, three story central portico with an octagonal cupola. The whole was announced by a campy wooden sign as "Administration Building 501." The car coasted away from the trees, and sunlight washed through the windshield. Past the dirty glass and a hood dotted with dusty water spots, beyond the stately building and its expansive lawns, another hodge-podge of brown and mint bungalows huddled at a distance.

Kristin asked, "Where are you going?"

"Not sure," Jared answered, casually guiding the car forward. "I'm following signs for 'Admissions.'" Kristin began to answer and Jared cut her off, "Before you say anything about, 'Oh, you always go for the tallest building,' I think it's the best call this time." Kristin again started to speak, but Jared continued, "We keep ending up in these facilities: army bases, hospitals. How are we supposed to know where to start? I figure most people start with 'Admissions,' so there should be someone there we can talk to."

Clifford

"If you're done," Kristin jumped in, "I was going to say that, in this case, the tallest building is where the map goes. At least I think it does: I'm still not sure what to do with those weird little loops at the end. Either way, the building looks important to me, and we just passed it."

"It doesn't look like a hospital, though."

"None of this looks like a hospital," Kristin observed.

"Well, the sign on the gate disagrees with you," Jared said confidently.

"That's the other thing," Kristin said as Jared eased to a stop at an intersection. "The gate, the fence, the signs… One of them said something about contraband and vehicle searches. Are we meant to be wandering around here?"

"I don't know," Jared said, "But now we are, so what's your point?"

Kristin continued thoughtfully, "If we find some admissions department and start asking questions, they might make us leave before we find anything. But if we follow the map, we could get to the end. Or, worst case, somebody asks what we're doing and we plead ignorance: tell them we're lost because no one told us where to go, which will still technically be true, so long as we don't ask anybody."

Unable to dispute her logic, Jared reprised, "So you advocate sneaking around."

Kristin sighed, "We're not *sneaking*, we're getting lost on purpose, like if... Just turn here. Loop back to the big building, find someplace to park."

Jared shook his head and followed her directions. Away from the main road, the buildings and grounds were less finished than functional: trees were spaced further apart, and the empty paths across the close cropped lawns were less even. Approaching the dignified administration building from behind, the limestone was darkened and mottled. The tall windows with small panes, that from a distance had given the impression of iron bars, were ill-fitting, and some of them were patched from the inside with

294

plywood panels. From those still made entirely of glass, air conditioners protruded at odd intervals along the first two floors.

At the rear of the peaked central section, Jared found a long parking lot. He pulled past a couple of smaller buildings and found a spot in the corner closest to their goal, behind a fenced-in transformer at the bottom of a long, lumber support that ran vertically nearly to the roof. Without comment, Jared quickly pulled the keys from the ignition and climbed out of the car, slamming the door behind him. Kristin sighed again to herself, unbuckled her seatbelt, and watched him proceed to the back of the building.

"Why you keep doing that?" she asked as she approached.

"Doing what?" Jared replied, oblivious.

"Every time we get somewhere, you just take off in a huff. Last time, things were tense and I thought you were just being pissy, but today we weren't even fighting, and you still just left me in the car."

"Oh," Jared nodded while he turned to lead briskly around the building. "Yeah, last time I was being pissy. This time, I did it on purpose, kind of. You said we want to get as far as we can before someone stops us."

"Yes," Kristin confirmed following closely.

"My experience," Jared explained as they crossed the lot, "Has been that people are less likely to stop you when you look like you're running late. If you look lost, then they want to offer help, but for some reason they don't want to be asked for help if it's urgent. Or they think that if you're supposed to be somewhere then you must know where it is you're supposed to be... I don't know why. In any case, it always works." Striding to the edge of the pavement he added, "It's all about moving fast and projecting confidence. And a little anger if you've got it."

He led Kristin around a large shade tree and into a closed corner. On the long wall that had materialized in front of them, a rusted fire escape snaked loosely down over its bolts and past weathered emergency doors on each of the three floors, before abruptly angling away from the building to land in a locked steel cage on the ground. Above this terminus, a pair of deeply oxidized five pointed stars capped ancient support rods. At every point where metal sat flush against stone, the wall wept darkly: black from the cast iron stars, reddish brown from the steel steps, a mossy green from the securing bolts, all deepened the shadows cast by the building and conspired with rotting window panes to heighten the impression of decrepitude. This place, at least this part of a once proud, graceful, and apparently important structure, had been forgotten, neglected, and clearly deprioritized.

"So you've confidently marched us in the wrong direction," Kristin jibed.

"Wrong is relative," Jared explained, "That's the difference between you're approach and mine. See, *you* just got lost and hit a dead end, as where *I*," he pulled back his shoulders and lifted his chin, "*found* this dead end because I wanted to." Turning about face he announced, "And now I've decided I want to go this way."

Kristin rolled her eyes and quietly followed in the opposite direction, back across the lot and around the stubby side of the building. As the pair stepped into the afternoon light, the building's character changed. From one side of the corner to the next, the stains on the white stone disappeared. Wide and well maintained steel emergency stairs zigzagged between freshly painted doors and window panes. Along the building's impressive front, Jared led Kristin past a small mass of shrubs and tastefully placed saplings, to a wide concrete staircase that bisected the half dozen Corinthian columns that supported the three tiered portico. Jared ascended with long strides to the lowest of those levels: a breezy porch surrounded by a low white railing and a sky blue ceiling. The angle of the sun reflected the brightly colored surfaces as a sort of soft glow against the front windows.

Nearing a double door with an arched transom and elaborate moldings between dark metal gas lamps, Jared slowed. The narrow floorboards, uneven and slightly squishy through a hardened coat of grey paint, groaned under his weight. He crossed carefully to a

The Beard

large plaque fastened to the wall. "Whatcha' got there?" Kristin called, climbing after him in a pace that was not leisurely, but was certainly less urgent than his.

"Watch your step," Jared suggested softly without turning, "Don't want to fall through."

Kristin shrugged, "It looks sturdy."

"*Looks* sturdy. Feels…" Jared trailed off.

Approaching within a few feet, Kristin repeated, "What do you got there?"

Jared read aloud from the plaque, "Austin State Hospital. While Texas was a frontier state and psychiatry a pioneer venture, the Texas legislature in 1856 created this hospital for the mentally ill; in 1925 named Austin State hospital. Oldest Texas Mental Hospital. Construction began in 1857. The institution then housed in the administration building was opened May 11, 1861, with about a dozen patients and has continued to be dedicated to mental health programs."

Kristin glanced over her shoulder without knowing exactly why. "So this used to be a Mental hospital?"

"This building used to be," Jared answered. Gesturing around them he added, "I think the rest of this still is."

Kristin shuddered, "No wonder it gives me the creeps."

Jared reached over to the handle of an incongruently new front door, half constructed of plate glass. "It's all in your head," he commented sideways, giving a tug. The latch rattled against a gleaming strike plate on the opposite door.

"Is it locked?" Kristin asked hopefully.

Jared tried again more subtly, for fear of drawing the attention of anyone inside. "It doesn't look like it should be," he said, "But it is."

"Maybe we should go back to the car and regroup," Kristin suggested.

Skeptically Jared answered, "No, that doesn't make any sense." He brushed past her and back down the stairs explaining,

Clifford

"People work in this building, there has to be an entrance. We just keep going around until we find it."

Kristin followed down the stairs and jogged to catch up with him on a sidewalk that ran parallel to the longer gleaming wing of the building. Under dense foliage, the path took a right angle toward the front of another parking lot. Approaching a hedgerow, Kristin touched Jared's arm and said, "Wait. I don't feel right sneaking around here. I don't like this."

Jared stopped and turned to face her. "But we're not sneaking," he said simply, "We're lost on purpose. And running late somewhere, I think we agreed."

"Jared," she said earnestly, "I don't *like* this."

Attempting to soften his tone, Jared answered, "If you forget about what you've seen in the movies, the place isn't so spooky. It's just a big, old hospital. It's built for a different era, and it's falling apart, but that's probably because it's as grossly underfunded as every other mental hospital in the world. And we're just walking through the office building of the hospital. Hell, this is less scary than a regular hospital if you think about it, because nobody in this one is contagious."

"You hope," Kristin nodded impatiently. "I know all of that, that's not the... I just... I don't like the vibe of this place. Can't you feel it?"

Jared made a sincere effort at picking up whatever it was that was bothering her. The air was still and hot, vaguely damp from an isolated shower that morning. The dapples of shade on the surrounding lawn danced almost imperceptibly, and were followed by the distant rustling of innumerable trees, only then chased by a warm breeze that grazed the droplets of sweat along Jared's hairline. Apart from that, nothing moved: no people, no cars, not even a stray cat. Finally he said, "Not really, no. I'm not getting what you're getting." Kristin stood quietly, indignant. Making another attempt to placate or to at least distract her, Jared said, "We have to go in, you know we do. But it doesn't have to take long. We'll find a door, then in and out, no sightseeing."

The Beard

Kristin furrowed her brow and pursed her lips before conceding, "I suppose. But if we don't find an honest way in, we're not breaking in. Deal?"

"Deal," Jared nodded. She retrieved her phone and pulled up the most recent pictures.

After settling on a close-up of a patch of what had been high on Jared's left cheek, Kristin repositioned herself further in the shade next to him, held up the phone and zoomed in. "This place where the blond gets really wide, it runs up on this black... looks like a Tetris block, you see it?"

Finishing her point, Jared gestured over his shoulder, "So it's definitely this building, but that goes straight through the front."

"Which we can't," she continued, "But it's a pretty big building, we have no idea what the floor plan is, or was, or how that fits with the map, or where we'll get in, so-"

Jared jumped in, "So wherever we go in, we should find the front door to get oriented."

"Yes, very good," Kristin said, her enthusiasm renewed by the problem solving exercise. "And when we find the front, we'll turn away from the door, go right, and then..."

Jared squinted at the picture. The blond line wrapped around over itself in two broad loops before hooking further to the right. "Then we do the hokey pokey?" he asked.

"Yeah, I still don't know what that's about," she said. "I'm hoping it will make more sense inside."

"Alright then," Jared said with an air of finality, "Let's get to checking more doors." He marched past the hedges, up the parking lot and down a shallow ramp. At the bottom, what had once been an arched carriage entrance had been permanently filled by a windowed wooden wall with a matching door in its center. Jared leaned tentatively on the door handle and felt the latch slide. "First try, not bad," he muttered to himself, holding the door open for Kristin.

Once the door had eased shut behind them, the light streaming through the low, arched windows at their back competed with a single row of fluorescents at their front, casting odd shadows down the length of a wide hallway with gleaming concrete floors and heavily scuffed white walls. In addition to the light fixtures, insulated pipes and electrical conduit ran above a mail cubby, a small wooden couch upholstered in yellow vinyl in the spirit of a 1970's Waiting Room, and several recessed doors with name plates above them. The hallway looked every bit the basement that it was, but tidy and well attended, if, at the moment, vacant.

"So front door then," Jared said, "Straight ahead?"

"No," Kristin corrected him, "We came down a ramp, but the front door had steps going up, so we'll need to find some stairs to find the front door."

"Which way?" Jared asked.

"Any way will do." Kristin impatiently took the lead. He followed her down the hall, past closed offices, fire extinguishers, and a large rolling trash can, toward what looked to be a locked door at the end of the tunnel. Just short of the obstruction, Kristin vanished through an alcove to the right. She was halfway up a dim stairwell with a PVC handrail by the time he caught up. Without a word she took his hand and pulled him from the final step through an aged wooden door and into another corridor. This new hall also relied on overhead fluorescents, but the windows that had seemed so dark, rotten, and foreboding from the outside, admitted sunlight inside from every possible angle. All the surrounding surfaces were white: a glossy eggshell for the walls and the high, pressed tin ceiling, a polished off-white with speckles for the gleaming floor tiles. From some unseen office, a man's laugh echoed down the hall: not maniacal or raucous, but polite, professional, the perfect supplement to the smell of judiciously applied floor cleaner in the air. The overall combination was jarringly normal.

Venturing cautiously around a corner, Kristin gestured to the front door of the building. Jared asked, "So we go right?" She shook her head and turned her body away from the door. Jared said "I see: we're looking left, then." Kristin confirmed by nodding and touching the tip of her nose with one finger. Keeping his voice low,

The Beard

Jared answered, "We're not raiding a terrorist compound for shit's sake. This could take a while if you pantomime everything."

Still not speaking, Kristin threw her hands up and headed to the left. Almost immediately, they found themselves in a long, wide hallway that ran to a tall, arched window. It was a scant distance from the welcoming front hall, and it was just as well lit, but this space was yellowed, aged, chipped, and peeling. Along its full length, every inch between one recessed door and the next was occupied with wooden furniture, like the world's least advertised yard sale: a pair of chairs at a side table, a glass and wood display case, a bureau with a tall mirror, a slatted bench under a long picture frame. In what little space remained, the walls were covered with photographs and felt-board displays, all black and white and under glass.

The couple took up positions at either end of a long glass case. In front of Jared, a dusty instrument resembling a small vice sat by a slip of white paper that bore the caption, 'Laryngoscope.' Arranged nearby, diagrams and photos demonstrated the proper way to insert the device down an unconscious person's throat. At the other end of the case, beyond an 'Optical Pressure Meter' and what looked like a miniature adding machine labelled 'Manual Cell Counter,' Kristin examined a small metal box with a shiny cover. Sloppily coiled wires ran from its face past the etched words 'ECT UNIT' and a handful of bakelite knobs and switches, one of which bore the instruction 'PRESS TO TREAT.'

Kristin finally broke her silence, "Why would you leave things like this sitting out?"

Jared shrugged, "They knew that people would be thinking about it anyway, so why not take it head on? I think it's interesting."

Kristin shook her head, "I think it's morbid. I just want to get this done and get out."

Jared nodded quietly and continued his review of the display while she turned her attention to a series of more benign pictures hanging nearby. He considered that before the items under glass

Clifford

had been treated as macabre novelties and antiques, back when they were shiny and new, each piece had been state of the art, a medical marvel: the absolute height of human achievement. The idea that a person's entire perception of reality could be 'cured' with a jolt from what amounted to a car battery with electrodes had at one time carried as much weight as the modern stream of well-advertised antipsychotics. Yet, as often as that button had been 'pressed to treat' no permanent cure had been affected. For all that people had known and would later learn about the mind, the ancient and very human problem of madness persisted. Jared wondered if there would ever come a day when an fMRI scan would be viewed in the same light as phrenology. It was less a question of denying science than an acknowledgement that explanations come and go, but true mysteries are forever.

Kristin resumed her hushed approach, issuing a "Pssst!" from halfway down the hall. She waved him over, past a low wooden chair and a squat chest of drawers, to a black felt-board with a handful of old photographs affixed under clear plastic. Pointing to a sepia image near the top, she asked, "Isn't that our guy?"

Jared shuffled closer and squinted. Above a typed label that read 'Patient Room ca. 1885,' was a picture of a slender man in a frock coat standing over an occupied bed. The patient, positioned with the crown of their head visible, appeared to be unconscious. The man was turned slightly toward the camera, partially concealed by deep shadow, with his face half covered by a long, dark beard that broke over his chest. Kristin retrieved her phone and flipped back through her pictures, finally holding up a snap shot she had taken of the marker at Arlington. "Kind of looks the same, yeah?"

Jared considered the resemblance for a moment. "Kind of," he said, "It's tough to tell. This black and white photo is so grainy. I can't really see the wrinkles around the eyes and stuff, you can't really make those out."

"The wrinkles won't be there anyways," Kristin stated, "He'd be twenty years younger in that photo."

The Beard

"I guess you're right," Jared said, "The style of his beard makes him look so old that I didn't even think about that. But there is a similarity, for sure. Something about the posture maybe? I don't know."

The man in the photograph stood sideways to the camera with an air of easy, self-assured dignity. His back was straight but his shoulders were slightly rounded; his gaze was direct but not challenging. He held what looked like a folio in one hand, but the other hung casually out the pocket of his trousers, parting his jacket to expose a high buttoned waistcoat. Jared's eye wandered from the figure to the patient room in which he stood. In a background stained and faded to reddish browns and tepid yellows the floor and walls gleamed dimly. The polished metal bed frame and spotless white linens gave the scene an antiseptic, truly clinical atmosphere. From just out of frame, a broad shaft of light suggested the existence of a window, further evidenced by the room's sole imperfection: the corner of a head casing with a square chunk of wood cut out, crept into the edge of the photo behind the man in the suit.

"It's definitely him," Kristin broke in.

"I think your right," Jared agreed, "It does feel right."

"Well that, and the fact that the map ends here."

Jared looked down from the picture, "Does it?"

"It does," Kristin confirmed, "Up the hall from the front door and hook to the right. And since this is where it goes and we found it, I think we can leave."

Ignoring the last sentence Jared repeated, "But what about the loops?"

"What about them?" she asked, "Who knows? Let's go."

"In a minute," Jared said unreassuringly, retracing their steps back toward the front entrance. Breaking in the opposite direction from the basement door, he rounded a corner and arrived at the bottom of a wide, open white staircase with rubber treads and a banister of polished natural wood. At the top of a short flight, the handrail curled back on itself to approach an unseen floor. Jared

Clifford

paused and looked over his shoulder at Kristin. Pointing upward he said simply, "That's the loop," before quickly ascending to disappear from view. Kristin grudgingly followed up and into a large vertical shaft, well lit by two tiers of windows on one side and punctuated by wide landings. Doubling back again, she found Jared standing in an open foyer. Directly above the corridor they had just investigated, a nearly identical hallway extended to a nearly identical arched window. Similarly cluttered with furniture and memorabilia, it was a bit less weathered, differentiated by a light green diamond pattern in the floor tiles, and separated from the area in which they stood by a sort of false wall: paned, upper side windows hung wide open on hinges while a central frame, its door long since removed, opened invitingly on the space.

Kristin noticed a man sitting with a magazine at the other end of the hall and tugged Jared's sleeve toward the stairs. Taking her meaning, he instead moved a few steps forward and squinted through one of the casings. "It's a mannequin," he said softly.

Kristin moved hesitantly into the door and peered closer. "It is," she said. "What the fuck? As if this place wasn't creepy enough. Why would they do that?"

Jared shook his head, "Yeah. I'm still less bothered than you, but that does seem excessive." Kristin moved cautiously down the hallway. "Hey," Jared said, "Where you going?"

"Hooking to the right. Right?"

"It's two loops," he corrected, pointing to the stairs, "I only stopped to let you catch up." Taking her hand, he said, "Don't worry, we're almost there, I think."

Approaching the top of the sunlit staircase, the varnish on the handrail became duller, the individual supports darker. The rubberized treads of the stairs groaned softly as they came to another landing which, even with no fewer windows, held deep shadows in the corners. When Jared and Kristin again hooked to the right, the cause of this became clear: yet another long hallway ran to another arched window, but this one stood gaping and empty, the fluorescent bulbs extinguished and by all indications

304

inoperable. There was a false wall similar to that of the second story, but on this one the side windows were grimy and buttoned up tight, the paint had chipped to expose bare wood, and the central doorway was blocked by a single strip of yellow 'Caution' tape.

Jared released Kristin's hand, ducked beneath the tape, and led the way. Beneath acoustic ceiling tiles that dangled flakes at their seams like fur, his silhouette against the distant arched window became one small shadow among many. He swung to his right into one of the recessed doorways. Taking advantage of the daylight that streamed through a mist of motes in the room beyond, Kristin pulled up the map once more. "Not this room," she said, stepping back into the hall and walking to the next alcove. She pressed gently on a solid wooden door with no knob or latch. It swung open under its dusty transom with a creak.

Kristin stood at the entrance with one arm extended, inviting Jared to proceed. He passed into a small, dim, rectangular room. "This is the one," he stated definitively. As he crossed a margin where the loose floor tiles vanished altogether, dirt and remnants of old adhesive crunched under his feet. Walking carefully around a system of wooden braces that supported a water damaged section of the ceiling, he pointed to the top of the single window, which was covered from the inside with butcher paper. "See that?" he asked. At a point where the taped edge had come loose, the paper fluttered in the perfectly still air of the room. The corner of the adjacent head casing had a square chunk of wood cut out of it. "That busted window frame was in the photo downstairs. So you were right, that had to be Strafford."

Wandering a slow circle back into the room, Jared looked to the door where Kristin still stood with her arms folded, watching him. "Come in here," he said, "Check it out. He was right here, in this spot..."

"No thanks," Kristin said softly, "We should probably not be here."

Jared continued his starry eyed promenade for a few more steps before coming to rest with his side facing her. Deep shadows

Clifford

cast by the wooden braces covered the lower half of his face and broke over his chest. The afternoon sun glowed through the paper on the windows and bathed the mottled white room in sepia tones. In reddish browns and tepid yellows, the floor and walls gleamed dimly. Jared, already more slender than Kristin was used to, looked especially lean at that moment, his shoulders slightly rounded even standing with his back straight, one hand hanging casually out of his hip pocket. Nonetheless, his satisfied expression gave him an air of self-assured dignity.

Only partially illuminated, he turned slightly toward Kristin and regarded her with a gaze that was direct but not challenging. "But he was *right here*. Can't you *feel* it?"

"Yes," Kristin said with a wary step backwards, "I can. And we should go."

Day 6

Crossing from Marysville on a pleasant afternoon, Louis observed the bright disc of the sun reflected off the glimmering, glassy surface of the Feather River, and could not help feeling disappointed. It was the same sort of mild distaste that he'd experienced crossing the Sacramento River. They just weren't rivers, not really. They were larger than creeks, but... It might not have been fair of him to contrast the Feather to the Mississippi, but running down a tally of the other rivers he'd seen recently: the Missouri, the Tennessee, the Ohio; all of these had been unmistakable water-highways, fully a mile-width of chop, marching a straight line to the horizon. These California "rivers," while they might be pretty enough in their own way, were too narrow, with sandy banks that twisted out of view in less than a hundred yards. But the thing about the Feather River that most annoyed Louis at that moment was what it had in common with all those other, mightier crossings he had made: he was travelling over it facing full west.

Louis had promised himself at the University Library that there would be no doubling back from that time on, but he hadn't accounted for the fact that south-southeast from the west edge of Chico would be more like due south from his RV park near Oroville, nor had he been aware of the abrupt eastward jog once he picked up Route 70. And so here he was, once again driving the opposite direction of what he had intended, but at least he knew that it wouldn't be far: the center point that he was skirting this time appeared to be less than a mile in front of him, in Yuba City.

Just this once he would make this minor exception and move backwards. "But ne'er again after this," Louis said aloud, causing Marlow to perk up, "Because them's the rules, boy: straight home, no deviatin', no researchin', no fact gatherin'." In short, the exact opposite of how he had handled every previous stop. And however else he was feeling: about his sense of direction, about the puny rivers, about how much longer he would be on the road with a dog that could not seem to stop farting that day, even for all of that, Louis was overcome with a sense of relief each time he considered how easy this stop would be.

He didn't expect to find any answers, didn't even care to. He would fulfill his bare minimum obligation to the spirit of this adventure and be done with it. It would be easy and straightforward, but also something else. Subdued, maybe. Concluded, pacified, controlled – yes, that was it, controlled. Louis was putting himself in control for the first time since he-couldn't-remember-when. He wasn't letting some object, or ghost, or circumstance dictate what he did or when he did it. If he felt like stopping in Yuba City he would stop, if he felt like driving on, he would do that. He didn't need to give a reason or even to know a reason. It would be his show.

As the roadway passed over a narrow earthen levee, Louis glanced at the compass and flicked his turn signal. He announced to Marlow, "And now we are leaving the highway 'cause I want to, not because that *thing* says so." He tapped the breaks to slow his rig as he chased the needle chasing an exit ramp that chased a chain link fence bounding a dried-up lot. Falling into a familiar pace, Louis snaked through a neighborhood best described as indecisive. He had seen this often on the outskirts of towns: a patch of widely spaced, nondescript office buildings came and went with the edges of a residential neighborhood, which graciously made way for a mobile home community, itself conveniently located near blocks of warehouses.

Sparsely planted rows of dusty trees followed a march of generic, if varied, beige structures. Louis took a corner past another overgrown fence, and found himself on a narrower road, between a few scattered houses and an empty parking lot. He hummed lightly to himself while he coasted to the center of the side street. He reflected that another, equally liberating consequence of his recent shift had been the demystification of his side trips. Not once since

The Beard

he had declared the journey over had Louis wondered or worried over what they would find next, because in giving up on any deeper meaning, he had in affect downgraded all those potential discoveries in one go: home was now the only real destination, the rest were just pit stops.

While in many obvious ways, this change had made travel simpler, it now presented a different set of complications. As where before he had located an RV park, fussed over how to handle the dog, found meals, plotted directions and similar, no longer having to do those things meant that those things weren't getting done. Wherever he happened to be or needed to go, he could now count on having Marlow accompany him, but that meant he had to look for pet friendly stops. He could also count on dragging the Shasta and on having no more guidance than the compass chose to provide, which meant making decisions of safety and navigability on the fly. The neighborhood in which he now found himself was a case in point: as he followed the needle over the crumbling edge of the asphalt and bounced his trailer slowly through an open steel gate to a weedy lot between an earthen levee and a corrugated metal fence, he could only pray that he wouldn't pick up a nail in his tires.

Louis carefully pulled past a mound of broken concrete and suddenly sensed that he was being watched by someone other than his dog. A heavyset homeless man sat perched on a lawn chair at the top of the levee, some seventy yards away. Surrounded by strewn newspapers, the man wore a full but neatly trimmed beard that concealed his throat and tucked into his wavy hair in a way that, from a distance, made his head look perfectly rounded, like a snowman come to life, or a sort of roly-poly garden gnome in wire rimmed glasses. At least Louis wouldn't be alone out here if he bottomed out, blew out, or otherwise broke down.

While maneuvering through the narrow gap between two gravel piles, he noticed the compass needle spinning west again, and he jammed down the breaks. Even at his low speed, the tires on the Shasta slid and kicked up a cloud of gray dust. "Sorry for that,"

Clifford

Louis mumbled, either to Marlow or to the truck, he wasn't sure which. With a more deliberate air, he put the truck in reverse and backed up until the needle swung east again. Finally satisfied, he dropped into park and cut the engine. As he prepared to pull his keys from the ignition, he returned his gaze to the levee and saw that the homeless guy was now peering at him through binoculars.

"Fuckin' great," Louis muttered, "I was hopin' for an audience." Of course, he didn't have to get out and put on a show. New rules and all, as he kept reminding himself: he could just drive off and assume, somewhat safely, that exploring a vacant lot would have been one more waste of his time. On the other hand, could he be certain of the lot's vacancy? For all of the research he'd had to do in Nebraska, there had just been a sign in St. Charles. And in Montana, a rock in the middle of a private gravel road had pointed him to Fort Custer with zero extra effort. As unimportant as this place seemed, maybe it was worth getting out and looking at the ground at least, now that he was here.

Marlow whined and pressed a front paw against Louis' thigh. "I think I can guess what you want," Louis answered. He generally avoided letting his dog make his decisions for him, but in this case Marlow's bladder might be a suitable tie-breaker. Worst case scenario, getting out for a couple minutes now could buy Louis an extra hour or two before they had to stop again. "Alright," he sighed, reaching for his cigarettes and compass, "You get five minutes, make it count."

The door was hardly open by the time the dog had bounded out and vanished into the tall grass. Louis followed slowly, staring at the compass while he stepped deliberately past a rock pile and into the space in front of his vehicle. No more than a few feet from the bumper, the needle went limp. He gave it a shake and watched it wobble loosely for a second before taking one large stride backwards to lean against the grill of the truck while he lit a cigarette and stared at the bare, rocky ground. Nothing. He could have hunkered down for a closer look, but there was so much absence of anything that he knew without contorting himself that there could only be nothing there.

He looked again to the compass: still lifeless, exhausted. Louis stared almost through it, half curious what might happen next. Up to now, the compass had given up once he got where it wanted him to go, and had only woken up after he'd found what it wanted him to find. But in this case, not only had he not found anything, he had no plans to. Would it snap back into action once it realized he was changing the rules? Or would it stay dead waiting for its next cue? Or was he going too far in personifying an inanimate object in the first place? There was no way of knowing, but in any case, he would find out: just as soon as Marlow came back, they would haul ass in the direction of home, and the compass could do as it pleased.

Louis noticed his cigarette burning closer to his fingers and guessed that it had been the five minutes he had promised. Preparing to call out, he paused to consider following Marlow's lead and taking a piss while he had the chance. No bathrooms out there, of course, but it's not like anyone would know except for... Louis looked up to the levee to check on his hairy hobo friend in the interest of putting the truck between the two of them. The garden gnome had vanished, leaving the newspapers that covered his lawn chair to flutter in a breeze that Louis couldn't feel. Scanning the lot in front of the truck, Louis spotted Marlow standing stock still and staring hard at the shallow ditch that ran along the bottom of the hill.

Still fifty yards off, the chubby man cautiously picked his way over from the levee to the lot, in the general direction of the dog. Louis didn't feel threatened by the man, not by a long shot, but something about the approach, the mere act of it, was a little off. More irritated than disturbed, Louis said, "Marlow. Les'go." He walked to the driver's side, opened the door, and turned. Marlow remained in place and lowered his head in the stranger's direction. "Mar-low!" Louis insisted. The dog relented and broke toward the truck. The hairy man began to run, but stumbled over a rock pile and bellowed something in a voice that was much lower than Louis had expected.

Marlow checked over his shoulder but shook off the impulse and trotted past Louis to climb back into the cab. Louis flicked his cigarette and turned to follow, when the man yelled out again from several feet closer.

Louis froze. He must have misheard. It didn't make any sense. God. Dammit.

He turned and looked down from behind the open door of the truck to the man, who now moved in a brisk hobble. The stranger hopped briefly on his left foot while attempting to brush gravel off a right knee skinned and bleeding below his cargo shorts. He hissed, "Ow... Fuck," before repeating his baritone call once more, "Henry Sullivan Strafford!"

Louis let the words hang in the air for a moment before nodding, "Yeh. I heard you. Who are you? What do you know about him?"

"*Every*-thing," Tim said, now close enough for a conversation, "I know *every*-thing about him. I've been waiting here a couple weeks now. I almost didn't recognize you without a beard."

The Beard

Day 8

The brittle brown plastic of the dashboard vibrated sharply as another seam in the asphalt passed beneath the truck then buzzed as an aftershock under the trailer behind. Outside the dusty windshield, the monotonous blur of the highway had finally surrendered to the true dark of a cloudy night, while inside, the instrument panel glowed out of sight like so many candles ensconced in the niches of a grotto. The combined effect of this impromptu nightlight, the empty outdoors, and the sound of a local country station turned too low for the words to be discernible, was a deep sort of peacefulness. Tim leaned the crown of his head against its dim reflection in the streaked passenger window and marveled at the whole situation.

To start with, he marveled that he had been right. Not that he was too surprised by that: not him, he was used to being right. But deep down, he hadn't entirely trusted the limb he'd climbed out on until this strange man with his strange dog had started grilling him. And the nature of that limb, the ways in which Tim was right, was more marvelous still: that this man had, with so much less information than even Tim possessed, driven across the country looking for those answers in this cramped little rig, feeling every bump and dip in the road from the Tennessee River to Sutter's Creek.

Almost in response to the thought, another unseen imperfection in the road zipped underneath the vehicle. The massive dog, without fully rousing, resituated himself, rolling to the side and pushing his hind legs against Tim's thigh to more deeply nuzzle his master on the other end of the bench seat. Tim pulled away, pressed closer to the door in effort to distance himself from the beast. A sharp, hollow twang reverberated from below the console, and the behemoth driver responded by pulling the glowing

Clifford

coil of the electric lighter from its socket, to press it with a sizzle against the tip of his off-brand cigarette.

What a goddamn hick, Tim thought, a fucking caricature. Big man with his big dog in his big truck full of stale smoke and country music, bumping and bouncing up out of the south. Though to be fair, in Tim's mind the man's region of origin didn't set him apart from any of the goobers and yokels Tim had met in Montana. At least he could be sure that this hick would be useful, if only he could keep his lung cancer to himself in the meantime. Tim sat up slightly, about to suggest cracking a window, but stopped and closed his mouth. It just wouldn't do to be impolite at this point, no matter how much the man deserved it.

Tim had already been required to make a serious case for why he should be allowed ride along with this hayseed. He was no longer sure what he had expected from that whole process; maybe that whoever arrived in that field in Yuba City would already know that they should be meeting with someone, or that they would at least be so curious and similarly focused on their destination as to cooperate more fully. At a minimum, following from Strafford's written account, Tim had expected to find a man with a very full beard who would be ecstatic to have help navigating from it.

What he had found instead was a guy with a compass who believed he could do everything himself: a man who first had to be convinced to go on, even after all he'd gone through up to that point, and then had to be sold on the notion that he couldn't reach the end goal without some guidance and context. The key, to Tim's thinking, was to strike a balance between claiming enough specific knowledge to make himself useful, and giving away enough of said knowledge that his new acquaintance could then do without him, which Louis had made pretty clear was his preference. To that end, Tim had engaged in what he felt were pretty impressive verbal acrobatics, but had gotten nowhere. Ultimately, he'd been forced to resort to, "One more stop. What do you have to lose?"

Tim should have guessed that simple would be best with such a man. But the unfortunate backside of that argument was that now

314

he had to be agreeable, to avoid a scenario in which he gave Louis something to lose, such as face, dignity, or pride, because it wouldn't matter where Louis chose to go next if Tim got himself tossed out on the way. The two of them had to arrive together, and it had to time out perfectly, so for now Tim saw a benefit in allowing the big guy to be in charge.

But was there no limit to that? Tim took a mental inventory of the indignities he had suffered thus far: his belongings had been stowed in the open truck bed because Louis, "Didn't want to catch something," from them. The radio station, while turned mercifully low, was certainly not to Tim's taste. The conversation had been virtually non-existent despite Tim's very best efforts, and the dog, of course... the goddamn dog. Stretched out as comfy as you please, that bastard was actually snoring now, while Tim pulled his arms tighter against his body, his knees forced together against the door to accommodate this mindless, drooling, smug, goddamn dog.

And now, in case that sensory combination wasn't grating enough, Tim should be expected to take in Louis's cigarette. It was more than too much, it was Tim's personal hell, and he decided he should say something. He turned to his driver, opened his mouth, and abruptly closed it again with a huff.

Without looking away from the road, Louis asked, "What's that now?"

Tim's mouth flapped inaudibly once more before he finally verbalized, "Didn't say anything."

Louis took a drag off his cigarette and inhaled before allowing the smoke to lazily escape with the words, "Naw, you didn't say nothin'. But it's the third time you made a noise like you wanted to."

Unable to determine whether Louis's tone was combative or just blunt, Tim mumbled, "I don't know what you heard... Maybe the dog..."

"Wait," Louis laughed, "Blamin' Marlow now? After how much time in close quarters with that dog, you think I don't know the whole catalogue a' his noises? Naw..." He shook his head at the road in his headlights, "You don't gotta say whatever you was gonna say if you don't want. You should, but I won't make you. Any case, you needn't blame the dog."

Tim allowed a few seconds to lapse while he mentally tried on different responses. Eventually he went with, "I was going to ask… if…. Would you mind if I took a closer look at the compass?"

"That all?" Louis asked. He plucked the item off of the dash and tossed it over Marlow's tail onto Tim's lap. "Don't gotta be timid. Maybe keep it quick, though: I'm still usin' it off and on: got a system goin', y'know."

Tim took up the object gingerly, delicately, with the pad of his thumb on one side and the tip of his forefinger barely touching the other. He stared at the thin, silver needle wagging gently, almost imperceptibly, but still with metronomic regularity. The brass case was mottled and oxidized on one side, the overly elaborate gradations on the paper face darkened, discolored, and in places barely visible under the hazy recessed glass that had somehow survived without a crack, even as the lid of the thing had clearly been punished beyond repair. As an object viewed objectively, the thing was basically worthless. But it had been the property of the doctor Henry Sullivan Strafford. It had been in the man's pocket when everything had happened, and again afterword.

Tim placed the cold metal in the palm of his other hand. This bauble had born witness to something that so few people would ever be a part of, and pretty soon Tim would as well. He could feel something, the importance of that history or perhaps the anticipation of that relationship: something flowed into his hand like electricity. For the moment, he did not care whether the feeling was real or imagined.

Suddenly realizing how long he'd been lost in thought, Tim carefully reseated the compass above a photograph of a woman and two children. Partly to break a silence that others might consider awkward, and partly out of simple boredom, Tim politely asked, "You say you have a system? How's that been working for you?"

The Beard

"Oh, that," Louis replied. He lifted his cap and scratched his head for a second before continuing, "Workin' okay I suppose. Not much to it, really. When I drive past somethin', the needle moves to point at it. I catch that early as I can, then I start circling back that way. Where I can, I try to use access roads, frontage streets, what have you. Get off the highway basically, so's to slow down and follow the needle without circlin' back more'n once. If I can. Main thing is to check in regular." Gesturing with his right index finger, Louis emphasized his conclusion, "That's the main thing."

"Mm hmm," Tim nodded with feigned attention, "It sounds like you're pretty practiced at this."

"Yeh," Louis shrugged, "Well, couple thousand miles. Feels like a dozen stops that damn thing pointed to."

"Really," Tim said, now with actual interest. "That many?"

"Naw, *felt* like," Louis said. He continued at half the volume, "Real number must be more like... let's see... Missouri was the first, just outside St. Louis. Then up through Iowa at Keokuk, was two. Then stopped in York, Nebraska, Wheatland, Wyoming-,"

"No kidding," Tim interrupted. "Was there something left to find in Wheatland?"

"Sure," Louis said, mildly gratified by Tim's attention, "Why you ask?"

Ignoring the question, Tim fired back, "What was it you found there?"

"A photo," Louis said plainly, "In a display case at a local history museum north a' town. They had a photo a' Strafford with a bunch a' guys diggin' a tunnel."

"He was in that?" Tim asked, perturbed, "Are you sure?"

"Yeh," Louis answered. "He was a few years younger'n the photo I saw in Missouri, but it was definitely him."

Tim grumbled, "In front of me that whole time. Damn."

"Right," Louis said warily. Shifting his tone, he resumed, "So Wheatland was what, my fourth stop? Then after that was Montana, then Jacinto, and then Yuba City, makes seven. Shit, is that all? Really felt like more-,"

Clifford

Tim jumped back in with his previous zeal, "I'm sorry, did I hear Montana in there?"

"Yeh," Louis confirmed, "Fort Custer, was outside a town called Hardin, which is-"

"East of Billings, I know where it is," Tim said impatiently. "But that doesn't make any sense: you're supposed to be following..." Tim stopped himself.

Oblivious to Tim's reticence, Louis replied, "It was right on the way, it makes perfect sense to me. At least as much sense as any of this. More than it made comin' across you."

"I don't know what you mean," Tim said defensively, "Yuba City was a sensible place for us to meet. And it was also on the way, if that helps you: It was the first place Strafford went, after the place we're going to right now."

"Fine, but how did *you* know that?"

Tim thought for a split second longer than was called for, before attempting, "I came across it by accident. When I was researching... something else."

"'Something else'," Louis repeated, "What 'something else'?"

"The history... of...Wheat in Northern California?"

"Hmmm," Louis nodded, "And researchin' wheat farms tol' you where we're goin' next?"

"Not the wheat farms, not..." Tim vacillated. With what he hoped was more authority, he tried again, "I started with wheat farming, but that led to Strafford which, yes, led to where we're going next."

Softly insistent, Louis asked, "So where we goin'? An' why is it special? An' how can you be sure it's the last stop? Was Strafford born there or somethin'?"

Tim said thoughtfully, "In a manner of speaking, I suppose he was." He halted again, realizing how counterproductive it would be for him to follow this train of thought. "You know, there isn't too much point in talking about this. You'll understand when we get where we're going. And until we get there, I can't really explain it to you."

318

The Beard

"Is that so?" Louis asked with raised eyebrows. "Seems like a long enough drive that you could try. An' you might be surprised. I might be able to understand more'n you think."

"Now, really," Tim began, "You know I didn't mean –," He paused and closed his eyes. He knew where this was heading, the way dumb people react when you explain to them how they are dumb. The anger, the end of rational conversation, it was a place that Tim knew well, practically where he lived. But he could not afford to go there yet. He drew a long, calming breath: in through the nose and out slowly through the mouth. He was quite sure that the dog had farted. He could actually taste it now.

Tim forced his attention back to the big man across from him. "I'm sorry if I wasn't clear," he resumed cautiously. "What I meant to say was that the whole thing is difficult to explain, and I don't think *I* can do it justice. There's just too much difference of approach at this point."

"Apology accepted," Louis said magnanimously. After a beat he followed up, "But how do you mean 'Difference of approach'? If you don't mind my askin'."

"Not at all," Tim said offhandedly. "Just that you've been working backwards: starting in Missouri, which was late in Strafford's life and consequently closer to the end of his story. To understand this next part, you'd have to see things from the beginning."

Clifford

August 16, 1881

The merciless Arizona sun passed its zenith and forced its way westward, driving out the shadows cast by the dense band of foliage that ran the bank of the Gila River. On the other side of those dusty trees, the water gurgled softly, quickly, and higher this summer than anyone had ever seen. But here, just a few dozen yards to the southeast, the higher ground ran dry: the rocky soil was held down by small, hard bushes and tufts of brown grass that stretched from the belt of cottonwoods on the right to the dark blue silhouettes of the distant, low-slung hills that sprang up in every other direction.

William Grafton lowered his head under the wide brim of his black campaign hat. Every step he took squeezed water from his socks to between his toes, even as he felt his boots baking into a hard shell. He had known better than to enjoy his accidental dip in the river. He had known that such cool relief in late morning would leave his clothes oppressive and scalding in the windless afternoon. Saturated from his armpits to his toes, he could feel every fiber of his shirt clinging to his skin. William widened his stride into a sort of waddle, doing what little he could to keep his soaked drawers off his crotch. He hated every moment of every sensation, he cursed his luck, but more than that, William cursed his travelling companion, the young Private Sanders, who now followed in an equally awkward gait a few paces behind.

To be fair, William was no officer and at twenty-one was only a couple years older than Sanders. But every day of those years weighed a great deal in this god-forsaken territory, and Private Sanders was as cocky as he was inexperienced, in a way that suggested he was somehow connected to someone that mattered. William had no proof of this and didn't want to be seen as caring enough to ask, but because the private had showed up at around the same time as Colonel Carr a few weeks earlier, William thought it

320

The Beard

safest to assume that the boy was at least attached to someone on the officer's staff. In any case William wasn't impressed. Nor was he inclined to risk crossing someone important by arguing with the young man.

That was why William had acquiesced to Sanders' insistence that they cross by canoe near the road instead of hiking to the gentler embankment a few miles upstream. It may also have been why Sanders was comfortable ignoring William's instructions on the water, with the consequence of tipping the canoe far enough to dump both men out. It did not explain why Sanders had only then confessed that he couldn't swim, turning a relatively minor discomfort into a desperate rescue which ended with William grasping at tree limbs in the shallows to drag ashore the capsized vessel with little Private Sanders breathlessly astride. But it did explain why William had not let Sanders drown, and why he chose to not choke the young man now.

It also explained why William, uncomfortable though he was, refused to undress or to even open the top button on the wool sack coat that now smothered him: not for the sake of modesty, but for a safe, hierarchal spite. William knew that making his own situation more bearable would give Sanders leave to make *his* situation more bearable. And even more than William wanted to be comfortable, he very much wanted for Sanders to be miserable. And thus he trudged on, dripping on the dry dirt, wishing for a stiff breeze that might offer him, but only him, relief.

William focused on stepping over and around the low shrubbery while Sanders' high, percussive voice called, "Are we getting close at least?" William clenched his jaw and exhaled heavily through his nose, doing his best to both march faster and hide under his hat. The sound of shoes slapping and twigs snapping came up quickly behind him. "Hey," Sanders resumed, "I said-,"

"I heard you," William snapped. "What you askin' me for? I should be askin' you."

"Well, how would I know?" Sanders asked impatiently.

Clifford

William stopped and turned to face the young man. "You sayin' you don't know where the line picks up? 'Cause you sure seemed to know this morning."

"I don't know what you mean," Sanders replied casually.

"This morning," William said, feeling the frustration build in his chest, "You said you could show me where the line was. Whole reason you come out with me."

"No," Sanders shrugged, "I never said I knew where it was."

William quickly replayed the day's events in his head, searching for evidence with which he could escalate his argument. Privates Grafton and Sanders, along with several other infantrymen and an equal number of Indian scouts, had set out from Fort Apache the previous afternoon to inspect the sole line to the Fort's telegraph, which had stopped receiving messages earlier that day. Out of consideration for recent tensions on the nearest reservations, and in service to a healthy superstition, no one had wanted or needed to admit the real reason for such a large and experienced inspection party: to scout for a possible ambush that might use a downed telegraph wire as bait. It had taken the rest of the day and most of that morning for the group to get within sight of the Gila River, but took less than two seconds on the flooded bank to work out what had happened to the telegraph. Once they were sure there was nothing lying in wait for them, a sergeant had called for a volunteer to cross where the line had washed out, to inspect the other side of the break. William, more tired of making conversation with his comrades than from travel, had raised his hand. And that was when Sanders had piped up and asked what William quoted presently:

"'Does *William* know what direction the line picks up across the river?' That's what you said," William reminded him.

"Yeh," Sanders nodded, "Then the sergeant told me to show you. I never said *I* knew where it went."

"But you said crossing upstream was further from the line," William argued.

The Beard

"Said it was further from the *break*," Sanders corrected, "Which stands to reason, since we were standing by the break, and you wanted to go a mile up."

"But now we've washed more than two miles *down*str-," William cut himself off and turned with a shake of his head, bewildered by the pointlessness of the debate. Angling his body away from the water, he returned his attention to the ground in front of him and pressed on.

"Hey," Sanders said chasing after, tugging his soaked pant legs away from the ground, "Are we almost there? You never said." William continued his lopsided march. "Hey! Can you tell me where we're going at least?"

"Thomas!" William barked over his shoulder. Camp Thomas was where William had decided to go, anyways. Much as he might like to tell Sanders where to go, he instead resumed his silent seething, leading ever so gradually away from the water. The sunlight screamed from the bleached ground cover and desiccated soil, in a way that was almost hypnotic against the arrhythmic slapping and shuffling of the men's boots.

After travelling over William-didn't-know-how-far for William-couldn't-say-how-long, Sanders suddenly shoved past his right side, breaking back toward the trees with a mumbled, "Thank the Lord for that." William squinted past the boy and made out the dark shape of a man in a foraging cap against the trees. Sanders paused near the figure, still holding his trousers off the ground, and spoke briefly before marching purposefully into the brush along the embankment. The second he was out of sight, William turned to follow at a distance while unbuttoning and removing his wet coat.

A previously imperceptible breeze brought a wave of relief through William's muslin shirt as he approached the soldier to whom Sanders had spoken: a ruddy man a few years older than William, smoking a pipe in the deep shade. Pointing to the button on his own pants, William asked, "D'you mind?" The man shrugged his assent and William proceeded to strip to his drawers and hang his dripping clothes from a nearby branch.

Clifford

The older man waited until William had crouched to pull his boots back on before calmly observing, "Your friend there was in some kind of hurry."

"Oh. Him," William replied. "Where'd you send him?"

Staring from his dim post into the aggressively bright distance, the man's words wafted lazily on a cloud of rich tobacco smoke. "Sergeant Grant. 'Round the way there. Your man has concerns about the telegraph, and that'll be Grant's department."

With an air of idle curiosity, William stood quietly for a moment before saying, "Saw the line got washed out. Think they can fix it?"

The other man shrugged again and knocked his pipe against a tree. He turned into a stretch of the bank with well-trampled vegetation, and William followed a half step behind. "I truthfully give up on that the minute I saw the water," the man said. William nodded in agreement and the soldier continued, "There again, we still out here, so I'd guess Grant thinks it's possible."

"Maybe," William said, "Or maybe he just don't want to go back to camp and say it can't be done."

"Officers is funny that way," the other soldier said, "Even Sergeants." A hundred yards into low cover, yellowish-brown water collected in slow eddies and still pools on either side of the raised path. As the pair progressed, the water moved faster, until the trees surrounding them opened up to reveal the flooded river immediately below. Broken twigs and branches collected against the embankment where the trail vanished into the wide current that rushed flat through an impromptu channel beyond. The older soldier stopped at the water's edge and picked up where he had left off, "But in Grant's defense, there could be some cause for his persistence: I believe he was told there might be trouble up your way. You all request two cavalry companies and field guns, then the telegraph drops out. I half expected hostiles had cut the line to attack you."

The Beard

"Not that kind of trouble yet," William said stoically, "But some might be coming. It's that Chief up at Cibicu again, Nock-ay-det-klinne."

"The Medicine Man with the dances," the other man replied, "Heard about him, a'course. He up to something new?"

William took his time and chose his words carefully, "Not new so much as more of the old: tellin' his people he can bring back the dead for the price o' some horses, some stock, maybe grain. Except lately, when the dead don't get up, he's been blamin' it on the White Man."

"Makes sense," the other man nodded. "No reason he wouldn't. I don't guess that'll appease them what's been givin' him their horses though. But there's where you could use some extra cavalry and field guns to stop his swindled neighbors comin' for him."

"I think that was Colonel Carr's plan a few weeks ago," William said, looking a short distance out to the water, "Instead we have the opposite problem: his neighbors all stayed peaceful, and now they're gettin' on too well. Got Sanchez's people goin' to dances with Pedro's people, got Coyoteros mixin' with Tontos… But no one is talkin' to us, not even half of our scouts."

The older man shook his head slowly and muttered, "Last time they *all* kept a secret like that…"

"Half of 'em rode off with Victorio," William finished.

The other man flinched at the mention of that name. After taking a moment to absorb the full picture, he suggested, "Old Nana, what rode with Victorio; I suppose you heard he's back north."

William nodded, "Carrizo Canyon, I heard."

The man asked softly "Suppose he'll come this way if the White Mountains break out?"

"God help us if he does," William said gravely.

"God help you indeed," the other soldier sighed, "'Cause I don't guess our cavalry will."

William turned quizzically to his compatriot, "Why not?"

Clifford

The older man shrugged and motioned to the river, "No chance they'll cross when it's like this. We've about drowned two men just trying to fix the telegraph. I don't expect you'll see more guns and horses cross for some time."

William nodded cynically, "How about if I trade you Private Sanders for them?"

The older man chuckled, "Not even then I'm afraid. You'll have to drown that pup yourself, on the way home."

William nodded, "He *is* awful clumsy. I expect he could fall in on accident."

They laughed darkly before settling into a heavy silence, only occasionally interrupted by the sound of men working and talking elsewhere in the wooded corridor. Dazzling sunlight reached over the canopy of their trees and glared against the far bank. Even at this notably narrow point in the river, the low but unusually steep embankment opposite was more than fifty yards away. It was at this distance that William spotted something tall and brown moving amongst green leaves. Before he could identify the object, his new friend observed, "Speaking of drowning on accident, what's this ol' jackass doing?"

Across the water, a thin man, whose long and expansive grey beard covered most of the space between the floppy brim of his hat and his chest, was picking his way along the edge of the embankment, dangling a pack behind him. Relieved at a distraction that was clearly not a threat, William cupped his hands to his mouth and yelled, "Hey jackass! What are you doing?"

The elderly man's eyes shot up in surprise for the briefest moment before disappearing, along with the rest of him, into the sickly water.

"Oh, there he goes!" the other soldier exclaimed.

William muttered, "God damn this day," before tossing his hat at the other man and throwing himself down the bank and into the flow.

As it had that morning, the calm surface of the stream, like so much mud-smeared glass, concealed a silty torrent below. Apart

326

The Beard

from the sound of William's blood pumping in his ears, only a soft gurgle and the noise of his splashing could be heard, while the banks on both sides, the standing trees, and the drifting logs, all rushed by in their relative silence. It was only when he'd swum hard to the middle of the channel that William realized he didn't have a plan, not really. Given how fast he was being swept along, and with such little control and visibility, he didn't know how he'd expected to catch up with the old man. And once he did reach him, assuming he could, William now wondered how to best drag the victim to shore: if he caught the back of the man's shirt, would paddling with his free hand be enough to move the both of them?

Before William could make up his mind on that last point, something dark and round broke the surface just past center and a little downstream: the crown of a hat or the crown of a head, it was impossible to tell. Without another thought, William took a deep breath, dropped into the muffled dark, and gave a hard kick, extending both of his arms in front of him. He felt something of substance roll up his arm and hit his shoulder, before making a soft impact against his skull. William angled himself what he assumed to be upward, brought his hands toward one another, and kicked once more.

As a sudden brightness and the thump of his hand pounding the surface sharpened William's senses, he became aware of two things: the first was the grown man's armpit pinched tight in the crook of his elbow, and the second was a barrage of hard kicks against his shins. "Ow! Stop, would you?!... Quit fightin'!" William shouted into the brim of a felt hat.

In response, the mass in front of him gave a sharp hiss and sprayed water in the air before growling something akin to, "Kahhh! Buuhh!" and throwing out a second cloud of spittle.

Beginning to sink backwards, William yelled, "If you don't stop, I swear I will drown you!" After one last strike to William's ankle, the figure went limp, and much of the slender man floated into view beneath the hat. As William turned onto his side and pulled them through the water, the other man settled into a rhythm of soft kicks to propel them toward the shore, trailing his long beard behind them. Back amongst the leaves, William dragged them into the muck of the bank, and wrenched the other man ashore until his back bumped hollowly against wooden planks.

William finally released his charge to collapse against the obstruction- and discovered that it was the curved keel of the canoe he and Sanders had run aground hours earlier. "God damn this day," he mumbled.

The man attached to the floppy hat at William's feet coughed, sputtered, and in a much more youthful voice than William had expected asked, "What did you do that for?"

William looked down past the felt brim to find that the old man was not very old at all. The small patches of exposed skin between his clothing and hair was a healthy tan, but smooth as porcelain. And the long beard that looked dirty-grey from a distance was in fact quite dark, except when it wasn't: a chestnut backdrop shot through with light splotches and streaks, bands of yellow and red intersected then split away against coarse strips of nearly white hair. William shook off his surprise: the illusion of the young-old-man's age should not have been important. But it felt like it was.

The knowledge that the grizzled old man who required rescuing was actually young and able bodied infuriated William. Ignoring the man's question, he yelled, "What in hell were you thinkin'?!? Why would you climb that close to the water not knowin' how to swim? What did you think would happen?!?"

The victim rolled over and pushed himself into a seated position facing William. Stunned by the sudden interrogation he stammered, "I- I- East. I wanted to cross 'cause I need to be… New Mexico I think I need to… East, I know for certain."

William shook his head, nonplussed but not for long. "New Mexico you *think*?" With raised voice and raised eyebrows William continued, "If you don't know then you shouldn't be goin'! And if you are goin', you should at least know that the river bends back around!"

328

The Beard

"Oh," the man mumbled, perplexed, "I don't guess I-,"

William resumed, "So now you got to cross back over a second time! And seein' as the first time near killed you-,"

"Hey, now!" the other man interjected, beginning to get his bearings. "That ain't fair. I'm really a very good swimmer: would've been fine if you hadn't almost drowned me."

William stared, wide-eyed and dumbfounded. He sternly replied "If *I* hadn't-,"

"Yea," the man nodded, calmly, "I was wrestling with my pack a little, but I about had that settled when you showed up and made me drop it. You know really, I should be mad at you."

William shook his head and mumbled something unintelligible that he would later remember as a quiet and ceaseless string of obscenities. Without reengaging, he pushed himself away from the canoe and back to his feet, to return to a narrow path of vegetation still flattened from his earlier walk with Sanders. Breaking once again from the thick smell of sopping green, into the merciless Arizona sun, every step he took squeezed water from his socks to between his toes. William heard clattering and rustling in the bushes behind him, followed by a thump and the uneven sound of shoes slapping against the bare dirt. "Hey," the man called, "Where are we going?"

William answered with determined silence.

After nearly half a mile of awkward following, the man tried again, "I don't know where you want me to go. Because now I need provisions, and really you owe me a pack because I had provisions, and then you made me drop my pack and so you... I know you hear me. Hey, I'm coming with you! Are we getting close at least?"

Having already given up his hat, William lowered his gaze and squinted at the nearby shade. He jealously wished for respite from the cloudless sky, but refused to sacrifice his ankles or one more minute of his day traipsing through the brush. The bearded man's voice cut again through the thick afternoon, "I'm Hugh, by the way. In case you were interested."

Clifford

Relenting, William mused sourly over his shoulder, "You're me?"

"I'm...," the voice started confusedly. "No, I'm not *you*. I'm *Hugh*. Carroll. Hugh Carroll. Is me."

Wordlessly, William Grafton soldiered on, widening his stride into a sort of waddle, doing what little he could to keep his soaked drawers off his crotch while his boots baked into a hard shell.

Day 9

"I've gotta go!!!" Kristin insisted.

"Alright," Jared answered calmly, "I heard you. There aren't many options out here. You'll have to be patient."

"But…" Kristin moaned, beginning to rock back and forth in her seat, "C'maahhwwn… I gotta gooooo."

Jared smiled in spite of himself and eased the accelerator toward the floor. He hadn't seen a posted speed limit for almost as long as he hadn't seen a public restroom. He had assumed that 50 miles an hour was acceptable on this two lane highway, but since the road was straight as an arrow, flat as could be, and virtually abandoned (also paved, which he thought might be special for this stretch of country), he guessed that he could push their pace.

But whether Jared ran twenty miles an hour or seventy-five, it would feel as though they were sitting still. The deep West Texas landscape was so broad and featureless, in color as well as texture, that every pebble and bush took on special significance: on the limitless horizon that divided the cloudless sky from the brown earth and roadway, even a cactus less than five-foot tall could serve as a landmark. For not the first time in his life, Jared was struck by the notion that in a uniform place, distinction was easy.

As a case in point, Jared found his eye uncontrollably drawn to a distant, subtle variation in the endless row of telephone poles that ran parallel to the road: one dark vertical was more tightly spaced and just out of line with those nearest it. Was it a mile up the road? Two? Ten? On this oceanic plain it was impossible to tell. As they drew gradually closer, it became clear that the forks atop the post were not forks at all, but the square edges of a blank marquee. From the sundrenched haze at the base of the pole materialized a squat, single story building. With every yard the vehicle covered, the structure gained additional detail: maroon siding, a boxy asphalt shingle roof, a large awning near the road, and eventually a narrow gap between that shelter and the building.

"Gas station," Kristin said breathlessly, "Gas station! Jared, pull over at the gas station!"

Jared lifted his foot and allowed the car to coast to the outlet of a gravel driveway. Creeping around the building, he leaned to look past Kristin, who still bounced and swayed in the passenger seat. Something was off. "There's no pumps," Jared announced.

"Stop the car," Kristin answered, "Lemme out."

"But there's no pumps," Jared repeated evenly, "And no sign. I don't think the place is open."

"I don't think I give a shit," Kristin said. "I'll try the front door, and if there's no one inside I will piss behind the building like a man. Now stop the damn car!"

Jared braked deliberately, respectful of Kristin's hurry but careful not to cause any jarring movement. By the time Jared shifted into 'Park,' Kristin had her door open. She made a strange, frantic sound as she threw off her seatbelt then bolted for the front of the building a few dozen feet away. The place looked extremely abandoned. Faux brick ran the façade from the cracked pavement up to about chest height. Above that, plate glass stretched the full length of the wall; or rather, it had at one time. The window nearest the car had been filled in with cinder blocks. The opposite side was still technically made of glass, but one corner had been heavily duct-taped, and the entirety had been coated in a darkly tinted film that now peeled at odd intervals across the top.

Kristin raced to a solid aluminum door that would have been more suited to a house: clearly a recent addition slapped into the middle of the front. She pushed on a small brass knob, and the door swung easily, far enough for her to poke her head through for a second before shuffling inside. "I'll be damned," Jared muttered to himself. It was only then that he noticed a straw welcome mat on the broken sidewalk and three late model pickup trucks parked in the shade by the side of the building. He was still very sure that no one sold gasoline here, but whatever the new owners were up to, he

The Beard

could assume they kept the public restrooms open. Jared cut the engine and climbed slowly out of the driver's seat, taking an extra minute to stretch from his knees to his shoulders in the dusty smelling sunlight.

Jared felt good. He had for several days, and he couldn't explain why: if anything, he supposed, he should feel worse the longer and further they went, but he didn't. It was as though a switch had flipped in his head while he wasn't looking, and instead of anxiously racing a clock, he found himself enthusiastically pursuing a goal. What that goal was he still couldn't say, but his newfound good vibes had prompted him to push forward as soon as possible. According to Kristin, it may have been too soon, in that the end of the map was still thin and non-descript when they had left Austin, but Jared had deciphered enough of the next leg to get them started, and now that they could see the end of it, they were already two-thirds of the way there. Their related arguments notwithstanding, it made Jared wish that they would have moved faster all along.

As he meandered around the front of the car, he casually observed that Kristin had been gone a couple minutes. Not long enough to cause concern, but enough that she must have at least discovered a business with a restroom inside, and Jared's combination of energy, curiosity, and boredom compelled him to learn what that business was. He departed the shade of the awning to stroll quickly to the building and found himself automatically wiping his feet on the straw mat in front of the entrance as he turned the warm brass knob. With a thick smack, swollen weather stripping let go of the incongruous door which swung open to reveal an equally incongruous interior.

A pair of polished billiard tables sat to the left of the door, under the tinted windows. Directly across from where Jared stood, a small hardwood dance floor with a slightly smaller stage was surrounded by a half dozen wooden tables, cleaned to gleaming save a couple of old drink rings. On the far end of the space, a long, solid oak bar ran in front of refrigerator cases that likely dated to the building's previous incarnation. The length of this was now tastefully illuminated with track lighting, apart from a large section of blank wall devoted to a flat screen TV, which was in turn devoted to *The Price is Right*. While the descriptor 'sleek' might have been a stretch for the establishment, modern and tidy would have been fair, if not for the stale, urine-esque odor of long-dead off-brand cigarettes.

Behind the bar, a woman in her early fifties with curly grey hair and a blue gingham shirt drew glass mugs of beer from a line of ceramic taps for a trio of slightly disheveled, though not unkempt, customers. Wanting to be neither rude nor overly familiar, Jared approached the bar and took a seat, leaving one empty stool between him and a grizzled looking man in his forties who wore large wire rimmed glasses and oil stained denim coveralls. The bar tender placed the last draught in front of a man at the end of the counter and disinterestedly asked, "That blonde in the powder room yours?"

"Yeh," Jared nodded. The other three men quietly alternated their focus between their drinks and the game show.

The woman followed up, "Can I get you anything while you wait?"

Jared took stock of his surroundings again: it really felt like a whiskey place, in spite of the fact that the room was drinking beer. And while he didn't want to spend all morning nursing a beverage, it wouldn't be right to not buy alcohol: after all, the woman was running a business and was considerate enough to let them use her restroom. "Yes," Jared declared, "I wouldn't fight a shot of bourbon."

The middle of the other three patrons gave a low chortle. The woman, incredulous but not contrary, moved to the middle of the bar and came back holding a full shot glass. With blithe obliviousness, Jared tossed back the drink and slammed the bottom of the glass to the bar, causing the collected assembly to start. He held the liquor in his mouth, rapidly drummed on the bar with both hands and issued an abrupt "MMMHH!!!" before swallowing.

The Beard

In the moment that followed, the group tacitly agreed to lock away from Jared to each other, before renewing their interest in the show playing softly on the television. Just as they began to relax back into their stools, Jared said loudly, "Y'know on second thought, I think I'll have what they're having. In a bottle though, if you got it." The bartender accommodated him without further discussion. As Jared noisily slurped the foam from the neck of his beer, Kristin appeared from somewhere around the side of the refrigerator cases.

"Oh," she said unobtrusively, "There you are." She walked past the customers to Jared's far side, before continuing quietly, "Are you ready to...?" Acknowledging his drink she answered herself, "I guess you are not." Leaning in to lower her volume still further, Kristin asked, "Isn't it maybe early for that?"

At full volume, Jared answered, "Why? It's not too early for these guys."

At the end of the bar, a man in a dirty blue t-shirt and a ball cap clarified, "Don't bring us into it: we on eleven to seven. Only been off work a couple hours."

With a note of impatience, the man nearest Jared added, "So it's *late* for us. Too early for *you*."

On the flat screen over the bar, Drew Carey invited another contestant to come on down.

Jared ignored the lot of them and told Kristin, "I just sat down, and we're not in a hurry. As soon as I finish this, we'll go."

Kristin glanced at the strangers glaring back at her while Jared stared straight ahead at the TV. Exchanging a look with the bartender, she said firmly, "Really, Jared, I don't wanna be here all day."

"I gotcha," he said sideways without turning his head. More directly at the program, Jared shouted, "One Dollar BOB!!"

Once again, the other patrons jolted in their seats, but this time they answered with assorted groans. The man at the end of the bar demanded, "What the hell man? You gotta have somethin' to say 'bout everything?"

Clifford

"Not my fault," Jared insisted, "Every one of those morons over bid. There is clearly no way-,"

"I gotta spell it out for you?" the man nearest him growled. "We work a full shift. We stop at a quiet place for a quiet drink, which we are goddamned entitled to. If you can't appreciate that and shut the fuck up, you best find another place to drink."

Kristin put a hand on Jared's arm and immediately answered, "I think that's a good idea." But by the time she finished the sentence, Jared had wrenched his arm away to turn and glower at the man.

The other spat, "Best listen to your girl."

Jared's mind raced in a way that surprised him, for both the rapidity and the clarity of his thoughts, like a laser shot into space. He first recognized the absurdity of the argument: of course, he could shut the fuck up or move the fuck on, as suggested. Realistically, he knew there was no practical reason for him to shout at this or any other television, and he understood the pointlessness of pursuing any path of more resistance than the one that ran out the door. At the same time, he had been insulted, even mildly embarrassed, and right or wrong, as a man, he felt he was entitled to some recompense. But then again, the other man had a point: he, Jared, was in their backyard acting inappropriately, and possibly, hell, probably, deserved the admonition, unpleasant though it may be. In context, it was hard for him to get upset by it.

And in truth, Jared wasn't upset. Not even a little. Actually, he still felt pretty good.

Which was why he was astonished to discover, on the cusp of a reasonable response, that his left hand was already in motion, sweeping impulsively over the empty stool beside him and toward the bespectacled face. Jared half stood in detached fascination at the feeling of the other man's teeth against the back of his hand, and marveled at how easily his adversary was knocked off balance, out of his seat, and onto the floor.

For all his wonderment, Jared's mind continued to whir, discerning that it no longer mattered how he would have liked for

The Beard

this to go. Much as he might regret the escalation, Jared was committed now: he had just bitch slapped a man twice his size, and if he hesitated long enough to let the guy up, he would be made to regret it. As the man rolled onto his side, Jared began to throw his weight forward, but was stopped by a flash of inspiration. He reached to his right and felt his hand close around the neck of his beer bottle. In a single, smooth motion, he smashed the end against the rounded edge of the bar and leapt gleefully off of his stool.

Jared brought his knees forward to plant them on the other man's back, but found himself unexpectedly forced to the side, with shouts and hands coming at him from every direction. Jared blinked once and discovered he was no longer looking at the big dude with glasses but rather at the acoustic ceiling tiles. Another blink, and he saw the bartender's screaming face, somewhere between panic and rage. One more blink brought the vision of a beefy, flannel covered elbow coming towards him, the next, an extreme close-up of the light colored carpet. Forcing himself away from the noise and contact, Jared rolled backwards and somehow, without meaning to, put his feet back underneath him.

He was pushed and pulled by unseen forces: a hand on each of his wrists, two more at one arm, something blunt against his stomach, maybe a shoulder or the crown of someone's head, all moving him haltingly away from the bar, stumbling until he felt a brass doorknob in his ribs. Over the chaos of indiscriminate yelling, weather stripping loudly peeled free again. Something pulled Jared's shirt taught across his chest and around his throat as he tumbled into searing daylight. The monotonous, blinding brown landscape spun around him twice as he was tossed face first into the gravel.

For what felt like several minutes, Jared lay on his belly with his limbs outstretched, listening to the commotion continue deep beneath the sound of his heart beating in his ears. Eventually, he pulled his right arm nearer his body and raised the palm of his hand a few inches from his face. As Jared watched, a set of small scrapes began to fill with blood, and individual words materialized behind him.

A man's voice bellowed, "That don't matter! He ain't never *even* drunk, just a goddamned *psych*-o!"

"Yes," Kristin's voice pleaded, "I have him. I'll take care of it!"

An older woman's husky voice yelled over the others, "I don't wanna call the sheriff's! Don't you make me call the sheriff's, now!"

"Yes!" Kristin yelled from nearby. "No, I won't make you! Just let me... we're going now!"

Satisfied or not, the voices subsided for the moment. On the other side of Jared's bloodied hand, Kristin's white sneakers stopped in a cloud of yellow-brown dust. Jared followed her bare ankles to her calves to the cuff of her jean shorts mid-thigh, working his way over her black tank top to her face. He expected to see tears tracking down her cheeks, a brow furrowed with concern for his safety, his sanity, his well-being, his whatever.

What Jared found instead was abject fury. Even in silhouette, with the halo of the late morning sun behind her, Jared could make out the intensity of Kristin's eyes, the flared nostrils, and rigidly set jaw. With far more than her share of restraint, but in a tone that burned hotter than the rocks buried in Jared's wounded hand, Kristin commanded in a low voice, "Get up."

Jared lowered his right arm and levered his left to raise himself as far as his scraped knees. "I'm sorry," he mumbled, "That got away from me, I-,"

Kristin repeated, "Get up."

Jared slowly stood the rest of the way, continuing to blubber, "But I had to though. When he called you a cunt, I had to-,"

Kristin's seething rage momentarily turned to confusion. "No," she said, perplexed, "No one said that. Not until you, just now."

"But... But he said," Jared stammered, "Didn't he say?"

The Beard

The more noises that came out of Jared, the more acute Kristin's anger became. Forgoing debate, she resumed her original posture. "Get. In. The fucking. Car."

Sheepishly, Jared put one foot in front of the other and shuffled away to the sound of raucous laughter. Climbing into the driver's side, he felt a dry crunch against his thigh: blood from his palm smeared against the tail of his shirt as he gingerly pulled his shattered phone from his hip pocket. Jared raised his head, and was forced again to look to the front of the establishment. Outside, Kristin said something over her shoulder and moved quickly toward the car. Behind her, the two men from the end of the bar mocked Jared, while the bartender nodded fretfully. To the other side of the entrance, the man with glasses, much older and much heavier than Jared had realized, shook his head in a kind of saddened disgust.

"Fine," Jared muttered to himself. What could it possibly matter? Not like they would see any of those people again anyways.

Ninth Growth

August 22, 1881

On a small patch of bare earth, amongst low grass and scrub, William worked a narrow limb into a shallow pile of kindling. A row of squat, wood-sided barracks cast long shadows that faded with as much calm inevitability as the orange and red sky above the distant ridgeline, all victims to the ceaseless march of the wide-open darkness rising in the East. On the far side of William's anemic excuse for a fire, Sanders sat in the dirt beside a short bench that he had pressed into service as a writing desk. Sanders leaned closer to his work and asked over his shoulder, "Do you think you'll be much longer? I can't hardly see what I'm doing."

"Not buildin' it for light," William answered gruffly. "It's meant for warmth. An' it's still plenty warm out yet, so I'm in no hurry." Not that it would matter much: William knew that any attempt at real comfort was an exercise in futility. He and every one of his comrades would wake shivering more than once before dawn, at which time they could look forward to another day of searing heat. But William insisted on doing what little he could to solve a problem before he complained about it, and he planned to have no shortage of complaints about the temperature.

"If it's heat you want," Sanders said, still squinting through the twilight to scribble on the paper in front of him, "Then you should see the girl I'm writing to. This girl, I am tellin' you, shapely don't begin to describe. You'll never see a neck that long with tits that big, I am tellin' you. And those eyes, the looks she give me... I hate thinking what she could get up to with me gone away this long. I have to write her every day, make sure she knows I'm keeping an eye on her."

"I didn't ask," William said, knowing as he did that it would make no more difference than the fire he was building.

"But how," Sanders continued, "Can I write something new for her every day, when nothing ever happens around here?"

Clifford

William blandly admonished, "You don't want nothin' to happen around here. Out here, things happenin' don't ever end well, and when things *really* happen, the people you'd like to tell won't have the stomach to hear it."

Sanders grunted in reply. It was his usual response, William had noticed, any time he was told something he didn't want to hear. The habit was exacerbated by Sanders' discriminating tastes when it came to other people's words, which made it unrewarding to say much to him and was probably why so few people did. William wasn't sure why he continued to bother with the boy. He figured someone had to, he had the time, and, despite what he had just said, he was bored too.

"Dammit," Sanders muttered at the page, "I can't see a damned thing. When you goin' to put some damned wood on that fire so's I can see what I'm doing?"

"Yes," a voice boomed mockingly from out of sight around the closest cabin, causing Sanders to startle, "When *are* you goin' to put some damned wood on that fire?"

William stopped what he was doing and stood, beaming, to approach the speaker. "I wasn't sure whether to expect you," he called back. The meager light of his nascent fire-for-warmth caught streaks of silver, crimson, and blonde as Hugh's massive beard swayed into view ahead of his sparkling eyes, full seconds before the appearance of his well-tanned cheeks. The two men shook hands while Sanders glowered at his bench-desk below. "Have a seat, why don't you," William said, reaching down to half fold Sanders' paper out of the way.

Sanders snatched a page to his chest and Hugh nodded to him politely as he sat on the end of the bench, "You may want to wait on your reading until the fire gets a little bigger."

William strolled around and settled back into his task of gingerly adding kindling. "Fire ain't for light. Meant for warmth."

"Oh," Hugh answered brightly, "No hurry then. Still pretty warm out, seems to me." William shrugged his agreement. Lowering his volume, Hugh inquired, "But wouldn't you be

344

The Beard

warmer sleeping *inside* the barracks? And you," he said gesturing to Sanders, still seated on the ground "Wouldn't a lamp at a table indoors solve your problem?"

"What do you care?" Sanders shot back, gathering his pencil and paper, and standing brusquely, "An' why are you still here?" Not waiting for reply, he stormed out of sight into the evening from whence Hugh had come, while the latter man shook his head, and William laughed.

"Well, I can think of one reason to keep you around!" William chortled, "I don't know how you get so far under that boy's skin, but my God! You have a talent for running him off!"

Hugh shrugged, "It's only jealousy."

"It's what now?" William asked, as his laughter tapered off.

"Jealousy," Hugh repeated, "He admires you, but you and I get on better'n you and him. He can't make out how to impress you, so instead he gets angry with me."

"Ad-mire," William scoffed, "The hell you say. That boy is a constant thorn in my side: always underfoot, always talkin' himself up..."

"Exactly as I say," Hugh nodded, "He wants to impress you, doesn't know how. I speak from experience: I once had a dog was just like that. Damn thing barked all the time, chased after me, nipped at me, for no reason but he wanted attention, didn't know how else to get it. So, I taught him to do things, to sit, roll over, to beg, and the like. After that, instead of pesterin' all day, he would just sit tall or play dead, because he knowed that was what I wanted from him."

"Right, so I should rub Sanders' belly and call him a good boy?"

"In a manner of speaking," Hugh smiled. "Try givin' him something to do: any old nonsense task you want done, but one you don't much care about. Then if he does it, then yes, you tell him he did good. Over time maybe he'll stop talking, maybe wait for you to talk instead." Answering William's curious expression, Hugh insisted, "People aren't as complicated as they'd like to believe.

Clifford

Most I've seen just do what they must to get what they want. If my mongrel dog could work that out, I bet even Sanders can."

William gave a short chuckle and continued feeding the fire. As much a consequence of the approaching darkness as of the growing flames, the circle of light around the two men drove past the exposed dirt to the short brown grass of the parade grounds beyond. Picking through his kindling to select a poker, William offhandedly said, "Bedbugs."

"How's that now?" Hugh asked easily.

"Why we don't sleep in the barracks," William explained. "In winter, sure, got no choice, but in August, those damned bed bugs about carry you off in the night." Hugh nodded and William continued, "So that speaks to your earlier point. But as to Sanders' question... Why *do* you keep coming around?"

Thoughtfully, Hugh answered, "I don't know anyone else here." Smiling, he added, "And I figure you still owe me for the gear you made me drop in the river."

"See if I ever save your life again, y'damned ingrate," William said sarcastically.

"I know it," Hugh laughed, "And then you bring me here, get me work in the steam mill and all-,"

William waved off the comment, "But neither I, nor the miller, nor anyone else expected you'd stay for long. Not that you have to leave: I'm told you're a fine worker an' all, but the way you talk, don't seem like you're making any plans. Weren't you on your way somewheres?"

"Yes," Hugh nodded simply, "New Mexico. But you've said it ain't safe."

"Oh," William said, gently setting a log on the fire, "Well, I haven't heard anything one way or other for some time, but that stretch of road will never be completely safe, no matter how long you wait. Same time, dangerous roads didn't stop you gettin' this far from home."

"Exactly right," Hugh affirmed, "That swim we took was not my first scrape, not by a mile. Nearly got myself killed a dozen

346

The Beard

times comin' south, and the further I go the tougher things seem to get. But I'm so close to the end now, I shouldn't get careless when I'm this close to the end-,"

In exasperation, William demanded, "End of what? Every night you say somethin' sideways about how you're close, not much further, but you never say closer to what. How can I tell you if the road is safe, when you won't say what road you mean, or where it's goin'?"

Staring at the low flames, Hugh shrugged again, but this time followed with silence.

William couldn't say why, but he found the gesture infuriating: in some way dishonest and in every way melodramatic. He had set this man up proper at the fort, and while he didn't require any thanks, he also didn't expect this caginess. He added another small log and growled accusingly, "If you *really* care about gettin' wherever it is, you'd explain yourself so maybe I could help, get you prepared, stocked up, moved on… *if* you really care about that. Turnin' up at the steam mill every morning and the barracks every night… That won't get you nowhere. Or maybe you too scared for whatever comes next. I suppose what you doin' now would make some sense if you was a coward."

Hugh sank back onto the bench, his eyes fading inscrutably into shadows while William tersely tended the fire. Finally relenting to the awkwardness, Hugh confessed, "Maybe I am scared. Maybe got reason to be scared."

"More reason than any of us?" William asked harshly. "You ain't seen what I seen, I don't guess. I ain't been hiding away here like you have. What could you possibly be after out there, to keep you cowering in here?"

Hugh resignedly sighed, "Ezekiel Gates."

"What are those now?" William asked.

"Not what, it's…" Hugh paused. After a moment he cleared his throat and leaned forward to place his elbows on his knees. In the dancing firelight, his beard swung thick near his ankles, almost sweeping the dirt between his feet. Lowering his volume, but

347

Clifford

directing his words, Hugh continued with purpose, "It's a story. It's the story of two widows."

William sat back to watch through the rising smoke. He wasn't sure how seriously to take whatever he was about to hear, and if it wasn't sincere after the adamancy of his prompting, then he wasn't sure that he shouldn't be insulted. All the same, even if the story was false, William figured he had time for it. And a tale involving two widows held some promise. He raised his palms quietly, gesturing for his companion to proceed.

Hugh spoke softly into the fire, the light behind his eyes floating further into the distance with every word, "The story begins back where I'm from in Yuba City. There's this boy I growed up with there, his name don't much matter now, but me and him was like you and Sanders, only I was the mutt in that friendship. He was a year older y'see, and he was always ahead of me at everything. Better'n me at everything. An' since he knowed he was better'n me, he found he could make about anything into a contest: couldn't go up the road without it bein' a race, couldn't fish in the summer without seein' who brung back more, an' it was always him what won, an' some ways that made me happy I guess, seein' my friend happy, but somehow I still come to hate him for it. Then one day last fall, he starts growin' a beard, so naturally I had to try to-"

"Wait," William interrupted, "You mean to tell me you grew that in less than a year?!? I'd have guessed that monstrosity took five times as long!"

"Fair t'say," Hugh continued nonchalantly, "I finally found somethin' I's better at than he was. Hardly a fortnight and I had more whiskers than both of our fathers, my uncles, and every other man in town, hell, every man I've spoke with since. But boy did it chap my friend, just the sight of me… I expect it's the reason I kept it, t'bother him. And for his part, at a certain point he decided he should make merciless fun of me. There was no room for him to challenge my manliness on its face, or on my face as it were, but the color of the thing, well, you see it… calico was an easy insult.

348

The Beard

For a time he tried out Autumn, on account of the fall colors, or 'Hugh of Many Hues,' that was a favorite. Then one day he asked me by his family's place to show me somethin'. His father was havin' some dispute with a neighbor that called for a engineer's map of their property. Pretty thing, colorful, showed every tract in the county, but really he just brought me over so's he could mock me, tell me my beard had as many colors as his map.

"Thing is, he was right: the lines in my beard very nearly looked like the lines on the page. Very nearly, though not exactly. He spotted some red parts of my beard that pushed out further than the Feather River did on his map. I didn't tell him what I heard that summer from a couple other boys I knew, that some irrigation ditches were bein' dug south of Marysville right where those lines pushed out. So y'see, my beard wasn't just like his map of the confluence at Yuba City, because *it was more accurate than his map*. Except," Hugh leaned in toward the firelight and ran his finger down a long, blond streak at his sideburn, "For this part. This one line... the top of it I knew aligned with a road out along the levee, but the bottom then meandered off, I couldn't say where. So I set out to find where it went. Didn't tell nobody, least of all my friend, woulda never hear-ed the end of that. One morning last winter, I borrowed a looking glass from my mother's dressing table and I used it to follow that line on my face, down the road and off of it, through forest and field, a good fifteen miles before I came to a cabin in a clearing where the trail faded.

"But before I could get to the porch, I tripped and fell over a tiny monument in the lawn. Smaller than most grave stones, a little marker just read "Ezekiel Gates. 1807 – 1836." That was all, just a name and some dates, and no other graves about. I can't explain, but it seemed to me that this was what I come for, so I sat and I looked at it, I don't know how long. I didn't even notice when a very old lady with a very old rifle come down from the house, not until she took aim and asked me my business. I couldn't think what to tell her, so I asked her the first thing t'mind: 'how did he die?' It

Clifford

turned out to be the best thing to say. Turned out she wanted to tell about her long-lost love, but nobody ever bothered ask.

"The old gal invited me in, and all that evening and into the night, she told about her girlhood in Texas, about the dashing young man who appeared as if from heaven near her family place in the late spring in 1824, and about how she'd pined for him until one day he gave her a second look and asked her to be his wife. She told me about their brief marriage, five years of bliss before he got his self caught up in a fight for revolution. She allowed she could share his affections with the Texian Army for a time, but in less than a year he went and got massacred at the Alamo."

"Wait," William interrupted, "If... You say you found his grave in California? How did that come about?"

"I wondered the same," Hugh nodded, "And she told me that anything really left of him was somewhere in Texas. There were no remains y'see, or none that reached her, but it didn't seem right to let her husband go forgotten after he died for his country. She said she couldn't stop the country keeping his body, but she would never give over his memory, so she had this stone made, put it on a family plot with no bones under it. Twenty years on, she followed a sister north, and she figured she ought to bring Ezekiel with her: no one would visit his stone once she left, and settin' it down on virgin soil in California or Texas, wouldn't be no difference really."

"Practical," William chimed. Turning a log with his poker he added "May I tell you that your tale of two widows is much sadder than I'd hoped it would be?"

"Oh," Hugh resumed, "It got worse. For a few days I kept thinkin' about her, this sad old widow out there by herself. I got thinkin' that she wasn't so far from me that I couldn't be of some help, at least be a comfort to her. After about a week of thinkin' I went back, but she wasn't at her little house. A neighbor was there, and they told me she had just died, just dropped on the road on her way God knows where, would have been the very day after I spoke to her."

The Beard

William somberly intoned, "And now there is no one left to tend the grave that never truly held her love."

Hugh winced. "Good lord," he muttered, "Hadn't considered that part of it. Now *you've* put *me* in a state." He shook his head and rejoined his story, "See, I didn't have too long to meditate on any of that, because the next day I was thinking I might like to saw off my beard after everything, and while I was contemplatin' that in the looking glass, I discovered that this line," he gestured again to the blonde streak, "Which had ended up here the day before, suddenly extended down t'here."

"It grew that much overnight?" William asked skeptically.

"No," Hugh clarified, "The hair was already that long, but the color around it turned, pulled me further and further afield, and since I already covered so much of it on the first trek, it only seemed reasonable that I follow the new section to the end. Again, I took my glass and set out, past the widow's cabin a good ten miles, and there I found…" Hugh paused for effect and raised his hands in a sweeping gesture, "Another cabin. It was a little larger, with a smaller lot, no graves that I could see, so I went directly to call at the door.

"A woman answered. She looked to be younger than the first woman I'd met, but not by too much. Not anything like youthful, but still healthy and spry. She seemed as wary as you might expect her to be with a strange man calling, and I hadn't given much thought to what I would say if I found someone at home, so I went with the first thing t'mind again: first thing t'mind that day was that I's looking for a man named Ezekiel Gates. I didn't guess she would know what I was on about, thought she might send me on my way, but I figured that if I could get her talkin', maybe she knew more than she realized.

"Turns out I didn't have to work that hard. She heard the name, 'Ezekiel Gates' and swooned, nearly fainted, right there on the porch. I helped her find a seat on the steps, and once she had composed herself she told me the *Exact. Same. Story.* Or very nearly the same, anyways. See, she had met Ezekiel, an older man than herself, in Texas in 1838. They fell in love immediately and were married that same year. Then there was a short, and to her mind wonderful marriage. But then in 1846... I don't guess you heard of the Thornton Affair?"

"Huh?" William asked, "You mean Thornton Massacre? Before my time, but have I not mentioned I'm from Texas?"

"Only every day," Hugh said, "That's why I guessed you might know it."

"More than 1600 Mexican soldiers lighting on eighty Americans? It started the whole damn war with Mexico, of course I know it."

"Yep, well," Hugh explained, "It seems that Ezekiel Gates, this woman's husband Ezekiel Gates, was among the seven people killed in that ambush."

"Wait," William interjected, "So this man, Ezekiel Gates, gets his self declared dead at the Alamo, then instead of going home to his wife, he leaves her for a widow while he goes and finds a second wife? All to end up gunned down in that Thornton business?"

"It seems so," Hugh confirmed, "Assuming he actually was gunned down. If he walked away and reappeared the first time, I'm not certain that he didn't do it again. But there again, I didn't have much time to contemplate: the line in my beard grew longer, as before, and every time I followed to the end, next day I found it longer still. The path travelled down t'the tip of my beard and back up the other side. It's run me as far south as the border, and as far west as the sea. And every time it stopped for a moment was a time I'd find more of Ezekiel: a name carved into a tree, a sign painted on a building advertising Ezekiel Gates Dry Goods, a street in a farming village in Nevada called Ezekiel Gates' Road. Everywhere I go he has been one step ahead of me. But doing what? I do not know, except that his widows were only the beginning."

Hugh's voice trailed off. The two men sat in perfect stillness, staring into a fire whose crackling and light served as the only

The Beard

respite in a featureless night. A long and weighty moment passed before William delicately ventured, "And?"

Hugh returned his attention, "'Scuse me?"

"If the widows were the beginning of your story," William stated, "Then what's the end?"

Hugh cocked his head and regarded William sternly, "How should I know? It's still going on: these events are still happening to me."

The two maintained eye contact for another long silence before William burst into laughter, "The hell you say! I hand it to you though, you spin a good yarn. I thank you for passing the time..."

Hugh snapped, "How well you do know the terrain out here?"

Humoring him, William considered, "Very well, I'd say. Been patrolling these en-vi-rons a few years now."

Hugh half stood and shuffled around the fire toward William. Holding the bottom of his beard away from the flames, he leaned in to the fire and pointed to a quadrangle of black hair nestled inside a red curve near his jaw line. "If we here, and this," he traced a few inches down to a smaller black square, "is Fort Thomas, then we met," he moved his hand slightly to a winding red swirl, "Around here."

William scooted closer and squinted to distinguish one color from another. Through his assessment William mumbled, "I can see why you might think that, but the Gila River would have to be three times wider than..."

Holding his pose, Hugh interrupted, "Yes. It would have to be as high as anyone has ever seen it, which everyone around here keeps tellin' me it is."

The words were lost on William. As his eyes adjusted to the firelight he ceased to see the other man's face. Neither could he make out individual hairs or isolated patterns. The lines and curves, colors and limits, stood suddenly in high relief. William saw mountains and plateaus that he had ranged a hundred times, and every stream and wash from the San Carlos substation to the White River and well beyond. And through it all a thin blonde streak cut,

353

meandered, slithered, and reached, into oblivion in front of Hugh's ear. "Incredible," William whispered, "It shouldn't... it can't... just incredible."

Sliding back around the fire to face William from a greater distance, Hugh said, "Also nearly finished. The path looks to finally be done growing." He pointed again, low on the blonde line, "Fort Thomas." Pointing slightly higher up, "Fort Apache."

As Hugh pointed to his hairline, William finished, "New Mexico."

"Precisely," Hugh nodded.

William sat, absorbing that information for a time before cautiously asking, "What do you think is waiting at the end then?"

Hugh answered without hesitation, "I've given up guessing. But if you help me, we can find out together."

The Beard

Day 1

Amongst the low grass and scrub, small patches of bare earth screamed in red and orange from the roadside. The violating glare of the wide open landscape collapsed beneath the gradually lengthening shadow of a vehicle on a two lane highway. Kristin viewed all of it as a marked improvement: they were finally travelling with the sun at their back, and were finally, *finally,* on paved roads instead of dirt. The dark hood in front of them allowed Kristin to stop squinting, but that was the only comfort of travelling through the desert in a black car with a sunroof in summer. Even with the A/C at full tilt, she had to practically plank in her seat and peel her clothing away from her skin to stop the feeling that she might develop bedsores.

Repeating that maneuver, she told herself (as she was increasingly wont to do) to make some small effort at finding something positive in their situation. She considered how lucky it was that they couldn't afford a car with leather seats.

Noting her discomfort, Jared enthusiastically asked, "You okay?" clearly demonstrating his interest if not ability to help her keep her shorts from riding up her ass crack in the car.

"Yeah," Kristin shot back tersely, "I'm fine." For a moment she considered apologizing for her tone, or adjusting it and finding something else to say, just to clear the air so that Jared might not feel bad. But then she didn't. She wasn't completely sure that he shouldn't feel bad. She knew she was irritated, had been for several days, and she wasn't sure why, but she suspected it was Jared's fault. It was easy to see how it could be, and if it was then maybe he deserved her ire.

At the very least, Kristin's shittiness had been keeping Jared on his best behavior, but she hated sustaining it all the same. She reassured herself that she wasn't that kind of girlfriend (or now fiancé), that she was positive and grateful as a rule, and that even throughout these unusual circumstances, she had been especially accommodating and supportive. But wasn't there a limit to that kind of support? At what point did encouragement become enablement? She wasn't sure, but when she had watched Jared lunge at that old man two days earlier, she had realized that wherever the line was they'd crossed it.

And so she had done what she'd felt would be most helpful to him: she had laced into him, nonstop like a harpy, for the better part of an hour. After that, she had instituted total silence for the remainder of that day and for most of the day after. Not until last evening had she relented to begin the long and ongoing thaw. In some ways she hated this part most of all. She couldn't let him think that his previous actions were acceptable, but punishing him was exhausting, and for her own sake she couldn't keep it up indefinitely. So instead, she vacillated between wanting to forgive and not being fool enough to forget, between wanting to turn homeward, so they could recover from their proverbial wounds, and resenting Jared for the possibility that he might come to resent her for forcing that decision on him.

In the end, Kristin had negotiated a series of bargains with herself. Among the most important: she would trust that this entire misadventure was anomalous, that once they got back to their home, to their routine, that she would find herself able to forget whatever mistakes had been made on their journey. She also tacitly agreed to see this quest through, but only up to such point as she had already promised, namely as far as Nevada and no further. That should be soon, Kristin thought: they were already out of New Mexico, though the very end of this map did double back, which worried her a little.

Additionally, she had promised herself that, as she allowed Jared back into her good graces, she would complete the trip one day at a time. Given Jared's recent volatility, she wasn't sure how to get by without fully resetting her expectations each day. In that context, all told, today had been reasonably good... so far. After forcing herself to swallow every conscious effort at forgiveness and

356

The Beard

open-mindedness (or short-sightedness: the terms varied with her mood), she couldn't shed the gut sense of dread at finding their upcoming destination. Maybe the next one she'd feel better about, but at this point she braced herself, not for what they might find but for whatever reaction it might provoke from Jared.

She also recognized that the only way to put this all behind them was to do exactly that: to continue forward from one map to the next until they reached a place where Kristin was allowed to set their course home. "Four more miles," Kristin said simply, "There will be a right turn there."

Gesturing to the featureless landscape, Jared asked somewhat sarcastically, "How can you tell with no streets and no landmarks?"

Kristin pursed her lips, squinted, and shook her head at him. She was prepared to move forward, but only if Jared stayed on the narrow path with her.

Adjusting his tone, Jared said casually, "I mean... how *can* you tell? Sweetie? Sugar plum?"

Kristin let him twist a second longer, then nodded, "That's better." In the interest of positive reinforcement, she made her own deliberate adjustment and overcorrected to slightly saccharine, "Mile markers and waterways." Dialing it back a bit she expounded, "The last few weeks I've been working out a scale for the maps."

Jared resumed a comfortable tone, "Doesn't the scale change all the time though? It looks like it does."

"For a while it does," Kristin nodded, enthusiastic about the normalcy of the dialogue. "But it stabilizes between changes. So if we're going a long distance at one scale, I can count the mile markers between the waterways. Say there's is a river at mile marker 10, and then a canal or something at mile marker 20, I measure the distance on my pictures of the map between those red lines, and the scale is 10 miles to however many inches, or fractions of an inch, or... you get it."

"Yeah," Jared said, basking in her fresh positivity. "So in a couple miles-,"

Clifford

"Less than a mile now, but yes," Kristin corrected sweetly, "There will be a stream or a creek, looks like, and *immediately* after that a right turn. And from there, only ten miles or so before you take a sharp left. It's actually easier with fewer streets and landmarks. Limits your options."

"So you have it all figured out," Jared observed.

"Pretty much," Kristin said, "But I still wish the online maps would work already. I'm getting kind of bored of reinventing the wheel."

They continued for another mile in a silence that suggested calm rather than tension for the first time in days. Eventually Jared asked, "So *are* you okay?"

Kristin raised her arm to point at a guard rail sweeping in on the side of the road. "Bridge," she said, "Over a stream. You want to take a right and follow parallel to the water."

Jared slowed the vehicle, leaned forward in his seat and said, "Not seeing it."

Kristin leaned back to clear his line of sight and scanned every inch of the shoulder. He was correct: there was a bridge, and though currently devoid of water, there was a sandy creek bed below, but for the several miles that were visible there was no road parallel to the dry wash, just a ditch in front of a fence row in front of tall scrub brush. Turning frantically to her phone and her photos, Kristin muttered, "Can't be right... we're nowhere close to the end, it has to be somewhere..."

Jared allowed to the car to idle for more than half a mile while she checked and re-checked her work. Apparently making an effort to stay upbeat, Jared said, "Maybe it was right. Not all of our stops have been next to the road. Think back to Tennessee: that was off in the woods-,"

"Within sight of the road!" Kristin almost shouted. She felt her palms begin to sweat as an inexplicable panic took root in her chest. She continued rapidly, "You're not hearing me. It's like, another ten miles just to the next turn. And that's at least fifteen

The Beard

more miles from where we're trying to go, maybe more! We can't just wander into a desert for a minimum twenty-five miles!"

"Well, now, hang on," Jared said struggling to sound soothing rather than trivializing. "Even if we have twenty-five miles left on the map, maybe we can use your systems and find a shortcut. We try driving around some more, look for a cross street, and maybe end up within a mile or two that way."

Kristin took a deep breath. They had done so well for a second. Maybe, she thought, she was looking for something to go wrong, to rekindle her anger and take her back to a place where she was surer of herself. Or maybe she was looking for an excuse for them to fail. Forcing her thoughts into line, Kristin regained her composure. "We can try that," she stated, "That sounds safe enough." Stretching her confidence slightly, she ventured, "If we don't find a closer way though, in your mind what is the worst case scenario?"

"Oh, worst case," Jared sighed. With an obvious attempt at compassion he explained, "I know twenty-five miles *sounds* like a long way, but it looks pretty flat. With some water and some sunscreen, if we pace ourselves right, we can hike that in a day." Jared paused to gage Kristin's response. She sat perfectly still, staring out the windshield. Expressionless, she gave an almost imperceptible nod and Jared went on, "We haven't really talked about it before, but you know I grew up tent camping. If we can find a sporting goods store, someplace to grab some supplies, I don't think one night in nature should stand in our way. But don't worry: one way or another, I will get us to the end of this thing."

Kristin decided to not focus on that.

Day 3

As the water hit Louis' fingertips, he remembered that both of the hand dryers were out of order. By the time the cold reached his knuckles, he was quietly admonishing himself for having come unprepared, but as he rolled his broad shoulders forward to douse one meaty palm after the other, he got past it. It wasn't like he could go without washing his hands after what he'd just done, and even if he had remembered to bring a towel, there wouldn't have been anywhere clean for him to set it while he'd been in the can. All he could do was make do. He used his elbow to turn off the faucet and dried his hands with the inside of the bottom of his shirt.

That was the hygienic thing, he told himself: just don't use the outside of the shirt, at least not until they'd come across a laundromat. And for god's sake, don't touch anything in this bathroom. He assumed. It was difficult to tell how clean or filthy the place might be, as the only light was what filtered through a row of narrow, screened in windows beneath the eaves, which also served as the only ventilation. Come to think, Louis thought, he hadn't noticed any electrical fixtures in the dank, bleach-smelling outbuilding. He wondered if the hand dryers were even wired in, or if they were glued to the wall just for show. He couldn't check without touching them, which would violate his rule about not touching anything, so he decided he'd never find out.

Clean or unclean, electricity or no, Louis never cared for public restrooms. Apart from more obvious concerns, bathrooms had always struck him as the worst possible circumstance in which to meet a stranger. He was awkward enough around new faces; the idea of mixing with random peckers in a trough toilet or semi-separated shower was a nightmare. He counted bathroom exclusivity as one of the greatest advantages of travelling in an RV. Or rather, he had until recently. Tim hadn't run him out of the trailer to go shit in the woods or anything, but something about the

The Beard

man was so unwelcoming as to make Louis feel that his very existence was a faux pas.

To be clear, Louis was unapologetic and for the most part not obliged to conceal his resentment. But he felt that if he were to commit actual slights (stinking up the trailer as an example), it might objectively validate Tim's treatment of him. Louis could not stop Tim from believing he was always right, but it was important that, whenever possible, he not allow Tim to be correct.

Louis crossed the threshold of the dismal john into a temperate and sun dappled morning. Across from the cinder block structure, on the opposite side of a neatly maintained gravel road, Marlow lounged in the shade of one of the loosely planted stands of pine that filled the interior of the campground. However much the proprietors had skimped on the facilities, Louis had to give them credit for the landscaping. Assuming they had done anything purposeful with it: Louis didn't know what vegetation occurred naturally in Northern Arizona, he'd pretty much just imagined the Grand Canyon and moved on.

Marlow lifted his head from his front paws and Louis called, "Okay! All done, thanks for waiting." The dog half stretched as he stood and Louis waved him over. "C'mon this way. Take the scenic route back." The pair walked leisurely past the restrooms and down a gradual slope. The gravel crunched pleasantly beneath their feet. "I know we're going the wrong way," Louis narrated, "But we take this path down to the pond, we can circle back on the other side. I think the air might do us some good, don't you?"

Marlow kept an easy pace on Louis' right, but didn't so much as look up to acknowledge him. Louis was unoffended by this, as he realized he had been unusually chatty with the dog as of late. "It's strange," Louis said as they walked, "I mean, we always shared secrets, you an' me, that ain't new. But now that we have another person around, why would that cause me to spend more time talkin' to a dog then I did when it was just you an' me? Strange. Maybe, what with *that guy* bein' so off putting, maybe it makes me appreciate you more as a conversation partner, as a partner in crime… you know?"

Marlow sniffed the grass on the shoulder of the road and huffed without looking up. Louis wasn't sure the dog knew. But Louis knew: knew better than to waste his time talking to Tim. The more either of the men spoke, the more obvious and insurmountable their differences. The more obvious their differences, the clearer it became that they viewed one another purely as a means to an end. At least that was how Tim viewed Louis. Tim had said so outright, several times.

For Louis' part, as mutual as his dislike was, he was having problems with Tim's quid pro quo model. For one thing, Louis despised usury as a concept. He found trading favors distasteful, and found the idea of owing someone humiliating. At times in his life that humiliation had been necessary, but unpleasant all the same. Beyond that, Louis had as much as given up his quest for the end of the compass before discovering Tim, so there was no upside to travelling with him.

Approaching a wide, glassy pond, Louis led to the right at a fork in the road. "So why we keep him around?" he asked aloud. The dog stopped and looked up quizzically, practically shrugging before turning to follow. "Hell, why we keep going at all? We own the truck an' trailer, we could cut and go home any time." Shifting to a subdued sigh, Louis answered, "But then the whole mystery thing don't get solved. An' ten, twenty years from now, we tell people about this rainbow you an' me followed', they gonna want to know what's at the end. So we gotta see what's out there. Basically a obligation at this point."

There was another obligation that Louis was reluctant to admit, even to Marlow. In accepting another person to their travels, Louis had made himself beholden to that person's expectations. Many times each day, Tim, in his own words, 'counseled patience'. In actuality this 'counsel' had been an excuse to talk up how patient *he* had been in his weeks waiting for Louis on the levee in Yuba City, with the intended consequence of making Louis feel guilty for wanting to pack up instead of waiting for the compass, which had suddenly gone limp five days earlier, to decide their next move. And the stupid thing was that the ploy worked. Louis saw what Tim was doing, he resented it and found it obnoxious, and yet he felt a deep and inexplicable shame at the thought of disappointing this horrible person.

"Dunno," Louis mumbled, "Maybe I've just let down my quota of people already. Maybe one more shouldn't matter. But maybe one more, maybe that's the bridge too far." And maybe that was why Louis had recently been so chatty with his drooling sidekick: Marlow never judged, never shamed, and was never let down. At least not that he'd ever let on.

But even if Louis's four-legged support system made the current situation more tolerable, there was no clear way to make it pleasant, and the thought of it stretching on indefinitely was downright unbearable. It was for that reason that two days earlier, Louis had offered to sell Tim the compass so they could go their separate ways. Tim had refused, which Louis still didn't understand, given how much Tim clearly disliked both him and his dog, but there it was. Tim had insisted that they had to go together, had said, 'the whole thing won't work' for either of them by themselves. That argument made no sense to Louis, but another of Tim's points had merit: that Louis should see some return on the investment of time he'd already made crossing the country.

So, as the three of them had waited for the needle to move, they'd settled into an uneasy routine. It defined much of their days together, but wasn't something they bothered to question, largely because, in the absence of everything else, they knew that the routine could be depended upon.

"Shouldn't take much more time, anyways," Louis observed. "Compass don't ever stay down for too long. An' dickhead says it ain't much farther from here. A'course, if he knows it ain't much farther, don't that mean he knows where we goin'? An' if he already knows where we goin', then why don't we just go?"

Clifford

Following the road around a final stand of pines, Louis stated, "That guy is a fuckin' ass hat."

Marlow paused halfway through the bend, cocked his head and perked his ears forward. As Louis came abreast, he heard a man shouting angrily. Fifty yards distant, Tim stood in front of Louis' truck, animatedly berating an elderly couple whom Louis supposed were camping nearby. "Wonder what they did to lay a hair across his ass," Louis breathed. "I'm 'a guess it was somethin' small." After standing unnoticed for several seconds, the big man turned to his big dog and stated "Well, at least we get better treatment than people who don't have somethin' he wants. Guess that's somethin'."

Marlow answered with a bass huff, then did an about face and sauntered back towards the pond. "Yeh," Louis grunted in agreement, "Time enough for another lap."

Day 4

With high, deliberate steps, Jared picked his way through dusty gaps in the seemingly endless scrub brush. His whole life, when he'd heard the word 'desert,' he'd imagined rolling dunes overlooking dramatic salt flats that would stretch to a colorful horizon that shimmered in hot, dry air. Something on the order of the Sahara, he had assumed, although now he couldn't be confident that even the Sahara would look how he'd thought. Until several hours ago, without realizing it, Jared had held onto that notion deep in his psyche, somewhere beyond the reach of observations he should have made as they'd driven through the actual desert. It had seemed that the badlands from the movies must have been just out of sight, that the terrible boredom of infinite shrubbery they could see from the road was just window dressing, like the trees that blocked the cookie cutter subdivisions from the view of the parkway back home.

But now they were well off the road, and the fact that should have been obvious had become inescapable: the only set piece capable of hiding behind a flat and withered brown landscape is more of the same. So, for at least ten miles now, Jared had led Kristin further and further, rhythmically slogging, scraping hypnotically through such parched brambles as had managed to claw their way out of the rocky soil. Chancing to look up from under a dusty white ball cap to which he had affixed a dish towel to drape over the back of his neck, Jared discovered that they had apparently wandered into a sort of shallow bowl, that the monotony now rose gently in front of and behind them in a disorienting and isolating gesture.

But that made no sense. To be in a bowl they would've had to walk down a slope, which should have felt much easier than it had. And if walking downhill had been that much work, then how much was it going to suck to hike back up? Jared felt suddenly nauseous.

Clifford

He wasn't sure if it was the emptiness, the brightness, and the hopelessness of their surroundings, or maybe the smothering combination of the sun lotion on his face and the smell of the new nylon tent slung over his shoulder.

There was also another smell under that: the sour smell of sweat in the still afternoon. Was it his sweat, or Kristin's? Probably his. He couldn't risk getting dehydrated out here. At best it wouldn't help with his nausea. He stopped with one foot on either side of a hard bush and dug a canteen on a shoulder strap from behind the collapsed tent. After taking a long pull, he replaced the cap and let the container clatter against his other cargo, while he pulled the narrow strap of a folded-up camp chair on his other shoulder to resettle a canvas tote containing two gallon-jugs of water.

A few feet behind Jared, Kristin's sneakers scraped to a halt in the dust. She asked, "Are you alright? We need to take a break?"

Jared took a moment to survey the horizon: there was no shade for them here. But given that there hadn't been any for at least three miles behind them, who knew how much further they'd have to go to find that. Fuck it. Jared was hot, and the water was digging into his collarbone. He swung the jugs off his shoulder and dropped them in the dirt before unburdening himself of his remaining items. Even without any breeze, exposing his sweat-soaked shoulders and back to the open air came as an instant relief. Regaining his focus, Jared took a deep breath and slowly twisted to stretch out his back muscles before bending to pick up the bag full of chair.

By the time Jared had assembled his seat, Kristin was already perched atop the small cooler she had been carrying, and was slurping from her own canteen in one hand while using the other to secure a massive, floppy straw hat on top of her head. She shook the canteen sharply and, with her mouth still full of water, pointed past Jared to the canvas tote. Jared quietly dug out and passed along one of the full jugs. Kristin nodded and grunted her thanks before swallowing.

The Beard

Still catching her breath from the long drink, Kristin surprised herself with a burp. She set the sealed jug on the cooler beside her, and sat with the fingers of her left hand looped casually through the handle. "'Scuse me!" she barked. Jared nodded his assent and Kristin followed with, "*Are* you okay over there? You're like, right, directly in the sun."

Gesturing around them Jared asked, "Where else could I be?"

"Touché," Kristin replied. "I told you we should've splurged on that folding chair with the awning attached to it."

Almost in alarm, Jared scoffed, "Sixty dollars more for a canopy... I mean, really?"

"Or," Kristin joked animatedly, "You could've split the difference and dropped thirty dollars on a sweet straw hat like I did. I wouldn't have judged you for wearing one."

"Hmmp," Jared grunted humorlessly before uncapping his canteen again. He wasn't especially pleased by the thought of that thirty-dollar hat. Objectively cute as it might be, he had tried to talk Kristin out of buying it. But he had taken the hit on that one, because he didn't want to seem defensive, didn't want his concerns to be too obvious. And the hat aside, Jared thought they had done alright on both value and preparedness. By delaying this leg of the map by a couple days, they had bought themselves time to make judicious choices. From the motel he had (finally) talked Kristin into, to the pared-down-two-day-camping list for the sporting goods store two towns over, Jared figured that a little extra time and care had likely saved them hundreds of dollars.

Of course, they'd still spent... Jared ran a rough tally in his mind: too much, he decided, still too much. At least thirty dollars too much, with her damn hat. But Jared had had to buy her something, offer some placation. Kristin had gotten sullen over the last couple weeks, and Jared was becoming concerned that she might give up.

Far more than any financial misgivings, that was the idea he found truly terrifying: that he might be forced back at this late stage. They were well past the point of no return in Jared's view.

Clifford

There was no more going 'back' per se, because anything but forward would be failure. And if events were moving one way, and Jared retreated in the other…

"Hey there," Kristin said, reaching out with the toe of her dusty sneaker to nudge Jared's leg, "Watcha' thinkin' about?"

Jared snapped off his train of thought to return to his chair in the desert. "Nothing really," he said simply, "Nothing important."

"Oh," Kristin said, "Just that I've been seeing a lot of that thousand-yard stare lately. Nothing on your mind?"

Jared shrugged and took another drink, almost compulsively. Kristin answered his stare with one of her own, drilling full eye contact as he lowered his canteen.

Jared cast about for a plausible response, "I… It's… I'm thinking about what we might find soon, is all. Won't be long now, I can feel it."

Kristin nodded slowly, "I hope you're right. But you've been saying that for three states now."

"Well sure," Jared said, "But this time is different. We're definitely getting closer. Don't you feel that, like we're getting close?"

Airily, philosophically, Kristin asked, "Close to what, though?"

Jared shrugged, more emphatically this time, "I don't know. That's what I've been thinking about."

Kristin half stood, grasped the cooler underneath her, and slid her seat closer to Jared. "I think it's about time we revisit that," she said sympathetically. "It's starting to look like there might be a chance, an outside possibility maybe, that we might not find anything at the end of all this."

Jared cocked his head, trying to make sense of her suggestion. "There has to be *some*-thing. Even a rock or a hole in the ground is *some*-thing. Whatever it is that exists at the end of the map won't be *nuh*-thing."

"Okay," Kristin conceded patiently, "But what if we don't find the end?"

The Beard

Jared squinted stupidly, "How can we not find it? We have a map."

Kristin took a deep breath and sighed, "I know that you know what I mean-,"

"Of course," Jared jumped in, "I know what you mean, but you can't *mean* it. We have to keep going, we're so close to seeing where it goes, and that is what you said you wanted."

Confused, Kristin asked, "What *I* said?"

"Yeah," Jared nodded, "*You* were the one who saw the Lincoln Memorial in the first place. *I* said you were crazy, but you said we should follow it. So, *you* were right."

"Oh," Kristin answered, mildly startled. She paused to adopt a soothing, conciliatory tone. "But that was so long ago, and we were at home where it was comfortable and we were safe and we weren't worried about... It didn't occur to me to talk about... where was the limit, I guess? Before we'd even left, it didn't seem relevant to bring up where the limit would be. I mean, these maps, they could go on forever. At some point we have to turn around."

Still incredulous, Jared scoffed, "But we can't, not now. The universe is pushing me, pushing *us*. It *gave* us these maps: that has to *mean* something, and if that means something, then *I* mean something, and if we give up, then-,"

Kristin lightly touched Jared's arm, "Sweetie you always meant something, that's why I-,"

Jared yanked his arm away and stood up, knocking over his chair, "Don't you fucking patronize me!" Registering Kristin's startled expression he took a small step back and lowered his volume, "You want to go home. So fine, say we go home. We get to where it's safe and comfortable, and then we say that in a year or two we'll try again. But then we don't, we just never get around to it, or worse: we do, but when I try to grow another beard it comes in all slow and solid brown, and either way I'm just like every other asshole on the planet again. Is that what you want, to be like them? Because you *said* you wanted this," he finished, gesturing around them.

Clifford

Her hand still balanced atop the water jug, Kristin stood to look Jared in the eye. Calmly but firmly she stated, "I said 'we should see where this goes,' not that we should never look back. I happen to love how we live at home, and I *thought* you did too."

"Don't you twist my words around," Jared shot back. "And anyways, why are we even talking about 'back home' and whatever all else is be-*hind* us? Why now?!?"

Kristin shouted back, "Because we're in the middle of a fucking desert! Because the further we go, the worse things get! We can't just keep going indefinitely! We have to go back soon! We have a life, responsibilities…"

Jared saw her mouth continue to move, but ceased to concern himself with what was coming out of it. He suddenly understood the problem, the fundamental misconception (on Kristin's part, of course) driving their argument. Relieved by how ridiculously simple the whole thing was, Jared cheerfully interjected, "Sweetie, there is no 'going back.' Even if we went home now, always knowing we'd had this opportunity in front of us but gave it up, nothing could ever be the same as it was, not once we know that. But if we see this through to the end, once we find what we're meant to find, nothing can ever be the same after that either. So, you see, there is no 'going back' because there is no more 'back' to go to. That's all just the past, and we have all the time in the world to figure out the future."

Dumbstruck, Kristin took a step back and shook her head. Beginning to pace she mumbled, "All the time in the world? We don't have… Jesus, and you dragged us clear out…" Kristin took a deep breath and tried to reclaim her earlier, gentler tone, "Jared I… *We*… we *have* to go home, and it has to be soon, baby. Our life, our friends, our jobs, I mean, I mean *your* job: how many more weeks of leave can you possibly get? I can't even remember the last time you checked in with Mr. Sherman, he needs to see your face, and soon."

"Wait," Jared said, "Is that what's bothering you? Deadlines at home? With my work?"

370

The Beard

Kristin half shrugged, "Sure, if that helps you. It's definitely on my list."

"Oh, okay," Jared waved dismissively, "You don't need to worry about deadlines for my work. I got no more deadlines for that."

Kristin stared in disbelief, a shimmering panic taking shape inside her rib cage. "Tell me you don't mean…"

Wondering at her terse response, Jared enthusiastically repeated, "But there are no deadlines, and you were worried about that. So now you don't have to worry about my work deadlines anymore."

Forcing back a lump in her throat Kristin asked softly, "When did he fire you?"

"It's for the best really." Jared said calmly, "That job wasn't going anywhere special, Sherman did me a favor-,"

Kristin closed her eyes and focused all her energy on forcing out the words, "Jared, when the *FUCK* did you stop getting paid?!?"

Jared held up his hands defensively and said, "Hang on now, because those are two different questions. To be fair, I've only been jobless since San Antonio, but I'm certain I told you we'd be into unpaid leave back in Arkansas."

Pacing nervously, Kristin muttered to herself, "And you had us keep going? Just driving around spending money…" She trailed off and absently bit her thumbnail whilst running the numbers through her head: she had already planned for them to spend down eighty percent of their savings by Arkansas, the point where she remembered Jared had casually mentioned they would *eventually* have unpaid leave as an *option* at some point. Subtracting their monthly bills, not to mention the grocery runs, gasoline, hotel rooms, and now camping equipment from the remaining twenty percent, even with the available balance on Jared's credit card, it wasn't adding up. They should've been broke weeks earlier. Something was missing. Lighting on a possible explanation, Kristin turned suddenly and with frantic focus said, "Rent. Did you pay the rent when I told you to?"

Jared patiently explained, "When we left, I thought we'd only be gone a couple weeks. So, I figured I should wait, hang onto that money in case of emergency. I thought that being prepared was worth the penalty for paying a few days late. And it's really a good thing too, if you think about it, because that's how we've kept up with our more immediate needs."

"More immediate then paying our bills?!?"

"Yeah," Jared shot back, "More immediate. Like a room for the night *last* night, or the food in the cooler that we have to eat *today*: immediate."

"Wait," Kristin jumped in again, the color draining from her face, "Because I was talking about when I told you to pay rent three weeks ago. Did you just say that you haven't paid it since the month before we left? Our shit could be out in the street right now!"

"I don't think that will have happened yet," Jared argued.

"But you haven't heard anything? You're seriously telling me no one has called about it?"

Jared rolled his eyes, "Well sure, they leave messages. They say shit to try and scare you, but I'm pretty sure there's like, a whole process or something to evicting people."

Without thinking, Kristin picked up the water jug near her hand and clutched it to her chest with both arms. She started to wander away mumbling, "ohmygodohmygodohmygod..."

Jared took two long steps to catch up to her. He tried to reassure her, "It's not as bad as all that. You don't have to worry about the things behind us, let's... we need to stay focused on what happens next."

"No," Kristin said shakily, still staring somewhere past Jared, "Ohmygod no, no we have to go back. You should have said a month ago, we have to go back..."

Jared stepped around in front of Kristin, halting her progress as a warm breeze pushed up the massive brim of her hat. Kristin

The Beard

squinted against the sun. In returning Jared's gaze, she could not escape his sunken eyes, his sallow cheeks, or the full weight of his pathetic obstinacy.

Disturbingly sweet and sincere, he asked, "But what do we *have* to go *back* to?"

Kristin felt tears welling up from somewhere clear down in her chest. But it was a place far deeper, more visceral, that produced her scream, "FUCK! YOU!!!"

Kristin swung the water jug hard against Jared's streaked sideburn, knocking him out of her path and freeing her to storm off into the direction from whence they had come.

Jared shifted his weight to control his stumble. Having taken the time to regain both his balance and all the righteous indignation of a man clearly in the wrong, he called out into the distance already between them, "YOU SAID YOU WANTED THIS!"

August 28, 1881

Hugh marched purposefully around the first row of small barracks and across a stretch of open parade ground to the second. As he worked his way quickly up the other side, he paused frequently to peer between his coarse facial hair and the soft, narrow, brim of his hat, into the darkening lawns surrounding the structures. Between the nondescript clapboard buildings, he occasionally found nondescript faces staring back at him: men who Hugh, having now lived amongst them for weeks, could not help but recognize, but whose names and stories he would never learn. He had nothing against the soldiers. Introducing himself simply wasn't his way.

Hugh sometimes perceived, especially back home in California, that his unwillingness to seek out new friends or to engage new neighbors might seem haughty or self-important, but, to his mind, that would only be true if that behavior somehow obligated the other party to initiate contact. It never did, and he never would, because he generally had no interest in speaking to those people in the first place, and moreover couldn't imagine why any of them would be interested in speaking to him. Thus, by remaining as much an island as any man in a small town could, Hugh had felt he was doing right by all interested (or disinterested) parties including himself.

That is, until recently.

Over the preceding weeks, Hugh had found himself both propelled and compelled well outside his preferences. For all his hatred and dread of new things, new people, and new obligations, his current pursuit required all three. He had resisted that idea for a fleeting moment at the start of his journey, and had found himself every day more nervous, more anxious. For lack of a comfortable alternative, he had finally given in to the process. He believed that resignation had helped him, though not to feel better.

The Beard

In truth, by doggedly following this trail wherever it led, he had only exchanged his weird anxiety for an equally weird drive. Now that he was moving, he couldn't seem to stop, and he couldn't seem to form a rationale for why he had started. He had begun sleeping less and worrying more, but the cause of his concern was... elusive? Vague? For a time, Hugh had convinced himself that the underlying problem was about his immediate needs: that day's food, that night's shelter, or safety at times in between. But now he had all of those. Hell, he had the security of a job and the protection of an army, and he was right back to feeling unsettled.

It was because Hugh had the humility to acknowledge when he chose to torture himself that he could be confident that this time he was being driven to it by something, something out... out there. After all, something out there must be pulling this map from his face, something external drawing this thing out from inside him until his very countenance was unrecognizable. Whatever it was, whether god, or devil, or a force beyond his descriptive powers, and wherever it spoke from, Hugh could hear it calling him again. It was taking shape out there, beyond the fort and its outbuildings, past the soldiers and the natives and their settlements, it was growing, getting stronger, and its momentum would soon escape his grasp. Events would soon move with or without him. He couldn't stay here much longer.

But he definitely wanted, and sensed he might need, William's help. It had been almost a week since they'd agreed to a general plan, but after a few days of Hugh relentlessly following up, William had made him promise to stop talking about it. Hugh had grudgingly assented, but he had also assumed that William would have mentioned it on his own by now. All of that day at the mill, a thin animosity had simmered in Hugh's mind. He didn't want to break his word and be obnoxious, but there had to be a limit. They had to move soon.

He continued across the final stretch of the tidy parade grounds, around the end of a long building with a longer shadow. As he moved westward around a corner, the grays and browns of the raw wood wall sharply switched to a burnt orange, dully reflecting the still expansive if unremarkable sunset. It was getting late, and William had not yet returned to barracks. Hugh began to wonder if the man was dodging him. Deeply dissatisfied but unsure what to do next, Hugh followed the wall of the long building toward a cluster of officer's quarters.

He kept a brisk pace and got within sight of the stables before his mood was interrupted by what had become a familiar and truly grating giggle. No more than ten yards distant, William appeared from around the side of a building. Over his shoulder, he wryly offered a low commentary to a tittering Sanders, who followed a half step behind. Noticing Hugh, Sanders's face fell, which prompted William to look in front of them. Smiling more broadly, William said, "Well hey! There he is, just the man I hoped to see." With each word from William, Sanders's expression dropped further into a grimace.

"Gentlemen," Hugh greeted them, "Say Pvt. Grafton, may I have a word?"

"Certainly," William answered, "I wish you would."

Hugh quickly replied, "Privately?"

Sanders crossed his arms and turned from Hugh to William, who knowingly nodded in response. As Sanders returned dejectedly to their original path, William called, "Don't forget what we talked about, now. I really need your help with this. Countin' on you Sanders!"

Sanders answered enthusiastically, "You won't be disappointed." He locked eyes with Hugh and gave a smug nod as he passed.

Hugh allowed Sanders to distance himself before approaching within a pace of William to lower his voice. "A pleasant evening for it," he said drily. William shrugged. Not caring to waste more time, Hugh jumped in, "I plan to leave forty-eight hours from now, with or without you. I'd prefer you join me, but either way I need to go."

William asked, "Has something happened?"

The Beard

Hugh shook his head, "We need to go. I've tried to be patient, but I can't keep waiting on you. Now, I realize you can't just up and walk out any time, but we need to leave soon, simple as that."

William's eyes narrowed as he moved from dumbstruck to intensely irritated, "You tried to be patient? You? Patient with me?" William straightened and continued sharply, "Well, at least you 'realize' what I done tol' you a hundred times: I *can't* just up and leave, that's called *desertion*. Which I might not mind if I had no desire to return, but soldiering is my livelihood. So, if you're in a hurry, you can go on and leave right now. But I predict you'll be a corpse by the end of your forty-eight hours from now. Or you can wait and I will find a chance to lead you outta here. But not if you talk about it in front of god and everyone and wreck my plans."

Hugh protested, "Look now, I *have* been patient-,"

William spat, "I *told* you to be quiet about this, an' you only managed it by avoidin' me for days. Then first time I see you again, here you is, talkin' about what I said you don't talk about!" With each sentence, Pvt. Grafton stood a bit taller in contrast to a withering Hugh. "And you call that patient! *Follow. Orders. Boy.*"

Hugh, as admonished as he cared to be, seized on William's pause, stammering, "I didn't mean to- I'm- I don't know what-,"

"No, you don't know," William barked, "So I'm 'a tell you what. You hear a'that medicine man up at Cibicu? The one caused a stir a couple weeks back?" Hugh nodded while William settled into a brusque, less commanding tone, "Things bein' a bit quieter the past few days, Colonel Carr sent Mose and Chapeau up to fetch him, for a conversation. Only I saw Chapeau come through this morning all by his self. Then I noticed Cruse let the Indian scouts keep their rifles after their drills. He didn't make a show of it, but I know he's been keepin' those weapons locked up lately. So, I ask around, and I just got it direct from Bowman that the whole cavalry moves out in the morning to collect Nock-Ay-Det-Klinne. They takin' all the scouts to find him, but none of the infantry."

Hugh stared, his shame replaced with confusion. "What does any of that mean?"

Clifford

William shook his head in exasperation, "Means that most the officers and all the Indians ride out for Cibicu in the morning, is what. All we got to do is disappear at about the same time. As infantry, I'm not meant to be with them, and seventy men gone to find one ol' chief, I don't guess they'll need reinforcement from the fort. They should be two days each way before anyone who goes with them, meanin' most the officers, notices that we left when they did."

"Oh," Hugh blinked, "But what about the officers who don't leave?"

"Got that managed as well," William explained. "You were right about that dog a' mine, Sanders, I give him a task an' he took right to it. It'll be his job to convince everyone here that I volunteered as a packer for the cavalry move up North. An' then, after they come back, to convince everyone I volunteered for a sentry detail up on Seven Mile Hill. That detail don't exist, but with everyone having mobilized an' all, I don't guess anyone checks up for much of the week after. By then I ought to be back. Since your map winds all around, but my return route will run straight home, I figure we can walk out for six, even seven days."

Hugh smiled, "Sanders agreed to cover us? And here I thought he didn't like me."

"He don't," William answered sternly, "He's covering me. On condition that I take you away from here and come back alone. Seemed like that fit with your plans, so I didn't think you'd mind."

"That makes more sense," Hugh said sadly. Suddenly perking up he asked, "You already planned all that for tomorrow?"

"I did," William nodded.

"Then why did you argue when I gave you two whole days from now?"

William shot back, "Because I didn't care for your tone, is why. I won't tolerate it once we're under way, and you've precious little time to correct it." Moving past, he concluded, "Find me after mess call. May as well get breakfast on the way out."

Day 5

Jared slid from his nylon camp chair and dropped one knee in the dust to pluck a few egg shell fragments from the brush beside him. As he reached to snag another, he reflected that no one in the world would know or care whether he picked up after himself out here. But a lifetime of lectures about littering had left him unsure if he could walk away from his trash in good conscience. Besides, whenever Kristin came back, Jared was sure she'd notice he'd been tidy. Or rather, she would notice if he hadn't.

The non-biodegradable plastic from the cheese slices he'd unwrapped earlier were already gathered, bagged, and crammed into a corner of the cooler with his empty soda bottles, but he tossed the egg shells alongside an apple core and a paper plate in what he only wished he could call his "fire pit." Any functional label for his pathetic attempt at a fire would have been extremely generous: the area of scratched earth with its loose, charred scrub stood merely as testament to how little Jared remembered from his time as a boy scout. But he hadn't forgotten that the safest way to prevent setting the wilderness aflame was to bury any coals, and here he saw an opportunity to compost. Even if his fire pit were neither fire nor pit, it could at least qualify as a trash hole.

Whatever its intended function, Jared was grateful that he had not depended on his trash hole for cooking: had that been the case, he would've had eggs ala Rocky Balboa. Instead, he had used a brand new propane burner under a precious little skillet, a rig that had been a bit costly but was one of his concessions to Kristin. He had assumed at the time that if he bought her the tools to cook she might continue to do all the cooking. Having now fended for himself on a couple meals, he was even more pleased with their purchase. He would be sure to tell her so, to thank her for her sound decisions on their provisioning. He would remember to do that. As soon as she came back, he would do that.

Clifford

And not only for the cookware and the groceries, but for all the equipment that had worked out so well: the name-brand cooler, the durable chairs, the tent, and the sleeping bags (even if they hadn't been enough to keep him warm out there by himself)... he had fought her on all of them but would now tell her that he had been wrong. They shouldn't have spent that much money, he had said so at the store, and she hadn't listened then. But he wouldn't mention any of that now, it wasn't important anymore.

Truthfully, Jared hadn't actually found it that important at the store, either. He'd made a show of controlling their spending but had ultimately given in because it just didn't *feel* consequential. He had been very aware that he ought to have been more worried, he just wasn't. Likewise, conceptually, he knew of the guilt he should be wracked with over lying to Kristin this whole time, and of the feelings of betrayal that had driven her away. He would apologize for all those things for which he was meant to, but secretly, again, he just didn't see the big hairy deal of it all. In the bigger picture those problems were all so insignificant. He saw them as minor blips, as specks of dust on a great golden orb of opportunity that he and Kristin now shared. And given that such a view of things was not only sincere in Jared's mind but attractive to it, he did not understand how or why anyone would consider the situation differently than he did, especially anyone who understood him as well as Kristin did.

This was why he had been so surprised when the sun had set and then risen again with nary a sign of her. Jared knew Kristin would be angry, and he knew that she would want some space to work out her anger before she came back to forgive him, but he had expected that the next part, the one where she showed up suddenly to berate him for ten minutes before dropping the issue, would be well concluded by now.

He didn't guess he would have to wait much longer, but as he balanced their remaining supplies against the delay, he decided that he should be as ready as possible to commence the final phase of their journey by the time she arrived.

The Beard

He crawled through the front door of the tent. The smell of new plastic warming, in a dry morning light tinted green and black by nylon walls, left the impression of an oven preheating. It was as good a time as any to strike camp.

Leaning forward, Jared wondered how far Kristin had walked, and how long it might take her to walk back to him. Only now, as he pressed the air out of his lightweight sleeping bag, did it occur to him that Kristin had left her own bed roll and compact pillow in the bag she had dropped by the cooler. He supposed it was possible that she'd gone clear back to the car, but they'd already walked for well over half the day by the time she had left, and that could mean she might not return for hours yet.

Or she may have gone just out of sight and followed the directions from the last map to some shelter, before looping around to their next destination. That would make some sense, Jared thought: it would keep them moving, of course, but it would also guarantee that, had he not waited for Kristin where she'd left him, she would still be able to intercept him. On the other hand, if she cut ahead and Jared did wait for her (as he had), then she could assume that making him wait like that would put the fear of god into him. Jared decided that was what she had done.

Her plan might prove effective in terms of their reconnecting later in the day, but Jared would have to fake the fear she had on order. This was not to say that he didn't care if she was okay, but he knew that she must be. She hadn't just wandered off without any notion of the terrain, she had the directions and the map and-

Jared looked up from his tent tidying and said aloud, "Holy shit... She has the directions *and* the map."

To be more precise, she had their only pictures of the map. It now dawned on Jared that the original map had been scraped off and washed down the sink of a gas station bathroom nearly a week earlier.

Jared rolled back on his heels and launched himself out the door of the tent, scrambling through the dirt to throw the lid off the cooler. Maybe somewhere in her stuff, he thought, maybe she'd left an old note card or a scribble on the back of a napkin or something. He pushed aside the meats and cheeses that were already softening in the shallow puddle of the thawing ice pack. Jared swiveled frantically to the large nylon bag she had carried. It didn't take him long to go through, as it contained only a few large items. None of them were paper, not so much as a loose receipt.

Jared stood and turned back to his trash hole, his eyes alighting across each item in his campsite. What might be useful, what could he use? What did he have that could show him where to go? He backed up to widen his view and tripped over the cooler. Flailing and stumbling back and around, Jared stayed on his feet, looking into the horizon. As he squinted against the morning sun, it occurred to him that this must be east. He only then realized that it didn't matter, as he couldn't remember which direction they'd been facing when they had arrived at that spot. They had started the day going west over the creek, but they turned north for a time and then…

Jared stepped away from his gear and slowly turned 360 degrees. Nothing. Everywhere he looked, nothing but dust and scrub, light and heat, not a hill, not a tree, nor a cloud. Where would he go next? How should he know? If he couldn't even say where he'd come from, there was no clear way back, let alone forward. He had to stay calm, had to think, had to… He knew there had to be something he'd missed.

In a sudden burst of clarity Jared said serenely to himself, "Of course. It's just the end of the beginning." Kristin had the old map, but Jared had the next one growing in nicely. And since each map started where the last had left off, the start of the map on his face should give him some indication where to end. There would be blanks to fill in, but he would get a cardinal direction at least, and all he had to do was consult his reflection.

Jared strode purposefully to the door of the tent and crouched inside beside a small knapsack. He examined the contents: a plastic mess kit. An empty canteen. A small toiletries bag but no mirror. One of those little things a person takes for granted, Jared mused.

The Beard

After all, the only time he was not in some proximity to a bathroom mirror was typically when he was driving, and even then there was his rearview. As he pictured the mirror in the car, Jared found he could also picture exactly where he'd left his broken cell phone, so that option was eliminated as well.

He ran a pointless second inventory: the plastic mess kit, the empty canteen, the small toiletries bag... Moving his hands constantly, quickly through the same items, it gradually dawned on Jared that at no point had he actually envisioned anything helpful in that bag, in that tent, in his campsite... Plastic-mess-kit-empty-canteen-toiletries-bag... what else was there, what the fuck else did he have that he could use?!?

With renewed frustration, Jared launched the bag against the wall of the tent, scattering what little he did have across his half-rolled sleeping bag. Turning back to the portal, he pulled himself desperately back into the daylight, bending a tent pole and partially collapsing the structure behind him. He must have missed something, there must be something out there...

Pushing back onto his feet, Jared looked frantically from object to object. Water! He had a whole jug of it, and a pool of standing water would cast a reflection. So he needed a pool of it, just a small one, he didn't want to be wasteful. He dropped gratefully to his knees once again and began scratching what should become a puddle from the dirt. As he dug, Jared imagined the outcome: having hollowed out a perfectly round abscess, he would splash in the tiniest amount of liquid and watch the contours of his face waver into view like a cartoon Narcissus. Satisfied with the depth and shape of the hole, he yanked the cap off the gallon jug, and sloshed out ever-so-slightly more than he'd anticipated.

Every drop absorbed instantly, darkening and clotting the parched ground as it vanished.

Leaning forward on his palms, Jared screamed into the earth, "God Dammit!!" He snapped his focus back up and in front of him, his eyes darting wildly about the campsite. He zeroed in on the small, seasoned, cast-iron skillet he had used to cook his eggs.

Clifford

There was nothing porous about that: it would definitely hold water. Jared grabbed the plastic jug with one grimy hand and, ignoring that he had just smeared his left knee in the mud he'd created, hobbled lopsided past the trash hole to the pan.

"Okay, alright," Jared muttered to himself, "This will work, there's no way this won't work." Forcing down his panic, Jared shakily tilted the jug over the skillet. He leaned over the thin layer of water and saw nothing but cooked-on breakfast. "Little more," he intoned, spilling into the pan until the food scraps started to float. He looked again and saw that he was backlit, blocking out details of his own reflection.

Jared stood, carefully holding the pan level, and began to turn. He shifted, tilted, and turned again like a dog chasing its tail, struggling to make out his dark silhouette, all the while mumbling, "I can't... how am I supposed to when I can't..." Against the glistening iron, Jared appeared as a vague shadow, the outline of a bearded face against an infinite, cloudless sky, his only clear feature the whites of his eyes as they widened and welled with tears.

Finally breaking, Jared retreated from his accusatory stare, threw the pan away and screamed into the empty landscape, "How am I supposed to know?!? I can't see myself!"

Day 6

The long, perfectly straight stretch of blacktop cut a ribbon through the wide-open landscape. Amongst the low grass and scrub on the roadside, small patches of bare earth screamed in red and burnt orange. The midday sun bored through a film of yellow dust on the wind screen and painted the interior of the crowded truck cab. The noise of tepid air blasting from the vents competed with the static-obscured country station on the radio. The recirculated air did little to alleviate the smell of two men and a dog that mingled with the odor of hot plastic, but, for once, Tim was oblivious to all of it. He fixated on the face of the compass, fascinated by every slight twitch of the needle.

An imperceptible dip in the roadway bounced the trailer on its hitch and shook the truck slightly from behind. Tim held up the compass and turned his body away, as though the movement of the vehicle might disturb it. Marlow pulled his feet in and pressed closer to Louis to distance himself from the man. Under the combined background noise, Tim declared, "It's doing something."

Louis answered loudly, "What's that now?"

Tim reached for the radio dial in front of a perturbed Marlow and turned it completely off. "It's doing something," he repeated, "The compass is pointing at something."

"Oh," Louis said, underwhelmed, "Yeah, it does that."

As Louis began to reach for the radio, Tim interjected, "But it's turning, don't you think we should turn?"

Louis waved his hand in front of them, "Nowhere *to* turn, not for miles yet."

"Shall we pull over then?"

Louis answered his question with a question, "That depends: is it pointing straight to the side of us?"

"Not quite," Tim said excitedly, "Out front at an angle."

"Like at that smokestack way off in the distance?"

Clifford

"Closer than that," Tim insisted, "And there doesn't seem to be many places wide enough to park, so maybe you should look for something before we miss it." For twenty-four hours, Tim's anxious sense of inevitability had bubbled from a simmer to a boil. He had only known enough from the manuscript to guide them as far as Arizona, after that there had been nothing to do but wait on the compass. He had tried to make good use of that time, but the second he'd noticed the needle bobbling around in its case, he'd felt giddy. Louis had been right to delay until daylight, but Tim was certain they were getting close, based not only on the historic account, but on his own gut as well.

"Fine," Louis relented flatly, "But you shouldn't worry so damn much." He gestured out his window at the flat, empty expanse beyond, "All I see out there is free parking."

Tim shot back, "I don't trust you to not get stuck in a sinkhole or something."

Ignoring this, Louis lifted off the accelerator and squinted into the distance. He locked in on the dull glare of a parked car fifty yards out and mumbled, "Well... looks like this spot was good enough for them. But will it be big enough for us?" Nearing the end of a rusty guard rail, at the footing of a short bridge, Louis slowed to a crawl and signaled to no one's benefit. He idled the vehicle across the road, dropping one wheel at a time over the two inches from the asphalt to the flat, rocky soil beyond. Hard scrub brush dragged audibly across sheet metal on the driver's side while the rig creaked and moaned to a halt three feet from the front bumper of the parked car: a black VW Jetta with an angry scratch on the driver's door and a thick coat of the same dust that covered the landscape. "There it is," Louis stated proudly as he put the truck in park. "This a fine, *fine* parking space... But I wonder what *they're* up to this far from the world."

Tim mumbled, "Bet I could guess." Getting no reply, he said more forcefully, "So, you want to cut the engine, get going?"

Louis stretched in his seat, twisting with one arm in front of him. Marlow took advantage of the movement by laying his large

386

The Beard

head in Louis' lap. "No need for all that," Louis said. Leaning back in his seat, he gestured with his hands as he explained, "Usually the compass leads me to something that looks like nothing, but it's always pretty close to the road. My guess is that if we cut the engine and get out, we'll be gone just long enough for it to warm up in here, and then we'll be broiling until the next town, which is where we'll have to go to find out what the compass was pointing to. So, my vote is that we keep the engine running while one of us gets out and follows the compass. And bein' as your holding it, I nominate you for that."

Tim squinted sideways at Louis, visibly annoyed, "We're nowhere close to what we're looking for. It will not be anywhere near the road. Why do you think I've been filling up the trailer with supplies the last couple days?"

"Well, I wondered about that," Louis said, "I didn't want to spoil your good time, but that ain't how this thing works. It's been my experience that every time," he continued as a matter of fact, "Not far from the car, I find somethin' looks like nothin'-,"

"Every time until *this* time," Tim interrupted. "*This* time is different: it *will* look like something and it *won't* be nearby. Things are about to change, Louis. And your experience has not prepared you for what will come next."

"Fine," Louis said forcefully. He wrenched back the ignition, jerked the keys from the steering column and popped the handle by his knee. The door fell open with a metallic groan, followed by a rush of hot air. "But ten minutes from now, when we back on the road and you stewin' in yer ball sweat, you just remember that you knew everything." He reached for his cigarettes and stepped down into the brush, and by the time he'd pulled one from the pack, Marlow had followed. Louis threw the door shut behind them.

Tim winced at the hollow thud and watched Louis turn and light up. Instantly the truck began to warm, but Tim stayed perfectly still, feeling the sweat begin to bead along his hairline. He knew himself well enough. He had to wait for his wave of irritation to pass. He couldn't risk losing his temper and saying something to

387

jeopardize his progress, not this far in, because even if Louis wasn't ready for the next leg of their journey, Tim had made damn sure he would be.

Really, he had made damn sure *they* would be. Tim had paid for everything they would need, had generated the entire shopping list, had even done the heavy lifting of the actual shopping, and what had Louis done in exchange? Nothing. Not a goddamn thing, besides wait in the parking lot, chain smoke, and mock Tim to his damn dog. It galled Tim, absolutely *galled* him: the lack of appreciation, but even more so, the lack of responsibility, of accountability. Tim had been left to do everything himself, and any time he had asked anything of Louis, all he had gotten were questions: Why do we need this? What are we doing next? Where are we going anyways? Setting aside that Tim wasn't sure he could explain those things to Louis without risking a fight, he knew for certain that he couldn't count on Louis being grown up enough to do what had to be done, once it was explained.

Tim breathed in through his nose and out through his mouth and focused on calming himself. Their next conversation couldn't be avoided any longer. And even Tim would concede that what needed to be done now would be difficult for any adult, let alone Louis. For a moment, he entertained the notion that maybe he should just do it, not talk about it just get it done on his own, as usual. Then again, playing out that hypothetical, he knew that Louis would rightly feel betrayed, and there would be no coming back from the fight that would follow.

Tim supposed it couldn't hurt to try giving Louis the benefit of the doubt. There was some slim chance that the man could listen to reason, and if he did, and it became a mutual if difficult decision between the two of them, perhaps it would create a bond that would make Louis more manageable. Doubtful, but Tim saw no downside in trying. He decided as he pushed open the passenger door, that in the spirit of cooperation he would prevail upon Louis to do the right thing. And after that had most probably failed, then he could

The Beard

take matters fully in hand. Arriving at this, he felt a sense of relief but chided his self to not visibly relish the idea.

Tim climbed down from the truck and retrieved a small blue satchel he'd stowed under his seat. Dangling the bag over one shoulder, he crossed between the bumpers of the truck and the Volkswagen. Louis stood near the back wheel, smoking and staring vacantly into the distance while his dog urinated obsessively on an emaciated bush ten yards away: in short, what appeared to Tim to be their favorite activities. Approaching slowly, Tim awkwardly attempted to strike a sympathetic tone, but landed somewhere closer to morose, "Hey, we need to talk."

Still gazing past the flat landscape from under his baseball cap, Louis sighed, "Yeh, imagine we should."

Ignoring the suggestion that Louis had any other topic in mind, Tim nodded toward the dog, who was now sniffing the next dry plant, and said, "About him."

Louis suddenly snapped back into the moment and turned to look at Tim, "What, about Marlow?"

Hearing his name, the dog padded toward the strip of bare ground where the two men spoke, looking from his master's face to the interloper and back again.

Calling back to an earlier point, Tim over-adjusted his tone to the saccharine empathy of a kindergarten teacher: "This time, we aren't going to be stopping nearby. As you may have noticed, we've been accumulating some supplies, all portable, some potable."

"I tried tellin' you at the store," Louis chuckled, "You buyin' and fillin' a 20-gallon water tank, when everything else is designed to fit in your pack... How in the hell you envision that workin'? You can't backpack that much water."

"I'm glad you mentioned that," Tim said more casually, "It's actually a big part of my concern. The next leg of our trip could take a few days, or a few weeks. It's impossible to tell, but we need to be prepared for any case, and water is an important part of that. Along with the tanks that you noted, I bought several large

Clifford

canteens, and also a ten-gallon bladder. Given how heavy those are, we shouldn't plan to haul more than fifteen gallons between us, and each person drinking a half gallon each day…"

Louis shook his head, "That's overdoin' it. No way this thing is gonna string us along for two more weeks."

"But it's already occupied us for months," Tim pointed out. "And I have reason to think we're in the home stretch, but that won't be easy."

"You and your, 'reasons,'" Louis scoffed, "Got all these reasons yer buyin' things, doin' things, but none of yer reasons been fit to share with me."

"You will know them when you need to know them," Tim shot back. Feeling his patience begin to wane, he decided to jump to the point. "Your dog is massive. And he drinks a lot, constantly, all the time."

"He's a Newfoundland," Louis shrugged, "They a water breed." He reached down to scratch behind Marlow's ear and the dog opened his mouth in a heavy pant, releasing a solid thread of drool that extended gradually to the dirt. "Why don't you just say what you tryin' to say?"

Tim bit his bottom lip and quietly cursed his luck. It was bad enough that he had been saddled with a hayseed that couldn't read between the lines, but to have to pretend to care about said hayseed's feelings… He told himself that this must be some kind of karmic credit, that the universe was just making him earn what would come after, that showing minimal sensitivity to this drooling moron and his drooling companion animal would ultimately be in *his* best interest.

Tim regained his earlier, sing-song condescension, "If there is a limit to how much water we can carry, and we need as much water as possible for ourselves, then we can't have a dog drinking all our water while contributing nothing to this process. If we bring Marlow with us, we will run dry in two days, and all three of us will be dead of heat exhaustion in five. Which is a shitty way to go, even for a dog." Louis opened his mouth to speak and Tim
390

The Beard

interrupted emphatically, "Before you even say that you're willing to risk it not taking that long: I know you don't have the will power to let your dog go thirsty, you're not the type. There is no point getting out there just to watch you give away our supplies and ultimately cause the dog, and us, to die of thirst." Tim let this sink in for a second before concluding, "It would be *kind*-est if we just made this the end of the road for Marlow."

Louis took a long drag from his cigarette, exhaled, and dropped the butt. He ground it out with the toe of his boot, put his hands in his pockets, and casually looked to the horizon, "If you through dancin' around tellin' me to kill my dog, I would *kind*-ly invite you t'fuck yerself."

Tim shrugged, unaffected and unaffectionate, "If you can think of a better way, I'm all ears. Maybe you find someone to take him off your hands or... Whatever you come up with, though, we need to do it quick."

Louis turned, cocked his head slightly, and regarded Tim with something between disbelief and amusement. "He's *my* dog. You ain't killin' him, and I ain't givin' him away, especially not when, like I say: we won't have to go far. Now, you wanna take all that shit you bought for a walk, be my guest. I'll sell you the compass an' we can go our separate ways."

Tim saw that civility was lost on this man, that his attempt at compassion would not be rewarded. Exasperated, he allowed his voice to rise, derogatory and shrill, while the veins on his neck made an appearance. Ticking off points on his fingers, Tim shouted, "No! It is like I say, like *I* say: we *do* have far to go. You *do* have to go with me. The dog can-*not* come. That *is* just how it is!"

Louis turned slowly toward Tim, taking his hands from his pockets. In one, large, step, he closed the distance between them, straightened his posture, and widened his shoulders, consuming Tim's field of vision. With his chin almost touching Louis's chest, Tim looked up nearly a foot into the tanned, stubbly, face beneath the ball cap, which now growled in an acrid haze of expirated cigarette smoke, "*You* don't tell *me* how shit is."

Louis allowed a long pause before he broke away, motioned to his dog, and started sauntering to the truck.

Tim quietly rolled his eyes. He had known that this was how the conversation would end, but no one could ever say he hadn't tried to be decent about it.

With a resigned sigh, Tim reached into his satchel, wrapped his fingers around the grip of his 9mm, and dropped the bag to the ground. The sound of canvas landing in the dirt prompted Marlow to stop and look back over his shoulder. Tim squinted at Marlow's forehead while he calmly retrieved a full magazine from his jacket pocket and inserted it into the firearm.

Marlow tilted his head curiously. Louis, noticing the dog's distraction, followed his gaze and looked to Tim, who was pointing the Glock at the ground while he racked the slide to chamber a round. Tim kept his eyes on his target but, aware of the mass of Louis approaching in his periphery, moved fast to bring the gun back in front of him. As Tim squeezed back the trigger, he found his view wholly blocked by Louis's chest, and his arm forced out to the side.

Struggling to keep his grip on the gun, Tim grabbed Louis's shirt front with his free hand and pressed his foot against Louis's knee, quickly climbing the front of the man until he could see over a mountainous shoulder. Tim pushed forward, accidentally squeezing the trigger and firing straight up into the air. A few feet away, Marlow startled backwards, apparently unharmed. Tim felt Louis's bicep beginning to snake around his thick waist, and responded by forcing his other boot against Louis's leg to twist his whole body up and toward his gun arm. Tim felt his hand lower as the rest of him broke loose into the open air; he landed hard on his side in the dirt, knocking the wind out of him.

Even in his breathlessness, Tim stayed focused on pulling the pistol from under his body. As he wrenched his arm free, he saw Marlow bare his teeth and begin to charge. Tim brought the gun up,

The Beard

but he barely had time to consider what a good target the dog was making of itself before Louis appeared between them again, this time facing down Marlow. Louis threw his self forward to shove the beast, launching it out of Tim's sights and ten or twelve feet besides. With a mental shrug, Tim aimed at the ground where he guessed the dog would land and squeezed the trigger.

Marlow let out a squeal, surprisingly high-pitched for such a large animal, and bounced as he hit the dirt, his head jerking sharply in the other direction. Both men froze expectantly as Marlow's bulk settled from the impact. It was five full seconds before the dog suddenly struggled to his feet and looked confusedly at his master, who then shuffled forward on his knees, waving his arms and shouting, "GO! Fuckin' MOVE y'dumb bastard!"

From behind Louis's frantic gesticulations, Tim could only glimpse the dog skittering backwards with the look of horrified betrayal, before it loped away, tail tucked under, around the bridge footing and presumably to the dry wash below. Tim let the dog go, and Louis let his arms drop to his sides, his knuckles almost in the dust as he stayed on his knees. Louis lowered his chin and looked absently to a trail of blood that now led from where Marlow had landed to the darkness beneath the bridge.

Tim rolled onto his back and sat up, keeping his attention trained on Louis, who was now several feet away. The noise of Tim's boots scraping the dirt as he stood seemed to jar Louis out of his desperate trance: in one explosive move, he was back on his feet and turned around, his cheeks flushed, eyes dark, animalistic. Louis looked ten feet tall as he stepped forward and spat, "Fuckin' shoot me if you want, I will murder you still."

Straining to conceal his terror, Tim raised the gun with both hands, snapping the barrel to a forty-five-degree angle from his body. "I won't kill you, but I will knee-cap you," he said sternly. "Hand to God, I will drop you where you stand and drag your ass through the desert on a sled if you don't stop there."

Louis froze about four feet distant. Looking down at the smaller man, he shook his head and sneered, "You pussy. Fuck you." With that, he turned on his heel to start after the trail of blood in the dust.

Tim shouted after him, "I said stop! I mean it!"

In answer, Louis took another large, deliberate step. Tim turned the gun slightly to the left, pointed at the ground near Louis's boot, and squeezed the trigger.

That sound again: it was definitely real, she was sure that time. But was it? What was it?

Kristin paused in the middle of the gravel road that she had been walking for the better part of the past hour. It was three sounds she'd heard, three sharp, cracking sounds, at short intervals and extremely faint. Whatever it was, assuming it was anything at all, it was happening very far away. The only reason Kristin could hear the sounds in the first place was the absolute quiet, but that quiet had begun to make her feel crazy. A day and a half without seeing other people, she was fine with that, that part was almost a respite. But a day and a half with no people, no cars, no animals, nor clouds, nor wind: a day and a half with no *movement*, and then... Then somewhere very far away were three sharp sounds, evidence, if of nothing else, that somewhere outside Kristin, the world still existed. Or that she was losing her mind.

Either way, whatever or whoever was causing the noise, they were distant enough to reinforce what Kristin had become increasingly aware of over the previous thirty-six hours, that she was alone, very and truly alone. Her newfound appreciation of just how isolated she was had begun with Jared's betrayal. During the hours that followed their argument, stunned silence had propelled Kristin forward for longer than she could now recall. In trying to see her next move, *their* next move, her mind had moved so quickly, but arrived at so little, that she had only noticed nightfall by way of observing the moonlight reflected on patches of bare rock.

The Beard

By the time she had reached the car, water jug still in tow, Kristin had no clue how late it must be. She had turned off her phone to conserve battery earlier in the day, and it was only as she was standing on that empty stretch of road in the middle of the night about to turn it back on, that Kristin realized there was no point. What did it matter what time it was?

And who would she call to come get her? Kristin hadn't spoken to her family in over two years. There had been no falling out, she had simply realized in the course of living her life how little they had in common. But even if they would pick up the phone in spite of what she knew they had long ago labeled her snobbery, none of them could afford to help her, nor would she presume to burden them that way. Similarly, she had never actively cut off any of her old friends, but in the course of moving in with Jared, Kristin had allowed herself to fall out of touch with everyone outside her home and her job, to sink into a comfortable isolation focused on a day to day routine. Kristin's coworkers liked to act as though they cared, but most days they could only barely carry that off as long as she gave them an audience to ramble on about themselves. There was no way any of them would travel cross country to her rescue, and if they did, they would never let her forget it.

In any case, if Kristin called family or friend, she would end up owing someone a lot, and at this juncture she was forced to ask herself what help, specifically, would be worth that. She had no choice but to entertain Jared's point about what was left of home, even if he was to blame for it. If he had no income, she had no social or family obligations, and they had no housing or possessions, then the only thing left would be a part-time retail job in a Virginia suburb. Was that by itself worth the cost of getting back to it? Kristin wasn't so sure. Not about that or anything else.

With no alternative in mind, Kristin had climbed into the back of the Jetta and fallen into a dreamless sleep. When she awoke, the sun was already high in the sky, and she was already a sweaty mess. She and her half empty water jug had found some shade and privacy down a nearby dry wash where she had spent what she assumed to be the rest of the morning.

Kristin realized early on that whether or not she had made the conscious choice to, she was waiting for Jared. She was mad at him of course, she wasn't sure she could ever forgive him, but she also loved him, also worried about him, also wanted him to come back unscathed even if she would ultimately break with him. She considered that she could start back out to find him, but she assumed that he was on his way to find her, and if they passed each other, then she didn't have enough water to be getting lost in the desert. Unless he wasn't coming after her, and if that were true and she did go back out to him, then what? More of the same? And what did it say about them, that there was any question of whether he was looking for her? Perhaps, Kristin decided, that was the true litmus test. Whatever Jared did, he had most of their water, all of their supplies, and the keys to the car, so he was amply provisioned to do what Kristin could not. If he used that to come to her, then maybe it was meant to be, but if not then maybe...

It was ultimately Kristin's indecisiveness that had been the deciding factor: after sitting in the wash for most of the day, she had found herself dangerously low on water. If that meant that waiting for Jared was not going to be an option, then neither was hoping for immediate help from anyone she might call two thousand miles away. She considered dialing 911, but if even if a sheriff's deputy was dispatched, where would they take her, an ostensibly homeless woman stuck on the side of a county road? On the other hand, Kristin thought, if she could find help for herself, then maybe she could do better than a holding cell, or a women's shelter, or a ride to the state line. And if whomever she found to help her called the sheriff on her, she would be no worse off.

Having climbed back up to the road where they'd parked, Kristin had walked for a mile without seeing anyone. For a time, off in the distance, she'd been able to make out an industrial looking smokestack, but orienting herself toward that somehow didn't feel like the right move: she wasn't sure what she was

396

The Beard

looking for, but after ignoring all her best instincts for the last few weeks of following Jared and his maps, Kristin was choosing now to trust her gut. It was this, her empty and hungry gut, which had encouraged her to try anything different, namely to turn from the two-lane county highway onto a nameless road set at a gradual angle toward the direction from whence she had come. And now, after hours of tramping through curves and bends, arcing with the thin, loose gravel around low hills of bare, striated rock, Kristin wasn't sure where she stood relative to where she'd started. She could be six or seven miles away, or she could have doubled back to within a half mile of the wash, the road, the car, she really had no way of knowing.

Kristin told herself, for the one-thousandth time, that it didn't matter how far she'd gotten, that she had to forget what was behind her, at least for the moment, and stay focused on whatever came next. Whatever distance she had or had not covered, Kristin had to at least believe that she was that much closer to help, that if she kept putting one foot in front of the other, she would soon find something and would be less picky about how she 'felt' toward that something: any structure, any vehicle, anything, wherever she might find it.

As it happened, she found it around the next bend, in the form of a modest, single story house with a few scattered outbuildings. The home itself was wood framed over an exposed cinderblock foundation, with peeling blue siding and a gently sloped roof that just overhung a small front porch. The long, dirt driveway that Kristin now traversed, almost indistinguishable from the rocky 'lawn' of the property, curved away from the front steps to circle past a newer detached garage and what looked to be an old stable. From between the buildings, Kristin caught flashes of green: carefully planted rows of small, hard plants, growing in that desiccated country by virtue of either a miracle or a sick cosmic joke.

The sun's constant slide had already begun to paint the sky in stripes of red, burnt orange, and yellow that seemed to mimic the

397

small crags surrounding the property, but even as the temperature matched the descent, and even far beneath the brim of her straw hat, Kristin judged as she climbed the steps that the deep shade of the porch must've cooled the front of the house by ten degrees. For good measure, a window air conditioner buzzed from a purpose-cut whole in the wall near the aluminum screen door. Kristin hunted fruitlessly along the casing for a doorbell. Finding none, she tentatively pulled open the outer door far enough to knock on the solid wood portal behind.

Even before the noisy springs could snap the screen closed again, Kristin heard movement from somewhere inside: something being dropped or maybe picked up, or tripped over, impossible to say which. In any case, the noise was followed by an excruciatingly long pause. Kristin backed up two feet and stood perfectly still for the duration. She did not worry or wonder what to do next. There was no next beyond this that she could think of. If waiting here was her only option, then second guessing that was pointless.

As the front door peeled back from the threshold a few inches, Kristin realized that she hadn't planned anything to say. She stood quietly while a hand, slight but strong with long, dirty fingernails, appeared through the crack in the doorway and grasped the inside handle of the screen to hold it shut. Near the level of Kristin's shoulder, a face followed the hand into the waning light: that of a woman in her mid-fifties, with angular features and deep creases at the corners of her eyes. Her oft tanned skin was approaching leathery, and her thick, coarse hair was pulled back in a long, brown-and-silver pony tail.

The woman peered intensely through the screen to under Kristin's hat. Finally, she said, "Well, you're here... Speak!"

Kristin felt herself blushing self-consciously. "I'm sorry," she stammered, "I was walking by and I saw your place, and I'm lost, and do you know you're the only house for miles? And I can't even hitch-hike, there's no cars and there's nothing out here, and-,"

"No," the woman interrupted emphatically, "There isn't. So, what the hell you doin' here?" Leaning closer to the wire mesh to

The Beard

look suspiciously past Kristin up the drive, the woman asked, "You break down or something? Where's your car?"

Struggling to regain her bearings, Kristin answered haltingly, somewhat pleadingly, "I don't know. It still works. It's not my car. It's my boyfriend's. And we had a fight. And now I'm lost, and... And now I don't know."

The woman's face visibly relaxed as her accusatory squint melted into sympathy and raised eyebrows. As abruptly as she had yanked wooden door, she shoved open the screen to inspect Kristin more closely. "Are you hurt?" she asked with a brusque sort of sincerity. "Do you need to call somebody?"

From somewhere outside of herself Kristin observed in amazement that even in her numbness, her exhaustion, in her want and dehydration, she had still found tears to weep.

The aluminum storm door of the RV shuddered to a close behind Louis, the consequence of gravity as he had parked the trailer at a list. Perhaps it was silly how much that bothered him under the circumstances. He would have liked very much to take the time to pull one side onto a ramp, but he wasn't sure if there was much point since they would be leaving it soon. Besides, he didn't think he would be allowed back into the vehicle alone in the meantime, so he resigned himself to fighting the door. At least there was that one thing he could fight. With his hands full, Louis turned on his heel, kicked the door open, and threw a camp stove onto a pile of nylon and canvas gear outside.

"Hey!" Tim shouted from behind the nearby table. Louis turned to glare at him. Tim leaned back casually with one arm stretched across the back of the booth seat and the handgun laid in front of him. "You wanna pout," Tim continued, "Pout all you like. But you break that stove and we don't eat."

Louis shook his head angrily and turned back to the task of packing.

Clifford

"You know," Tim reflected loudly, "I understand why you're mad at me, really, I do. But at the same time, I'm not sure you didn't give up the right to be mad when you threw that tantrum out there. Even if you couldn't listen to reason, if you had stood aside and let me handle things, then you could maybe blame me for killing your dog. But now, *you're* the one who chased it off, and out there on its own, it will die just the same, only *slooow...* so really, now, *you* killed the damn thing." Stretching, Tim added, "But you wanna be mad at me, that's fine, *juuust fine.*"

Louis felt every muscle in his shoulders and neck tense involuntarily. Clenching his jaw, he forced his hands to continue quietly in their work.

"A'course," Tim continued, "It might have gotten lucky and bled out in the bushes. Then I guess maybe I killed it."

Louis let his handfuls of plastic cookware clatter to the floor and turned angrily toward Tim. Before he could lift a foot to approach, Tim had the gun back in his hand and aimed at Louis's knee. He said calmly, "If I could trust you enough to turn my back, then maybe I could help you pack up and carry all this gear. But as it stands-,"

"Why?" Louis barked in frustration, "Just fucking *Why*? Why wouldn't you let us go? I offered you the compass, you could've stolen the truck and the trailer, but you don't even want them. More than half this food and water is for me, and if you know where you're going now-,"

"Where *we're* going," Tim corrected him, "And that's half the reason you can't leave, right there. The universe didn't just choose me. The compass chose you and *then* led you to me, and you don't get to walk away from that, it doesn't work that way. The other half of the reason I've already told you, and I keep on telling you: I can't do this part by myself. So, like it or not, I am stuck with you. And since I can't trust you, you are stuck hauling these water jugs. So, strap up buttercup, and let's get marching already."

Louis stared at Tim and his gun, unsure what to say, until he realized that nothing he might say would matter. He was not in
400

The Beard

control, and Tim wasn't going to give him enough information to argue effectively. And no argument, no matter how effective, would make any difference anyhow, because this guy held the cards and apparently wanted to torture him. Grasping on the nearest point he could find, Louis muttered, "What's the goddamn hurry? We still have a roof over us for tonight, and it'll be cooler first thing in the morning."

Tim leaned back and laid the gun on the table, this time keeping his hand on the grip. Absently inspecting the fingernails of his free hand, Tim answered, "Out there in the heat, there is already someone waiting on us. And for all the same reasons that I can't do this part alone, for the part after this, we will need a third."

September 3, 1881

The merciless Arizona sun approached its zenith, gradually degrading the long shadows of the dusty crags that guarded either side of the trail. After days' worth of hard shrubs on the Mogollon Plateau, the landscape had finally broken, leaving Hugh and William to follow curves and bends that arced around low hills of bare, striated rock. The red and brown layers of stone were more stimulating country than Hugh had seen in some time, but his most frequent view remained unchanged: the dirt directly in front of his boots and, a little higher up, the dirt on William's back between the carbine he'd slung from a strap on one shoulder and the knapsack he'd slung from the other.

For the first couple days of their march, William had been the only one of them who'd known where they were, which had proved important as they tacked from creek to wash to spring in an effort to keep their canteens filled. But by William's own admission, at some point they had crossed into unfamiliar territory, and had thereby negated his advantage and placed more emphasis on Hugh's map and mirror as a means of navigation. Still, William had led, and Hugh had followed, and neither had suggested otherwise. In their constant quest for water, water had found its level.

Hugh looked again past his swaying beard to the uneven ground before him. Suddenly aware of William's shadow breaking away up a hill to the left, he inquired, "You gotta piss? You wanna stop for a bit?"

"Nah," William called back, "This is where we go now, up this hill to points north."

"Alright then," Hugh said. "But as I recall, my map says east."

Without looking back, William continued trudging on, "I know you love going downhill, and I know that the path is pretty level, but there is a certain safety in keeping to higher ground when we can. The map also says there's a stream or something to the North."

"Oh that," Hugh said, having turned to follow up the ridge. "I saw that, but it's a mile out the way, and I thought we had plenty of water."

"Plenty," William said loudly, "Is never enough." Hugh looked from the speaker's back to the loose, rocky soil as he picked his way forward. Both men focused on their footing as the climb became steeper. The scraping of their boots and their labored breathing filled the silence. As they emerged from behind the hill, sunlight exploded onto their exposed arms, and the ground abruptly leveled off before descending into a more gradual slope. Catching his breath, William carried on speaking, wistfully nigh absently, "Do you know that you're fortunate to be undertaking this journey in such a wet summer? Couple years back, when we's chasin' Victorio, now *that* was brutal. I won't pass up a stream ever again after that."

"How's that?" Hugh asked, just making conversation. "Seems like everyone at the fort made mention of Victorio, but none of 'em said anythin' specific."

William chuckled, "You would too, an' then you wouldn't either. Some is afraid they'll call him back from the dead. More likely though… see, Victorio an' his raiders were our last hard fight. Everyone wants the glory of that, you live yer life waitin' for it, you never stop talkin' about it. But nobody *really* wants the horror of it, the depredations, de-*pri*-vations. Nobody smart wants it, anyhow. An' if anyone had a knack for makin' war look ugly, Victorio was the man for that.

"He was an Apache chief who knew how to get the army's attention an', later on, how to avoid it. He hated bein' at San Carlos, as everyone does, so he set out with a couple hundred riders. To get him back in, somebody promised him a place at Ojo Caliente, where his group come from in the first place. But then, the War Department wanted to keep a closer eye, an' the Peace Department wants all the Indians concentrated, so they sent him back to San Carlos to live near the White Mountain Apache, and the Pima, and all the rest of his father's and grandfather's worst enemies. He didn't stay long, an' on his way back East, he carved up a handful o' soldiers: staked their earthly remains to the ground, so I heard, before magically vanishing with hundreds of men and dozens of army horses.

"We went out after him a number of times: we was better manned, armed, an' provisioned than him in every case. But as close as we come to gettin' him, Victorio was too smart for it. Y'see, he knew that causin' you to die was just as good as killin' you. And in that, thirst can be a powerful weapon. There was one drive south we was chasin' him well into October, late in the season, so dry to start with. But we cut a straight line after him. Day an' night we marched to catch up, an' every drop of water he beat us to, he tainted. The first little stream we come across he'd had his men ride through 'til they'd churned it into mud and horse piss. An' we was so thirsty, some men tried drinkin' that mud. Not that it worked, but can you imagine? A little later on, we come across a fresh water tank, but Victorio had killed a coyote, pulled its guts out an' tossed the whole mess in t'poison it.

"Three days like that, in that heat without water. But you don't dare risk gettin' poisoned out there... out here. Victorio taught us that one as well, when he come back north the next year. We had him surrounded in the mountains, but then a whole company got poisoned drinkin' from a spring what had gypsum in it. Good lesson in that though: if they'd brought Indian scouts with 'em like we did, those boys would'a knowed to not drink it."

As William trailed off, Hugh responded, "But you got him that time? When you had him surrounded?"

"Nah," William sighed, "We got caught up rescuin' them poisoned bastards. Y'know, it's disheartening just how often soldierin' comes down to shittin' yer way across the countryside. In the end it was the Mexicans got Victorio. Their army sent word of a glorious battle down south, but I hear it was a massacre, just Victorio an' a bunch a' old squaws. An' in any case, they didn't get

404

ol' Nana: that's one of Victorio's chiefs, said to be raidin' as we speak in the territory where we're goin'. I expect the fort will march against him any time now, with more glorious shittin' to follow. That is, once they get this whole medicine-man-ghost-dance problem squared, because I don't guess you'd wanna undertake a pursuit with all your Indian scouts lookin' askance at your cavalrymen. Army can't function without trust, an' our scouts can't be trusted at the moment."

Sensing a rare opportunity to relate from his own experience, Hugh offered, "I saw some of what you mean when I was there. Them scouts skulkin' around… you can tell they're pretty sneaky."

William replied defensively, "Well, now, I wouldn't go that far: you're talkin' about dependable soldiers. But this is an unusual time. A few bad apples got the whole country stirred up this summer."

"That may be," Hugh said, only debating to pass the time, "But you say that Nana and the medicine man are bad apples. For years before that, there was Victorio, and before that I'm guessin' someone else-,"

William stopped and turned around to clarify his point, "So sometimes the same apples, sometimes different. Either way, it's only a few of 'em holding forth on the same worn argument: that white men have come to take and live on their lands."

Curious now, Hugh observed, "You look as though you disagree with that."

"A'course I do," William scoffed, "Takin' the land. Don't be absurd: the land hasn't gone anywhere."

"I don't believe that part is at issue," Hugh said.

Turning back to the trail, William spoke casually over his shoulder, "We're not livin' on their land. We were, back when we were fewer, an' there was enough of them to kill us all. Then the settlers come and kept on comin', until there was enough of *us* to kill all *them*. So now they live on our land, what we stole fair and square."

Clifford

Hugh let the discussion peter out, choosing instead to renew his focus on his footing. The pair travelled across a low ridge that was slung between the hills they'd just climbed. Had Hugh looked up, he might have been struck by the hard transition from low vegetation to bare rock, or by the odd uniformity of the striations from hilltop to disparate hilltop. Instead, he balanced the pack on his back and peered through the gap between the brim of his hat and the apron of his beard at William's boot prints in the red and yellow dust.

William resumed unprovoked, "Yeh, them scouts is alright, as a rule. Y'know, more than once they saved my life, saved the lives of every man in my company."

"But you can't trust them," Hugh repeated back.

William laughed, "Now you're seein' it. It confuses you?"

Hugh shrugged his concession, then realized William wouldn't have seen the gesture as he walked with his back turned. Even so, William continued magnanimously, "Forget for a moment that the White Mountain Apaches what saved us soldiers were savin' us from their Warm Springs brethren… Apart from that… It's… It's tough to explain. Here, just as an example, there was a time, around when I arrived at Apache, so must be three years or more now, but we was out on patrol, and we come across a Indian campsite full 'a dead men. Not too many, maybe fifteen, sixteen dead warriors in and around a few of their huts. I don't know what group they was with, or who attacked 'em, but some of 'em was full of arrows, and most of 'em had faces beat in."

"Jesus," Hugh muttered, "I see why you're distrustful."

"No. Haven't got to my point yet, don't interrupt," William loudly interrupted. "Men die in the mountains, that happens every day. What impressed me though, about this time, was that in one of them huts, we found ammunition. No rifle, just ammunition, a broken war club, and a body with a crushed face. That says to me that an enemy warrior strode in and beat to death a man guarding his hut with a gun. Can you imagine? I mean, I've killed an' all, once or twice, but it's one thing to fire on the enemy, fire a volley I

406

mean, an' see them fall up on a hillside where they's tryin' to fire on you: that's my job. But to beat a man like that, what must that require?"

Still unsure of his footing, Hugh treaded carefully in William's footsteps. Offhandedly he hazarded, "Savagery?"

William stopped again to turn towards him. Firmly he insisted, "Courage. Incredible courage, at least at first. To run after a man who's hopin' to kill you, to look him in the eye, and then you can't flinch, you can't hold back, you have to put him in the dirt quick, before he pulls a trigger against you. That might be more courage than I got, an' certainly more than yer store. So you see, that kind of a man can be relied upon. But the kind of man who can do what comes after, who can finish an enemy that way… Consider the sound of that, all the blood an' the brains… and you'd have to keep bringing that club down, over and over and… I'm sure I'm not illustrating my point here."

Hugh stood for a long somber moment before offering, "That you'll never see a dime novel end with the hero beating in a man's skull?"

William's face broke into a grin. Returning to the trail, he said, "As fair a conclusion as any, I suppose."

Hugh followed. Relieved to have taken his foot out of his mouth, he sighed, "This is a lawless place-,"

"No!" William shouted in exasperation, "Dammit, no, that is the opposite…" He walked more slowly to speak more rapidly, "There *are* laws. There's our laws, there's Apache laws, Pueblo laws, then the army, the territory: everybody got laws out here, far more than they got out East. An' I'd speculate that the average Papago knows his people's laws better'n I know the latest regulations handed down by our government. But their peoples' laws are the kind that might compel a man to face down death, an' then beat it with a club."

Hugh committed to silence, hoping that William would treat it as either acquiescence or disinterest, whichever might draw the least ridicule.

Clifford

"You can't make sense of it," William bloviated, "Because you been talkin' about Indians. I been tryin' to talk of the wide world. Every man of every stripe lives by rules, boy, whether they know it or not, whether they know those rules to repeat them or not. There's rules that everyone agrees on, and still others that lie beyond our descriptive powers, but if ever you should meet a man whose rules you don't fully understand then, *then*, you don't dare trust him. An' you don't know the Apache's rules. Hell, Apache don't know Pueblo rules nor the other way 'round neither, but at least they all know enough to not trust each other, and sure as hell to not trust us white folk. That's the meaning of my little morality speech."

Hugh shuffled wordlessly through the dust. He didn't spend much time considering William's diatribe: whatever point he had or had not made was of less concern to Hugh than the passionate impatience with which he had made it. For weeks before they had left, the two of them had related quite well. At the time that Hugh had entrusted William with this mission, he had found him to be trustworthy. But in the days since that disclosure, Hugh could not seem to avoid saying the wrong things: the rhythms of their conversations had been consistently out of step. Or perhaps Hugh was only now spending enough time with William to discover how mercurial he was. Either way, in increasing measure, silence seemed Hugh's safest course. On the other hand, the awkwardness of the moment was more than he could bear.

Hugh opened his mouth, still unclear on what words would come out, when he was mercifully interrupted by distant laughter. His first reaction was jealousy: whoever was out there had been blessed with better humor than he had enjoyed the last few days. It was only as he nearly collided with William's back that he realized the implications of coming across other people out here. William turned and held a finger to his own lips to signal quiet, before gesturing to the craggy hilltop a few feet to their right.

Hugh climbed to a ledge where William lay on his stomach, peering over with his gun at hand beside him. Hugh lowered to his hands and knees, taking care to balance his pack between his shoulder blades, and inched forward to avoid kneeling on his beard. As he came even with William, the other man growled sarcastically, "Just two men takin' their donkey for a turn in the garden." It only took a glance to see exactly what he meant.

Down a gradual slope near their perch, the crumbling earth had worn into a dusty red bowl, devoid of vegetation or shade. Almost a hundred yards down this searing, desolate landscape, a pair of respectably dressed men strolled leisurely on either side of a mule. The taller of them wore a dark suit with a black, wide-brimmed hat, and held the reins loosely in one hand, offering the animal more guidance than discipline. He made a comment without turning his head and the other man, shorter and wearing a bowler with a curled brim that matched his tan waistcoat and complemented his meticulously rounded beard, replied with a laugh that echoed from the surrounding hills.

Hugh began pushing himself to his feet when William caught his sleeve and pulled him back. "What are you doin'?" William hissed. "If we gotta ambush these two, this is a fine spot to do it."

"Why would we want to ambush anyone?" Hugh whispered in disbelief.

"D'you even listen when I talk?" William asked angrily. "We ain't on reservation rules no more, you don't know what they's about. And when you got an advantage like this hidy hole on high ground, you don't give that up unless you're sure there is no threat."

Losing patience, Hugh said at conversational volume, "They're not hostiles, not bandits, and you're the only one I see has a weapon. I'm 'a go talk to 'em."

Realizing that there would be no argument to win, William sniffed, "Fine then. Your funeral. But I'm stayin' on the high ground in case they try anything." As Hugh climbed over the ridge and bounced awkwardly down the slope, William called after in a stage whisper, "You should ask 'em the nearest place to fill our canteens!"

Clifford

Between the weight of his pack and the instability of the red soil, Hugh was forced by gravity into an accelerating trot: rapid, tiny steps to repeatedly catch himself from falling forward and sliding downhill on his face. He might have been able to throw his weight back, to take more time getting to the bottom, but beyond his momentum, he found himself propelled by his enthusiasm for company of greater variety, if as yet undetermined quality. Even as his shuffling quickened into a dusty skid, Hugh saw his quarry moving gradually away over the bottom of the basin. He shouted, a sort of sharp bark, and waved his arms.

The other men startled. The shorter of them vanished nimbly around the front of the mule, while the taller spun to face the source of the noise. Hugh's boots slapped the hardened earth at the bottom of the slope, and he finally took an easier pace, making every effort to appear casual while he caught his breath. As he approached the back end of the mule, he found the man in the dark suit to be a good head taller than he, broad shouldered, with an olive complexion and straight black hair left just long enough to sweep behind his ears. Under the wide brim of the man's hat and above his sharp features, his dark eyes surveyed Hugh from top to toe. In a rich, deep voice the man said, "Impossible. Simply impossible."

Hugh squinted and cocked his head, "What's that now?"

Around the other man's shoulder, the top of the tan bowler hat slid cautiously into view. Following close behind, the shorter man's grey eyes peered at Hugh, at first furrowed in concern and then wrinkling at the corners over a smile. With a careful agility, the smaller man stepped around his companion and strolled in Hugh's direction. He left his hands in his pockets while he articulated, "He only means that we hadn't expected to see anyone for some time yet."

"Sure," Hugh said, looking from one man to the other. "We haven't run across anyone ourselves for a couple days."

"We?" the short man asked. The larger man tapped him on the shoulder and pointed to the hillside where William now picked his way down. "Ah... We... I see."

410

The Beard

Noticing their stares and nearing the bottom of the basin, William called over, "You ask 'em yet? Where to find water out here?"

"He hasn't had the chance," the small man yelled back. Returning his attention to Hugh he said, "But you're both welcome to share in ours. We have plenty: we only left St. Johns late this morning, and we were told we would find a creek twenty miles or so out. We had thought to spend the night there, and tomorrow travel... east?" He turned to his companion for confirmation but was answered with an apprehensive silence.

"We're going east as well," Hugh said cheerily.

"Then you must join us!" the man in the bowler declared, "For at least as long as our trails converge."

Surprisingly close to Hugh's elbow, William's voice stated, "That'll be a couple days and no more. Hugh, two more days, three nights, an' we start back in, now, I'm serious."

To either or both of them, the small man grinned curiously, "Back to where, in such hurry?"

Out of hand, Hugh offered, "Fort Apache," before turning to explain to William, "Another day should get us to the end. So long as they don't slow us down, I see no harm in it." Hugh returned to his newfound friends and discovered the larger man opening his mouth to speak, while the smaller shook his head vigorously in response. The former nodded, prompting the latter to spin around and espouse, "Then it is settled! We must all be going!"

Hugh turned to William. William shrugged. The men fell in beside their new companions, with Hugh and the smaller man to the left of the mule and William next to the larger on the right. Hugh added, "This other one is William, by the way, and I'll be Hugh."

"Very good," the small man nodded. "The talkative gentleman tolerating my company is called Benjamin. My name is Dr. Henry Strafford."

Day 7

In abject defiance of time, the sun refused to descend. The flat landscape extended under an otherwise empty sky, featureless but for desiccated scrub brush. It had been hours since Jared had stopped looking at all of it, yet it was all he could see, even now, even while he stared unblinking at the translucent camouflage ceiling of his tent. He considered the irony of camouflage in a desert: in this world where everything, including him, wore the same layer of dust, where every plant and rock was the same sickly tan, the deep green and black of his tent was the only thing that stood out. Moving his eyes without lifting his head, he allowed for the splotchy shadows that the pattern cast on his bare calves. He supposed that meant that he was camouflaged to match the tent that then matched nothing but him.

None of it belonged out there. Nothing belonged out there. And before Jared had come along, nothing was exactly what had been there.

Perhaps it was appropriate then, that Jared had accomplished nothing since his arrival. Three days earlier, he had been plagued by too many options: he could've wandered in any direction, could've gotten more lost, or found a road, could've explored the wilderness in search of civilization, but not knowing the right way to go he'd elected to sit still and wait. In the end it was Jared's indecisiveness that had been the deciding factor. That first day, sure of Kristin's impending return, Jared had drunk more than half of his water. On the second, he'd tried a combination of rationing and relying on fate to deliver him quickly, but by evening it had not, and so Jared had consumed the last of what little condensation had collected at the bottom of the cooler.

Now, twenty hours later, Jared was thirsty, but he didn't dare go searching for water for fear of either overheating or losing moisture by breaking a sweat. "Maybe after dark," he thought, "It's cold out there at night, and maybe I could search for water then." But then what if Kristin followed her directions back to look for him, and he had gotten more lost by wandering off their path? He didn't know if it was worth the risk, but he wasn't sure he had a choice. He would decide later. For now, the only option he recognized was to stay in what shade was available to him, lying on his back in the camouflage tent with the door unzipped near his feet.

For a time, Jared's mind had made up for his conscious effort to stay as still as possible. It had continued to move, to seek out the solution that must exist out there in the wilderness, but at some point he had arrived organically at the futility of that exercise, and all thought had then come to a halt as well. Thusly Jared sat, broiling in his shelter but frozen in body and spirit, aware only of the narrow slice of landscape visible between his outstretched feet.

It was from that direction that the sound came: a man's voice, faint, muffled, invisible, and vaguely unintelligible. It left an impression less of words than of tone, communicated a feeling more than an idea, and that feeling was haughty and imperious, not shouting but lecturing. In the back of Jared's immobilized brain, he accepted that somewhere out there, it sounded like *someone* knew what *they* wanted to do next.

And then it was quiet. Remaining on his back, Jared was roused only far enough to wonder whether he had heard anything at all. Or was it a mirage? Could sounds be called mirages, or was the term 'mirage' meant to cover specific optical illusions, as it was used in cartoons? In his first real decision since morning, Jared determined that what he'd heard was not a mirage, but rather a good, old-fashioned auditory hallucination. But why couldn't it be Kristin's voice he hallucinated? Why did it have to be some guy's, and why did that guy have to sound like such a dick?

On the horizon beyond Jared's sneakers, a long, hazy figure materialized. "There," he sighed aloud, "*That's* a mirage then. Problem solved." As the nondescript shape gradually grew in size, it morphed from a black bar against the bright sky into a pair of distinct silhouettes. Slowly, silently now, the independent shapes wavered into something more recognizable, the edges of the shadows hardened into the image of a small man laden with baggage marching beside a much larger man hauling something still larger on his back. Jared wondered quietly why his subconscious would conjure furniture delivery in the desert. Soon enough, given the shades' progress, he assumed he would have the chance to address the voices in his head more directly.

The smaller figure turned toward the larger and issued that sound again: a distant, authoritative bark. Jared regarded the activity with the bored attention one would pay to the dancing flames of a campfire: the flickering shapes and movement, while necessarily indicative of something, didn't seem to require his attention. He found it exhausting to wait on them to do something worthwhile. He leaned his head back into his pillow and stared blankly at the glowing camouflage above.

At length and still at some distance (whether outside or inside his skull he wasn't sure), Jared heard scraping and shuffling, then a gravelly baritone, "Jesus, is he dead?"

The first voice, now less screechy than it was whiny, replied, "No he can't be dead, that isn't possible. Bring that over here, will you?" Sharper, the voice cut through the haze, "Hey! Hey we're here to help!"

Something massive hit the ground with a thump, followed by a sloshing sound. Slightly labored, the baritone growled, "Well, if he ain't dead, he's most certainly shat his self."

The higher voice admonished, "Now don't be..." After a beat, "Y'know, I guess I can't speak to that either way. Hey buddy! We're here to-," In another direction it quietly instructed, "Hand me that canteen already."

By the time Jared registered the sudden cold against his face and arms and the tick and slap of water hitting the walls of his nylon enclosure, he discovered he had already crab walked as far from the entrance as was possible. With eyes wide and wild, Jared was baffled by the appearance of hard objects through his as yet

414

The Beard

fuzzy perception. In front of him crouched a man best described as round: not fat, or not aggressively so, but thick at the waist and joints, with soft wavy hair and a neatly rounded beard broken by an exaggerated smile and sun burnt cheeks. Behind that man was a far less jolly giant, six foot six at the very least, with broad shoulders and a barrel chest pulled awkwardly toward one knee as he carefully repositioned a rubber bag full of liquid one third the size of a waterbed. This second man wore a dour expression, unmanaged gray stubble, and a tired orange baseball cap pulled far enough to conceal his eyes.

The comprehension crept in slowly that Jared's only hallucination had been the existence of any hallucination at all. These men were real, and their water was cold.

The cheerful face at the door inquired, "So how 'bout it, guy? Did you shit yourself?"

Jared's panicked, haunted eyes continued to dart between the two men as he raised his right arm to point beyond the wall of the tent.

Following this gesture with the fraying bill of his ball cap, the larger man flinched and pulled back his head. He wrinkled his nose in disgust, "C'mon dude... Latrine should be twenty yards from camp, minimum." Shaking his head, he continued, "Didn't even pretend to throw dirt over it... You a fuckin' animal or somethin'?"

While the round man was distracted by his companion's critique, Jared leaned his extended arm forward and snatched the canteen from his hand. Reacting on impulse, the other man began reaching to take it back, and then thought better of it. Jared tipped it, filling his maw to overflowing and taking no notice of the cold running down from the corners of his mouth. Outside, the baritone chuckled darkly, "Better keep an eye on this one, Tim. He may be too quick for you."

As Jared swallowed repeatedly, as his most pressing need was met, the light in the tent assumed a new character. The green and yellow glare lost its intensity, hard edges softened while blurry objects reclaimed a certain depth, and the wheels spinning in his

Clifford

mind began to catch, to gain traction and make sense of the scene. He was with people. They might know what to do next. Realizing that the canteen was empty and unsure of when that had happened, Jared dropped it heavily to the floor and panted to get his breath.

The others stared quietly, waiting for something, not saying what that something was. Finally, Jared looked to the nearer of the two and breathed, "Kristin."

Tim raised his eyebrows, "Christian? Is that your name, Christian?"

"No, I said-," Jared stopped short. He knew what he'd said and why he'd said it. He was concerned, intensely concerned, about her wellbeing and her whereabouts. For a split second he thought that these men ought to know those things, assumed that she had sent them to find him. But if they had seen her, then they would've known Jared's name. And by asking his name, the round man had also informed Jared what was expected of him. "Jared," he muttered quickly. After a pause, he more clearly enunciated, "My name is Jared. And I am lost."

Tim smiled broadly, "On the contrary, Jared. You're the only one of us who has any clue where we're going."

The Beard

September 4, 1881

William worked a narrow limb into a shallow pile of kindling and watched the beveled edge begin to smoke, then catch: a wispy flame slithered across to blacken the least of it, while the surrounding bed of dry brush smoldered gently. Above the dusty fire pit, the sky was still light, the sun having retreated only just below the bare hills. This had the effect of yellowing the hilltops, washing out the pink and brown striations, even as their bases sunk deeper into shadowed reds and blues. William didn't love where his comrades had elected to camp. He had argued that they should strike for higher ground, that they would make easy targets down in a bowl like this, but the counter to that, which had won out, was that if they and their one rifle were attacked they would likely lose regardless of position, so their best bet was to stay as hidden as possible, and that might prove easier away in the shadows.

William believed that his companions had been taken in by the notion that the cliffs and hills that surrounded them were some kind of natural defense, rather than the shooting platform they actually were, but the men were insistent and William supposed they had a point: the group would be vulnerable no matter what they did. So, they had come to recline in this dusty pocket in the rocks, with dark stretching ever closer to their fire, concealing them from the world beyond, and likewise concealing the world from them.

Them, that is, with the exception of Hugh, who had volunteered earlier to strike out for the creek that hadn't materialized. William had been a bit surprised by Hugh's decision, it was generally William who was most concerned about such things, and he was not yet worried at all. He suspected that Hugh was as interested in the solitude that came with the mission as he was in full canteens. Still, that had been hours ago. To no one in particular William thought aloud, "Hope that boy gets back afore dark."

Clifford

On the other side of the fledgling flames, the dark man in the dark suit laid stretched out with his head on a knapsack, his hat tilted forward over his eyes. Without moving, he grunted, "For as long as he's taken, we can hope he's at least found *something* worth his while."

William glanced briefly from the outstretched Indian to the doctor, who now sat against a rock nearer the mule, his legs in front of him while he stared blankly over his boots at the fire. Returning his attention to the former, William said to Benjamin's hat, "I don't mean to offend, but might I ask why you aren't out there with him? You are meant to be a Indian guide after all. Shouldn't you be *guiding* us to water?"

Without moving, Benjamin answered warmly, "Perhaps if I knew the area I would. But as I've never been this far west, any one of us would more accurately be *scouting* for water, and I shouldn't like to get in the way, given that the two of you are meant to be army scouts-,"

"Wait," William interrupted, "You don't know the area? Then why were we told you were a guide?"

Strafford released a single sharp laugh, loud and jarring enough to startle the other men. With a mischievous grin he observed, "When you ask like that, it makes me sound ridiculous for hiring him."

Benjamin laughed along enthusiastically, "Yes! It *is* ridiculous that you've hired me. I've been telling you that since Kansas City."

With sincere disbelief William pressed, "This is dangerous country. If you're agreed that neither of you know where you're going, then why are you out here? What are you doing?" Turning to Benjamin he demanded, "And how could you offer yourself as a guide?"

Strafford interjected defensively, "Well now, don't judge him too harshly. As he said, he has tried to convince me of his ineptitude. But, as I've told him in each case, he is overly modest about his contribution. Among other things, he is rather a skilled linguist."

The Beard

"Hardly," Benjamin answered, exasperated. He finally sat up, using his erstwhile pillow as a cushion. Placing his hat on one knee, he clarified, "I speak some Chickasaw from my youth, of course, and a few Creek phrases from a boy who came to our school. But there hasn't been much call for that lo my last decade in Philadelphia. These days, my Latin is more practiced."

Exaggeratedly, Strafford said, "It was your *Latin* to which I was *refer*-ing. It certainly didn't hurt in deciphering the directions we got from those three Spaniards in Santa Fe. And it isn't as though you've had any trouble communicating with the Pueblo we've met."

"Yes," Benjamin said, "Because they've all spoken English-,"

"All the same," Strafford argued, "I found your presence on those occasions to be helpful."

William poked plaintively at the fire and silently cursed Hugh for leaving him alone with these two. They weren't intentionally obnoxious: in fact, he was tempted to find them entertaining. But he hated being outnumbered by new company, of trying to avoid their insecurities, work out their views, and fit himself into the existing rhythms of their conversation. It was challenging enough to allow one newcomer into his ranks, but to make a newcomer of his self was unbearable, especially when the other men were so given to sarcasm. At this moment, for example, William couldn't be sure whether he'd been party to good natured ribbing, or been witness to an argument. In either case it seemed unfair that he should be the one left in awkward silence. William tried again to find his footing amongst their dialogue. Without looking up he grumbled, "What was a Chickasaw gettin' up to in Philadelphia?"

"I was a clerk," Benjamin answered simply, "At a legal practice. We dealt primarily in property disputes. I spent most of my time on matters related to probate administration."

"Ah," William said. Now at an even greater loss for direction he tried, "There many Chickasaw up that way?"

Benjamin answered drily, "Almost as many as there are estate lawyers in Indian Territory."

Clifford

William nodded quietly and continued stirring the coals, well aware of the almost childishly sullen look he wore.

With a deliberately easier tone, Benjamin continued, "By which I only mean that I finished what education was available to me in Indian Territory and struck out in pursuit of more. I had an interest in law, and Philadelphia seemed as good a town as any for that." Leaning back, putting his weight on one elbow, Benjamin winked, "For reasons I will never understand, my colleagues all thought I was Punjabi. They seemed to find that agreeable, and I enjoyed the irony of the error, so I never corrected them."

William chuckled, less amused than gratified to finally be invited to a joke, "That's good. Punjabi. So, you an Indian six different ways then."

"There it is," Benjamin nodded graciously. "And it all went exactly to plan until this one," he reached out and slapped the toe of Strafford's boot, "Came around *looking* for Indians."

"In Philadelphia," William grinned.

"I know it," Strafford shrugged, "It may sound ridiculous now, but you can't argue with my results." The three men laughed together for a moment. In the broken tension that followed, Strafford clarified, "I stopped in Philadelphia for supplies. That I found this Indian there was a happy accident."

Concerned at losing the momentum of the conversation, William followed, "Supplies for what? Where were you on your way to?"

"Why, here," Strafford said, gesturing widely around them, "Or some approximation of it. The ends of the earth, is where I wanted to go."

William nodded, "I suppose you're heading the right direction after all. Though I still couldn't' guess why."

"Ah," Strafford said brightly. He folded his legs over and scooted out of the shadows. The growing firelight danced across his glistening eyes. Gesturing with his index finger next to the narrow brim of his bowler he exclaimed, "'Why' is a much bigger question."

420

The Beard

"With a much longer answer," Benjamin finished. He returned his head to his knapsack, but this time set his hat on his chest.

Strafford ignored the last and continued, "Our journey, like all journeys I suppose, began with an idea. No... 'Idea,' might be too vague... with *expectations*, perhaps, a desire more than a purpose. It must have been ten years ago now: I had recently returned to my family home in Boston from a year abroad, and one of my shipmates had invited me to join him at an exhibition of paintings in New York. The artist was well past his prime by then, but before the war he might have been called important.

"He had spent his youth traveling the Western frontier, recording the people he found there for posterity. You see, he was convinced, remained convinced until his death, that the noble natives of this continent are not long for this world, that European civilization would and must destroy them and their way of life, that only their likenesses on canvas might be rescued, and, of course, only by him. The actual permanence of that 'rescue' might be open to debate, as by the time of the exhibition in question, the artist had already given up every one of his original portraits to pay off personal debts. The collection on display in New York was based entirely on rough charcoal studies and his forty-year-old memories. He called them his cartoons, and for all their detail, one could not but scoff at the notion of preserving likenesses which in all likelihood looked nothing like their subjects.

"And scoff is exactly what we did, me and the few members of the public who attended the gallery. I thanked my friend for having invited me, I went back to Boston, and I scoffed. But for all my ridicule, there was something about it that I could not let go. For weeks, the faces from those portraits, whosesoever they were, would spring to mind at odd moments; for months those chiefs and squaws would find me in my dreams. It wasn't until a year later that I realized: I could no longer remember exactly what any of them looked like, and yet I could not give up the *idea* of them, even then. I struggled to understand why. What was causing my obsession with this sad old artist and his inaccurate pictures?

Clifford

"I eventually realized that it wasn't the people that had interested me at all, but the place that might produce those people and the world that they might produce in their turn. It was built on a concept I had carried back from my time in Europe, but all of the exotics of that year had run together in my memory. Have you ever seen a castle?"

William sat dumbly for a long moment. The soft crackle of the fire filled the void in the conversation while he realized that the abrupt question had not been rhetorical, and that the other man stared at him expectantly from the shadows. Annoyedly he asked, "What, me? You know I ain't seen no damn castles. Maybe years ago, in a storybook-,"

"Exactly!" Strafford exclaimed excitedly, "Always and in every storybook, we talk of castles, knights, and princesses, and we call those stories 'make believe,' because no person we know on this continent has experienced them. But that's only because we're all separated from them by a great distance. All of those things still exist in the world: I've seen them, and the people who live near them think nothing of them. The stories that *those* people tell are of monsters and magic, stories *they* call 'make believe,' because they are separated from them by the expanse of time, so that no living person they know has experienced them. If it's possible that the castles and kings from our stories are real, could it not be possible that the creatures from theirs were as well, at a time? And if they were, then what became of them? Did our nations, our progress, claim some victory over them, not simply over their physical being, but over our very memory of them? Is it a universal truth that the light of our civilization should extinguish all the shadowy mysteries beyond?

"That idea brought me back to the artist, to his notions of extinction. Even if he was wrong, and his subjects and their families survive, I wonder what will remain of their stories a century from now. What will become fairy tale, and what parts of those tales might in fact be real today? If there is still some magic hiding in the world, some strange force left in some unseen corner, would the people living next to it even realize its significance? Or would they, like those living in the shadows of castles, accept it as commonplace? It isn't a question of the *people*'s stories," Strafford said emphatically, "But of the place, as it was... as it is. And of what becomes of the place once the people who know what it was have gone."

Strafford leaned back and took an easier tone, "Once I arrived at that question, I could not seem to turn away. The impressions of the faces from the gallery suddenly visited every night, and then every morning after. Going west, not in the spirit that others had gone west, mind you, but in search of my own strange vision, this... this call... That became my obsession. By some chance, I found myself living at a time of great, irreversible change, and with news of every unrest on the frontier, I could feel the moment passing. I fought with the idea for six years, and in the end, it was not my courage, but my horror at missing that moment that drove me to act. For another three years I planned, and by the end of last summer, I had sold most of my belongings and closed up the house in Boston. It was not long after, when I was provisioning in Philadelphia, that Benjamin's and my paths crossed."

William sat and stared over the top of the fire, sure that there must be more to the story. Darkness had now completely fallen in the valley around them, and the contrast of the other men's figures in firelight gave their features renewed clarity, caused Strafford's eyes to shimmer beyond the flames. Finally, William observed, "Not meaning to offend, Doctor, but that seems fairly foolish of you. If there was some mystery to be found out here, you think it would still be secret? Don't you guess there would be endless reports of that back east?"

Strafford laughed openly, "You mean reports from better men than I?"

William smiled in spite of himself, "So to speak. More prepared than you, at the very least."

"It is my belief," Strafford answered grandly, "That better men than I don't know what they are looking at. And at any event, wiser men would not look in the first place. Have you ever taken a tumble and seen stars? Haven't you ever seen a spark in your periphery, a spot in the corner of your vision that disappears when you try to look on it directly? That is how I imagine this: the very presence of the people who would report these things is the cause of its demise. To tread softly and listen carefully, that is the only thing to be done. That is the core of my mission."

Shifting his focus around the fire, William asked, "And you Benjamin? How does this mission suit your dreams?"

Benjamin laughed deeply, "How does the *mission* suit? Not at all. But you may have surmised that our friendly doctor is a man of some means. He promised to be a generous employer, and being well paid suits all men's dreams equally, I think."

"Generosity," Henry interrupted, "Had nothing to do with it. Hiring Benjamin was an investment, and one that I stand by. As you suggested, I could have hired local guides with experience of the immediate terrain, but to trust a dozen or more men over the course of my journey... Even if the majority were perfectly reliable, just one untrustworthy guide could jeopardize my pursuit, if not my very life. I could tell that Benjamin could be trusted: there are some people you can put your faith in almost immediately."

William could not dispute that Benjamin projected a rare sort of honesty. It occurred to him now that Hugh had that same quality. Some men, however vague their sense of direction, enjoined you to follow, it seemed.

"I also saw some value," Strafford continued, "In engaging a competent conversationalist, not only for selfish reasons related to the length of the journey. It occurred to me that a well-spoken man with a dusky complexion might inspire the confidence of the people whose stories I want to know. If I trust Benjamin, might the natives trust him as well?"

Benjamin answered, "We still disagree on that thesis."

William laughed, "So you say you're a disappointment?"

"Only the doctor can speak to continuing returns on his investments," Benjamin shrugged, "But my expectations were low

424

enough at the outset that 'disappointment' might be impossible. I will say that I haven't found these native conversations productive."

Aghast, Strafford demanded, "Now how can you say that? We've learned so many amazing things."

To William, Benjamin clarified, "Superstitions mostly, and many of those are contradictory. Two thousand miles to hear superstitions and children's stories-,"

"Precisely!" Strafford interrupted. "Stories direct from the source: stories and fables not worth compiling back East. And offered up as though they were commonplace, simple, everyday parables! You take for example the story we're following now-,"

With feigned exhaustion Benjamin asked, "Must we?"

"Oh, we must," Strafford said, "We already are." Strafford scooted himself around Benjamin and closer to the fire, into a direct line of sight with William. Against the backdrop of the dark hills, the firelight streaked across his tight cropped beard and around his twinkling eyes to the brim of his bowler, now tipped back and illuminated like the graying halo of a neglected icon. "No fewer than four separate bands have now asked of us the same question, as if the answer were obvious: whether we are answering a call of some kind. Apparently there is a local legend that once in every generation a group of strangers will come this way to answer the call of an ancient power. They suspect us of being those strangers, and because they accept the story as history, none of these bands would call it a legend. What's more, as the story concerns strangers, none of the natives claim that history as their own."

William interjected, "So when you say you're following this story, do you mean you're following their group of strangers? Do you have any idea the number of 'strangers,' who wander through these parts in a given season?"

Benjamin clarified, "Not strangers. I believe they said 'travelers': the men they described will have come a great distance, be unknown to everyone, be moving in a particular direction, and

Clifford

will arrive at an approximate time. And I don't recall anyone saying they'd answer the call of a 'power'. All four bands used the phrase, 'ancient evil.'"

"Well, continue then," Strafford waved, nonchalant, "You tell it better than I do."

Unmoved and without embellishment, Benjamin stated simply, "I just told it: Once in every generation, a group of travelers answers the call of an ancient evil. This call can only be heard by those intended to answer it, and has rung out since before there were men to hear. No one seems to know where it draws the travelers or what it demands of them, but it is widely believed that they are due at any moment now."

Strafford clapped his hands once excitedly before shouting, "You see? Such a faithful retelling, so clear, so succinct! How can you help but trust what this man says?"

Ignoring the outburst, William turned to Benjamin. With casual curiosity he observed, "Much as anything, I'm surprised t'hear they admitted to a thing ringing out before there were men. Most Indians I know say their people been here since the dawn of time."

"Perhaps," Benjamin shrugged, "But then, was the serpent not in Eden before Adam arrived? Inconsistencies are not what make these stories fantastic."

Strafford jumped in, "The both of you are so intent on missing the point. However inaccurate the story may be, we've heard it repeated as fact, with the same precise details and requirements, from bands hundreds of miles apart who appear to have little else in common. Certainly, much of it is exaggerated, and it likely came from a single source long ago, but the story has survived that long, which says to me that there must be something to it."

"And if there is," William said, "You think it wise to go to all this trouble searching for something evil?"

Benjamin replied, "I don't worry much that there is such a thing to search for."

426

The Beard

"Exactly!" Strafford exclaimed. "If such a thing cannot possibly exist, then what is the danger in seeking it out?"

William answered quickly, "Hunger. Hostiles. Injury, illness, bad water, no water... There is plenty of danger in wandering unprepared in this country."

Strafford answered, "I don't think it's fair to say unprepared, not wholly. In the event of medical emergency, I am a trained and experienced doctor. Benjamin may not know the terrain, but he is quite resourceful and has a talent for negotiating with white men and Indians alike." Gesturing past the fire to William he added, "And now that we've found a soldier who appears to be travelling a seasoned adventurer, well, what really could interfere with us?"

"No," William chuckled good naturedly, "You'll want to leave Hugh and me out of your plans. We'll stay with you again tonight, but in the morning, we have to split off, get back to our detachment."

"Ahh," said Strafford, "Your detachment."

"Yeh," William nodded.

Strafford let the word hang in the air for a moment before elaborating, "An infantry detachment. From Fort Apache. Sent to make contact with the Zuni Pueblo."

Incredulous, William firmly stated, "That's what I said, ain't it?"

Strafford laughed, "Yes, yes that is what you said."

A heavy silence settled over the group. A thick log in the fire collapsed into the coals, prompting a burst of sparks to hiss directly upward to a windless sky. The erratic light conspired with an anemic heat to form a flickering corona around them, purely a product of contrast with the rising dark and lowering temperatures.

Benjamin said softly, "We know that's a lie. If you're going to use that story in the future, you'll want to choose a different fort."

William cocked his head quizzically, "Beg pardon?"

"Fort Apache," Benjamin said, "By now everyone will know you can't be from there, so you and Hugh should agree on a different story."

Clifford

"I don't know what you think you know," William insisted, "But for whatever else, that is where we came from."

Strafford's answer was brisk, matter-of-fact, "There are no detachments from Fort Apache, because Fort Apache was burned. There were no units sent out from there, because everyone stationed there is dead, and by now the whole countryside knows about it."

William stammered, "I... What are you..." Abandoning pretense, he cast about for some truthful counterpoint, "I'm sorry, but you must be mistaken. We left there just one week ago-,"

"Yet less than two days ago, all of St. Johns was abuzz with the news," Strafford interrupted. "The cavalry at Fort Apache rode north last week to arrest some medicine man. They then killed said medicine man and their scouts turned on them. After those soldiers were massacred, their enemies used the captured guns and horses to ride on the Fort, and the remaining infantry couldn't hold it. Reports are that there were no survivors, that the whole of the White Mountains have broken out, and that the Fort itself was reduced to ash. One rider we encountered in town claimed to have personally seen the place burning before he raced out to spread the word."

"But that," William snorted, "That can't be true." As he prepared to offer evidence of that assertion, William considered the series of events. He and Hugh had departed seven days prior. If the cavalry had ridden for a day before a rout, and the Fort had fallen by the evening after, a witness to that could easily have ridden as far as St. Johns in time to meet Benjamin and Doctor Strafford. William sat dumbly as the fact sunk in: it could be true.

"So, you see," Strafford concluded, "If the cavalry was slaughtered at Cibecu, leaving all the infantrymen to be massacred at the Fort, then you and Hugh must be ghosts. Or more likely you've lied to us, which didn't offend me at first, but I must say, now that I've been quite honest with you, your persistence is a little disappointing."

The Beard

William's thoughts raced, tramping over the doctor's final sentiment. Nothing was supposed to have happened, just an uneventful action that might allow him to fall through the cracks for a couple days. And now, when he had turned his back on them, even for less than a week, now all his friends and fellows had been slaughtered. He should have been there to fight alongside them. He should never have left. He had to get back, had to see the truth of it and face the fate he had avoided. He would require some explanation: others would note what Strafford just had, and he would want to be prepared to justify his absence. But that could come later, he would have more than two day's hiking to consider what to say, and if no one who knew him was left to ask questions…

William's ideas ran around and piled over themselves, rolling into a boil that spilled from his lips, "I have to leave. I have to go back. This wasn't meant to happen, now I have to get back there."

Strafford raised an eyebrow, "Back to where?"

Benjamin leaned forward and suggested, "I think he was telling the truth. Not about his unit or his mission perhaps, but about where he came from."

Strafford winced, "Well then. I suppose I might have done that differently."

The deafening torrent of William's thoughts fell off into a void, leaving him silent and numb. Without a word, he stood, turned away from the fire and stepped into the dark. At his back Benjamin called, "What about Hugh?"

William paused, "You'll tell him where I've gone."

Strafford replied, "To the Fort that no longer exists? Or into the arms of the enemy with no army to support you? Or shall you muster into another unit to avenge your fallen comrades? If you do that of course, they are bound to recognize you and force you to explain your desertion."

William stopped, facing the shadows, searching for any retort. Finally, he tried, "I can tell them I survived the attack."

Clifford

"Ah," Strafford said, pulling himself to his feet, "Very good. And so long as not one of your friends made it through to contradict you, your new friends will be quite pleased with your detailed description of enemy forces and positions. Assuming, once again, that you can break through every band in the White Mountains to tell that story." William stood blinking at the obscured hills while Strafford's voice moved calmly around the fire, "Or you may join us. We've discussed it, Benjamin and I, and even not knowing what you and Hugh were up to, we feel your presence could be helpful, especially at what seems to be a dangerous time."

From his respectful distance opposite the fire, Benjamin offered, "It would give you some time to decide where to go next. There's no reason not to, if you think about it."

William stared forward, absorbing but not fully grasping. From somewhere beside and in front of him came a scraping sound, a shuffle, the dull tick of a pebble bouncing down a dusty hill. From William's periphery, Hugh called, "Hey there! Hey gents! I found it just two miles North, I did! Ain't as much as you'd expect, this creek, but it is close, no more'n two miles. I don't guess it's worth going out again tonight, but directly at dawn, I can show y'all, before we all split up."

"About that," William said. He forced his gaze down and turned back to the fire, to the silhouettes before the flames, "Good news: you won't have to hurry yourself in the morning. Seems we'll be following the Doctor for a spell."

Day 10

"…But I realize I have to go back soon. Don't worry, I realize that," Kristin stated.

A woman's gravelly voice, pitted and scored by age and off-brand cigarettes, answered impatiently, "Just hand it over. You're making a mess."

Kristin leaned back, away from the stained porcelain sink, and noted four errant drops of water on the scratched, green laminate countertop. As she watched, two healthy sized drips broke free from the rim of the plastic salad bowl she was holding. Even before they spattered against the bare floorboards, her small companion had snatched the dish away from her to vigorously rub it with a towel. It was rather an overreaction, by Kristin's standards, but the more time she'd spent with this woman, the less comfortable she was correcting her.

"You know," Kristin said tentatively, "I can wash and dry. I do both at home, most of the time."

"That may be," the woman growled, "But this ain't your home. An' I don't trust you alone with the good silver."

Confused, Kristin dipped a hand in the filthy dish water to dredge up a mass of stamped steel flatware. She raised an eyebrow in spite of herself, "Good silver?"

Not missing a beat, the older woman said, "Onliest silver I got. That counts. Now scrub or stand down, I ain't got all night."

Kristin was fairly sure that the other was just messing with her: fairly sure, but less than entirely certain. The woman's name was Diane, as far as anyone knew. She claimed to have lived in that house for 'thirty-some-odd-years,' but had given Kristin the impression that, in all that time, she had yet to be on a first name basis with any of her neighbors. Diane was either the most sarcastic or most humorless and thin-skinned person Kristin had ever met. By the end of their first day together, Kristin had decided to assume

Clifford

the former, because to do otherwise would have been unbearably awkward.

Either way, Diane had been a decent and generous hostess. She had given Kristin one end of the couch from which to watch T.V. in daylight and the whole thing to sleep on at night. Beyond that, she'd made up for any want of conversation with a surprising excess of food. In return, she had asked for help with some of the chores, but it was really no more than Kristin regularly did around the house, and back East she had worked part time on top of that. Really, as long as Diane didn't turn out to be a serial killer, it was quite a reasonable arrangement for Kristin.

It was largely due to that reasonability that Kristin had to remind herself of the point she had repeated aloud moments earlier. It would be too easy for her to slip into a sort of odd routine with someone as predictable, albeit predictably unpleasant, as Diane seemed to be. It would be too simple for Kristin to rationalize overstaying her welcome, especially since she had not yet worked out where that limit would be, so she tried to keep the issue near the front of her mind, and occasionally found opportunities to reassure Diane that she was taking seriously the decision of how to get out, even though she couldn't envision a first step to save her life.

Kristin finished working the frayed edge of a soapy rag between the tines of a fork then dutifully held up the utensil beside her. Diane snatched the object away and attacked it with the towel. With inexplicable contrition, Kristin repeated the maneuver. Casting about for something to break the tension, Kristin muttered, "It seems like I was talking about something, can't remember what now, that's okay."

Diane responded loudly, "You were talkin' about leaving. Again. Ain't nobody stoppin' ya'. Far as I'm concerned you can take your little pink backpack and get out right now."

Kristin felt a sudden flutter in her chest. "What?" she asked quickly, "Are you... You want me to... Right now?"

432

The Beard

Tossing a spoon into a nearby drawer, Diane said, "Sure. Why not? Sounds like you hate it here. I'm sorry," she added in a tone that said otherwise, "that you think my place is beneath you. Maybe you'd be better off out there."

Even soaked in dishwater, Kristin felt her palms begin to sweat. She could tell that her cheeks were getting flushed, her hairline hot and then suddenly cold as the blood drained from her face. "But I never said... I would never say..." A rising throb in Kristin's ears fell off into a hollow ring. She choked out a whisper, "But I don't want to go."

"No," Diane said firmly, "I know you don't. Because you say you do ten times a day, an' yet here you still are: not packin', but not comfortable neither." Lowering her voice, Diane settled on a grave tone, "If it don't suit ya' here, then go. For your own sake, it might be best if you did. After all, what's the wait for? On the outside chance that the man you don't love comes back lookin' for ya', the best he can offer you is the life you run away from."

For reasons she couldn't put her finger on, Kristin felt compelled to correct Diane, to make her understand, but she wasn't sure that she understood herself, or not enough to put her feelings into words. Struggling to make out what was on the tip of her tongue, Kristin startled both of them by loudly blurting, "But it's not that! It's the opposite of that! I want my life back very much, and I want him back, and that's why I have to stay here where he won't find me!"

Diane cocked her head curiously, "Go on."

"I want all those things, but all those things are gone now," Kristin stated forcefully. "If I go back to Virginia, then eventually he'll come find me. And he'll still want to marry me because he loves me so much, and I'll still say yes because I love him so much, even though I don't trust him. After everything he did and he looked me in the face and he lied to me for weeks, and I can't ever trust him, never again, but I can't not love him now, so I'll say yes, but then I'll live my whole life just waiting for him to disappoint me, and he'll see that too." Faintly aware of her vision blurring, of

433

wet streaming down her cheeks, Kristin breathlessly forced the words out, desperate to find the bottom of them. "But he can't change it, any of it, there won't be any way for him to fix things ever, and we'll just be stuck like that, loving each other and resenting each other because I can't trust him, and that's his fault, he *did* that, and love and trust are not the same thing and-,"

Kristin's soliloquy devolved into a full-bodied sob. As she moved to cover her face with her trembling hands, several pieces of the good silver clattered to the floor. Even before she could wipe her eyes, Diane had stepped over the mess, reached up with her thin arms and pinned Kristin's biceps to her ribs with a bear hug. Swaddled in this way, trapped but also protected from the harsh realities of her options, Kristin fully and finally gave in to the indignities of a good cry.

Diane spoke softly, reassuringly, and for the moment inaudibly under the raucous moans that were hardly dampened by her bony shoulder. Struggling to communicate her support in this way, she rocked from foot to foot, the height difference between the two women creating a lopsided waltz.

After a time, the wailing gave way to ragged breathing, and Kristin became suddenly self-conscious, of her loss of composure, her display of emotion, of the fact that she almost certainly had snot smeared across her upper lip. The shabby kitchen around her gradually faded to the front of her mind along with Diane's raspy voice, "Hush now, I won't send you away, don't you worry." After a long moment of silence, the woman loosened her hold. "I understand what you mean, better than you know." Stepping back to look Kristin in the eye she added, "Besides, you've been a real help around here. When you're not making things messier."

Kristin looked down at the puddle of dishwater by her feet and beyond, to the dried bits of cast-off-dinner that hardened next to discarded serving utensils. She held down a sob and brought up a smile to let Diane see that she appreciated the joke. Starting to crouch, Kristin muttered, "I'm sorry, I can clean it, I just got carried-,"

434

The Beard

"Oh, no you don't," Diane interrupted catching the young woman's arms and standing her upright. "You done enough to my floors for one night. Just you go an' watch some T.V."

Kristin forced another smile, a brave one she thought, and nodded her gratitude before obediently crossing the small kitchen to pass through a threshold with hinges but no door. On the far side lay a dim room with heavy curtains, wall-to-wall shag, and a surprising amount of too-large furniture for the home of someone who seldom entertained. Set in the wall beside a walnut console television, a window air conditioner worked overtime, blasting near hard enough to push Kristin's bangs from her eyes. She settled herself on the coarse overstuffed sofa and wrapped a quilt around her bare shoulders. From the next room Diane called, "Then in the morning when you're fresh, *then* we'll let you finish with them dishes."

Tenth Growth

Day 2

It was tough to say which was worse: the heat or the monotony of the place. For all of that morning, the shrubs had gotten smaller, harder, spread further apart until, for the last mile or so, they had given up altogether. Now, finally out of sight of the nearest vegetation, the dusty earth spread behind them like a broken moonscape to the white horizon of an empty sky. Louis wondered if this wasn't similar to being becalmed at sea. Out in the wide open, exposed to the windless glare, the low hill in front of the group could just as easily have been a cresting wave, Louis thought. Although he had to allow that he had been thinking about water a lot of late.

For a time, he had tried to keep his focus on the fact that less water meant less weight on his back, to make his nearly empty canteen into a glass half full. But beyond a certain point, even Louis's power of denial found its limit, and he'd become concerned in spite of himself. He was sure that the other two men were thinking the same thing, but that was why none of them could say so: out there with no help, with no roof, and no cell signal, staying on the right side of that line between worry and panic was crucial. After this many days, that was no small trick.

Unwilling to risk even slight validation of what was becoming their worst fear and unable to think of much else, the men trudged on in silence. Louis pulled down his cap to fend off the worst of the world, zeroing in on where he was about to step. A pebble clattered against the toe of his boot. Eight feet in front of him, the rhythmic crunch of Jared's sneakers in the loose soil slowed, while a few feet in front of that, the sound of Tim's breathing became more rapid. The other men's footprints were more pronounced as the gradient changed, and Louis adjusted his pace to avoid overtaking them.

After a few minutes of pressing up a crumbling hill, Louis got the sense that they had been tacking: zig-zagging. Assessing the landscape behind them, he saw their rough, chewed track running at odd angles around the steepest and least stable ground. In front of him... he didn't need to check, he knew he'd find the same view he'd had for two days: Tim and the compass overzealously out front like he knew what the fuck he was about, and Jared close behind, faithfully consulting the back of an eight-inch section of cardboard with wandering pencil lines scratched into it. A few evenings prior, Louis had torn that flap off of an empty box at the campsite and had used it to craft a map based on the beard Jared was about to shave. Louis still wasn't sure how much of Jared's story he believed, but the younger man had insisted on his drawing the route, and Louis had indulged him because he didn't see the harm. As the days progressed, he was glad that he had, as the map seemed to comfort Jared, to give him a sense of purpose and control.

Even if Jared was chasing a delusion, his peace gave all three of them quiet, so that was all upside, really. But it also meant that each of the other two men now had a means of navigation, and where did that leave Louis? As he turned to resume his shuffling pursuit of the group, Louis wondered at his role as pack mule. He wondered if this was a case of water finding its level, or if it was yet another preventable outcome that he had failed to avoid.

When Marlow had fallen out of view through the brush and down the wash to whatever fate had awaited him, Louis's sense of agency had gone as well. Not that the two were directly related, although Louis did fear that it said something about him as a man that he'd been unable to protect his dog, yet managed to save himself. In any case, Louis could pinpoint that as the moment when he'd affectively stopped making decisions. The gun at his back had not been liberating, and being told what to do upon pain of death was not something he'd welcomed. But it had been easy. To unquestioningly do as he was told had been easy.

It had also been easy to justify: his life was in danger, better follow directions, with the caveat (he told himself), that he would look for opportunities to escape when Tim wasn't watching. And he might have done, but then they had found that demolished campsite, with its twitchy, emaciated architect, and Louis, without being so ordered, had discovered that he would have to look after their new companion. Jared had been weak for days: hungry, thirsty, struggling from exposure, and it wasn't as though Tim had the empathy to feign interest in any of that, so Louis had stepped up because he'd had no choice. Or maybe he'd had a choice, but he'd missed being depended on since he lost his dog. More than once in the last couple years he had wondered if the real reason he'd kept Marlow around was that he'd missed being needed by his kids.

Whatever his underlying motives, he had constructed a new, more functional campsite a few hundred yards from Jared's latrine, had moved the young man into his own tent while he lovingly struck and relocated Jared's things, and had spent the following four days nursemaid-ing, at least to the extent that he felt was within both their dignities: staying available, helping Jared get up and move short distances, preparing and fetching him food and water while he got back his strength, and making conversation to stay sane.

Tim had not participated in those conversations, but Louis didn't guess that *staying* sane was the issue for him. It seemed like all Tim had done with every minute of light on those days was to read and reread a sheaf of papers that he refused to allow anyone else to see. On the other hand, he hadn't made any more threats. But then again, he probably knew he didn't have to: Louis was very aware that to make a break for it would be to turn Jared into Tim's de facto hostage. And even without bringing it up, Louis knew that Jared would refuse to escape with him, because Jared was following something else, something all consuming that Louis couldn't fully get his head around.

That first day, when Jared had frantically stated his business, jabbering aimlessly for over an hour about where he'd been and how he'd gotten there, Louis would have thought the man was delirious from the heat, but Tim had been completely underwhelmed, even seemed to anticipate the most fantastic
441

elements of Jared's story. Louis had been bothered that this left him in the minority, but Jared was a nice guy, and he really seemed to care that Louis believe him, so Louis had nodded along, had set aside his skepticism to draw the harmless map that Jared now clung to, and had kept on dragging most of their gear and his own sorry ass behind them.

Farther up the incline, the scraping and shuffling abruptly ceased. A few paces ahead of Jared, Tim had reached the top of the slope, and now stood sideways, his boots dug hard into the gravel while he surveyed something on the other side. Without looking back, Tim announced, "There it is!" before vanishing over the hill. Jared disappeared after him while Louis resituated his pack. He followed deliberately over the top to find the others already halfway down the other side, their feet a blur of quick, tiny steps racing against gravity. A hundred yards from where the ground leveled off there was a string of sparsely situated trees. Through the dusty leaves, the sun glinted on a thin vein of muddy water.

The sight of the creek, relief that it was, drove home still another point that Louis wanted to forget: that even if he could sneak away, and even if he wouldn't be abandoning Jared, and even if he could count on getting very far without Tim catching up to inexplicably blow out his kneecaps, even then he would still be in the middle of the damned desert, hopelessly turned around, with less water every hour. So whatever Louis believed or didn't believe about where they were headed, until they came within sight of a town he would have no alternative to looking out for Jared and following Tim.

He tried to emulate the other men's descent, but thought better of it as his pack began to swing around his side. He threw his weight backward into the hill to compensate, and bounced off his ass back up to his heels. In this fashion Louis half slid, half scooted to the bottom. Unclear as to whether the others had witnessed his graceless maneuver, and unsure of whether that mattered, Louis regained his composure with a casual stroll to the tree line.

442

By the time he arrived, the others had filled one of the group's two water filtration bags, and had hung it on a twisted branch to begin filling their canteens. As Louis sloughed off the near empty 10-gallon bladder that hung from his shoulders, he commented to no one in particular, "Been kinda nice not having too much weight in that thing. This stream is a lucky break, though."

Without looking at him, Tim scoffed, "Don't be stupid: it's not luck if I lead you straight to it."

Louis let that one hang in the air for a few seconds. He knew that the comment was in character for Tim, and that it would be foolish and pointless to react. All the same, if Tim insisted on Louis being there against his will, then it was only fair to make Tim share in that frustration. Louis dropped the last of their things and in one slow, giant stride, put himself within an inch of the other man. Towering over him, looking straight down to make eye contact, Louis growled, "What you fuckin' say boy?" Tim's eyes darted nervously to the satchel near his ankle, where he and Louis both knew his gun was stowed.

Jared's voice floated tentatively through the moment, "H-Hey… I think he only meant that he thought you already knew the stream was here. Because it's on my map that you helped me with. But I didn't tell you what it was when you drew it, so really, I think it's my fault. No big deal?"

Louis held his hard stare, stone-faced as he reflected that this dynamic was really panning out for him. He could make life as uncomfortable as he pleased for the man with the gun, secure in the knowledge that a third man would intercede. And with someone as skittish as Jared acting as that third man, things would never escalate too far. To Tim, Louis cocked an eyebrow, "Is that what you meant?"

Tim glared back at Louis, unwilling to give any ground but too frightened to take any either.

Louis sniffed, "That's what I thought."

"C'mere," Jared said brightly, "Come over here, I'll show you what I'm talking about."

Louis finally broke away. He knelt to rifle through a pack he had dropped and pulled out the other water filtration bag before approaching Jared, who now sat on the ground with his legs folded, holding out his cardboard scrap as though presenting a wine list. "You might remember," Jared continued, "That when you drew this, I had you make the blonde parts a solid line, with the black parts as dashes and the red parts dots. Remember?"

"I do," Louis nodded as he took a knee.

"That's because, and Kristin figured this out, that the red lines are water, but the black lines are other boundaries like that hill. So you see here how the solid line crosses the dash to come alongside those dots here. That's the stream, that's how I know where we are. I'm not sure I'm explaining very well. Kristin had a better handle on it, she could tell you better-,"

"Nah," Louis interrupted, "That makes sense. Ya' did good." He stood and proceeded to the bank of a slow moving, thirty-foot wide creek. He picked his way along the edge and eventually hunkered down. Leaning out, he drew his bag along the surface to fill it. The large rubber bladder he'd been carrying would probably take a half dozen of these, in which case the group would be stopped for a bit while he filtered them. To keep out of trouble, Louis returned in a wide loop away from Tim and around Jared's opposite side. "Yeh," Louis said picking up from where he'd left off ten minutes before, "That map o' yours still blows me away. I mean, it bein' magical and a treasure map a' course. But even just to grow a beard that fast is impressive, fuckin' manly! Who ever heard of that much hair in less'n two weeks?"

From his corner, Tim said jealously, "I've heard of it. He's not the first one, you know. I know all about it."

Louis prepared to respond, but Jared lunged sideways into his field of vision, nearly falling over in his bid to distract them from an argument. He said cheerily, "But where it leads is always the best part."

Louis narrowed his eyes at Tim for a second before taking Jared's less toxic bait. He grabbed the corner of the large bladder

444

and attached it to the full filtration bag which he hooked over a tree limb. "No offense, but I'm 'a have to disagree with you, Jared. These destinations are depressing at the best of times. Why couldn't anything nice ever happen to Henry Strafford?"

"I don't know what you mean," Jared answered, "So far, it's led me to a mansion, fairgrounds, a fort…"

"Figures," Louis chuckled darkly, "You get all of his good times, an' I get the bad."

"Well there was Arlington Cemetery," Jared offered, "And the mental hospital, not sure how you characterize that."

"There," Louis said enthusiastically, "Now that makes more sense to me. With what I know 'a Henry Sullivan Strafford, I could see why he'd end up in a mental hospital."

"Huh?" Jared replied, "Oh! You mean- No, he wasn't a patient, he was on staff."

"On staff? Really. I'm havin' trouble picturing that."

"Yep," Jared nodded, "It was the earliest medical post I found him in: the State Hospital in Austin, Texas. Would've been 1885 or so."

"In *Texas* in 1885," Louis said, "You're *sure* about that."

"Well yeah," Jared said, "That's what the picture said, anyways. I see no reason to question it. Austin in 1885 makes sense if he was just up in San Antonio the fall of 1886."

"San Antonio in '86," Louis repeated. He noticed his filtration bag had run limp, and he carefully unhooked it from the branch. "I'm 'a be right back, but we're gonna discuss that one." A few minutes later, trudging back with a full bag, Louis called, "Now how sure are you that he was in Texas that whole time?"

"Pretty sure!" Jared answered too loudly. He adjusted his volume when Louis appeared from the vegetation ten feet away, "Pretty sure. I guess I don't have any proof about San Antonio. The map led me there, so I *know* he was there, but the timing... Kristin found something that said 1886. I don't really remember the details. She's pretty good at those things, but I should've paid closer attention."

"Well," Louis said, taking his time to replace the bag and kneel down across from Jared, "I found evi-dance of his bein' in Nebraska by May of '86 through '87."

"Nebraska," Jared muttered to himself. "The thing Kristin showed me, it was handwritten, so maybe the six was really an eight or something. But even then, Nebraska? How'd he get up there?"

"I assumed," Louis explained, "That he went over from Wyoming. He'd dug a tunnel there a few years earlier. I guess for your 1885 in Austin, it woulda' been possible he come down to Texas in between those."

"Huh," Jared said. "Ditch digger to doctor to… what was he doing in Nebraska?"

"Takin' up collections for a church, then splitting town," Louis said casually.

"Really," Jared marveled, "How can this be the same guy? Where did he split town to?"

"All signs point to Fort Custer, Montana by end of 1887. An' after that he disappeared on me for a couple years. Then he got his self married in Iowa," Louis added.

Jared shook his head, "I can't figure this guy out."

Louis pushed himself to his feet to snag the empty bag off the tree limb, "Back in a bit."

Minutes later it was Jared who resumed the conversation as Louis retook his post, "You know, none of that tells us what he was doing out here. Or why he was doing it."

Louis asked, "How can you be sure he was out here?"

"Because *we're* out here," Jared said simply. "And we only get to go to where he was, even if we never know why. It's like that saying, 'If you forget history, then you have to repeat it-,'" Louis jumped in, "'Those who cannot remember the past are condemned to repeat it.' It's George Santayana said that. Sounds kinda like Carlos Santana, is how I remember him. Had me a history professor used to get all worked up about that quote."

Jared nodded, "It seems like something all history professors must have tattooed on themselves somewhere."

"Not this guy," Louis said, "This guy hated it. Used to go on for hours about how wrong an' stupid it was, an' about how too many people put too much stock in the idea."

"Really," Jared said, "Wouldn't it be better for him to have people wanting to remember things? He made you remember that quote, and that was part of the past."

"That wasn't the thing," Louis explained. "See, this guy, he was a sorta fatalist. At least he said he was. He said that if you boil things down enough, you see that the universe presents everyone at all times with the same basic choices in different contexts. Everything from whether it's better to walk in the sun or in the shade, to whether we get married or stay single, to whether we live quietly under a government or risk fighting to overthrow it, every generation is presented with basically the same options. It's the context of each of those what changes: some days it's cold instead of hot so sun is better'n shade, in some cultures marriages are arranged, and sometimes a government is fair instead of tyrannical. But the options themselves are always basically the same, and human nature will pull us in the same basic directions as it has everyone else throughout history. On top of that, we're all subject to the decisions of all the other people in the world who have the same basic choices and nature as everyone who came before them.

"So whether or not y'say things are preordained, a person can't help repeating history, y'see, because everyone has the same options, everyone has a familiar place in it, an' everyone is subject to the same archetypes, patterns… the same rules, I guess. So, his gripe was, he said it was arrogant to think that by remembering the past you'd be allowed to escape from it. He said that if anything it was the opposite: the people who forget the past are the only ones who don't realize they *are* repeating it, which he said was bad, like flying blind. An' he always finished with the same thing." Louis raised his hand to declare like a Roman senator, "'In reality, it is those who *can* remember the past that are *destined* to repeat it.'"

447

A few yards behind Louis, Tim interrupted, "You've finally surprised me. I never would have guessed that you once had a professor."

For a brief and merciful moment, Louis had forgotten that Tim was there. While the man's snobby words and snotty tone did not startle him per se, they so abruptly ended the conversation as to make him wince in something close to pain, closer still to rage. As a familiar tension flowed into his shoulders, he turned his head to the side in a crescendo, "Why... don't... you... just shut the FUCK UP?!?" He stood and turned on his heel to follow up, "If you got all the answers then either tell us all you know or shut the fuck up! You fucking know-it-all!" Beginning to walk toward Tim, he shouted, "You are worthless, you know that? FUCKING WORTHLESS!"

Jared leapt to his feet and stepped quickly in front of Louis. "HEY!" he said, as he reached up to hold back the monster's shoulders, "Hey calm down, man!"

Louis slid Jared several feet across the dirt as he continued forward two more steps. Only after he had demonstrated how powerless the smaller man was to stop him did Louis cease in his tracks.

Jared lowered his voice and said, "Not that big a deal dude. Just tap the brakes for a second. We're on the same team here. Don't know why you let him get under your skin like that..."

The three of them held that tableau for more than a minute: Tim seated on a tree stump, his hand on the satchel at his feet, Louis now a few feet away, looming, leaning in with the slight figure of Jared futilely braced against his chest.

Maintaining eye contact with Louis, Tim brightly addressed Jared, "Don't worry, it isn't personal. He just has less patience for me since I killed his dog."

Jared pushed himself back from Louis and forced the beginnings of a polite laugh. Looking up at his friend, his face fell, "Wait... Is he serious?"

Louis answered tightly, "I don' wanna talk about it."

448

"Good!" Tim shouted, "It's about damn time you didn't!" Raising his hand away from the satchel to gesture at Louis's now empty filtration bag Tim asked, "Could you get a move on? We're waiting on you."

Quietly, concernedly, Jared said, "Look, Louis, I'm sorry. I thought it was a bad joke. If I knew he was-,"

Tim interrupted, "You know what? Never mind! I'll just do it myself!" He snatched the small bag off its limb and stomped out of sight toward the creek. From the nearby trees he called, "We don't have time to sit here while you crybabies braid each other's hair! We still have a lot more of the past to repeat, and I'd like to get to Scarlet Butte before dark!"

September 7, 1881

Scarlet Butte was aptly named, at least at this time of morning. The previous evening, when the sun had been behind the rock formation, there had been no color: it had been all corners and edges, all spreading shadows as it devoured the desert sunset. But if it had had all the character of a tombstone before supper, the butte before breakfast was a different animal entirely. Striations of purple and brown at the base nurtured strong vertical cracks that burst into the signature red stone for how-many-feet-Hugh-could-not-say before breaking into an uneven tan. From the strong, flat, leading edge to the muted crags at the nearest corner, Scarlet butte shimmered like a bonfire in the morning.

Hugh wondered if it was rock that he was seeing, or if the immense face of the thing was somehow reflecting the sunrise, indirectly showing him more of the horizon behind him than his naked eyes would allow. Either way it was an easy view to stare at, and it made Hugh grateful that he'd gotten up to piss before dawn. Returning to camp, when his eye had first been drawn to the rays of light scattered across the distant stone, he'd allowed himself to sit down next to a small rise, remove his hat, and be fixated. But now, he didn't know how long ago that must have been and supposed that he should probably get up and move on. The others would have noticed his absence, and he didn't want them to think he'd gotten lost.

Not that one could really get lost near Scarlett Butte. The object was massive, a visible and singular point of reference in an otherwise empty landscape. Perhaps that was what made it so fascinating, Hugh thought, the days of nothing that a person had to pass through to reach that lonely, giant thing. So often in the preceding days, Hugh had been overwhelmed by the emptiness, at times it had seemed like he could see to the edges of the world.

450

But he knew that must not have been true, because he still couldn't see as far as Yuba City. He wondered how long it would take him to get back there. Once all this was finished and done and he was ready to go home, how far would home be? And could a person really *go* back, after so much time away from a place? Might 'home' have changed? Might he?

He wondered these things, but he also saw that there was no point guessing at things he would eventually see. With that, Hugh dropped his sagging hat back onto his greasy scalp, and rocked forward onto his feet. He had hardly taken three steps when he heard the slow trot of hooves just past the rise. As the sound halted, Hugh lowered into a half crouch and peered cautiously over the other side. Ten yards off, Benjamin sat atop the mule faced away from Hugh. Before Hugh could greet him, the other man turned to his side and called out, "Are you certain? I still object to this, doctor. I strenuously object. This seems an unnecessary risk."

Only then did Hugh spot Dr. Henry Strafford farther down the rise. "You needn't worry," Strafford smiled easily, "You just go on now. I'll see this thing through and be along before you know it."

Benjamin nodded, as much a goodbye as an affirmation, before turning to resume his slow ride away from camp.

Hugh watched Strafford watch Benjamin go. In one sense he did not want to interrupt, but it felt even more awkward to spy, so he straightened up and approached as casually as he could, announcing himself with, "Good morning, sir."

Strafford shifted focus quickly and fully, "Oh, there you are! And a fine morning it is!"

"Fine morning for a ride, I see," Hugh observed.

Strafford blinked, oblivious, "Is it?"

Patiently, Hugh persisted, "Where's he headed?"

"Oh, *Beehhhn-jamin*." With a dismissive wave, Strafford finished, "He's gone back to St. Johns."

Strafford turned back toward camp. Hugh cocked his head quizzically, but decided to let the matter drop for the moment, falling in behind the doctor. The crunch of running boots on the

451

hard soil carried across the silence from the direction of the butte. William's voice was close behind. "Hey!" he yelled, "Hey, where is he taking it?"

Strafford stopped to stare at the figure approaching them. He asked simply, "What's that now?"

"Where?" William demanded breathlessly, "Where's he takin' the mule? Where's he takin' the provisions in the saddle bags?"

With the same dismissive wave, Strafford repeated, "He's gone back to St. Johns."

Strafford turned again toward camp. Still winded, William hauled his self into Strafford's path. "Why? Why has he taken the mule to St. Johns?"

"The mule will act as collateral in the near term. As will the supplies, really." Strafford chuckled to himself, "I owe that man a fair amount of money at this point." He stepped around William and resumed, "But offering him those assurances shall liberate me to pursue the next leg of our journey."

William grabbed the doctor's arm as he passed. "And what do you mean by doing that?"

"Oh, sorry," Strafford said patiently. "'Collateral' means my guarantee of payment. If I fail to appear with Benjamin's pay, he may accept the mule and supplies as compensation."

"I know what damned 'Collateral' is," William shot back. "I want to know what you mean by sendin' away our fourth man with damn near all our supplies, and then turnin' yer nose up like you done the three of *us* a favor."

Exasperated, Strafford pulled his arm away from William, "I *did* do the three of us a favor. It *has* to be three people." He shifted his weight nervously and turned his argument to the both of them, "You know I *could* have sent you away instead, William. But Benjamin didn't think we should pursue this in the first place, and I thought that could become problematic."

Hugh felt himself losing patience, as much with William's ineffectual antagonism as with Strafford's vagaries. He took a step in and said, "Aw, for chrissakes doc, pursuing what? Why not spit it out already?"

Strafford squinted at him dumbly, "Pursuing you, of course." Neither of the other men spoke. The silence prompted Strafford to explain, "There were details of the legend we've been following that Benjamin felt I should not bother you with. I agreed in the beginning: I didn't want to make you uncomfortable before I was sure. But now we're getting close to the end, and I'm convinced it may be necessary." Strafford took a breath and turned toward Hugh, forcing William to step around them to hear. "As I have described, 'Once in every generation, a small group of travelers is said to answer an ancient call.' What I neglected was that the small group is to include three men only. And the call itself is said to come in the form of a map, which one man must carry on his face."

Hugh breathed, "Is that right? Isn't that something now?"

Strafford continued dramatically, "The map that the travelers bring is said to take them to a place that has been cleansed by fire, and it is in that place that they will be transformed!" Lowering his voice, he winked, "The exact wording of that last portion is my own. The moment seems to warrant some poeticism, I think."

Hugh searched for a response and came back blank, so continued to nod softly, "I see… I see…"

William appeared more decisive in the moment, "I also see. I see this asshole been lyin' from the start."

Retreating to his grand mannerisms, Strafford announced, "Of *coooourse* I lied to you. Benjamin thought that the truth would scare you off, and that would have been unhelpful. As for me, after your stories of an invisible infantry unit, I simply didn't trust you. But that has clearly changed, given that I've sent Benjamin away and have remained with the two of you."

"*You* didn't trust *us*?" William replied, "Now that is rich. And atop of it all you think you get to decide where we go next. The nerve of it! The effrontery! Hugh, I say we strike camp and go our own way right now."

Before Hugh could determine whether the suggestion was rhetorical, Strafford barked, "And to where exactly will you go? To follow that map on his beard? Don't think I don't know that you both know what you have there. I've known all along that is what you've been getting up to out here."

William spat, "You don't know a goddamn thing-,"

"I know plenty!" Strafford shouted. "For one thing, I know exactly where it's taking you!"

Having watched the argument bounce back and forth without him, Hugh intercepted the comment before William could run it down, shouting, "Where?!?"

Both of the others startled at the sound of him. Strafford, jarred into the direction of propriety, answered softly, "I believe you will go near San Marcial. It's a village not too far east of here. Or it was: Benjamin and I have been hearing for a month that the place mysteriously burned up. One end to the other is said to be ash, and no one knows how the fire caught. The line on your beard bends to the east, and if we're looking for a place that was cleansed by fire, it seems an obvious choice."

Hugh looked at William. William shrugged. Strafford resumed, "If the two of you would follow me to San Marcial, I would like that very much. Or, if you'd rather strike out to follow your beard where it goes, it would suit me equally well."

William opened his mouth to reply and Hugh made a point to interrupt, "That's fine then. We'll travel together." Hugh managed an air of finality by walking between the others, directly towards their camp.

Firm, but not angry, William asked, "You sure of this?" Without looking back, Hugh declared, "If we're all going to the same place, it's about damned time we got there."

454

Day 3

The landscape had become unreasonable, Jared thought. Not un-navigable: in a sense it was quite the opposite of that, but just… absurd at this point. He understood, the desert is the desert, it's dry and it doesn't contain much flora and/or fauna. But here, where Tim was determined to make camp, even the scattered bushes were burned away.

Jared had grown accustomed to desolation, so much so that even Scarlet Butte had resembled something, and that had only been a big-ass rock. They did seem to be approaching another, lower mesa in the distance, but in the meantime they'd meandered into something worse than nothing. It was the ashtray where nothing had once stood.

In the days that now felt like weeks since Jared and Kristin had abandoned the road, the silence had been so complete that the ringing in Jared's ears had at times been all consuming. But this was not to describe the silence as deafening, a phrase that Jared no longer understood, because he was constantly and painfully aware of how well he could hear that there was nothing to hear. The absence of sound was rivaled only by the absence of movement, yet somehow there was still the impression of movement. If anything, the emptier the landscape, the more important and pronounced every detail. Those coupled with a lack of distractions that heightened Jared's senses, and he could swear that from the corner of his eye he could see the desert shimmer.

No, not shimmer. Jared could see the desert breathe.

He was mostly sure that he'd have gone completely crazy by now if not for his companions. And by companions, he could only mean Louis, because talking to Tim made Jared feel more alone than when he had been alone. At the best of times the man was unresponsive: all he seemed inclined to do besides marching, clutching his little satchel, and barking orders, was to sit around re-

reading that damn sheaf of papers over and over again. Even now, while Jared and Louis busied themselves setting out supplies amongst the char, Tim sat at a short distance, using what remained of their daylight to squint at page after page of what Jared assumed the man should have memorized by now.

Jared shook his head and turned away from the myopic gnome. He shuffled ten feet through the dust to the spot where his friend was kneeling over a pile of twigs, carefully stacking them like a log cabin. He was sure that Louis had heard him approach but still softly cleared his throat to avoid startling the other man before asking, "You sure that's the best idea, building a fire out here? It looks like this spot might be kinda combustible."

Without looking up from his work, Louis said easily, "Yeh, that's why I ain't worried. See, it *was* combustible, now it's just com-busted. In fact, I think we might have the problem backward: with everything out here havin' already burnt, we got less kindling than charcoal."

Jared turned and Louis looked up. Gesturing at Tim poring over his manuscript, Jared said drily, "If you're short on kindling, I might have a lead on some paper you could light."

Louis laughed, "Tempting, ain't it? Then again, if it keeps the man occupied, maybe it's best left alone."

Jared stepped around their future campfire and took a knee nearby. He began dragging collapsed tent poles out of a nylon sack. "What do you think those papers of his are about, anyways?"

Louis shrugged, "The en-tire story of everything in the world. So he would have you believe."

"Like what's at the end of the map?" Jared asked.

"Sure," Louis said vaguely, "He thinks that's in there. I don't suppose that matters at this point: seems like we'll all find out together soon enough."

"Well yeah," Jared replied, "But you can't tell me you're not still curious what's coming up." For the first time since Kristin had broken from him, Jared allowed himself to speculate aloud, "What if it's a lost city or something?"

456

"Like a El Dorado situation," Louis followed along. "It's a fine idea, but I don't need a whole city. I'm not greedy. I would settle for a tidy treasure pile myself. An' since you bring it up, lost treasure would be well timed for me."

Jared paused in what he was doing, "Is there ever a wrong time for treasure?"

"Fair point," Louis nodded. Returning his attention to his delicate stack of twigs, he said, "I suppose I should warn you though, that with my luck it won't be anything at all. Might be a mark in the dirt where Henry Sullivan Strafford lost his virginity or some shit."

Projecting over the twenty yards between them, Tim interposed, "I wish you two would stop guessing. You're being ridiculous. I mean look at yourselves: one of you bumbles across a haunted compass at precisely the same time that the other finds a map growing out of his skin, and you really think the explanation is as simple as buried pirate's gold? You think this is a children's story?"

The other men sat for a moment, somewhere between chastised and defiant. Finally Jared said, "So Tim is out here *not* for gold. I guess we'll split our treasure two ways then."

Louis laughed. Tim snorted, "Fucking children," before pushing himself to his feet and turning away.

"Aww," Louis said, "Where you goin'? It don't need to be like that."

"Going for a piss," Tim called back, "It's a better use of my time."

Louis sighed mostly to himself, "A'course. *Every* conversation with that guy ends with him takin' a piss." The pair resumed their respective tasks for a minute before Louis absently reiterated, "Yeh, a little gold would go a good long way for me right now. I know you don't want my whole litany of complaints or nothin'-,"

"I don't mind," Jared said, "I've got time."

"Oh," Louis blinked, seemingly unprepared for genuine interest. "Well... See... Where to start. I got no job, firstly, got no real money comin' in. So I can't afford to look after my kids, an' that sucks. At least they're with their mom. But then, that means she has the house. It's only right, but then, they got that an' I don't so… Now that I say it out loud, I'm not sure if money fixes all of it. Wouldn't need the job, is one thing it would solve, and I'd get myself a house at least, but I don't know if even bein' rich would get Carolyn back. We fought about a lot of things. But you know, I always felt like money was at the back of it. Or that maybe there was things I might could buy t'help fix some of it at least, y'know what I mean. That's sort of the same thing, ain't it? You figure I could buy myself outta my whole mess?"

Slightly bewildered by the details Jared answered, "I think so. I might be the wrong one to ask about relationships though."

"Yeh," Louis resumed, "I think I could, but it seems like we could use a fe-male perspective on it. Maybe when we done here, we go find Kristin, she can give me some insight."

Jared chuckled darkly in spite of himself, "Now, that's a problem I know buried treasure won't solve. It might treat some of the symptoms, but I fucked that way up. Not sure what it will take to fix it."

"You'll figure out somethin'," Louis said. "For now at least, there's no sense thinkin' otherwise. An' tell you what, once you do work it out, an' we've had some time to spend some of our gold an' everything, you an' Kristin can ride down in yer limousine to me an' Carolyn's mansion in Tennessee, tell us all about how you won her back."

With the best rendition of a smile that he could manage, Jared said, "Sounds good. We'll do that."

Jared paused to feed a tent pole through a nylon sleeve, while Louis struck his plastic cigarette lighter several times to get a steady flame. The latter man transferred the fire to a withered twig, and Jared settled himself on both knees to reach for another collapsed part. "Did I tell you," Jared asked casually, "That Kristin and I recently stopped in Tennessee? A few weeks ago, as part of all this."

458

"Really?" Louis said. "Y'know, that almost pisses me off. I had to drive clear to Missouri to find anything. The idea that there was something right in my back yard, I mean..." Louis sighed resignedly. With a renewed pleasantness, he followed up, "So what part of Tennessee it take you through?"

"Nowhere recognizable," Jared offered. "We wound up in a town called Selmer, but the map didn't even take us there. It took us to a clearing sort of close to there, just dropped us in the woods next to an empty kennel. Looked like something out of a slasher film."

"Wait," Louis said, "A clearing with a kennel? Ten minutes east of Selmer, little more than a mile off the interstate?"

"Yes," Jared nodded slowly. "It *felt* like more than a mile, but the access road was slow. It may have only been that far."

"Damn," Louis marveled. "That is my actual, literal backyard. I built that kennel for my... Bought that land a couple years back, still live out there in my trailer."

"You know who used to own that land was Henry Strafford," Jared stated.

"I'll be damned," Louis shook his head. "This whole damn time. Y'know, by now I should expect shit like that, but goddamn. That is fuckin' creepy."

The two men sat in silence for a moment. Jared wasn't sure how to follow that news: it was neutral in the grand scheme, and not important. But he could see where, to Louis, it would not be unimportant either. Jared steered the conversation back to more familiar territory, "Speaking of creepy, what could be keeping our mutual friend out there?"

Louis visibly shook off his distraction, "What, Tim? Oh, I expect he's around the bend jerkin' off or somethin'. Or maybe a shit snuck up on him. Maybe both: maybe he jerked off 'till he shit his self, who cares?"

"It's just unusual for him to leave us alone long enough for a conversation," Jared observed. Walking over to where Tim had sat,

Jared leaned down to pick up the rubber-banded sheaf of papers, "Especially with these lying around."

"Ho-ly shit," Louis laughed, "The gospel according to Tim. He left that unsupervised?"

For whatever ancient wisdom Tim would assert they contained, the pages in Jared's hand appeared to be unremarkable, relatively new color copies. One side of each page featured the high resolution image of a slightly smaller page, each of those a mottled brown, occasionally punctuated by erstwhile creases and dog-ears, and apparently brittle and flaking at the edges. Though not so bad as the original appeared to be, even the copies had now become, if not worn, at least road weary: yellowed along the margins from exposure, slotted at the rubber band and riffled at the corners from use.

Legible nonetheless, a sometimes-compact-sometimes-florid handwritten script ran page after page after page. Letters crowded one another through lines packed surprisingly close, with few if any discernible paragraph breaks. Each figure slanted to the right, often shaky but always joined with hardly a blot or a lift, they carried a weight and momentum that could only be described as frantic. Starting at the top, Jared read aloud, "If you are reading this, I don't know who you are-."

Tim bellowed, "Hey! What the hell do you think you're doing?!?"

Jared startled but didn't miss a beat, "I wanted to know how it would feel to have all the answers."

Ignoring the rejoinder, Tim threw down his satchel and stomped quickly across the last few yards between them. Angrily he spat, "That's my personal property! You put that down!"

With a laugh Jared repeated, "If you are reading this, I don't know who you are-," Tim reached for the pages and Jared, taking full advantage of Tim's diminutive stature, twisted away and hoisted them over his head and out of reach. Tim pressed and hopped while Jared continued, "But I need for you to know me. No man desires to perish unremembered as I fear I soon must. I only

460

pray that providence shows you more kindness than it did those others in my confidence..."

Tim gave up on Jared's game of keep-away and crossed to where he had dropped his satchel. Louis, keeping his eyes on Tim, stood and in one smooth motion snatched the full stack out of Jared's hand to throw it haphazardly at Tim's ankles. The smaller man reacted quickly, immediately abandoning his bag to pounce on the bulk of the loose pages now scattered in the dirt. Pausing in his mad scramble, Tim looked to the other two men, "You can't just *do* that. If you read it now... you wouldn't under-*stand* it. You would think you understood, but you wouldn't *understand*, and it would ruin *every*-thing."

An imperceptible breeze caught at a single sheet of paper and pulled it toward the dimming wilderness. Gesturing to it, Louis said softly, "Best pay attention. It's getting away from you."

September 9, 1881

The wind whistled in a way that Henry Strafford was unused to. In his native New England, even a light breeze would bring with it the soft rustling of leaves or, in winter, the chattering of bare branches. During his brief periods at sea, gusts had roared unobstructed off the water in a bass drone across bare ears. In this place, though, an undulating terrain broken only by the burned-out carcasses of buildings provided resistance without cover. It was apparently just enough to channel the wind coming over the hard edge of the nearby mesa into a treble whoosh, complemented occasionally by the creak of a beam about to give way or the rattle of a dry twig. He had never considered what now seemed obvious: the impact of landscapes on the sounds that moved through them. Having observed the phenomenon, he knew that he would never again cross unfamiliar territory without noting it. Henry Strafford delighted in fresh observations.

This was fortunate, in that there was little else to delight in at that moment. The heat of the late afternoon was oppressive, trapped against the ground by thin clouds of a kind he'd seldom seen west of the Indian Territory: a white haze that concealed the sun and at the same time glowed in its own right, making the day both gloomy and distressingly bright. The place in which the small party found themselves was no less paradoxical. They walked past burnt shops with missing roofs and blackened walls, some of them partly rebuilt with patches of fresh cut lumber, but none of them inviting business or workmen in this heat.

Henry saw everywhere the trappings of civilization but not one single denizen. He knew the town's residents must be nearby, and in a way that made the place feel even lonelier and more unsettling. For days or possibly weeks now, he had felt as though there were eyes on him that he couldn't see: the lingering impression of being both watched and led by the nose. But now, their proximity to the slight and displaced community of San Marcial presented the possibility of actually being watched, and begged the question of how many unseen eyes were imagined and how many real.

None of the three men invited attention as they trudged single file out of the gutted business district. Beyond the furthest of the half-restored shops, they passed through a series of small, ruined shacks, then entered an area that looked to have been uninhabited before it had burned. Charred and broken stumps, some with skeletal branches, were scattered unevenly across the mottled ground for more than a quarter of a mile. Nearing the crest of a hill, the chaos abruptly ended at a clearing surrounded by an untouched paddock. Settled on a bed of dry but unburned grass inside a split rail fence stood a few rows of evenly spaced grave markers. "Well," Henry observed wryly, "At least these dwellings survived."

William turned back to speak around Henry, "Hugh, come up here. We should check to see if this is on your map." Standing amongst the tidy crosses before the striking backdrop of a smoldered village lording over a murky river that swept silently around the foot of the mesa, Hugh followed the instruction reverently. After a brief consultation, William announced, "Not much farther now."

Henry strode forward and shouldered William aside. "How can you tell?" he asked. Along the periphery of the beard, now fanned out across Hugh's shoulder, Henry followed the blonde streak he had come to know as their course. Against the brown background it wove through a hollow black square, presumably the fenced in graveyard in which they now stood, before winding past a small black cross. Just beyond that, looping now in the direction of Hugh's ear, the line ended at a disproportionately large symbol, also in black: it looked something like a misshapen, upside-down egg, but the fat end featured two round dots and the narrow part sported a straight line in the same brown as the background. To the right imagination, it looked like a skull with oversized eyes. "I see," Henry muttered thoughtfully.

Cooperatively holding his pose, Hugh quipped, "Didn't trust us to be honest with you?"

"Well, I don't *have* to trust your honesty, Hugh," Henry said politely, "Not when your face is so easy to read."

William laughed once loudly: a sort of bark made more jarring by the surroundings. "Clever," William said pointing to Henry, "Very good, you... you are clever." With that, he turned to the far side of the cemetery, inveigling the others to follow down the opposite slope.

Proud though Henry generally was of his cleverness, he had only been half joking. In addition to what he considered his obvious charm, Henry Strafford also thought himself a sound judge of character, and he had determined at first glance that Hugh was a sensitive and truthful person. As a rule, Henry strove to be the same, which was why it had required all his self-discipline and powers of rationalization to be less than forthcoming with the other two men.

It continued to be an issue. But Henry reminded himself that if he shared all that he knew, even now, it could only put him at a disadvantage: if the finer points of the legend were symbolic, as he told himself he wanted to expect, then disclosing them would benefit no one. But if the remainder of the story was literal, as Henry secretly hoped, then it might put him in personal danger, particularly from William and his rifle. After all they had seen, Henry allowed that even a reasonable man might kill for the sake of caution, hearing that, 'Once in every generation, three travelers are said to answer the call of an ancient evil that takes the form of a map which one man must carry on his face. Their path would take those Three to a place cleansed by fire where they would be transformed, so that One Great Name would emerge.'

William led the group through the burnt brush and limbs that crowded the bottom of the hill. As the dead trunks became denser, twigs scratched and tugged at the men's ankles and sleeves. It became apparent that, had portions of the area not been 'cleansed by fire,' the vegetation would have made it impassable. It would

464

also have fully concealed their next obstacle: three quarters of a mile from the graveyard, a waist high stack of exposed adobe blocks extended into a low-slung wall, reminiscent of an English garden. Looking over the wall, scattered bricks served as evidence that the structure had been far more substantial sometime in the distant past.

Without looking back, William talked as he walked, "Supposing this will be the cross on the map."

Henry called, "Or perhaps the graveyard was the cross, and whatever-this-was is the end of the thing."

"No," William replied, "The graveyard was the square."

"Unless the square was the town," Henry argued.

Hugh finally interjected, "Does it matter? We've arrived *near* the end. I very much doubt that what we're looking for will be ambiguous. Walk until you find it, then stop. Should be simple."

Faced with this logic, the men marched on in silence. Over the course of fifty yards, the ruined wall rose briefly to shoulder height and then to just above their heads, with the charred and shattered copses of trees close and constant on their other side. At the front of their column, William slowed and then vanished through the wall. Hugh followed. It wasn't until Henry stood directly beside it that he saw the gap through which they'd gone: an arched doorway framed by chipped stone beams. Like much of what remained of the place, that stonework suggested a graceful simplicity, now reduced by nature and neglect to precariously balanced blocks that wanted nothing more than the peace of rotten collapse.

Beyond the ruined portal, the theme of quiet desolation continued. Twenty yards away, the wall took a corner; whether the interior had once been dug out or the structure had caused some unevenness in the undergrowth, more of the wall was exposed on this side. Universally crumbling at the top, it still stood well over ten feet in places, interrupted occasionally by empty niches and crenellated where square windows had caved in. The surrounded expanse featured fewer tree trunks, but still contained its share of burnt grass and bushes, between which short courses and piles of earthen blocks marked the former sites of interior walls and chimneys.

Hugh asked, "You think this was a fort or some such?"

"Too old to be one of ours," William said.

"I suspect it was a Mission," Henry posited. "But you are right: this must have burned a hundred years or more before the town did."

Through it all Henry followed the soldier and the adventurer. He refused to think of them by any other name. Knowing what he would have to do, Henry saw no benefit in getting attached to either of them, and so considered them only according to their utility of the moment: the disciplined defender and the guileless navigator, neither of whom would he allow to outlive their usefulness.

Coming even with an interior corner of the high wall on their right, William stepped around a low stack of slabs to a small break in the wall opposite the arched doorway. Beyond the barrier, more blackened trunks rose and crowded his path, throwing deep shadows before him. William raised his hand to signal the others to stop. Not looking up from the ground, he disappeared from view with the sound of pebbles clattering down a slope.

Henry and Hugh stared for over a minute at the spot where William had stood, before his voice called back, "There, now! That is certainly the end of it!"

Henry strode impatiently around Hugh and through the gap. Looking down to the right of the opening, he discovered a steep set of stone stairs, their edges rounded and treads half packed with soil, curving down between the trees. As Henry cautiously observed each step, he heard water gurgling before the brown river burst into view with a flood of daylight. A second set of stairs forked off to the left, but Henry continued straight to a steep and sandy bank where he joined William in looking up the hill, whence they had come.

The adobe blocks stacked and scattered around them evinced that the wall they had passed through, as well as the stairs beyond

466

it, had once been inside of a building that had extended nearly to the water. At some point in the preceding century, the hundred-foot wide stream that now ran low and slow at their back must have flooded enough to consume half the hillside along with the rear of the ruins, from which Hugh still stood blinking at them.

The second set of stairs that Henry had passed led to a natural cave that might have been repurposed as a cellar: a rough, round opening in the limestone. Erstwhile occupants had lowered and flattened the bottom of the passage so that, now exposed, the whole looked something like a misshapen, upside-down egg. The shallow roots of some trees above had broken through the fat end to form two round cavities, and the narrow part sported a straight line in the form of the final landing. To the right imagination, it looked like a skull with oversized eyes.

Last Day

Kristin stared into the darkness.

The foam panels that Diane had jammed into the living room windows to keep in the air conditioning were equally effective at keeping out light, so that Kristin, now wedged on her back between the cushions of the overstuffed sofa, could not see even as far as the ceiling, could not begin to guess what time of day it was, could really only be sure she was still alive from the sound and smell of coffee brewing. She supposed it must have been that sound that had woken her since the smell, just as dark as the room now, had only recently seeped through the threadbare comforter that hung from a curtain rod over the kitchen doorway, to overtake the musty odor of the quilt pulled across her face.

Kristin wondered how long she had been lying there thinking, and she realized that she had not been thinking at all, at least not about any one thing. She wondered how long it had been since she was able to do that, to let her mind sit perfectly still like that. She then realized that such reflection was itself a train of thought, and cursed her curiosity for yet again ruining her clarity.

The door-comforter snapped open suddenly, blindingly, with Diane's silhouette looming disproportionately in the lighted frame. Holding the barrier to one side she blurted, "Up an' at 'em, Lazy Bones!"

And then she was gone, leaving her words to float on a waft of coffee behind her.

Kristin pushed aside the quilt and reached past her head to feel for a lamp chain. She snapped on the light without thinking to avert her eyes and mumbled, "Stop it!" as she took a direct hit in the retinas.

Diane's voice, punctuated by slamming cupboards and clinking dishes, carried on from the next room, "Time to get up now, missy! Can't have you spend all of another day on m'damn sofa, I mean… Has it occurred t'you that maybe I might like to use that room sometimes? Maybe I might like t'watch the T.V. sometimes or somethin'?"

Kristin rubbed her eyes as she sluggishly stood up. She waited until she had folded the quilt and laid it across the back of the couch before answering, "What channel you want?" Diane's reply came quietly from just behind Kristin's shoulder, causing her to startle, "How's that now?"

Kristin spun to find her hostess holding a brimming coffee mug in each hand. Barely catching her composure, she politely asked, "What channel would you like us to watch? I'll turn it on for you."

Diane wrinkled her nose and shook her head, "Mornin' shows? No *thank* you." She shoved one of the mugs into Kristin's hand and continued, "But that don't mean you should presume to think I *would*n't watch 'em. Besides, spendin' all yer time in this dark room: it ain't healthy. Yer not doin' yerself any good."

"And *you*'re not being fair," Kristin stated firmly. "I've spent hours outside with you every single day. And I always help out when you ask, and I've tried to do more around here, but you won't let me."

Diane scoffed, "Let you? Chores ain't a thing to be *allowed*, missy, they're a thing t'be done."

"Okay," Kristin said, "But every time I try to *do* them, you tell me to stop."

Diane nearly shouted, "Because you're doin' 'em wrong!"

Kristin crossed her arms, raised her eyebrows, and cocked her head, allowing Diane's retort to answer itself.

"Fine," Diane relented, melodramatically waving her free hand, "Alright, I get it. You wanna do somethin'? How 'bout you feed them cats then?"

Gently, Kristin pointed out, "You just fed them before bed."

"I know that," Diane snorted, "You think I don't know that? I ain't demented, y'know. They been eatin' a lot. An' it's a good thing too, 'cause that means they won't starve if you screw up."

Kristin took her turn on defense, "Now, how do you think I would screw up feeding cats?"

"There's ways, missy!" Diane allowed herself a moment to regroup. To appreciate the importance of each detail, she enunciated clearly and calmly, "They're barn cats an' they scare easy. An' they're real particular, so you gotta mind that. T'start, you gotta mash up a can of the soft stuff, but then you gotta sprinkle some hard food over that an' just around the edge. But that's for just the grey one though. The calico don't go for the fancy stuff, so he'll take a cup of the dry food straight, but on the side, an' most important-," she paused for emphasis before repeating, "*Most* important: they *do not* like an audience. You put out their breakfast on a paper plate so's you can leave it. But be sure to get the one from last night, 'cause those things get nasty if you let 'em pile up. Oh, an' don't forget t'leave the door open so's they can get to it, or otherwise, what's the point?"

It was only after enduring two more repetitions of the rules, plus the painstaking preparation of the dish, that Kristin was allowed to serve the barn cats without careful supervision. Balancing the paper plate to step down from the recently refinished wood deck behind the house, Kristin was surprised to find that the sun was still rising. There was something fundamentally dissatisfying about a dry sunrise: all the best parts were missing. There was no smell of damp grass, no dew to touch her bare ankles, only a tidy gravel walkway demarcated arbitrarily from the bare dust on either side of it. Kristin followed this trail a short distance to the barn, which was well more than twice the age and size of the house, replete with peeling paint, a sagging roof, and the building's finest feature at the other end of the path: a brand-new-man-sized-aluminum-door, which hung open, useless.

As she crossed the threshold, Kristin searched in the shadows near the entrance for a light switch, but found none. She gave up, and with her eyes still adjusting, she concentrated instead on a lone, bright shaft of sunlight near the center of the cavernous space. Filtered through a filthy, unseen window somewhere overhead, the

470

yellow stream of dancing motes poured over the front end of a disused tractor, the stern of which was covered by a sheet. Kristin shuffled cautiously to this focal point, still balancing the breakfast service, ever vigilant for unseen tripping hazards while the coarse dust of the place settled on her arms and filled her nose and throat. In the periphery of the room, and of her field of vision, Kristin sensed large objects in the stifling shadows: looming stacks of pallets, old machinery with menacing corners and rusting edges, piles of large, tarp-covered bags, of what she could not say.

The airless room made Kristin sweat, which transformed the floating dirt into a gritty paste wherever it made contact with exposed flesh. She would have sworn that the place had warmed by ten degrees in the seconds she'd been there. She hastened her pace to the tractor, quick baby steps now to keep her balance, until she could brace one hand against the machine to crouch and set the plate on the cracked cement floor.

It was in this moment, in this vulnerable position, that Kristin first heard the scraping sound: treble, staccato, short-lived, and then nothing.

Kristin stayed low, turned her head back the way she had come. She had almost decided she was imagining things when she heard it again, louder and more distinctly. Glancing nervously into the corners, she heard another noise which she recognized as her own heartbeat. Kristin chastised herself for being ridiculous and forced a deep breath of the noxious mustiness. In a trembling voice she exhaled, "Here kitty-kitty... Come'n get it."

In answer, another quick scrape, this one definitely originating from beside the barn's lone exit. Kristin stared as something dark and massive passed in front of the lighted opening and vanished to the other side. Her hands went cold, her fingertips tingled, and she couldn't discern if the door was ten feet away or a hundred, but it didn't matter anyways because she felt like her sneakers had suddenly filled with lead. As she fought to force herself into any action at all, the shadows in front of her gathered, their concentrated immensity rising slowly toward her, a tortured, lumbering, *scraaaa-pe* into being across the dusty, concrete slab.

The sound, still sharp and short, repeated in quicker and quicker succession, and the writhing darkness took on greater definition: something like the shape of a tall man bent nearly in half, and the sound... Was that... Was it the sound of his meaty knuckles scraping across the ground?

Kristin felt the cold front of the tractor against her lower back, not realizing she'd been shuffling away from the thing until she had nowhere else to go. The narrow shaft of sunlight that grew smaller around her by the second glinted off something, left the impression of wet eyes, of the glistening points of enormous lower teeth. Falling back onto her tailbone, Kristin tried to scout a path to the exit but the shadow grew larger in its approach, blotted out more of the light with every iteration of *that sound*. While Kristin fought to pull in enough air for a scream, the specter launched something at her. Bouncing, skittering, and rattling towards her, something bright bounced off the tractor tire next to Kristin's hand. Horror stricken, she forced herself to look.

An empty paper plate, stained brown at the center and covered in black hair, rolled on its edge back into the shadows.

The hulking shape pursued the item unhurriedly. As the monster passed more gradually in front of the door, Kristin was finally able to make out the snout of a very large dog. From this emerged a wide, pink tongue, which in licking the empty plate, pushed it across the floor with a scrape.

Kristin let her taut muscles relax, and dropped her full weight onto her ass. Her palms were clammy and her mouth was bone dry, though she took some small comfort in the fact she had not pissed herself. But relieved as she was to know what was stalking her, she still couldn't know if the dog was friendly, and she did know for sure that it could easily knock her down if it wasn't. Bearing all of this in mind, Kristin rolled herself around onto her hands and knees to slowly crawl in the direction of the door.

As she neared the beast, it froze. The dog looked up, turned its head directly to Kristin, then unconcernedly returned its affection to the empty plate.

From that distance, new details emerged: a thick black coat, soft where it was clean, but matted and dirty over much of the animal's side. Against her better instincts, Kristin reached slowly toward the mud encrusted face, and the giant flinched; there was no malice or aggression, just surprise, the suggestion of pain as it started and stumbled away from her, showing the whites of its eyes. Lowering her hand Kristin cooed, "Hey-hey-hey-hey there… You're alright, I won't-,"

Kristin half stood and scurried back to the tractor. She picked up the fresh plate of cat food and set it atop the empty one a few feet from the incredulous dog. It was now the other's turn to approach cautiously. The animal bowed its head, dropped its gaze, and came in low to accept the offering. Kristin inched in while the dog was absorbed in sniffing the edge of the plate. She began to slowly raise her hand again, but stopped herself.

In the wan light stretching from the open door, the mud on the dog's face took on a rusty hue against its black fur. Kristin gently stroked a shimmering patch and brought her hand back to confirm her suspicion. Not mud. Blood. And an incredible quantity of blood at that. She followed from the crusted spray at the dog's elbow up to a matted patch at its shoulder. Beyond the still wet stretch that she'd examined on the side of its neck, she found the source: most of the dog's left ear was missing. Ragged and torn away near the base, it looked to have stopped actively bleeding, but must have been opening and reopening for some time to produce that much mess while leaving the creature on its feet.

A single, smart scraping sound preceded one loud crunch. Kristin maneuvered around the dog's face and found that it had cleared the cup of hard food. While it took two whole licks to savor the soft stuff, Kristin examined the rest of its head. Apart from a thin, raw cut across its scalp behind the displaced ear, everything looked normal. The dog got down to the business of licking this plate, and Kristin moved deliberately around its uninjured side. The animal was unperturbed by her hand on the scruff of its neck.

Kristin kneaded her fingers deep in the dog's thick coat, and felt a wide, nylon collar. She turned the object gently around the dog's neck until she felt cold metal in her palm. Kristin leaned in, on her feet now, but bent part way over to shuffle along as the dog continued to chase the empty plate. In her hand, the light played off one of two dog tags: it was glossy and brass and shaped like a bone. On one side she found the name, 'Louis Garrett,' followed by a phone number and an address in Selmer, Tennessee. Across the back she discovered, etched in a much larger, florid script, the word 'Marlow.'

Following the dog in their waltz with her hand on the tag, she breathed the name aloud, "Marlow." The dog ignored her, kept after his prize, and Kristin repeated the word, easily, calmly, and, she hoped, invitingly, "Marlow, Marlow, Marlow..."

With its nose to the dusty concrete where its breakfast once stood, the dog emitted a sort of groan in response: a low mewling that transformed to a whine in its journey from Marlow's chest to his throat.

Kristin kept her running commentary to the dog. "All done, baby," she cooed, tugging at the collar, "You ate it all up. Time to go-,"

Unmoved, Marlow stepped toward the plate, taking his collar and Kristin along with him. "No, now," she said firmly while she grabbed the nylon band with both hands, "We have to go back to the house-,"

The dog groaned again, and casually dragged Kristin on her feet through the dust in a sort of skiing exercise. She turned sideways and, ever mindful of Marlow's wounds, wrapped her arms around his neck, using her shoulder against his cheek to steer his face back toward the door. The dog huffed once and then grudgingly plodded in that direction, though clearly by his choice and not Kristin's. Even with his tentative cooperation, Kristin expended all her energy in maneuvering Marlow. She pulled at his

474

collar, pushed at his armpits, and from what she could tell just plain worked much harder than he did to coax the front half of his body through the small door of the barn.

Kristin stumbled backward into the open morning. She paused to catch her breath in the fresh air, leaned forward with her hands on her knees facing a dance partner who stayed half out of the barn, half in. In the light, Marlow's coat looked even filthier and his wounds even nastier, but his face broke into a broad, smiling pant under warm and grateful eyes that gave Kristin the impression he was laughing at her efforts. She adopted his facial expression without realizing it, drily chuckling, "You're kind of a dick, aren't you?"

A distressed cry shattered their moment, "Oh for shit's sake, little girl!"

Kristin straightened up to look over her shoulder at the small and furious form of Diane, standing on the porch, hands on hips. "Y'see?" Diane demanded, "I told you. I *tooold* you! I *knew* you'd find a way to screw up feedin' them cats."

Somewhere behind Tim, something was jangling. No, not some*thing*, but some*one*. And not *some*one, but Louis. More specifically, some*thing* Louis was carrying on his back was jangling. It sounded like something small and round, maybe coated in fabric, or maybe made of a softer material like wood, bumping rhythmically against something larger and hollow made of metal: a pan, perhaps, or an empty canteen. Tim wasn't sure, but he'd been trying to guess every time he'd heard the sound. Which was every time Louis had taken a step for at least the last three miles.

The charitable thing would be to tell Louis to drop most of what he was hauling and all of what was clanging like a cowbell around his neck. Even forgetting the noise, the group was bound to reach their destination that day and would no longer need much of the gear Louis was carrying. But Tim was not charitable, for one thing. In fact, he somewhat enjoyed treating Louis like a pack animal; he thought it suitable punishment for the man's obstinacy. Also, people do put bells on cows for a reason, and he thought that the noise might be a simple way to keep tabs on Louis. So, he told himself to tune out the sound, to accept that it had a purpose and allow it to fade from his attention like the ticking of a clock.

Yet there it was, every second and a half, like the triple meter of a busted waltz: *Clang-tink-tink. Clang-tink-tink. Clang-tink-tink.* Constant. Infuriating. All Louis's fault and all that Tim could hear: *Clang-tink-tink. Clang-tink-tink.*

Thump. Rustle. Jared exclaiming, "Aw fuck!"

Tim continued marching. Sadly, that noise too had been recurring regularly, but unlike the jangling, it didn't serve any purpose.

This time though, Jared announced, "I *said* 'Aw fuck!'"

Behind Tim, the jangling stopped and Louis gently asked, "You okay, bud?"

"Yeah," Jared said, "I tripped over something. Looks like it's half-buried."

Tim stopped, sighed, and turned slowly to survey the ground. The rounded corners of a smooth-worn stone slab punched through the ground beside one of several evenly spaced mounds. "Don't sweat it," Tim instructed calmly, "It's just graves."

Jared blinked back at him, "Really? They don't look much like graves to me."

"Yeah, well," Tim shrugged, "They used to. C'mon, we're going this way."

Jared asked, "You're sure? We've been going that way for a while now. Maybe we should check the map."

"No need," Tim said, continuing his march, "I am one hundred percent certain. You can trust me." And for once, they actually could trust Tim, thanks to Jared's discovery. Prior to their stumbling over the cemetery, Tim had been much less than 100% that there would be any landmarks to guide them. Strafford's memoir gave the impression that the mission ruins had been largely

476

eroded 130 years earlier, so Tim thought it unlikely that there would be much left of them by this point. As it was, San Marcial had disappeared with nary a trace. Ironically, the little town situated in an area destined to be cleansed by fire once every generation had ultimately washed away. A series of floods had prompted the community to give up and abandon the place in the 1930's.

Whether the town had gone up in smoke or landed somewhere downstream, the outcome was the same: all that remained to greet the trio was a terrible monotony of charred plants and loose dirt, more of a lumpy dust really, extending behind them as far as the eye could see. Before them though, was something very different. Far down a slope from the cemetery, entering a recently wooded area near the shadow of a mesa, the terrain flattened into a sort of plateau divided by a series of straight, gentle ridges no more than a foot high, which intersected occasionally at right angles. In the large square spaces created by the ridges, the brown gravel was interspersed with chunkier, if equally jagged, red rocks, a pattern that continued to a similar but slightly taller berm that bounded the area, straight as an arrow along a row of bald, burnt trees.

Tim called back. "Watch your step, Jared." He took his own advice, stepping over the bumps in a direct line to the back berm, but no further. Tim was only vaguely aware of the other men behind him as he picked his way parallel to the trees. At odd intervals, blue sky and open air peeked through between the trunks, hinting at a sudden drop just out of view. Tim kept his eyes trained on the base of the barrier until he found a narrow break, what looked like a caved in section with a small flat spot just beyond.

He passed through to this landing, took a hard right, and followed a trail in his original direction of travel. In short order, the trail inclined down the hillside into a kind of ramp, impressed with short terraces that only hinted at the stone treads Tim knew to be packed under more than a century of ash and soil. He stopped to let Jared catch up, just before the trail punched through the trees. Gesturing back to the top, Tim said, "Go tell the big guy he can leave all that gear up there. Oh, but there's a pair of propane lanterns with him somewhere. We'll need both of those."

Jared nodded quickly and retreated uphill while Tim continued down, breaking into the daylight, still well above a long, sandy, bank. Past that, a row of healthier trees concealed whatever visible water, if any, was keeping the green space alive. Tim did not bother with any of that, but doubled back from the path onto the narrower ledge that had once been a second staircase, and shimmied sideways to a four-and-a-half-foot tall hole in the cliff. He reached above the opening, and looped each hand through the tree roots he knew would be exposed there. Tim extended his arms as he bent his knees, hanging like this until he saw Jared pop around the corner on his way to the beach. Tim called, "Hey! This way!"

Jared glanced around the open air for a moment. Finally spotting Tim, he paused, perplexed, and then called sarcastically into the trees, "Oh, you'll love this, Louis! Got some spider monkey shit comin' up for you!"

Tim did not wait to watch that play out, but swung himself through the hole, landing in a crouch. When he heard pebbles falling down the cliff just outside, he shuffled further into the short cave, allowing space for Jared to swing inside quickly to accommodate the much larger Louis just behind. Jared asked, "How did you know this was here? I didn't see anything like it on the map, just some weird dinosaur egg looking thing at the end of the trail."

"Don't worry about that," Tim reassured him, "Just trust that I will show you the way."

The others nodded quietly in the deep shadow, waiting.

Tim said, "I'll need some light for it."

"Oh, right," Louis mumbled, "Got that for you." From a cord he had looped over his shoulder, Louis swung a pair of small lanterns onto the floor. He settled on his knees, lit each in turn, and passed one over to Tim.

Tim held his lantern aloft and turned away from the entrance. The glow spread rapidly across the flaking yellow stone of the opposite wall, then jumped dramatically to illuminate the wall he had been leaning on. In between, there was darkness. Silence. The primordial stillness that can only exist underground.

Tim tried ambling on hand and knees behind his lamp, and the tunnel retreated apace into shadows. His thighs began to cramp, so he dropped onto his butt and scooted along, supposing from the sounds as he did so that the other men had followed his lead. Inching forward in this way, it was impossible to tell if the ceiling was gradually rising or the floor gently sloping, but whichever was the case, Tim found himself with enough head room to roll forward onto his feet. Picking up momentum, he decided they must be going downhill now, and before long he had straightened his slouch to stroll casually. Glancing back, he observed that the passage had gotten tall enough even for Louis, beyond whose lantern, Tim could no longer make out the entrance.

He could not tell how far they had come, how fast they were moving, or whether the incline had run straight or bent into the hill. He did, however, have a sense of some changing condition in front of them: the movement of air, the cool odor of damp rock. He lowered his lamp-hand to pay special attention to whatever the floor might do next. The light jumped over a shadow and glinted off a ledge a couple of feet in front of him. As Tim approached, the dark section narrowed, revealing the tread of a short stair, with another in front of it, and the dull horizontal lines of several more dug into the earth, proceeding steeply down and out of view.

Keeping the lantern in his left hand, Tim lightly ran his right along the wall, for reference as much as balance. His fingertips delicately brushed over something: a crack, he thought at first, until the hard line bent into a symmetrical curve with dots on either side. Tim raised his lamp high to prevent getting run over by his comrades, and found himself staring into a chiseled image of beady eyes on a bald cartoon head with a giant nose that swooped over a wall inscribed 'Kilroy was here.' Below the simple scratching, block letters in quotation marks signed the work, 'Ty Johnson.' The footsteps that had followed him onto the stairs scraped and slapped to a halt while he twisted to examine the wall in either direction.

Beside Jared, a pattern of two-foot tall, ill-defined blobs formed a psychedelic font in flaking, faded black marker that spelled out the compressed name, 'Joshua Carver.' Stretching from the final 'R,' of that name, a newer, double outlined, spray painted tag swooped up the wall past Louis to form the words: 'Frank Taylor.' Tim returned his attention down the stairs and discovered more writing, more names, some with elaborate illustrations and inscriptions. 'Theo Forbes,' left only his moniker in block letters; 'Charles Howard,' had spent considerably more time carving the likeness of an American flag with 48 stars over the words 'God and Country'.

On and on it went as the stairs leveled off into a narrow passage, where Tim stopped once more. There, in a careful and elaborate cursive, above his eye level but barely beyond his lamp, stood the carved name, 'Henry Sullivan Strafford.'

Louis softly exhaled, "I'll be damned."

Jared answered, "Let's hope not."

Tim ignored them to marvel, "I never considered how many others have come since Strafford by now."

Jared followed up, "How do you mean?"

Without answering, Tim directed his lamp light down the wall and over the next name: scratched in sharp, uneven letters were the simple words, 'Ezekial Gates.' "There!" Tim exclaimed, "Good! Now I know where we are."

Tim passed by the next signature. And then another. And another. Moving through the narrow passage, again unsure of the gradient, he could not say whether it was gravity or enthusiasm pulling him along, but he could not help but move faster and faster. And all along the graffiti continued: now English names were replaced by Spanish phrases; now an elaborate crucifix overlapped with intricate geometric patterns; now angles and circles gave way to interlocking animals, devilish faces, long forgotten deities

480

sneering at the men from what Tim thought might be an actual underworld.

Deeper and deeper, faster and faster, Tim knew where they were and where they were going. And he knew he was ready, but the figures marched on, reached up one wall and down the other, stretched across the ceiling, then crowded in tighter, from embrace to constriction and then…

Nothing. Darkness. The walls and ceiling vanished as the corridor emptied into a vast chamber. Tim tried raising his lantern, but only the floor was close enough to reflect it. He allowed his lamp-hand to hang slack alongside him and squinted into the shadows above, willing his eyes to adjust to the total absence of light. In answer he got nothing but an overriding sense of space and anticipation, as though he were standing on a stage in a darkened auditorium, waiting for his spotlight.

Tim mumbled, "Fuck it," and pressed on in search of what he knew awaited them.

Jared asked breathlessly, "What is this place?"

Truthful in the broadest sense, Tim answered, "Some centuries ago, there used to be a chapel above this cave."

Jared followed up, "So this was like, a crypt or something?"

"No," Tim said, "This place was thousands of years old by then. This was… something else entirely."

From just beyond the entrance to the room, Louis's lantern had floated silently off to explore in another direction. Tim and Jared persisted in a straight line for a surprisingly long time before their light finally ricocheted off of something solid: an irregularly mottled rock wall shooting straight up in front of them. An apparent cave-in eons before had deposited a nearly five-foot slope of rough rubble at its base, while leaving the surface near perfectly smooth. Without taking his eyes off the barrier, Tim asked over his shoulder, "You still have that drawing of the symbol from the end of your map?"

"Yeah," Jared said hurriedly. Tim heard paper crinkling behind him and assumed that the younger man was unfolding the design from his pocket. He knew Jared hadn't been carrying additional baggage: none of them had, save the lanterns and Tim's omnipresent satchel, Tim had made very sure of that.

With the sound of paper rustling nearer behind him, Tim picked his way up the piled debris to the largest of the splotches in the rock and raised his lantern to his limit. Well above his head floated dozens of painted figures, of various sizes but nearly uniform build. In dark red, brown, and black, most of the simple shapes only suggested the silhouettes of men: apparitions emerging from another era, their fading, tapered, legless bodies grew darker over the course of seven feet or more in some cases, before swooping in to form broad shoulders set under thin necks, which in turn supported round, filled-in heads. Tim slowly, reverently, followed the figures. Most were featureless, but some had limbs holding spears, a handful of others wore horns or antennae, and select few bore intricate white designs.

At the end of the ancient procession, three shadowy, limbless people gathered underneath a much larger creature that to Tim resembled a sarcophagus painted in red. He called back, "Hey, gimme that drawing." Jared obliged, and Tim took it up in his free hand for comparison. Both on the page and atop the broad neck of this central figure, an oblong oval stood like a misshapen, upside-down egg featuring large round eyes that stared from above a stern mouth depicted as a thick, horizontal line.

Before either man could speak, Louis's voice cut in from twenty yards further down the wall, "Hey! Found something here!" Tim's moment of awe was shattered, disintegrated. God how he hated that guy. Louis insisted, "Y'all wanna see this, I'm pretty sure!"

In his annoyance, Tim skidded down the loose stones, shoved the drawing back into Jared's hands, and all but hissed, "Follow me." He shuffled carefully to avoid twisting his ankle in one of many divots: as he had read in Strafford's manuscript, following from the edge of the paintings nearest Louis's lantern, the floor was dotted with carefully carved depressions, each no more than a few

482

inches across, and each set at the center of several concentric rings. These small glyphs clustered with increasing density around Louis and his discovery.

In the wan light that collected between Louis's well-worn boots was a monochrome pile: a dry, lumpy mash the color of the dust that coated every surface in that room. Shoved against the wall as it was, it was a very long moment before Tim's eyes could differentiate between shredded cloth and bare bone.

Darkly, almost smugly, Louis observed, "An' you said this wasn't a crypt."

For everyone's benefit, Tim ignored the comment and crouched for a closer inspection. He ran his lamp over the knobby end of a long bone set beside a cluster of small ones. Observing what he believed to be rotted shoe leather, Tim moved quickly along the bottom edge of the wall, amongst more carvings, past what he now recognized as ribs and vertebrae. Coming to the skull, Tim extended two fingers of his free hand and pressed lightly against the cheekbone, rolling the object to one side.

Something dark and narrow protruded from the back. The end of a rusted blade angled upward into the braincase with such force that the tip had punched through the opposing cranium from the inside.

"Holy shit," Tim breathed, "It's *him*."

Two steps behind, Jared demanded, "It's *who*?"

Hugh cried out from the dark.

William squinted at the last place he'd seen the man's shadow. He reached back to his torch as he called, "You alright?"

Hugh's reply was surprisingly calm, "Yeh. Just about fell, though. Somebody poked a mess 'a holes in the floor."

Ticking down his priorities, William followed up, "And the lamp? You drop it?"

"Yer precious lamp is safe. I broke its fall."

William was pleased, and so chose to not correct Hugh: the simple, tin signal lamp had actually come from Dr. Strafford's provisions. Over the years, though, William had developed the view that, any time comrades stand together in harm's way, practicality requires that all property be communal. To be fair, there had been a moment when William had considered exploiting this philosophy, demanding that the best equipment go to the man in front, knowing full well that he would be that man. But, speaking again to his practicality, he couldn't reconcile handing an open torch flame to a man with as much unkempt hair as Hugh had. And so, rather than burn Hugh's beard for light, William had given him their only lamp.

Even after giving up the lamp, William had insisted on leading. In order to responsibly do that, he'd used some small tree limbs and the remnants of the doctor's tattered coat to fashion torches for Strafford and his self. With his free hand, William had bravely pressed his rifle, bayonet fixed, from one end of the tunnel to the other, past Hugh's discovery of Ezekial Gates's John Hancock, and all the way down to this room. The others had thought it best to split up and explore, but William had worried over something pursuing them, so he'd stayed near the exit as a sentry. He had also worried about something confronting them, so was pleased to find a sconce on the wall nearby to make the exit more visible by torchlight.

William worried about many things these days.

Most consistently, he worried over what he should do at the conclusion of this adventure. He couldn't very well go back to Arizona. Or rather, he could, but there would be little to go back to. If any forces did remain in that part of the territory, he would have to explain where he'd been and how he'd survived. William would hardly be the first or last deserter in that part of the world, but to absent oneself during a battle... that would carry a stigma, even if it didn't leave a mark. Likewise, should he return to East Texas, he might still be labeled a deserter.

One obvious choice he'd considered was to attach himself to one of the other men. But little by little, he had formed the impression that Hugh did not like him very much. And William knew with some certainty that he did not like or trust Henry Strafford. Alternatively, he could strike out into the wilderness on his own, could avoid human contact altogether and thus avoid making excuses or peddling stories; truly, at moments like this, moments of change, William instinctively tended toward solitude. But after everything, something inside him craved the familiarity, the predictability, the security of civilization.

This was his dilemma, how to seek society and avoid socializing, and he could not reconcile the two. So instead he worried over simpler problems, like imaginary stalkers and flammable facial hair, or the ongoing mystery of whatever they were in the midst of discovering-

William's train of thought was abruptly derailed by Henry Strafford's voice reverberating, "Gentlemen! I have found it!"

William reached again for his torch, but thought better of it: it still seemed wise to leave their exit well-lit in case of emergency, so instead he grasped his rifle tightly across his body with both hands, and followed Strafford's voice toward the latter man's flickering light. William was surprised at how much distance he had to cover and was further surprised by the distance between himself and Hugh, whose lamp now floated eerily over a field of depressions in the floor.

Only when the men were close enough to see the excitement on Strafford's face did he dramatically sweep his torch as high above his head as he could reach. The flame diminished with a whoosh as it travelled, then flared at its apex, illuminating a stream of rudimentary paintings, just above eye level in front of William and Hugh. "I don't understand," William said, "What makes these more important than all the names and pictures we just come past."

Strafford replied cheerfully, "Here, look closer." He held his torch out to William, who took it in his free hand and climbed a small pile of loose stones to the wall. Strafford moved out of the way around the men and continued, "Along with my light, I would also offer my confession. You might recall that I originally withheld a portion of the legend that Benjamin and I had heard."

"Yes," William said, "I hadn't forgot you was a liar."

Strafford laughed cordially, "I maintain that I had good reason. All the same, I have continued to reserve the very last of it for this moment." Clearing his throat, Strafford announced, "Word for word, all that I know, the legend is as follows: 'Once in every generation, a group of three travelers is said to answer an ancient evil in the form of a map which one man must carry on his face. Their path will take them to a place cleansed by fire where they will be transformed, so that One Great Name will emerge.'

Disregarding the content of the oration, William observed, "So you been lyin' to us again, or lyin' to us still." He turned to face Strafford, who had backed away far enough to put Hugh in between them. William's voice rose as he demanded, "Now, if you still lyin', then why should we believe what you think you know, what you *say* you think you know?"

Hugh interceded, "Not to argue, Doc, but he does have a point. You keep holding back parts, makes it hard to believe you're telling us the whole story now. Not that what you've told us makes sense anyhow."

"Understood," Strafford shrugged, "But at this point there is no more reason to lie. I held back the more cryptic language of the story in order that we might all have the courage to find the end of the path together. And here it is before us: this is the end of it. You can observe for yourself," he gestured to three shadowy, painted figures congregating under a larger, red one. "Three travelers transformed so that one great name might emerge." Strafford strolled casually while he talked, removing to the edge of the lamplight immediately behind Hugh, who was now transfixed on the referenced paintings. "Now that I consider it," Strafford chuckled, "I don't guess it matters how much truth I've told you, or how much I've kept to myself... now we've arrived at the end, nothing said can be too important." With a sigh he concluded, "All

486

the same: if I am to transform a group of three people into one, I thought it only fair to offer the two of you some explanation."

For the briefest instant the lamplight flared, just long enough and bright enough for William to see the glint of metal in the doctor's hand. Even before Strafford propelled it upward, before the shining point sailed toward the back of Hugh's neck, William heard a shout issuing from his own mouth: a warning two steps ahead of his mind, any words unintelligible. But the noise and the look on William's face were jarring enough to prompt Hugh to glance over his shoulder.

The doctor's blade had too much momentum to change course along with its intended victim, and instead whizzed past Hugh's cheek to become entangled in the midst of his beard. Hugh's lantern clattered to the floor as he tried to back away, tried to wrest the knife from his attacker, but struggled to find it in the coarse hair draped in front of his chest. In an instant, William recognized his breathless suspense at whether Hugh would find Strafford's wrist before Strafford found Hugh's throat. A wave of shame at his own immobility washed William back down the rock pile. He threw the torch aside to grasp the butt of his rifle.

Now at attention, William's mind moved more rapidly than his instincts. He weighed his options as he raised his weapon. Even at such close range, the other men twisting and tangling in low light made the outcome of a shot unpredictable. With his gun halfway to his shoulder, William instead pushed forward, drove the triangular tip of his bayonet at Strafford's waistcoat. The point made contact, struck something hard that William at first believed to be bone. But the barrel of the rifle glanced away, and the power of William's thrust carried him past the other men. Stumbling, falling, William landed full on his chest in the dust, knocking the wind from him.

He rolled over and looked back, but the others had wrestled away from the lamplight. Still gasping, William crawled, dragged his rifle to the sound of their scuffle, finally spotting them not far from where his torch had landed amongst the depressions in the floor. In a half crouch he scrambled forward, made out the shape of

Strafford using his body to pin Hugh against the wall, face first. William closed the distance between them as Strafford again drew back his blade to increase the force of the blow. Still farther away than he would've liked, William lunged up at the back of them, stretching as far he could.

He felt his bayonet graze across the doctor's body then slow to an abrupt stop with a sickening squish followed by a metallic clack. William froze, all his weight on one knee with the other leg kicked out behind him, pushing, *pushing*, on the butt of his gun. Strafford's arms dropped to his sides, allowing the knife to clatter to the floor. Hugh wriggled free from the wall, and William felt himself slide forward, swung his other knee around to stop his fall.

Near William's face, the doctor's fingers jolted and fluttered as both his hands involuntarily flapped from the wrists by his thighs. William knelt there for a long moment, holding the doctor upright on the end of his pike, before a hand on his shoulder caused him to startle. The weight of the body that was attached to the skull that William had pierced, pulled his gun with it as it collapsed against the wall.

William let go and stared at what he had done. Behind him he heard Hugh say, "Slow up now, wait there and I'll…" William heard the scrape of the lantern being lifted from the floor, still too far off to be useful. He leaned forward and rolled Strafford's corpse further against the wall to grasp the stock of his rifle.

Tugging vainly, William could make out where the spike had entered, just above the hairline in the back of the man's neck, and was surprised, impressed really, how much of it had vanished into his head. But now it seemed to be stuck on something, and for some reason William felt uncomfortable with the jerking and rattling that he knew would be required to free it.

Instead, he twisted the rifle, felt the bayonet unlock with a scrape and a dry click, and carefully pulled the gun free, leaving the metal in his adversary.

488

By the time Hugh's lamp illuminated the grisly heap in front of them, William knew exactly what he would do next.

"But that doesn't make any sense," Jared shot back, "How can Henry Strafford have died here in 1881, when we've all seen how much he did after that? Up to and including dying elsewhere? At least twice?"

"Well," Tim resumed calmly, "This was Strafford before Strafford was Strafford. Let that sink in. It's the only explanation that does make sense, when you think about it."

Louis stood quietly, watching them haggle over reality. He wasn't sure how invested he was in this debate: it seemed to him that, regardless of the finer points, this whole odyssey had been all fucked up from the start. No matter how Tim presented it, there was no explanation that could knock the weirdness out of this, so Louis saw no choice but to embrace whatever was presented, however bizarre it was. Every inch of the scene begged suspension of disbelief: the emaciated, unshaven man gesturing wildly at the foot of a disintegrating skeleton, as he argued biographical details to a rude and rotund technician, himself sentimentally lifting a pierced skull from the floor like Hamlet reunited with Yorick. A pair of propane lanterns placed along the wall cast the shadows of all three men with the bones of the fourth long into the massive chamber.

Near Louis's foot, Tim gently replaced Strafford's head where he'd found it. He stood up awkwardly to avoid further contact with the dead man, or any contact with Louis, and wiped his hands on his pants as he stepped away. Walking a short distance past Jared, Tim dug into his satchel, and came up with a long, aluminum flashlight. He flicked it on and shined the beam over the bones while he continued talking, "Before that man arrived in this place, he was a doctor named Henry Sullivan Strafford. He came from New England looking for an adventure, which he found in a pretty final way. Really what he found was a local legend. That myth, in full, was as follows: 'Once in every generation, a group of three travelers is said to answer an ancient evil in the form of a map which one man must carry on his face. Their path will take them to a place cleansed by fire where they will be transformed, so that One Great Name would emerge.'

"But the doctor succumbed to an obvious temptation. Faced with a legend as vague as legends are wont to be, Henry Strafford filled in the gaps of what *he* thought it must mean; he daydreamed it, came up with a detailed scenario, and took everything that happened to him as confirmation of his dream. When he found a man with a map on his face, he made the positive choice to assemble three travelers to include himself. He then accompanied the other two, a man called Hugh and the other named William, to a place where he assumed three men would enter and one man would leave. He further assumed that in order for that to happen, he would have to kill the other men. Most of all though, and this was his big mistake, he assumed that the outcome of every event was fated, based on their having occurred in the first place."

Tim stepped further from the bones and waved his flashlight over the painted figures that reached high along the wall. As he used the light to gesture at three dark specters under one tall, red one, he said "It's fairly easy to see how he might assume this was pictorial confirmation of that fate. But this was where all his assumptions caught up with him." Turning to the other men, Tim added with a smear of irony, "I'm making some assumptions of my own here: he didn't leave any record of his intentions, all we have from the manuscript are his actions. And from that I surmise that he had two major problems. The first was that his assumptions all conspired to cede his sense of agency." Tim raised a hand toward Louis to preempt a follow up question, "*Meaning:* he made so many assumptions about his *fate,* that he treated his victory as guaranteed, unavoidable even, without accounting for free will and personal choices."

Louis nodded along, having understood without the clarification, but too used to Tim's condescension to feel insulted. He lifted his lamp from the floor and walked past Jared, around the edge of the broken rock pile to address Tim at a conversational volume. Patiently he asked, "And the second problem?"

Directing the light back over the skeleton Tim observed, "He was short. A shorter than average man. That plus his lack of modern lighting meant…" Tim whipped the beam back to the wall, to a point above the large red figure, "He'd have missed that top bit there." Unimpressive relative to what was painted below, two more red figures, identical to the first apart from being half the size, leaned at angles moving away from it. Tim concluded in a hurried tone that suggested that either he felt this was explanation in itself or that he'd grown bored with discussing it. "So, the late, great Dr. Henry Sullivan Strafford attempted to lead two men to a death that he thought it was his destiny to cause, and instead they killed him. Exactly as *they* were destined to do, you see."

This part Louis didn't see, and not for lack of trying. Tim's description was internally consistent, in that it explained how the dead man on the floor came to be dead. But giving Tim the benefit of the doubt on his clairvoyant accounting of Strafford's motive did nothing to answer Jared's question of how everything that happened after could have happened if the man that it had happened to had died here at that time. Louis wanted to point all that out, but something about Tim's smugness and Jared's silence suggested that he should infer the answer from what they'd just heard. If Louis reiterated the question, he would risk looking stupid, but at the same time he felt that the answer he didn't know was really the whole point of everything, so he tried a different tact: breezy as he could, he nodded as he ventured, "So Henry Strafford was *meant* to bring two men to kill *him* as part of some Indian curse."

Tim groaned loudly enough to echo from the unseen walls; even in near total darkness, Louis could see the man roll his eyes. He released his frustration in a shouted, "No. No. NO! You clearly don't underst-," Tim cut himself off, took a breath, and tried again, with patronizing calm, "Did that revered professor you spoke of the other day spend much time on Voltaire? 'The Holy Roman Empire was neither holy, nor Roman, nor an empire?'"

Jared interjected, "You might make your point faster if you spent less time being a dick."

Apparently accustomed to this advice, Tim bulldozed on, "There is no 'Indian curse,' don't be ignorant. By the time Spanish sailors declared the Caribbean 'India,' the locals here had only been static for a few hundred years, and the tenants previous to them for a thousand more before that. Those paintings on the wall were a thousand years old by the time those earlier folks showed up. Some of the carvings in that tunnel are likely from earlier millennia still, and it wouldn't shock me if those cup and ring petroglyphs in the floor were ancient before any of the other decorations came along. No one we know to have lived in this area, not New Mexicans, not American pioneers, not the Spanish, not Pueblo groups, nor their known ancestors, could have created this place. And surely none of those people would claim it, especially if everyone predicted to come here had to be a traveler from somewhere else.

"But for all of that time, five thousand years, maybe ten, maybe more, this spot has called out like clockwork, and people like us have answered it. Unknowing, unknown, over and over again... All to play out the exact same course of events. That isn't a curse, it's a pattern. There is no intent, just routine. Is the sunrise a curse? Are the tides? No. These are things that happen simply because they have to happen, whenever and wherever they have to happen. For everything else he got wrong, I'm certain Strafford understood that much."

Tim tapered off, having fully vented his spleen. Louis allowed the subsequent silence to settle for a second before trying again, very deliberately relaxed, "Okay. I hear you. I'm just trying to follow along here. So, you say that this is a pattern: one guy has a beard, he links up with two other guys, and they come here, and
492

then… what, then? Patterns are supposed to be predictable, right? So why did Henry Strafford die and how did he then go walkin' around for the rest of his life?"

"That is a fair question," Tim replied, flicking off the flashlight. He reached back to place the object in his satchel, saying as he did, "But a third thing that may have killed Strafford, the first time he died, was how long *he* spent explaining things."

Louis did not panic when he recognized the 'click' of the safety on Tim's pistol. He stood steadily, was impressed, really, by his own courage. Or was that resignation? Did the designation make any difference under the circumstance? Could anything make a difference now? Did anyone-anywhere-ever concern themselves with the pensive motives and restive thoughts of a sheep being led to slaughter? Louis reflected on this very deeply in the instant before the muzzle flashed.

Marlow leapt to his feet in a panic and flashed his bandaged head to the side, muzzle punching Kristin in the midsection hard enough to force a grunt from her chest. The dog stumbled sideways a few steps, dropped his broad, fluffy, tail to between his hind legs, and glanced wildly at each of the two women. By the time Kristin fully registered the sudden flurry, Marlow stood three feet away huffing confusedly, a sort of pained growl that undulated into a high-pitched whine. Diane had sprung to her feet quickly enough to knock over her wooden chair, and was poised to launch herself at him.

Kristin twisted sideways, extended her arms, and raised an open palm to each of them, without looking at either. "Everybody stop," she stated forcefully. "Bring it back down. We were having a nice time. What happened?"

"I'd tell you what happened," Diane snarled, refusing to relax her posture, "But I tol' you already, been tellin' you all day. You don't know what goes on in a animal's brain. You can't just be pickin' up strays. It could be crazed and rabid for all you know."

In an aside, Kristin countered, "He's not rabid. He's got a tag that says he had his shots."

Diane shook her head, "Nah. People fake those tags y'know."

"No. They don't." Kristin glanced up at the dog and then back down to the ground between them. She had read somewhere that this signaled submissiveness, would help to counter a dog's sense of a threat. Marlow continued to look through Kristin, his eyes darting, following, searching, and beneath it all he moaned in a hopeless and sorrowful drone. Still avoiding direct eye contact, Kristin slid toward the dog, cooing reassurances as she gently placed one hand on his shoulder.

Marlow twitched at the contact, but otherwise remained in place. His moaning ceased as abruptly as it had begun. He cocked his head in the direction he'd been staring. The base of his good ear pulled forward as far as the bandage would allow, and he swung his gaze around slowly as if he were tracking something, past garden path and porch decking, over a tense Diane, to settle on Kristin's furrowed brow. At this Marlow extended his wide tongue and slathered high across Kristin's cheek, only once, but hard enough to shove her head back.

Kristin leaned away to wipe her palm across her face. "C'mon dude," she protested, "Why you gotta lick my cornea? God... and that does not smell pleasant."

Marlow broke into a grin and lowered his head apologetically while Diane chortled in spite of herself, "I tol' you that bastard would make you sorry you helped him."

Kristin scooted across the top porch stair where she'd been seated, and dried her palm on her shorts. "Alright," she sighed, waving Marlow over, "You can come back now."

Marlow approached cautiously, his nose near the floorboards, his tail fanning slowly, gratefully. He plodded to Kristin's side and collapsed with his front leg running the length of her thigh, his head nuzzled against her bare knee. Kristin rested her elbow along

494

his spine and buried her fingers in his luxurious coat, full and thick, but surprisingly airy now that he'd dried. She filled her whole fist with just a portion of the scruff of Marlow's neck, and kneaded his skin while he moaned and pressed harder against her leg. Kristin patted the white bandage where it ran across the dog's crown, and settled herself back against the porch railing, as she had been for most of the previous hour.

The sun had only just dipped below the distant hills, and shadows that had been gaining length were now losing strength. The deepening purple of the sky to the right of the barn spread and corrupted what remained of the burnt orange sunset on the left, but as yet offered up no more than the very brightest of the stars in its stable. A half-hearted breeze, still warm and still dry, meandered through very occasionally, but the distant rattling of hard shrubs, the barely perceptible ticking of grit against broad leaves in the nearby garden, somehow spoke to the feeling of desolation, and in this way, paradoxically, to the stillness of the evening.

Kristin turned her head far enough that she could soften her voice and still be heard. "Damn," she said, "I really thought we had him calmed down."

Diane noisily righted her chair and projected, "Yeah, well, you do until you don't. Can't guess why you'd think a injured beast should act right. You can't trust the healthy ones as it is."

"Give it time," Kristin chided, "He's only been around us for a day." But what a long day it had been.

As little faith as Diane had claimed to have in Kristin's abilities, she had been none too pleased by the woman's decision to forgo all of the day's planned chores in the interest of caring for and fawning over the new dog. The sheer size of the animal had turned every minor task into a project. That morning's accidental feeding had turned out to be a very small drop in a large, furry bucket, but because Diane resented handing out any more of the cats' food than was necessary, and because Kristin had no desire to displease her, Marlow's bottomless dietary needs had been met with a near constant succession of very small, negotiated portions.

Bathing the dog had been another production, begun with the idea of a simple onceover with a garden hose, only to discover that his coat was so thick and so tangled, and that every tangle contained so much filth, that every knot and mat required special attention. Then, of course, there was the head wound, which had to be avoided during the bath but then delicately and especially cleaned, disinfected, bandaged, and wrapped afterward. Not that Kristin, or Diane, or really the vast majority of humanity, had any experience stanching and bandaging a dog's missing ear without obstructing other bits of his face.

So it was that the day had involved an exhausting amount of trial and error. At the same time, Kristin had been surprised to discover a kind of clarity in the work. The act of caring for another creature on such a basic and necessary level served to remind her that not all decisions were discretionary, that, like it or not, sometimes shit just needed to be done. The careful problem-solving required of Kristin had also served to remind her of her own ability to do said shit. All told, the stream of short-term decisions had primed Kristin to make some of the long-term decisions that deep down she knew she'd been avoiding. But, as she had feared, each decision she'd made begged follow up questions, and for everything she'd done, there was that much more to do.

Kristin sighed again at the sight of a gradually expanding dark spot on the white bandage. "It's bleeding less than it was, but I'm worried that'll get infected. I should probably take him to a vet soon."

In a tone that was crude but not cruel, Diane corrected her, "I'd say yer half right. He should prolly *see* a vet. As for you takin' him, well…" Diane exerted herself enough to hesitate before softly finishing, "Sweetie, you know he can't stay here, don't you?"

"Yes," Kristin said simply, "I know he can't stay. But that's okay, because I can't stay here either."

"Now wait a minute," Diane said hurriedly, "You don't hafta'… I mean, if it's really that important-,"

496

Kristin contorted herself to look Diane in the eye without disturbing her lap guest. With as sympathetic an expression as she knew, Kristin said, "No, I didn't mean it like that. I'm not storming out or protesting over Marlow or something. But you know that I never meant to stay forever. It's amazing that you took me in in the first place, and you've already given me so much help, and I don't want to take advantage, especially now that something has come along that needs *my* help and that, well… That seems like maybe sort of a sign, doesn't it? That maybe it's time for me to move on with Marlow?"

Diane opened her mouth to respond, then closed it again. Leaning back in her wooden chair, she shrugged, "Yer not wrong, I suppose. Can't keep ya' here. And if yer sure this is the time t'go, I shouldn't stop ya'."

Kristin nodded with quiet confidence, "I am sure. I can't explain why, but I know that if I go now, I'll be fine."

"Don't know why either, but I think that's true." The women sat in agreeable silence for more than a minute before Diane added, "Much as I'd like to, you know I can't get you clear back East."

"I didn't expect you would," Kristin reassured her, "And I still don't think I should go back there."

"So where should you go then?"

"To the vet," Kristin reiterated. "If I'm ever to get started, I need to focus on one step at a time, and getting his ear looked at has to be the first step."

"Can't argue with sense," Diane shrugged. "I can drop y'all in town in the morning. There's a vet there, owes me a favor."

"That's good," Kristin laughed, "Because I hadn't really thought of a way to pay them." She added thoughtfully, "I can't really pay you back for it either."

Diane waved off the comment, "Nah… You don't owe me nothin'."

Kristin knew better than to argue and had no real argument to make. The best she could do then was to feel bad, to feel guilty, but she didn't see how that would help. Kristin chose instead to feel good, to feel hopeful. The evening came on without further comment. She absently stroked Marlow's neck and thought about the following day, thought about how much better she would feel once she knew that her new friend was healthy and safe, and otherwise reflected on the virtues of being generous to a stray.

"Slow up now," Hugh said in a quavering voice, "Wait there and I'll..." He allowed his words to trail off. William, kneeling over the corpse of Henry Sullivan Strafford, did not appear to require further instruction. Hugh turned back into the chamber, casting about for what to do next. He might have assumed that witnessing the death of the man who seconds earlier had held a knife to his throat would offer some sense of relief, but Hugh's heart, having come so near to being stopped, was now making up for lost time: it pounded in his ears, so loud that he half expected to hear its echo from the distant ceiling; it raced, and it dragged his thoughts along with it.

Hugh's mind spun in a tight circle around what had just happened, looking for a way in, to relate, to understand the doctor's last words, the doctor's last actions, but even as it did, he recognized that none of it was over. He was still in a cave full of symbols that he couldn't make sense of, hell, couldn't even see at present, but now there was a dead man and his killer on the floor, and already the metallic reek of blood and piss soiled the dank air. Certainly, there was much to contemplate, but Hugh sensed that first there was much to be done, and he had no idea where to start.

Light, he decided, must be first; there was not much else they could do for lack of it. Hugh retraced his steps to where he had dropped the lantern. As he lifted it from the floor, he tried to picture what it would reveal, to imagine what they would do next by its light, but the only vision he could conjure was the one he had left: the vague outlines of the crumpled corpse and Hugh's despondent defender. Perhaps that was his answer, to resume his familiar role and follow William's lead. But confused as Hugh now found himself, he had to assume that William would be in worse shape. After all, William's recent violence would not be tempered by the relief of having been rescued. He had only just killed a man, and what does one do after that?

Resolved to find out, Hugh raised the lamp before him, and squinted past its glare to the gore in the corner. As he approached, the light reflected off something flying toward his leg. He jumped back to the sound of metal clinking to a stop beside him. Ten feet in front of Hugh, William called out, "Sorry! Overshot the mark on that one. Would you mind kickin' it back this way?"

Hugh stooped to investigate and discovered a small, ornate belt buckle near his foot. He picked it up more delicately than was necessary and carried it closer to the voice. As he approached, his mind ground nearly to a halt, struggling to sort the shapes from the shadows. William's gun, now freed from its victim, lay perpendicular to the wall. Beside the stock, William had unfolded a handkerchief with the initials H.S.S embroidered in the corner nearest Hugh. In the center of the white cloth was a small bunch of loose coins and a few matches. In front of it, William had positioned himself on both knees to more comfortably rifle through Strafford's pockets.

Straightening up suddenly, William declared, "Aha! I knew I caught him on the first pass! Boy, I couldn't a' hit that more on the nose if I'd been tryin' for it." Tossing another piece of flat metal onto the pile, he looked finally to Hugh. "Oh, there it is," he said, gesturing to the belt buckle, "You can toss that down there."

Hugh demanded, "What in the hell are you doing?"

William shrugged, "Don't guess it's all worth much, but it's still worth more to us than it is to him. An' it's not like he asked to be buried with any of it. To the victor go the spoils an' such."

"It… Well, it…" Hugh searched for the source of his consternation, "It don't seem… Don't seem *proper*, is all."

"Yeh, well…" William muttered as he inspected the inside of the dead man's waistcoat for hidden pockets. Emphatically dropping the edge of the garment, he asked, "Didn't he have more with him? I'm certain he was carryin' a saddlebag this morning."

"He was," Hugh confirmed, "I'm sure he left it out front with the rest of our things."

"You think he had papers? Photographs, diaries, personal effects an' the like?"

"How should I know?" Hugh stood in place, his lantern incidentally aiding William's ghoulish pursuits. "And why do you care? Pilfered coins not enough, you hoping for bank notes on top of it?"

"A man of his stature may have some, and he won't be needin' those neither," William stated. "But that ain't so much what I'm hopin' t'find." Turning his attention to Strafford's trousers, he continued, "Been workin' on a problem, lo' these many days. See, I'm a deserter. An' before you say it, I realize I'm far from the only deserter in the territory. But most a' them boys, they leave for a reason, to farm or to trade or to take on some other business… But soldiering is the only business I know. The only thing close to it in practice is banditry, an' I don't guess that's for me, so what else is there? Yeh, been workin' on that, but I could not see a solution. Then the doctor attacked you, and I had me a revelation."

Hugh's curiosity, having melted into confusion, now boiled into frustration. "Revelation?!" he shouted, "What can you mean by that? You just killed a man!"

"Oh, that's right," William blinked calmly, "I suppose you never have. Shall I assume from your reaction that you never *seen* a man killed neither?"

Hugh opened his mouth to answer, then closed it again, flabbergasted at the absurdity of the question.

William softened his tone, as though explaining to a child, "Well if ever you find it necessary to kill a man, you might be surprised at your response. There are few moments in life when a body can't account for what goes on in the mind. Birth of a child, I

500

hear. Or death of a loved one, that's a good'n: you can't tell a widow not to wail. Nor can you help what goes through *your* skull when you stick a knife through someone else's. For me, just now, it was a memory. I remembered the one time in my life when I wasn't a soldier. I was a child, and a sickly child at that. I remember doctors come out to our place, none of 'em named Strafford, though there might've been a Henry or two. I remember what they carried, how they carried themselves an' I thought, yes. Yes, I could do that. You gimme the right tools, the right references, an' I reckon I could."

"My God," Hugh shook his head, "You are cracked."

"I know that you're meant to have training and experience and all that too," William continued, "An' I don't mind workin' at that. But I'm behind schedule on all of it, an' in the meantime, here's a man who has the tools an' likely has the references an' can't use any of 'em. An' that was the revelation, what hit me like a lightning bolt, that I can't see any good options for William, but Henry Strafford may have better days ahead. He said he come South before he found us, so I'd guess nobody straight east of here knows what he looks like. I can take his papers that direction, an' then see how far they take me."

"You have lost your mind," Hugh reiterated.

Pausing in his task, William shifted his weight from his knees to his rear and swiveled, still seated with his legs folded, to face Hugh. "Maybe," William said simply. "All I know is that as I live and breathe I just watched a man die, and I had a revelation. What I'm going to do next, what I'm certain I have to-," With a sudden and jarring enthusiasm, William interrupted this thought with another, "Say! You could be Benjamin!"

With a look approaching horror-stricken, Hugh shouted, "I can't just *be* Benjamin! Benjamin is Benjamin!"

Raising his palms defensively, William said, "You do know that you wouldn't *actually* be anyone else. You could take Benjamin's story; wouldn't even need to take his name, you could call yourself anyone you like. Anyone except Henry Strafford.

Can't both of us be Henry Strafford. Unless," he chuckled, "If we split up, I guess we could both be the same person. Who would know the difference?" Serious again, William cautioned, "But if we do, I must still insist on taking possession of his letters and effects. I have plans... Revelations to consider."

Hugh shook his head slowly, his mouth hanging slack. His disapproval had not accomplished much, but he clearly could not entertain a word of what William was saying. He would've assumed that the death of a travelling companion, even under these circumstances, would command a certain respect, nothing formal perhaps, but a general gravitas that was lacking in William's odd combination of wistful planning and business-like looting. Hugh wanted to be gracious, deferential to the man who had just saved his life, but the very kindest assumption he could make was that William was in some sort of shock.

And was kindness wise? Hugh wanted to feel that he owed William time enough to regain his senses, but looking back now, Hugh couldn't be sure whether the senses William had lost had been there to begin with. After all, he'd only known William a few weeks: was it possible that the man was, and had always been, a lunatic? Had Hugh willfully ignored warnings of that in pursuit of his goal? He could not say for certain, and having just seen what William was capable of, even in their defense, Hugh decided that the stakes were too high for him to remain there with any uncertainty.

With deliberate calm, Hugh acquiesced, "You can keep his papers. I do think we should part company, though."

William's face fell as he nodded, "Oh. I see. No. You're right. I suppose it might be safest for the both of us to split up. I don't think anyone will come looking for the doctor, but if they do..."

"I'm glad you agree," Hugh agreed, but not too strenuously. "If I spot his bag, I'll move it near the entrance then."

"You're leaving already?" William asked. "You've come all this way. Shouldn't you want to explore more?"

502

Hugh answered drily, "I've seen just enough to not mind getting back to Yuba City."

"Well…" William began. Making no effort to stand, he cast his eyes around awkwardly, seeming to search for something appropriate to say or do. In short order he found both. Plucking a pair of objects from the ground, he presented one in each hand with the suggestion, "If you're striking out on your own, you might get some use out of these."

Hugh recoiled at the sight of Strafford's knife, offered handle first. Not wanting to be rude, he checked his revulsion and reached past the weapon to the mostly flat, round object in William's open palm. Hugh pinched it between his thumb and forefinger, and raised it in front of the lantern in his other hand. The face of a small compass peeked out from under a lid bent nearly in half.

"You'll have to excuse the top of it there," William explained, "Seems it got between Henry and my bayonet. But the glass looks to be sound."

Hugh nodded to the knife that still extended from William's other hand, "Thank you, but I think this will suffice."

"Suit yourself." William casually tossed the blade onto the handkerchief, where it jingled lightly amongst loose change. With that, he turned on his tailbone again to conclude examining the body.

Not wanting to interrupt further, Hugh gently set the lantern on the ground beside the gun, and moved to retrieve Strafford's diminishing torch. As he crossed the chamber back to the tunnel, as the darkness between the men grew in breadth and depth, William called through the shadows, "If you ever need to find me, ride to the east of here. And ask after *Doctor* Henry Sullivan Strafford!"

"What did you do?!?"

Jared knelt beside Louis, unsure of what he himself was doing. The pool of light around the propane lantern, which had come to rest beside Louis's opposite shoulder, strained to reach the nearly seven feet to the man's boots, and so instead highlighted the worst of the scene. The uneven spray of blood and gore across the dust betrayed a concealed exit wound, as did the position of Louis's head which, reclined at an ever-so-slightly-past-peaceful angle, leaned a bit further back than his skull should've allowed. The result was that Louis's barely opened eyes stared down his nose, unseeing from under the bill of a worn and faded red cap that was becoming redder by the second.

Jared marveled in spite of himself at how small was the hole in the front of that cap, and at how much damage such a mark could cause. The dark halo spreading across the floor above his new friend's shoulders brought Jared back to his senses. He had to do something. Something to help. But if nothing could help now then what could he do? There had to be something. Jared began to reach for Louis's wrist to check his pulse, but what was the point of that? He pulled his hand back and started reaching with his other to turn Louis over and check the wound, but again... Jared froze with his hands in front of him, palms down and fingers spread above the body as though he were warming them over a fire, unsure which direction to take them, where they might do some good.

Only then did it occur to Jared that Tim was still standing behind him holding a gun. That, he thought, might be worth doing something about. But again, what? Having returned to that problem late, Jared could still track the onset of adrenaline, could follow along as his stomach dropped and his heart thudded in his ears, before his palms started to sweat and his fingertips to shake, none of which was helpful. Fight or flight: with a gun at his back, either would have the same outcome.

Conceding to his obvious helplessness, Jared let his palms fall to his thighs. "What did you do..?" he demanded again, choked, almost petulant, "What did you do that for?"

"The answer to both those questions," Tim stated simply, "Is that I just did the hard part for us."

Jared wasn't sure if that comment should mean anything to him. He had no answer for it and so offered none. Instead, he settled his eyes on Louis's shirtfront and waited for whatever was next.

For once, Tim chose to clarify unprompted, "Louis had to die. Louis always had to die. Same as Strafford always had to die. He had to die, to stand aside, so that the men who killed him could become him."

Still unfocused, still at a loss, Jared turned his upper body to cock his head at the other man. Tim's features were mostly hidden behind his flashlight, a shape in shadow roughly defined by the dull glare off his spectacles and sidearm. The latter item was still close enough to terrify Jared, but Tim had relaxed his posture a bit, had lowered his elbow to his side to more casually point the loaded gun at Jared's head. He occasionally used it to gesture as he said, "On September 9 of 1881, three men came to this place. Henry Sullivan Strafford you already know, or rather, you think you do. The man you've really been following was at that point still called William Grafton. The third, once named Hugh Carroll, has been more influential in the sense that Louis was following his life backwards, and it was his memoir that I discovered. So, Henry, William, and Hugh. You follow so far?"

From the place they'd discovered to the corpses on the floor, to the dully reflected light waving and bouncing off the tip of the gun while Tim talked: taking all of it together without time to process, Jared was simply overwhelmed. To now add a history lesson on top of it all... there were no words, so Jared nodded dumbly, on his knees, passively absorbing Tim's story. This seemed to suit Tim especially well.

"Good," Tim stated. He continued to lecture as though he were reciting common knowledge, "So as happens once every 19.143 years, three men came to this place. Two of those men killed the third, in that case meaning Henry Sullivan Strafford, and in so doing, both of those men assumed his name, his identity, under which they were destined to do important things. That's how the name 'Henry Strafford' could be everywhere all at once, could even die in two different places. It should also explain what I've heard you observe once or twice, that it seemed like you and Louis weren't following the same person. In some sense you were, but not really. Two men serving the same identity, pulling in different directions to feed a single, gluttonous, biography: your Henry Strafford worked his way up through the ranks and then through society. When you get a chance to look closer, you'll find that he quietly revolutionized everything he touched. Louis's Henry Strafford, on the other hand, was a born loser whose greatest accomplishments involved being in the wrong place at the wrong time. It seems fitting that Louis followed *that* Strafford. But we'll come back to that in a minute."

Pulling himself from the tangent, Tim took a step backward and directed his flashlight to the mural. "The pattern as discussed thus far: 'Once in every generation, a group of three travelers is said to answer an ancient evil in the form of a map which one man must carry on his face." With this Tim illuminated the three dark figures at the bottom of the panel. Jared only now noticed that the two positioned on the outside held spears pointed at the third. Waving the light to the top of the scene, where two more specters broke away from the central character, Tim said, "Their path will take them to a place cleansed by fire where they will be transformed, so that," he swept the beam down in a slow circle around the large red creature, "One Great Name would emerge.' So you see," Tim finished triumphantly, "'Louis Garrett' may yet be a great name, with both of us putting great work behind it. And without him weighing it down, of course."

Jared turned back to the body. Even if what Tim was saying did fit, that didn't mean it made sense to him. Or maybe he just didn't want to make sense of it, because he didn't want Tim to have been right to kill Louis. Although, if Tim was right, then he and Jared would both have to leave there alive to fulfill their obligations. And if he was wrong, he would never admit it, not even to himself. That meant that Tim would insist they both survive this encounter, which in turn meant that Jared was safe from harm.

Jared inhaled deeply through his nose and relaxed his full weight onto his heels beneath him. Releasing his breath in a sigh, he challenged, "Whatever the hell we're meant to do, wouldn't three people have had an easier time doing it?"

"That's not how this works," Tim said slowly.

"Says who?" Jared's voice rose as he demanded, "God? The universe? Why would it make things so complicated? Why does the universe care whose name we go by?"

"Whoever said the universe cares?" Tim snarled. "You want complicated? Try looking at anything on earth under a microscope or anything in the cosmos through a telescope. The universe is nothing *but* complicated, certainly complicated enough without some bullshit motives you'd like to imagine. Hell, as these things go, our pattern is pretty straightforward: three travelers in, one man sacrificed, the other two take his name and do great things. Oh, and you're welcome, by the way. Not only did I choose for you to go forward, I didn't even make you kill your friend there."

"I wouldn't have killed my friend," Jared answered.

"I'm fully aware," Tim shot back. "Given your options, I expect either one of you would've killed me. I never said I got nothing out of making the decision, but you could at least acknowledge that you got as much from the decision *I* made."

Exasperated, Jared turned on his knees and shouted, "What did we get? Why did *anyone* have to die? If you knew what we were walking into, why did *any* of us have to come here?!?"

"Why does anyone do anything?!?" Tim screamed in response. "Why do you get out of bed every morning? What purpose were you serving before all this? This was just the next thing that you- that *we*- had to do in life." At a lower volume, but still annoyed, Tim said, "You know, of the three of us, you really have the least cause to bitch over this outcome. If the pattern is destined to run its course each generation, I arguably could've given up my part in it to someone else. *I* could've thrown out the manuscript, and
507

someone else would have picked it up. Louis: he could've quit at any time, could've tossed that compass out his car window and someone passing by would've found it. We had decisions to make in our actions and our outcomes, but you, you have the beard. There was no avoiding your role. You were born to this."

"I could've cut it off-"

"Sure," Tim patronized, "You could have cut it off, if you could help yourself. But how could you? And why would you? Hiding your face behind that thing, then chasing what it came to mean, it made you feel like somebody. You loved that feeling too much to stop it, and you followed it no matter where it took you, and you would have, whether with me and Louis or with two other people. You were desperate to be a part of something as interesting as you'd convinced yourself *you* were. And by now, hell: taking a new name, presenting yourself as someone you're not, should come easy to you."

Even as Jared spoke, he could hardly deny his descent into whining self-pity, "I just want to know the point. I need to know why."

"You want to know 'Why'?" Tim sneered. "I don't know 'Why', I know 'What'. You are part of a very, very large pattern now. And the part that you are is called Louis Garrett. You can embrace your life as a thing called Louis and succeed in everything you do, or you can fight and fail. One of the Straffords tried that, tried pretending he was still a man named Hugh, tried running back to his old life, and he struggled and suffered at every turn. Eventually, he learned the hard way: a person cannot succeed by pretending to be what they want at the expense of what they are."

More desperate than defiant, Jared asked, "Who are you to tell me what I am?"

"Same as you," Tim shrugged, "I'm Louis Garrett. And I'm not telling you any more than what the rest of the world will see when they look at you. When they looked at Hugh Carroll, they saw a man named Henry Sullivan Strafford. When they look at you, they will see a man named Louis Garrett." Tim finally

508

lowered the beam of the flashlight to the floor and turned around. Walking the few steps to where his satchel had landed, he called back, "I'll show you the manuscript. You can read all about it, then do whatever you want." Dropping the gun into the bag he added, "And I won't try to change your mind again, either. If you didn't have many options before I decided Louis should die, you sure as hell have no choice at this point."

Tim's words hung in the air, almost tangible in front of Jared's bleary eyes. No choice at this point? Had Jared ever had a choice? At this moment, he wasn't sure. He'd never been a man with a sense of destiny, but at the same time, he'd never put any effort into realizing a future that was less than guaranteed. Why did Jared get out of bed every morning? Because that's what people do. At what point could daily indecision be deemed a person's destiny? Could it truly be for lack of purpose that he walked the road plainly set in front of him each day? But what was fate if not that exact practice?

One thing that Jared and Tim agreed on was that the day he'd followed his first map, he'd had purpose. But that was a *choice* Jared had made. Likewise, it was his *choice* to grow the second map, to book the hotel in Asheville, to press cross country, to lie to the only person he cared about. He had *chosen* to pursue his purpose at the cost of every aspect of his life and livelihood, to push himself until he broke and then push harder to get here. Even if the few options presented to Jared were curated exclusively by fate, whatever he was and whatever his destiny now, he had *chosen* to pursue it. If anything, that had been his only purpose since hiding his face behind that beard: to choose, to decide, if not *what* he was, at least *who* he would be.

Jared's eyes had wandered behind his thoughts, had followed the edge of Louis's lamplight to settle on the pile of broken stones between Tim and what was left of Henry Strafford. Jared didn't much understand fate, was still new to destiny, to the machinations of the universe. He didn't know what name people would call him after this, or what the rest of the world would see when they looked at him, but he would have purpose: he must have options. He would not choose to subjugate himself to some insensate pattern. Jared would choose to wreck the universe's plan, in the most permanent fashion he could think of.

Not wanting to give himself time enough to think better of it, Jared scraped toward the wall, and reached into the rubble there with both hands. Unable to see much more than rough outlines in the dark, he came back with a jagged stone more than half the size of a cinder block and nearly as heavy. Jared shuffled sideways, swinging the rock in front of his thighs like a pendulum. The momentum of the third upswing was enough to carry the leading edge across the back of Tim's head.

There was a grunt followed by a thump. Jared sensed Tim moving, rolling over to face him, and he lunged with both knees at what turned out to be Tim's chest. Another grunt, not a word after that. As Jared lifted the rock above his head, he thought that perhaps Tim was stunned. Noting an expression on Tim's face that showed more annoyance than fear, Jared thought it more likely that Tim assumed that some divine providence would stay Jared's hand, that the forces that had brought them here would never allow one of their so-newly-christened-Louis-Garretts to die without having accomplished any great thing.

Jared half assumed the same. When he replayed that moment in his mind, as he often would for years to come, Jared would wonder if it wasn't the very expectation of failure that had freed him to bring the rock down on Tim's forehead. Either way, he was impressed by how easy it was, by how much of the work was accomplished by gravity alone, and by the fragility of the human skull. Jared tried it a second time. He found no compunction in the simple act of raising the stone, and, so long as he clung to that feeling, there was no physical challenge to releasing it. The hollow *thwop* that followed, the feeling of bone giving way like the rind of an under-ripe melon, told Jared that his task was accomplished.

But that did not mean he was finished. He had not *chosen* to be finished.

510

Again he lifted the rock and again he let it fall. Once more he hauled it up, and let its weight carry it down. With every repetition, after each pull but before every strike, Jared saw Tim's face become a bit less of what it was. The features had no chance to bruise or swell, only to flatten, to smear, to disintegrate. Jared was not blind with rage; of course he hated what Tim had done to Louis, and he resented that so much of what Tim had said afterwards had been true. But even so, Jared did not feel anger, not really. Rage would have been a force entirely of itself, but Jared, for once, felt completely in control.

And he raised his stone, and he let it fall. The gentle recoil of soft tissue made way for the scrape and crunch of what lie beneath, and eventually to a revolting combination of the two. As bone and flesh and line and curve dissolved, so must the pattern. Jared would still carve his friend's name in the wall as he left that place, might even use that name for himself, but as a memorial, not of necessity. And he would only do that based on his confidence that the name would never be tainted by what had been Tim Donaldson, or by anyone else of the universe's choosing. There would only be cne 'Louis Garrett'. Now there *could* only be one Louis Garrett, and that was *his* choice, destiny be damned.

Like Sisyphus, Jared committed every ounce of his strength, every ounce of himself, to raising a stone just to see it fall. But unlike the myth, when his stone dropped, every time it dropped, he escaped from the preordained, moved further from the pattern. Only Jared could choose how to live whatever life was given him.

The Day After

Kristin sat on the top tier of a terraced curb, what amounted to three irregular concrete steps that ran the length of the block. They appeared to have been painted yellow long before and to have faded and flaked shortly thereafter, so that now they served as a perfect spectral interval between the relentless tan, adobe store fronts behind her and the grey of the unnecessarily wide asphalt road in front. No traffic interrupted her view of the other side of the street, where more dusty browns and whites glared back from a weather-beaten, two-story motor court. Much nearer to Kristin's toes, the periphery of the shade patch in which she sat shimmered, as an imperceptible breeze disturbed what scant foliage clung to a pair of anemic ash trees wedged between the buildings nearest her.

Kristin decided that she had too many options. None seemed especially good, but that had not made them any less overwhelming. From where she was sitting at that moment, from that start point, Kristin could proceed in any direction, could pursue any goal, could be whatever and whomever she chose. And though she was too broke to view the world as her oyster, from her seat on the precipice of the roadside, she could see an infinite number of paths.

That would remain true, she knew, right up to the moment that she chose any one of them.

She couldn't stall forever. Hell, she probably wouldn't be allowed to stall past sundown, at least not in that spot, but she also felt that the moment was too important to waste on impulse. It was with that in mind that she stared vacantly at the vacant motor court, aware of her unwillingness to choose which choice to make and then lose.

Although, to be fair, Kristin had already managed one choice: that of what to have for lunch. Still staring straight ahead, still channeling her energies into her racing and circular thoughts, she brought a half-eaten peanut butter sandwich to her lips. Before she could even swallow, her bare shoulder was insistently slapped by cold, smooth plastic. Kristin absently pulled off a chunk of bread crust and reached forward to dangle it in front of a large white funnel, twice the size of her head. Out of sight beyond this barrier, she felt Marlow's tongue grasp the bread along with three of her fingers.

Kristin laughed, "Dammit..." She pulled her hand back to wipe the drool on her shorts. Turning to the massive cone-collar that the vet had given them to prevent the dog fussing with his freshly stitched ear, Kristin concluded, "It's a good thing you like peanut butter sandwiches though. That's the only thing we got plenty of."

Kristin was proud to have plenty of them, or plenty of anything, even if it had begun with more charity from Diane. Their goodbye had consisted of pulling up beside the yet-to-open vet's office while the older woman shouted, "Here you go," as prelude to shoving Kristin out the passenger door. But just as her eyes had started to well up, and before she had stomped on the accelerator, Diane had, through some sleight of hand, shoved two hundred dollars into Kristin's closed fist. It wasn't until the truck had vanished around the corner, not so fast as to squeal tires, but quick enough to kick up a cloud of dust, that Kristin had realized how many twenty dollar bills she was holding. She had reminded herself at that point, and several times since, that the parable of the loaves and fishes was not about conjuring something from nothing, it was about making a little go a long way. In that spirit she saw room to make miracles.

She'd had a moment of panic with the veterinarian, having thought that he might demand the whole wad of bills for his services. But her brief description of her time with Diane had been sufficient proof to him of their acquaintance, and the doctor had accepted as payment the solemn promise that Kristin would convince Diane that his treating Marlow made 'everything squared'. That promise had been a lie: Kristin didn't even know how to get back in touch with Diane. But lie or no, she hadn't felt too bad for saying it. She'd assumed they both knew that the old woman wouldn't have listened to anyone anyways.

In this way, Marlow's wounds had been treated gratis, and Kristin had spent the duration of that treatment mentally balancing their most pressing needs against their resources. The region in which she found herself was generally warm and dry, so shelter from the elements was not life or death in the nearest term, but those same qualities made water very important. Also, while she didn't mind sleeping under the stars, there were other activities for which Kristin very much preferred an actual bathroom. She still had a stock of all the toiletries she needed in the small pocket of her backpack, and she believed that she could get by on water and on privacy by sneaking empty bottles into any department store or gas station that had public restrooms.

But that still left food. To squeeze as much as possible from a non-existent budget, Kristin needed something high calorie, high protein, and compact enough to carry. That was how she'd ended up with a backpack full of all the bread, peanut butter, and granola bars on offer at the Circle K. Kristin wanted to consider her problem-solving thus far as an accomplishment, and she supposed that going from zero to a week's subsistence in a few hours wasn't nothing, but it so clearly wasn't enough. Not for her alone, and certainly not with Marlow depending on her. Kristin needed cash, and in her experience that meant she needed work. But going through the whole process of finding, applying for, and interviewing for a job that might then make her wait weeks for a check... she needed to get earning as quickly as possible. Perhaps at a small business, she thought, someplace without a payroll department, the kind of place that might not mind paying under the table.

The phrase, 'Gotta get earning,' rolled on a loop in Kristin's mind. For the moment she had most of her money, but she still didn't know how much food to give her new dog each day, or how much of that should be peanut butter. Kristin took a last dry, sticky

514

bite before setting the remainder of the sandwich on the lip of the funnel. It was so infuriating to be this near to having an idea. She knew what she needed to do, but she just couldn't see the next step to getting it done. One place more than any that she knew she would not see the answer was the empty parking lot of the abandoned looking motor court. Yet that is where Kristin continued to stare as the wide, pink tongue in the cone beside her pulled in the last bits of bread.

"D'you get the Albuquerque stations on that thing?"

Kristin discerned a man's voice, but not the meaning of his words. "Excuse me?" Blinking away sunspots, she turned away from Marlow toward the interruption, where she found a heavyset man in his late 60's accompanied by a slender woman of about the same age. Both wore wire framed glasses and straight white hair in a length and style similar to one another but for the fact that his was thinning. He had tucked a light-colored polo shirt around his large belly and into dark dress slacks, while she had draped a tasteful blouse over pleated khakis.

"Your poor dog," the man explained, "He looks like a satellite dish, so the Albuquerque stations…" He trailed off under the influence of Kristin's tight smile.

The three of them shared an excruciating moment. Finally, Kristin offered, "He's had a rough morning at the doctor's office."

The man gently asked, "Would it be okay if I say hello?"

His wife interjected with a statement made less apologetic by virtue of its having been so well rehearsed, "I'm sorry. He does this. We really should just get our own dog, but we travel so much, you know."

Kristin considered that none of her important concerns included pressing appointments. She sighed, "It's fine. Go ahead. Just mind the ear."

The couple moved together. It took them several steps to get around the length of the dog and his cone. In an overwrought baby-talk, the gentleman said, "You just look so pathetic wif yo' fancy cah-wa." Positioned directly in front of the cone so that he could be

515

seen, the man crouched down and stretched his arm around the outside, to Marlow's neck, where he could pet him without cornering him.

As the dog leaned into the petting, the plastic swung the opposite direction, almost far enough to smack Kristin in the face. She slid over, stood up, and stepped back beside the woman, who asked, "What happened to him?"

Kristin shrugged, "Not sure. He came home yesterday with an ear missing, so I brought him to get fixed up. Should be fine now, but I'm not letting him out of my sight for a while."

"I should think not," the woman said. Her tone was clipped: polite but with a forcefulness somewhere between self-assured and condescending. "That's just awful. The poor thing."

With much more ease, her husband echoed, "Poooor thiiiing…" Having now introduced himself, he drew back his arm and gently reached into the cone, toward Marlow's good side. Whatever it was that he scratched in that funnel, the dog lowered his shoulder to lean harder against the man's hand.

Without taking her eyes off Marlow, Kristin asked, "Are you from here? Can I ask you something?"

The woman took a step back and crossed her arms. "Our daughter lives here," she said. "We're regular visitors, but I'm not sure we can help you."

"Could you tell me," Kristin asked, "Where they keep their department stores? The Wal-Mart, the Kmart? I'm not picky."

"Oh," the woman said, relaxing slightly, "You won't find any of that in this town. There's a decent grocery I can point you to, but not much else."

Kristin weighed the suggestion carefully. "I guess that could work," she said. "I need to buy dog food, in bulk if I can, what with my dog being in bulk. It seems like something that would be easier to afford at one of the big chains."

Still intent on his borrowed pet, the man affably followed up, "You need some help with dog food? Our truck is around the corner. You could follow us to the grocery, I could pay."

516

His wife instantly tensed again, knees locked, arms drawn in. She hissed, "Albert, don't be rude."

"Nancy," he hissed back mockingly, "I'm being helpful." Looking over to Kristin, he said, "I didn't mean any offense."

Nancy pursed her lips and glared back at him, clearly communicating that *she* found his helpfulness offensive.

Kristin interceded airily, "It's alright. I appreciate the offer, but I'm happy to say that I don't need to take you up on it." This seemed to satisfy them both, so she added, "Or not yet. Completely unrelated: if you happen to know of anyone hiring…" She laughed at her own joke more loudly than was warranted, but the couple joined in anyway, grateful for the chance to break the tension. As they politely subsided, Kristin followed, "I am serious though, if you've heard anything."

A bit less guarded than she had been, Nancy answered, "I haven't. We haven't. As far as I know. And in a town this size, you probably would know if there were jobs popping up."

"That's true," Albert agreed, returning half his focus to Marlow, "Seems like everyone is hiring these days, everywhere but here. But I take it from your questions that you're not from here?"

"No," Kristin confirmed, "I'm just passing through. Passing through pretty quickly, if there's no work."

"Right," Nancy nodded, as she uncrossed her arms and stepped around the dog toward her husband. With an air of finality, she said, "That's probably the right idea. Maybe you'll have more luck someplace bigger. Albert, should we-,"

Albert continued conversationally, "Where we're from isn't even all that big, and the number of jobs popping up there, compared to a couple years ago-,"

Kristin asked quickly, "Where is that?"

He answered, "Flagstaff."

Kristin had no idea where Flagstaff was. Then again, she didn't have much idea of where she was now, and the potential of something in Flagstaff had to be better than the guarantee of nothing here. On top of which, it seemed unlikely that she'd find

517

anyone less threatening than these two to winch her out of her quagmire. "Don't guess you could give us a lift."

Albert shrugged and turned to his wife. Nancy's mouth hung open, the color draining from her face as she realized how quickly she'd lost control of the conversation. Kristin made a note of this, but still saw no risk in pressing the issue, apart from momentary social awkwardness. Focusing on Nancy she said, "If you can drop us at any discount store between here and there, it would be a lifesaver. A serious, for real, lifesaver. And I'll pay gas money, too, for the trip. Or... well, our share of the gas money, but that's still gotta be half, since Marlow's as big as a person. And you said you had a truck? Marlow can ride in the back. Or me *and* Marlow can ride in back. Or I can ride in back and Marlow can ride up front with you if you want and I'll still pay for gas."

Nancy stood over Albert with a pained expression on her face, not relenting, but slightly tempted to do something that every cautionary tale she'd ever heard had told her she should not do. Kristin half-crouched and set her hands upon Marlow's shoulders. She concealed herself behind the massive cone and used it to gently direct the dog's chin toward the couple. Replicating Albert's earlier baby-dog-talk, she said, "Pweeeease? How can you say no to this fwuffy face?"

Nancy quipped, "Do you mean your dog's or my husband's?"

Unsure if she should laugh, Kristin peeked innocently over the edge of the cone. Nancy maintained her stern expression, but after a beat, gave a dismissive wave and said, "Fine. And I don't know if you were joking, but there isn't much space in the cab, so you will have to ride in back. But if you don't mind that, and it's just you two, and if you pay your way..."

"Is it just you two?" While Nancy had been speaking, Albert had stood, both of his knees cracking audibly. The longer her concession had continued, the more bemused he had looked. He had sidled around the cone to rub the scruff of Marlow's neck, and had glanced at the dog's collar, before interrupting his wife. Now fingering the top of two tags, he elaborated, "Or should we be expecting someone named Louis Garrett?"

When she replayed that moment in her mind, as she often would for years to come, Kristin would first of all marvel at how unprepared she had been for that question. In retrospect, she should have had an explanation ready for the vet, who ought to have made similar inquiry, but, weirdly, had not. And because Kristin had not stolen the dog, had even gone through the cursory motions of trying the phone number on the tag a few times, the possible implications of her being in possession of a total stranger's pet hadn't occurred to her until that moment. At best, her deeply held belief that fate had brought her and Marlow together might appear from the outside as a base rationalization of 'Finders Keepers'. And if they didn't believe that she and Marlow had crossed paths incidentally, she didn't guess that she could count on their help.

Eventually, once Kristin had time to reflect on the full range of bullshit stories that she might have come up with to appease Nance and Al, she would notice the improbability of the one that she chose. She would also live out the problems of it, would realize the level of commitment required for her to follow it through. But at that time, the answer that came to her seemed the most natural, the simplest, the most elegant solution in the world. And it would always impress her that so many important decisions in life could, in their moment, appear so trivial and be so impulsive.

"Oh, that," Kristin said breezily, "No, that's a misprint. There was supposed to be an 'e' on 'Louise'." She confidently presented her hand for Albert to shake. "That's me. Louise Garrett."

7

www.ingramcontent.com/pod-product-compliance
Lightning Source LLC
Chambersburg PA
CBHW070539030726
47505CB00001B/96